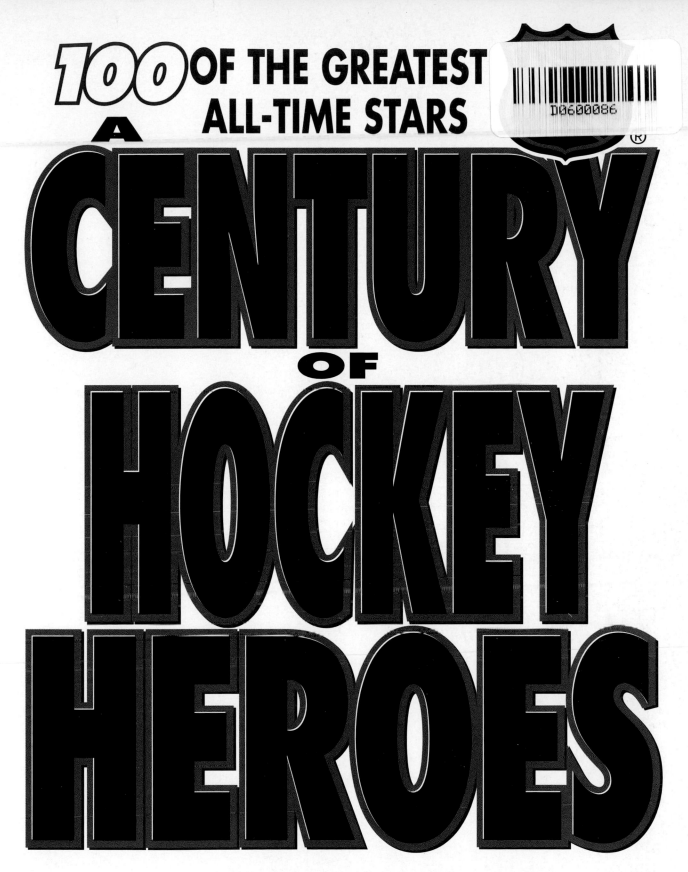

100 OF THE GREATEST ALL-TIME STARS

A CENTURY OF HOCKEY HEROES

James Duplacey and Eric Zweig

SOMERVILLE HOUSE, USA
NEW YORK

ISBN: 1-58184-062-4   A B C D E F G H I J

Printed in USA

Writers: James Duplacey and Eric Zweig
Designer: fiwired.com

Somerville House, USA is distributed by Penguin Putnam Books for Young Readers, 345 Hudson Street, New York, N.Y. 10014

Published in Canada by Somerville House Publishing a division of Somerville House Books Limited
3080 Yonge Street, Suite 5000
Toronto, ON
M4N 3N1

e-mail: sombooks@goodmedia.com
Web site: www.sombooks.com

Foreword

We are very excited at the National Hockey League about *A Century of Hockey Heroes*. As NHL Commissioner, I get to watch and enjoy the talents of so many of these great athletes. Moreover, I have had the opportunity to get to know them.

I think our athletes are the best of any sport: consider the power of Jaromir Jagr, the creativity of Paul Kariya, the agility of Dominik Hasek, the vision of Peter Forsberg, or the strength of Raymond Bourque.

When Wayne Gretzky retired last spring, we all lost the opportunity to watch the greatest team athlete in the history of professional sports. Wayne was dedicated to his sport and his team. But even more, he was dedicated to his family and friends. No matter how great "The Great One" became, he never lost sight of what was important. As you read *A Century of Hockey Heroes*, you will find many of the same outstanding traits that Wayne Gretzky had in each hockey hero.

You will learn of the fierce determination of Rocket Richard, the unbending strength of Gordie Howe, the unique style of Bobby Orr, the leadership skills of Steve Yzerman, and the blazing speed of Pavel Bure. You will learn about the pioneers of the game, too. When you read about players like Georges Vezina, Howie Morenz, and Newsy Lalonde, you will see how similar players of each era are.

There are also many stories about players whose success took place on another continent. I hope that you pay particular attention to such players as Vladislav Tretiak, Peter Stastny, and Vsevolod Bobrov. Because of them, hockey is the most international of sports.

The players of yesterday and the players of today are connected by the qualities that make a hockey star — determination, teamwork, speed, agility, hard work, courage. The players had those qualities when the 20th century began and they have them as the century ends. I suspect they will have them when the next century ends, too.

I hope that you enjoy *A Century of Hockey Heroes*.

Gary B. Bettman
Commissioner

Introduction

For many years historians have wondered about the origin of hockey. Did it evolve from the ball and stick games played on the frozen lakes and rivers of Nova Scotia and the New England states? Or do its roots date back even further? Ball and stick games have been popular in Europe for centuries. So is skating.

One thing is known for sure. The sport of hockey as it would become known in the 20th century first came indoors off frozen lakes and rivers for a demonstration at the Victoria Skating Rink in Montreal, Canada on March 3, 1875. The two teams that day used nine men per side. To keep the rubber ball from flying into the stands and harming spectators, the players cut off the top and bottom to make it flat — creating the first hockey puck!

Within 15 years of the first game in Montreal, the new sport of hockey had spread all across Canada. Interest was so high that in 1893 Canada's Governor General, Lord Stanley of Preston, donated a championship trophy that would become known as the Stanley Cup. Around this time hockey was also beginning to attract attention in American cities like Boston and New York, Baltimore and Pittsburgh, as well as in states like Michigan and Minnesota. At the same time, athletes began to play hockey in the colder countries of northern Europe — though it would take many years for them to catch up to their North American counterparts.

Still, by the dawn of the 20th century all the pieces were in place for what would become "The Coolest Game on Earth!"

If a hockey fan took a time machine and traveled back 100 years, that fan might have a hard time recognizing the game. Goalies had only just started wearing pads on their legs, while other players of this early era used very little visible protection. Some of them used catalogues or magazines under their socks and tucked a little something extra into their football-style pants. They wore long woolen socks and thick sweaters for warmth in drafty wooden arenas that relied on cold temperatures to keep the ice frozen. Many players also wore woolen hats. There were no hockey helmets or special hockey gloves, and games began when the referee placed the puck on the ice between two opposing centers and shouted, "Play!" Teams now used seven men on the ice at a time and players weren't allowed to pass the puck ahead of them. Goalies had to remain standing at all times.

The first professional hockey leagues were formed in the United States just a few years after 1900. By 1910 the American game was strictly amateur again, but professionalism was spreading in Canada. The National Hockey Association was formed in 1910 with professional teams in eastern Canada. In 1912, the Pacific Coast Hockey Association was formed in the west. These were hockey's top pro leagues.

The NHA and PCHA battled each other for the Stanley Cup, and between them they began to modernize the game — eliminating the seventh man, experimenting with forward passing, and letting goalies drop to the ice to stop the puck.

In 1917–18, the NHA became the NHL. The PCHA had teams in Canada and the United States, but the NHL only had teams in Toronto, Ottawa, and Montreal. In 1924, the NHL expanded into Boston while the New York Americans and Pittsburgh Pirates came on board one year later. Around this time, international hockey teams in Europe were beginning to take part in Olympic and World Championships. Still, by 1926–27 everyone agreed that the NHL was the top league in all of hockey. It was now the only league competing for the Stanley Cup.

The NHL had as many as 10 teams during the 1930s, but in 1942–43 it settled in as a six-team league. Those teams, which have become known as "The Original Six," were the Toronto Maple Leafs, Montreal Canadiens, Boston Bruins, New York Rangers, Chicago Blackhawks, and Detroit Red Wings. Today, many old-timers will say that the era of the six-team NHL was the greatest in hockey. Fans were familiar with all the star players, and great rivalries existed between teams that played each other 14 times a year! But things change.

In 1967–68, the NHL doubled in size to 12 teams. More teams meant more players and more fans in new cities. This resulted in more scoring and even more excitement! The NHL continued to expand throughout the 1970s, creating more star players for even more fans to follow. There were 21 teams during the 1980s, and there will be 30 by the time the NHL reaches the 2000–2001 season. Bolstered by an influx of European stars, the NHL of today has more talented players than ever. Who knows what new advancements await us?

To determine the greatest players of the 20th century the authors looked to their fellow editors of *Total Hockey* and *The NHL Guide and Record Book*. By studying Hall of Fame members, All-Star Teams, and top trophy winners, they compiled a list that reflects all of the game's eras: from the pre-NHL years, to the Original Six, to today's worldwide game. Also included are the best international stars from leading hockey nations like Sweden, Russia, Slovakia, and the Czech Republic who never had a chance to play in the NHL. And who knows? With the inclusion of women's hockey at the 1998 Winter Olympic Games in Nagano, perhaps the greatest players of the next century will include names like Canada's Hayley Wickenheiser, Finland's Riikka Nieminen, and American gold medalist Cammi Granato.

Syl Apps

Position: **Center**   Height: **6'0" (183 cm)**   Weight: **185 lbs (84 kg)**   Born: **January 18, 1915 in Paris, ON.**

Regular Season								Playoffs					
Season	Team	GP	G	A	Pts	PIM	+/−	Season	Team	GP	G	A	Pts	PIM
1936-37	Toronto	48	16	29	45	10	—	1936-37	Toronto	2	0	1	1	0
1937-38	Toronto	47	21	29	50	9	—	1937-38	Toronto	7	1	4	5	0
1938-39	Toronto	44	15	25	40	4	—	1938-39	Toronto	10	2	6	8	2
1939-40	Toronto	27	13	17	30	5	—	1939-40	Toronto	10	5	2	7	2
1940-41	Toronto	41	20	24	44	6	—	1940-41	Toronto	7	3	2	5	2
1941-42	Toronto ♟	38	18	23	41	0	—	1941-42	Toronto ♟	13	5	9	14	2
1942-43	Toronto	29	23	17	40	2	—	1942-43	Toronto	—	—	—	—	—
1945-46	Toronto	40	24	16	40	2	—	1945-46	Toronto	—	—	—	—	—
1946-47	Toronto ♟	54	25	24	49	6	—	1946-47	Toronto ♟	11	5	1	6	0
1947-48	Toronto ♟	55	26	27	53	12	—	1947-48	Toronto ♟	9	4	4	8	0
	NHL Totals:	423	201	231	432	56	—		Playoff Totals:	69	25	29	54	8

Syl Apps was more than just a great hockey player; he was also a college football star and the Canadian pole vaulting champion. In 1936, he finished sixth in the world in pole vaulting at the Summer Olympics. That fall, he began his NHL career with the Toronto Maple Leafs.

With his handsome looks and graceful style, Syl Apps was one of hockey's true gentlemen. He didn't smoke, he didn't drink, and he never swore. Like Wayne Gretzky, Apps was a center who seemed happier to set up his teammates than to score goals himself. He led the NHL with 29 assists in 1936-37 and won the Calder Trophy as rookie of the year. His fine passing skills helped teammate Gordie Drillon lead the NHL with 26 goals and 52 points in 1937-38, while Apps led the league in assists again that year.

By the 1941-42 season, Apps was one of the top stars in hockey. He had been either a First- or Second-Team All-Star four times in six seasons. He had been a top-10 scorer five times. He'd been named captain of the Leafs in 1940-41. In 1942, he won the Lady Byng Trophy awarded for most sportsman like player in the league. Apps also led the Leafs to the Stanley Cup that year. Toronto lost the first three games of the final to Detroit, then won the next four in a row. No other team in sports history has made such a dramatic comeback in a championship series.

After the 1942-43 season, Apps left the Maple Leafs to become a soldier in World War II. He spent two years in the army. When the War was over, he returned to Toronto for the 1945-46 season. Apps was better than ever! He set a new career high with 24 goals that year, then broke it with 25 in 1946-47. He also led the Leafs to another Stanley Cup title in 1947.

At the start of the 1947-48 season, Apps hinted that he was getting ready to retire. He said that before he did, he wanted to score his 200th career goal. (In those days, 200 goals was the kind of milestone that 500 goals is today.) Apps reached his goal with a hat trick during the final game of the season! His three goals that night gave him 26 for the season and 201 for his career. In the playoffs that year Apps led the Leafs to another Stanley Cup championship. Once the season was over, he retired. He was elected to the Hockey Hall of Fame in 1961.

Only 16 players have captained the Toronto Maple Leafs over more than 70 years of team history. Syl Apps led the Leafs to three Stanley Cup titles in his six years as captain.

Hobey Baker

Position: **Rover**   Height: **5'9" (175 cm)**   Weight: **160 lbs (73 kg)**   Born: **Wissachiken, PA.**

Year	Team	Event/League	GP	G	A	Pts
1906-07	St. Paul's	Not available	—	—	—	—
1907-08	St. Paul's	Not available	—	—	—	—
1908-09	St. Paul's	Not available	—	—	—	—
1909-10	St. Paul's	Not available	—	—	—	—
1910-11	Princeton	Not available	—	—	—	—
1911-12	Princeton	Not available	—	—	—	—
1912-13	Princeton	Not available	—	—	—	—
1913-14	St. Nicholas	AHA Sr	—	—	—	—
1914-15	St. Nicholas	AHA Sr.	8	18	0	18
1915-16	St. Nicholas	AHA Sr.	—	—	—	—

Hockey was still a new sport in the United States when Hobart Amery Baker began to play the game around 1906. Baker first made a name for himself in hockey at St. Paul's School in Concord, New Hampshire. By the time he reached Princeton University in 1910, Hobey Baker was ready to become America's first hockey star. But Baker was more than just a hockey player; he also excelled at golf, gymnastics, track and field, and swimming. He was an All-American football hero during his days at Princeton, where he captained the team in his final year. Baker was a handsome man with "a twinkle in his eye" and an impish grin. His blond good looks won him fans both on the ice and off.

During his days at Princeton, Baker was also the captain of the hockey team for two years. When his team played, they were often referred to as "Baker and six other players." Baker was not happy with that description because he believed teamwork was essential to success. Still, Baker was by far the school's best player. He was a speedy skater with slick stickhandling skills. Newspaper stories would be filled with accounts of his dazzling displays. They often talked about Baker jumping over sticks and legs to score a goal.

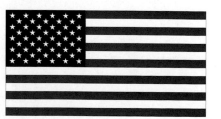

Some stories say that he once jumped up and ran on top of the boards to outrace an opponent!

Baker came from a wealthy Philadelphia family and grew up with a spirit of sportsmanship and fair play. Even when other players broke the rules to try and stop him, Baker would always shake hands with the opposing team.

Baker played the position of rover in the days when hockey teams used seven men on the ice. The rover was responsible for helping the forwards score goals, but also had to help the defensemen prevent them. Baker had many offers to play professional hockey in Canada after he graduated from Princeton in 1914, but he chose to play with the St. Nicholas amateur team in New York. Soon after arriving, Baker joined the American air force and flew as a pilot during World War I. He was killed in a plane crash on December 21, 1918 — five weeks after the war ended. In 1945, Hobey Baker was one of the first players elected to the Hockey Hall of Fame. Every year since 1981, the best player in U.S. college hockey has been presented with the Hobey Baker Memorial Award.

After he joined the St. Nicholas team in New York, limousines would line up outside the arena. The big cars were bringing high society fans to watch Hobey Baker (top row, middle) play hockey.

Andy Bathgate

Position: **Right Wing**   Height: **6'0" (183 cm)**   Weight: **205 lbs (93 kg)**   Born: **March 31, 1928 in Winnipeg, MN.**

		Regular Season									Playoffs				
Season	Team	GP	G	A	Pts	PIM	+/-	Season	Team	GP	G	A	Pts	PIM
1952-53	NY Rangers	18	0	1	1	6	—	1952-53	NY Rangers	—	—	—	—	—
1953-54	NY Rangers	20	2	2	4	18	—	1953-54	NY Rangers	—	—	—	—	—
1954-55	NY Rangers	70	20	20	40	37	—	1954-55	NY Rangers	—	—	—	—	—
1955-56	NY Rangers	70	19	47	66	59	—	1955-56	NY Rangers	5	1	2	3	2
1956-57	NY Rangers	70	27	50	77	60	—	1956-57	NY Rangers	5	2	0	2	27
1957-58	NY Rangers	65	30	48	78	42	—	1957-58	NY Rangers	6	5	3	8	6
1958-59	NY Rangers	70	40	48	88	48	—	1958-59	NY Rangers	—	—	—	—	—
1959-60	NY Rangers	70	26	48	74	28	—	1959-60	NY Rangers	—	—	—	—	—
1960-61	NY Rangers	70	29	48	77	22	—	1960-61	NY Rangers	—	—	—	—	—
1961-62	NY Rangers	70	28	56	84	44	—	1961-62	NY Rangers	6	1	2	3	4
1962-63	NY Rangers	70	35	46	81	54	—	1962-63	NY Rangers	—	—	—	—	—
1963-64	NY Rangers	56	16	43	59	26	—	1963-64	NY Rangers	—	—	—	—	—
	Toronto 🏆	15	3	15	18	8	—		Toronto 🏆	14	5	4	9	25
1964-65	Toronto	55	16	29	45	34	—	1964-65	Toronto	6	1	0	1	6
1965-66	Detroit	70	15	32	47	25	—	1965-66	Detroit	12	6	3	9	6
1966-67	Detroit	60	8	23	31	24	—	1966-67	Detroit	—	—	—	—	—
1967-68	Pittsburgh	74	20	39	59	55	-11	1967-68	Pittsburgh	—	—	—	—	—
1970-71	Pittsburgh	76	15	29	44	34	-11	1970-71	Pittsburgh	—	—	—	—	—
	NHL Totals:	961	327	601	928	563			Playoff Totals:	54	21	14	35	76

Andy Bathgate was a hockey player who did everything well. He was a strong skater, a slick stickhandler, and had a quick release, which gave him one of the hardest shots in hockey. He was also a talented playmaker who always ranked among the NHL's leaders in assists. Bathgate prided himself on staying in top condition long before most athletes concentrated on keeping in shape.

At only 16 years of age Bathgate joined the New York Rangers organization. He played with New York's farm club in Guelph, Ontario, and helped them win the Memorial Cup as Canada's junior hockey champions in 1952. Bathgate suffered a serious knee injury while playing in Guelph, forcing him to wear a special brace for the rest of his career. It didn't stop him from becoming a star. Bathgate became a regular in the Rangers lineup in 1954-55. From 1955-56 to 1962-63, he led his team in scoring for eight straight seasons!

Unfortunately, Bathgate was a great player on a team that was not very good. His best season was 1958-59 when he ranked third in the NHL with 40 goals and 88 points. He was so good that year that he won the Hart Trophy as the NHL's most valuable player even though his team didn't make the playoffs. Bathgate was a First-Team All-Star at right wing that season. He made it to the First All-Star Team again in 1961-62 when he tied Bobby Hull for the NHL scoring title with 84 points. Hull won the Art Ross Trophy that year because he scored 54 goals. Bathgate scored only 28 goals that season, but his 56 assists were by far the most in the NHL.

After starring for years with the Rangers, Bathgate finally got a chance to play for a championship team in 1964. Traded to the Toronto Maple Leafs, Bathgate led the NHL in assists again in 1963-64, and helped Toronto win the Stanley Cup. Before the 1965-66 season, Bathgate was traded for a second time to the

Detroit Red Wings. Bathgate helped the Red Wings reach the Stanley Cup Final, but they lost to the Montreal Canadiens. Later Bathgate played for the Pittsburgh Penguins, then coached in Europe. In 1974-75, Bathgate was a "playing coach" with the Vancouver Blazers of the World

In his nine full seasons in New York, the Rangers never got past the first round of the playoffs. Andy Bathgate finally won the Stanley Cup with Toronto.

Hockey Association. Bathgate was elected to the Hockey Hall of Fame in 1978.

Jean Beliveau

Position: **Center**   Height: **6'3" (191 cm)**   Weight: **205 lbs (93 kg)**   Born: **August 31, 1931 in Trois Rivieres, QC.**

Season	Team	GP	G	A	Pts	PIM	+/-		Season	Team	GP	G	A	Pts	PIM
1950-51	Montreal	2	1	1	2	0	—		1950-51	Montreal	—	—	—	—	—
1952-53	Montreal	3	5	0	5	0	—		1952-53	Montreal	—	—	—	—	—
1953-54	Montreal	44	13	21	34	22	—		1953-54	Montreal	10	2	8	10	4
1954-55	Montreal	70	37	36	73	58	—		1954-55	Montreal	12	6	7	13	18
1955-56	Montreal	70	47	41	88	143	—		1955-56	Montreal	10	12	7	19	22
1956-57	Montreal	69	33	51	84	105	—		1956-57	Montreal	10	6	6	12	15
1957-58	Montreal	55	27	32	59	93	—		1957-58	Montreal	10	4	8	12	10
1958-59	Montreal	64	45	46	91	67	—		1958-59	Montreal	3	1	4	5	4
1959-60	Montreal	60	34	40	74	57	—		1959-60	Montreal	8	5	2	7	6
1960-61	Montreal	69	32	58	90	57	—		1960-61	Montreal	6	0	5	5	0
1961-62	Montreal	43	18	23	41	36	—		1961-62	Montreal	6	2	1	3	4
1962-63	Montreal	69	18	49	67	68	—		1962-63	Montreal	5	2	1	3	2
1963-64	Montreal	68	28	50	78	42	—		1963-64	Montreal	5	2	0	2	18
1964-65	Montreal	58	20	23	43	76	—		1964-65	Montreal	13	8	8	16	34
1965-66	Montreal	67	29	48	77	50	—		1965-66	Montreal	10	5	5	10	6
1966-67	Montreal	53	12	26	38	22	—		1966-67	Montreal	10	6	5	11	26
1967-68	Montreal	59	31	37	68	28	27		1967-68	Montreal	10	7	4	11	6
1968-69	Montreal	69	33	49	82	55	15		1968-69	Montreal	14	5	10	15	8
1969-70	Montreal	63	19	30	49	10	1		1969-70	Montreal	—	—	—	—	—
1970-71	Montreal	70	25	51	76	40	24		1970-71	Montreal	20	6	16	22	28
NHL Totals:		**1125**	**507**	**712**	**1219**	**1029**			**Playoff Totals:**		**162**	**79**	**97**	**176**	**211**

Standing 6'3" (191 cm) and weighing 205 pounds (93 kg), Jean Beliveau was a rare combination of power and grace. His long legs moved with a sweeping skating style that gave him surprising speed. His long arms helped give him wonderful puck control. It was hard for other players to check him because of his size, but Beliveau always behaved like a gentleman — on the ice and off.

Jean Beliveau spent 20 years with the Montreal Canadiens between 1950-51 and 1970-71. He played 18 full seasons with the team and helped them win the Stanley Cup 10 times! Beliveau has become one of hockey's most legendary players, but he was being hailed as a hero even before he joined the Canadiens.

These days, the annual NHL Draft sees many young players enter the league with a lot of hype. They're expected to become superstars. Beliveau was the first player to carry such high expectations into the NHL. He certainly lived up to it in Montreal, but not until he had thanked the fans who supported him in Quebec City. Beliveau played an extra year with the Quebec Aces before he finally signed with the Canadiens in 1953-54.

By 1954-55, Beliveau was the NHL's First-Team All-Star at center. In 1955-56, Beliveau led the league with 47 goals and 88 points. His goal total that year was the third highest in NHL history at the time, and he was rewarded with the Hart Trophy as the league's most valuable player. In the playoffs that year, Beliveau helped the Canadiens win the first of five Stanley Cup victories in a row! During that time Beliveau also recorded the league's fourth-highest goal total when he scored 45 times in 1958-59. His 46 assists that year gave him a career-high 91 points.

Beliveau was named captain of the Canadiens in 1961-62. Unfortunately, injuries

that year ended his All-Star streak at seven straight seasons. Beliveau's health was much better by 1963-64, and he won the Hart Trophy again that year. Beliveau retired after the Canadiens won yet another Stanley Cup in 1970-71. At the time, Beliveau's 1,219 career points was second only to Gordie Howe in the history

Jean Beliveau was just the fourth player in NHL history to score 500 goals in regular-season play. Here, the great Canadiens captain celebrates one of the 507 goals he scored during his career.

of the NHL. Beliveau was elected to the Hockey Hall of Fame in 1972.

Clint Benedict

Position: **Goaltender**   Height: **(unknown)**   Weight: **(unknown)**   Born: **September 26, 1892 in Ottawa, ON.**

Regular Season										Playoffs									
Season	Team	GP	W	L	T	MINS	GA	SO	AVG.	Season	Team	GP	W	L	T	MINS	GA	SO	AVG.
1917-18	Ottawa	22	9	13	0	1337	114	1	5.12	1917-18	Ottawa	—	—	—	—	—	—	—	—
1918-19	Ottawa	18	12	6	0	1152	53	2	2.86	1918-19	Ottawa	5	1	4	0	300	26	0	5.20
1919-20	Ottawa 🏆	24	19	5	0	1443	64	5	2.66	1919-20	Ottawa 🏆	5	3	2	0	300	11	1	2.20
1920-21	Ottawa 🏆	24	14	10	0	1457	75	2	3.09	1920-21	Ottawa 🏆	7	5	2	0	420	12	2	1.71
1921-22	Ottawa	24	14	8	2	1508	84	2	3.34	1921-22	Ottawa	2	0	1	1	120	5	1	2.50
1922-23	Ottawa 🏆	24	14	9	1	1486	54	4	2.18	1922-23	Ottawa 🏆	8	6	2	0	480	10	3	1.25
1923-24	Ottawa	22	16	6	0	1356	45	3	1.99	1923-24	Ottawa	2	0	2	0	120	5	0	2.50
1924-25	Mtl. Maroons	30	9	19	2	1843	65	2	2.12	1924-25	Mtl. Maroons	—	—	—	—	—	—	—	—
1925-26	Mtl. Maroons 🏆	36	20	11	5	2288	73	6	1.91	1925-26	Mtl. Maroons 🏆	8	5	1	2	480	8	4	1.00
1926-27	Mtl. Maroons	43	20	19	4	2748	65	13	1.42	1926-27	Mtl. Maroons	2	0	1	1	132	2	0	0.91
1927-28	Mtl. Maroons	44	24	14	6	2690	76	7	1.70	1927-28	Mtl. Maroons	9	5	3	1	555	8	4	0.86
1928-29	Mtl. Maroons	37	14	16	7	2300	57	11	1.49	1928-29	Mtl. Maroons	—	—	—	—	—	—	—	—
1929-30	Mtl. Maroons	14	6	6	1	752	33	0	2.63	1929-30	Mtl. Maroons	—	—	—	—	—	—	—	—
NHL Totals:		362	191	142	28	22360	858	58	2.30	Playoff Totals:		48	25	18	5	2907	87	15	1.80

Even though his name is not as famous as Georges Vezina, Clint Benedict was probably a better goaltender. Their careers cover many of the same years, and Benedict's statistics were usually better. He also helped change the way goaltenders were allowed to play. Benedict had a habit of "accidentally" falling to the ice to make saves. At the time, the NHL rules forced goalies to remain standing at all times. Rather than calling a penalty every time he did it, the NHL decided to change the rule and allow goalies to fall and block shots.

Clint Benedict began playing hockey as a six-year-old in his hometown of Ottawa. By the time he was 15, he was playing with grown men. At the age of 20, he joined the Ottawa Senators of the National Hockey Association for the 1912-13 season. He became the club's number-one netminder in 1914-15 and led Ottawa to the Stanley Cup Finals that year. The Senators lost the championship to the Vancouver Millionaires of the rival Pacific Coast Hockey Association. (In this era, the Stanley Cup was decided in a series between the NHA and the PCHA. When the NHA became the NHL in 1917-18 it continued

the series against the PCHA for several more years.)

When Benedict entered the NHL, he soon established himself as the best goalie in hockey. He had the lowest goals-against average in the NHL from 1918-19 to 1922-23. He also led (or shared the lead) in shutouts during each of the league's first six seasons. Benedict helped the Senators win back-to-back Stanley Cup championships in 1920 and 1921. Ottawa won again in 1923.

Even though he had a 1.99 goals-against average in 1923-24, the Senators decided to trade Benedict to the Montreal Maroons. The Maroons were an expansion team in 1924-25, but Benedict helped them win the Stanley Cup in 1925-26. The next season was his best ever. He had a 1.42 goals-against average and 13 shutouts.

Benedict remained with the Maroons until the 1929-30 season. On January 7, 1930, his nose was broken on a shot fired by Howie Morenz. Benedict was out of action until February 20. When he returned he became the first goalie in the NHL to wear a mask. The mask was made of leather and did not provide a

lot of protection. Soon, Benedict's nose was injured again. Benedict also feared the mask was blocking part of his vision, so he stopped wearing it. No goalie wore a mask again until Jacques Plante, 29 years later. At the end of the season, Benedict retired from the NHL. He was elected to the Hockey Hall of Fame in 1965.

Even though equipment looked primitive in the early days, Clint Benedict was a great goalie. Benedict still holds the NHL record of 15 career shutouts in the playoffs.

Doug Bentley

Position: **Left Wing**   Height: **5'8" (173 cm)**   Weight: **145 lbs (66 kg)**   Born: **September 3, 1916 in Delisle, SK.**

Regular Season									Playoffs					
Season	Team	GP	G	A	Pts	PIM	+/-		Season	Team	GP	G	A	Pts	PIM
1939-40	Chicago	39	12	7	19	12	—		1939-40	Chicago	2	0	0	0	0
1940-41	Chicago	47	8	20	28	12	—		1940-41	Chicago	5	1	1	2	
1941-42	Chicago	38	12	14	26	11	—		1941-42	Chicago	3	0	1	1	4
1942-43	Chicago	50	33	40	73	18	—		1942-43	Chicago	—	—	—	—	—
1943-44	Chicago	50	38	39	77	22	—		1943-44	Chicago	9	8	4	12	4
1945-46	Chicago	36	19	21	40	16	—		1945-46	Chicago	4	0	2	2	0
1946-47	Chicago	52	21	34	55	18	—		1946-47	Chicago	—	—	—	—	—
1947-48	Chicago	60	20	37	57	16	—		1947-48	Chicago	—	—	—	—	—
1948-49	Chicago	58	23	43	66	38	—		1948-49	Chicago	—	—	—	—	—
1949-50	Chicago	64	20	33	53	28	—		1949-50	Chicago	—	—	—	—	—
1950-51	Chicago	44	9	23	32	20	—		1950-51	Chicago	—	—	—	—	—
1951-52	Chicago	8	2	3	5	4	—		1951-52	Chicago	—	—	—	—	—
1953-54	NY Rangers	20	2	10	12	2	—		1953-54	NY Rangers	—	—	—	—	—
	NHL Totals:	566	219	324	543	217				Playoff Totals:	23	9	8	17	8

Doug Bentley didn't look like a hockey star. He stood just 5'8" (173 cm) and weighed only 145 pounds (66 kg) — but could he play! Bentley was a speedy skater and slick stickhandler. He became one of the top players in the NHL during the 1940s.

Bentley began playing hockey in his hometown of Delisle, Saskatchewan. He moved up the ranks quickly and was soon starring on a team in Drumheller, Alberta that featured three of his brothers! In 1939-40, Bentley made it to the NHL with the Chicago Blackhawks. His brother Max joined the team the following season. They both became stars in 1942-43, when Max won the Lady Byng Trophy for sportsmanlike play and Doug won the NHL scoring title with 33 goals and 73 points. His point total tied an NHL record that had stood unbroken for 13 years. In 1943-44, Doug collected 38 goals and 77 points, but had to settle for second place in the scoring race. Herb Cain of the Boston Bruins won the title with a new record of 82 points.

Doug Bentley joined the army during World War II and didn't play in 1944-45. He rejoined the team for the 1945-46 season, and he and Max were placed on a line with Bill Mosienko. The Pony Line, as they were called, became the best combination in the NHL. Doug's play in 1946-47 earned him a selection as the left winger on the First All-Star Team for the third time of his career.

The next season, Chicago traded Max to the Toronto Maple Leafs. Doug remained with the Blackhawks and continued to be one of the NHL's best scorers. In 1948-49, Doug was second in league scoring with 66 points, while new teammate Roy Conacher won the scoring title with 68 points.

In 1950, Chicago fans voted Doug Bentley as the greatest player in Blackhawks history. But his career was coming to an end. He played only eight games in 1951-52, then returned home to Saskatchewan. In 1953-54, he made a brief comeback with the New York Rangers, where his brother Max also played, but it would turn out to be the final NHL season for both Bentley brothers. In 1964, Doug was elected to the Hockey Hall of Fame.

Though older than Max, Doug Bentley was two years younger than brother Reg, who played just 11 games in the NHL. The three Bentley brothers played on the same line in Chicago on New Year's Day, 1943.

Max Bentley

Position: **Center**   Height: **5'10" (178 cm)**   Weight: **155 lbs (70 kg)**   Born: **March 1, 1920 in Delisle, SK.**

Regular Season								Playoffs						
Season	Team	GP	G	A	Pts	PIM	+/-	Season	Team	GP	G	A	Pts	PIM
1940-41	Chicago	36	7	10	17	6	—	1940-41	Chicago	4	1	3	4	2
1941-42	Chicago	39	13	17	30	2	—	1941-42	Chicago	3	2	0	2	0
1942-43	Chicago	47	26	44	70	2	—	1942-43	Chicago	—	—	—	—	—
1945-46	Chicago	47	31	30	61	6	—	1945-46	Chicago	4	1	0	1	4
1946-47	Chicago	60	29	43	72	12	—	1946-47	Chicago	—	—	—	—	—
1947-48	Chicago	6	3	3	6	4	—	1947-48	Chicago	—	—	—	—	—
	Toronto 🏆	53	23	25	48	10	—		Toronto 🏆	9	4	7	11	0
1948-49	Toronto 🏆	60	19	22	41	18	—	1948-49	Toronto 🏆	9	4	3	7	2
1949-50	Toronto	69	23	18	41	14	—	1949-50	Toronto	7	3	3	6	0
1950-51	Toronto 🏆	67	21	41	62	34	—	1950-51	Toronto 🏆	11	2	11	13	4
1951-52	Toronto	69	24	17	41	40	—	1951-52	Toronto	4	1	0	1	2
1952-53	Toronto	36	12	11	23	16	—	1952-53	Toronto	—	—	—	—	—
1953-54	NY Rangers	57	14	18	32	15	—	1953-54	NY Rangers	—	—	—	—	—
NHL Totals:		646	245	299	544	179		Playoff Totals:		51	18	27	45	14

Max Bentley was a magician with the puck. He was called "The Dipsy Doodle Dandy" because of the way he could stickhandle around his opponents. Bentley would dash and dart back and forth, and he could stop and start faster than any other player. He looked skinny and frail, but hard-hitting defensemen couldn't hurt him, because they could never catch him!

Max Bentley grew up in a hockey-playing family in Delisle, Saskatchewan. Three Bentley brothers eventually made it to the NHL. Both Max and Doug Bentley made it all the way to the Hockey Hall of Fame. Doug was the oldest Bentley brother. He broke into the NHL with the Blackhawks in 1939-40. Max joined him in Chicago the following year. By 1942-43, both Bentleys had become stars. Doug won the NHL scoring title that year, while Max finished third and won the Lady Byng Trophy for his sportsmanlike play.

Max missed the next two seasons while training with the Canadian army during World War II. When he returned to Chicago in 1945-46, he was better than ever. Max was teamed on a line with his brother Doug and Bill Mosienko. Together, they were called the Pony Line and they were three of the most dangerous scorers in the NHL. In fact, Max won the NHL scoring title in 1945-46. He was also awarded the Hart Trophy as the league's most valuable player. The following season, he was the league scoring leader for the second year in a row.

Max Bentley was now at the height of his fame, but the Blackhawks were not doing as well as he was. In November 1947, Chicago traded him to Toronto and received five players in return! The Maple Leafs were a much better team: they had won the Stanley Cup the year before they got Bentley. He helped them repeat as champions in 1947-48, then win again in 1949 and 1951. He remained with the Leafs through the 1952-53 season.

In 1953-54, Bentley was reunited with his brother when both players joined the New York Rangers. Unfortunately, the aging veterans were past their prime, and it was the final NHL season for both of them.

Toronto's Max Bentley – one of three Bentley brothers to play in the NHL – tries to dipsy doodle past Red Wings defenseman Leo Reise, Jr., whose father – Leo Reise, Sr. – played in the NHL from 1920 to 1930.

Vsevolod Bobrov

Position: **Left Wing**   Height: **6'1" (185 cm)**   Weight: **185 lbs (84 kg)**   Born: **December 1, 1922 in Bestroretsk, USSR.**

Year	Team	Event/League	GP	G	A	Pts	PIM
1954	Soviet Union	World Championships	7	8	1	9	2
1955	Soviet Union	World Championships	6	4	—	—	—
1956	Soviet Union	Olympics	7	9	—	—	—
1957	Soviet Union	World Championships	5	13	—	—	—
1946 - 1957	"CDKA Moscow, VVS MVO Moscow"	Soviet Union League	130	254	—	—	—
	Career Totals:		155	288	—	—	—

Not too many years ago, almost every player in the NHL came from Canada. A few came from the United States. Today, the NHL has many players from all around the world. Some of the league's top stars, like Pavel Bure, come from Russia. Russia has been producing great hockey players for more than half a century, but Russian players were not allowed to play in the NHL until the 1990s. That's because until then Russia was a part of the Soviet Union, and the Soviet Union had a very different system of government than Canada and the United States. The Communist government of the Soviet Union kept its hockey players at home.

When they could not play in the NHL, Russian hockey players concentrated on winning at the Olympics and the World Championships instead. These international tournaments were not open to professional players, so the Russian players did not get paid. Usually, they were given jobs in the army instead, though they trained more to play hockey than to be soldiers. And they trained well! The Soviet Union did not even have its first official hockey league until 1946, but by 1954 the Soviet national team was good enough to win the World Championship. The first Soviet hockey star was Vsevolod Bobrov. His

career began in 1946, and by his final season in 1957 he had led his teams to seven Soviet championships in 10 years. In 130 league games during that time, Bobrov scored an amazing 254 goals!

Bobrov was a natural athlete who also starred on the Soviet Olympic soccer team in 1952. He was an excellent stickhandler with blazing speed, and he always wanted to have the puck. As soon as he got himself into position, he would call out to his teammates to pass him the puck. They would always try their best to get it to him right away because, when they did, it usually wound up in the net.

In addition to starring in the Soviet hockey league, Vsevolod Bobrov was also the captain of the national team from 1954 to 1957. He was named the Best Forward at the 1954 World Championships after leading the Soviets to their surprising victory. In 1956, he captained his team to the gold medal at the Olympics. After his playing days, Bobrov became a coach in Moscow. He later coached the Soviet national team from 1972 to 1974. In those three years, Bobrov guided the Soviet National hockey team to two World Championship titles.

Vsevolod Bobrov poses with the 1954 World and European Championship Trophy. This was the Soviet team's debut at the tournament, which saw them reach the finals undefeated. Canada was heavily favored to beat the Soviets for the Gold Medal. However, the Soviets skill and speed proved to difficult to handle, and the Soviets beat the Canadians easily by a score of 7 - 2.

Mike Bossy

Position: **Right Wing**   Height: **6'0" (183 cm)**   Weight: **186 lbs (84 kg)**   Born: **January 22, 1957 in Montreal, QC.**

Regular Season								Playoffs						
Season	Team	GP	G	A	Pts	PIM	+/-	Season	Team	GP	G	A	Pts	PIM
1977-78	NY Islanders	73	53	38	91	6	31	1977-78	NY Islanders	7	2	2	4	2
1978-79	NY Islanders	80	69	57	126	25	63	1978-79	NY Islanders	10	6	2	8	2
1979-80	NY Islanders	75	51	41	92	12	28	1979-80	NY Islanders	16	10	13	23	8
1980-81	NY Islanders	79	68	51	119	52	37	1980-81	NY Islanders	18	17	18	35	4
1981-82	NY Islanders	80	64	83	147	22	69	1981-82	NY Islanders	19	17	10	27	0
1982-83	NY Islanders	79	60	58	118	20	27	1982-83	NY Islanders	19	17	9	26	10
1983-84	NY Islanders	67	51	67	118	8	66	1983-84	NY Islanders	21	8	10	18	4
1984-85	NY Islanders	76	58	59	117	38	37	1984-85	NY Islanders	10	5	6	11	4
1985-86	NY Islanders	80	61	62	123	14	30	1985-86	NY Islanders	3	1	2	3	4
1986-87	NY Islanders	63	38	37	75	33	7	1986-87	NY Islanders	6	2	3	5	0
	NHL Totals:	752	573	553	1126	210			Playoff Totals:	129	85	75	160	38

Mike Bossy was one of the most gifted goal scorers to ever play in the NHL. Blessed with a laser-like shot, Bossy is the only player to score 50 goals in each of his first nine seasons.

Even though Bossy averaged better than 70 goals a year in junior, most NHL teams didn't seem to want him. That's because his talents were hard to see. He wasn't very fast, or big, or strong, but he had a hockey sense that could not be taught. He knew how to get open, and when the puck touched his stick, it was gone in a blur. Fourteen teams chose somebody else before the New York Islanders drafted Mike Bossy. He went on to score 573 goals in his career—all of them wearing an Islanders uniform.

Bossy was a star from his very first season of 1977–78. That year he set a new rookie record with 53 goals; no other rookie had ever scored more than 44. In just his second season, Bossy led the league with 69 goals. A great team player, Bossy helped the Islanders win the Stanley Cup four years in a row from 1980 to 1983.

The Montreal native was the most accurate shooter of his era. He scored on better than 20% of his shots in each of his first nine years in the league. Even the great Gretzky and the marvellous Mario did not match that mark.

Although Bossy is one of only two players in NHL history to score 60 or more goals in five different seasons, he was also a gifted playmaker. He collected 50 or more assists in seven of his 10 NHL campaigns, including a career-high 83 helpers in 1981-82.

On January 21, 1981, Bossy tied a record many people thought unreachable. On that night, he scored his 50th goal in his 50th game of the season. Only the immortal Rocket Richard had ever been able to do that!

Many of Bossy's classic goals were scored in the area near the crease known as the slot. When you stand in the slot, you get hit. While Bossy could take a hit, his back couldn't and, during his 10th NHL season, back problems forced Bossy to stop playing. He was only 30 years old. If he could have continued, Wayne Gretzky may have been chasing Bossy instead of Gordie Howe for the all-time scoring record.

Mike Bossy raised his stick to celebrate a goal 573 times in his career. Bossy averaged more than three goals for every four games he played in the NHL! Only Mario Lemieux has a higher scoring rate.

Frank Boucher

Position: **Center**   Height: **5'9" (175 cm)**   Weight: **185 lbs (84 kg)**   Born: **October 7, 1901 in Ottawa, ON.**

Regular Season								Playoffs						
Season	Team	GP	G	A	Pts	PIM	+/-	Season	Team	GP	G	A	Pts	PIM
1921-22	Ottawa	24	8	2	10	4	—	1921-22	Ottawa	1	0	0	0	0
1926-27	NY Rangers	44	13	15	28	17	—	1926-27	NY Rangers	2	0	0	0	4
1927-28	NY Rangers 🏆	44	23	12	35	15	—	1927-28	NY Rangers 🏆	9	7	1	8	2
1928-29	NY Rangers	44	10	16	26	8	—	1928-29	NY Rangers	1	0	1	0	—
1929-30	NY Rangers	42	26	36	62	16	—	1929-30	NY Rangers	1	1	2	0	—
1930-31	NY Rangers	44	12	27	39	20	—	1930-31	NY Rangers	0	2	2	0	—
1931-32	NY Rangers	48	12	23	35	18	—	1931-32	NY Rangers	3	6	9	0	—
1932-33	NY Rangers 🏆	46	7	28	35	4	—	1932-33	NY Rangers 🏆	2	2	4	6	—
1933-34	NY Rangers	48	14	30	44	4	—	1933-34	NY Rangers	0	0	0	0	—
1934-35	NY Rangers	48	13	32	45	2	—	1934-35	NY Rangers	4	0	3	3	0
1935-36	NY Rangers	48	11	18	29	2	—	1935-36	NY Rangers	—	—	—	—	—
1936-37	NY Rangers	44	7	13	20	5	—	1936-37	NY Rangers	9	2	3	5	0
1937-38	NY Rangers	18	0	1	1	2	—	1937-38	NY Rangers	—	—	—	—	—
1943-44	NY Rangers	15	4	10	14	2	—	1943-44	NY Rangers	—	—	—	—	—
NHL Totals:		557	160	263	423	119		Playoff Totals:		55	16	18	34	12

Hockey was a very different game in the early years of the NHL. At first, players were not allowed to pass the puck forward. This meant that the best players had to be able to stickhandle the puck all the way from one end of the ice to the other. Gradually, the rules were changed to allow more and more passing. That means teams had to find players who could play well together on lines. The NHL's first great forward line featured Frank Boucher with brothers Bill and Bun Cook.

Like the Cooks, Frank Boucher came from a hockey-playing family. Four Bouchers played in the NHL, and Frank and his brother George made it all the way to the Hockey Hall of Fame. During his days in the league, Frank Boucher was considered the top playmaker in hockey. He was at his best when he was setting up goals for his teammates.

Boucher's NHL career began in his hometown with the Ottawa Senators in 1921-22. George Boucher was a top player with the team, but Frank didn't get many chances to play. He spent the next four seasons in other professional hockey leagues. Frank finally returned to the NHL in 1926-27, when he joined a brand-new team called the New York Rangers. Bill and Bun Cook were already there. In their first season together, Boucher's pretty passes allowed Bill Cook to lead the league in goals and points. Boucher himself was seventh in the NHL scoring race. The next season, all three linemates finished in the top 10 and the Rangers won the Stanley Cup. (They would win it again in 1933.) When the NHL began to choose an annual All-Star Team in 1930-31, Frank Boucher was selected as the center on the Second Team. He was chosen as a First-Team All-Star for the next three years.

Talented as he was, what really made Frank Boucher stand out was his classy style of play. Hockey was a rough game, but Boucher was always a sportsman. He won the Lady Byng Trophy seven times in eight seasons. Boucher won it so often that he was given the original trophy to keep!

Boucher retired as a player in 1938 and took over as the Rangers coach. He coached the

team to another Stanley Cup victory in 1940. Later, he became the general manager of the Rangers and remained with the team until 1955.

Frank Boucher's skill with the puck helped change the way hockey was played. Like a quarterback in football, Boucher practiced set passing plays with linemates Bill and Bun Cook.

Raymond Bourque

Position: **Defense** Height: **5'11" (180 cm)** Weight: **219 lbs (100 kg)** Born: **December 28, 1960 in Montreal, QC.**

| Regular Season | | | | | | | | Playoffs | | | | | |
Season	Team	GP	G	A	Pts	PIM	+/-	Season	Team	GP	G	A	Pts	PIM
1979-80	Boston	80	17	48	65	73	52	1979-80	Boston	10	2	9	11	27
1980-81	Boston	67	27	29	56	96	29	1980-81	Boston	3	0	1	1	2
1981-82	Boston	65	17	49	66	51	22	1981-82	Boston	9	1	5	6	16
1982-83	Boston	65	22	51	73	20	49	1982-83	Boston	17	8	15	23	10
1983-84	Boston	78	31	65	96	57	51	1983-84	Boston	3	0	2	2	0
1984-85	Boston	73	20	66	86	53	30	1984-85	Boston	5	0	3	3	4
1985-86	Boston	74	19	58	77	68	17	1985-86	Boston	3	0	0	0	0
1986-87	Boston	78	23	72	95	36	44	1986-87	Boston	4	1	2	3	0
1987-88	Boston	78	17	64	81	72	34	1987-88	Boston	23	3	18	21	26
1988-89	Boston	60	18	43	61	52	20	1988-89	Boston	10	0	4	4	6
1989-90	Boston	76	19	65	84	50	31	1989-90	Boston	17	5	12	17	16
1990-91	Boston	76	21	73	94	75	33	1990-91	Boston	19	7	18	25	12
1991-92	Boston	80	21	60	81	56	11	1991-92	Boston	12	3	6	9	12
1992-93	Boston	78	19	63	82	40	38	1992-93	Boston	4	1	0	1	2
1993-94	Boston	72	20	71	91	58	26	1993-94	Boston	13	2	8	10	0
1994-95	Boston	46	12	31	43	20	3	1994-95	Boston	5	0	3	3	0
1995-96	Boston	82	20	62	82	58	31	1995-96	Boston	5	1	6	7	2
1996-97	Boston	62	19	31	50	18	-11	1996-97	Boston	—	—	—	—	—
1997-98	Boston	82	13	35	48	80	2	1997-98	Boston	6	1	4	5	2
1998-99	Boston	81	10	47	57	34	-7	1998-99	Boston	12	1	9	10	14
NHL Totals:		**1453**	**385**	**1083**	**1468**	**1066**		**Playoff Totals:**		**180**	**36**	**125**	**161**	**151**

It's rare for any player to play 20 seasons in the NHL with the same team. Yet Raymond Bourque has managed to do exactly that. He has remained a solid fixture on the Bruins' blueline for two decades with no signs of slowing down.

Bourque was Boston's first selection in the 1979 draft, the richest, most productive draft ever. Bourque is the answer to a unique trivia question: Who was the NHL's top rookie in Wayne Gretzky's first year in the league? It was just the beginning of the most consistent career of any defenseman in NHL history.

Bourque has scored at least 20 goals in a season nine times. Not even Bobby Orr or Paul  Coffey managed to do that! He was an All-Star 18 times, second only to Gordie Howe, and his name has been etched on the Norris Trophy five times. In 1998-99,

Bourque passed Gordie Howe to move into third place on the all-time assists leaders' list.

How has Bourque done it? He plays a calm, quiet game and rarely takes chances.

Off-ice training keeps Bourque in tiptop shape. The most important part of Bourque's body is his legs. Bourque is a smooth skater, and his easy, gliding style has kept his legs fresh. That's important because he still plays 25 to 30 minutes a game!

The only item missing on Bourque's honor roll is a Stanley Cup title. The Bruins have reached the finals twice in his career, but they fell short both times. The Bruins offered to trade their long-serving rear guard to a contending team, but he humbly refused. He didn't want to uproot his family, who love the Boston area, which tells you as much about Raymond Bourque as a man, as it does about him as a player.

Hockey is played at high speed, but a talented defenseman like Raymond Bourque can calmly control the play. Bourque doesn't panic when he has the puck, so he rarely makes a bad play.

Turk Broda

Position: Goaltender   Height: **5'9" (175 cm)**   Weight: **180 lbs (82 kg)**   Born: **May 15, 1914 in Brandon, MB.**

Regular Season										Playoffs								
Season	Team	GP	W	L	T	MINS	GA	SO	AVG.	Season	Team	GP	W	L	MINS	GA	SO	AVG.
1936-37	Toronto	45	22	19	4	2770	106	3	2.30	1936-37	Toronto	2	0	2	133	5	0	2.26
1937-38	Toronto	48	24	15	9	2980	127	6	2.56	1937-38	Toronto	7	4	3	452	13	1	1.73
1938-39	Toronto	48	19	20	9	2990	107	8	2.15	1938-39	Toronto	10	5	5	617	20	2	1.94
1939-40	Toronto	47	25	17	5	2900	108	4	2.23	1939-40	Toronto	10	6	4	657	19	1	1.74
1940-41	Toronto	48	28	14	6	2970	99	5	2.00	1940-41	Toronto	7	3	4	438	15	0	2.05
1941-42	Toronto 🏆	48	27	18	3	2960	136	6	2.76	1941-42	Toronto 🏆	13	8	5	780	31	1	2.38
1942-43	Toronto	50	22	19	9	3000	159	1	3.18	1942-43	Toronto	6	2	4	439	20	0	2.73
1945-46	Toronto	15	6	6	3	900	53	0	3.53	1945-46	Toronto	—	—	—	—	—	—	—
1946-47	Toronto 🏆	60	31	19	10	3600	172	4	2.87	1946-47	Toronto 🏆	11	8	3	680	27	1	2.38
1947-48	Toronto 🏆	60	32	15	13	3600	143	5	2.38	1947-48	Toronto 🏆	9	8	1	557	20	1	2.15
1948-49	Toronto 🏆	60	22	25	13	3600	161	5	2.68	1948-49	Toronto 🏆	9	8	1	574	15	1	1.57
1949-50	Toronto	68	30	25	12	4040	167	9	2.48	1949-50	Toronto	7	3	4	450	10	3	1.33
1950-51	Toronto 🏆	31	14	11	5	1827	68	6	2.23	1950-51	Toronto 🏆	8	5	1	492	9	2	1.10
1951-52	Toronto	1	0	1	0	30	3	0	6.00	1951-52	Toronto	2	0	2	120	7	0	3.50
NHL Totals:		**629**	**302**	**224**	**101**	**38167**	**1609**	**62**	**2.53**	**Playoff Totals:**		**101**	**60**	**39**	**6389**	**211**	**13**	**1.98**

Turk Broda's real name was Walter. He was given his nickname because, as a boy, he had freckles and people would tease him and say that his skin looked like a turkey egg. He never let the teasing bother him though. He never seemed to let anything affect his cheerful personality — not even the pressure of being an NHL goalie. The more important a game was, the better Broda played.

He was the first goalie in NHL history to win 300 regular-season games, but it was his performance in the playoffs that made him truly special. Broda led the Toronto Maple Leafs to five Stanley Cup championships in his 13 seasons with the team. His lifetime playoff goals-against average is an amazing 1.98! His 13 playoff shutouts have been topped only by Clint Benedict and Jacques Plante.

The only thing that ever bothered the roly-poly goalie was his weight — though it always seemed to be more of a problem for other people. Once the Maple Leafs suspended Broda until he lost 10 pounds!

Turk Broda became a Maple Leaf in 1936 when Toronto owner Conn Smythe bought his contract from a Detroit Red Wings farm team for $8,000. Broda immediately took over Toronto's number-one goaltending job and led the Leafs to

the Stanley Cup Finals in each of his first two seasons. In 1940-41, he won the Vezina Trophy as the best goaltender in the NHL for the first time. His goals-against average that year was 2.00. The following season, Broda and the Maple Leafs won the Stanley Cup.

Turk played one more year in Toronto, then left the team to become a sailor in the Royal Canadian Navy during World War II. At the time, he announced his retirement from hockey, but when the war ended he returned to the Maple Leafs late in the 1945-46 season. With Broda back in goal in 1946-47, the Leafs began their most successful run in team history. They won the Stanley Cup three years in a row from 1947 to 1949, then won it again in 1950-51. Broda was at his best during the 1947-48 season. That year he won 32 games and set a Leafs record that lasted for 11 years. He also led the league with a 2.38 goals-against average and won the Vezina Trophy for the second time.

Turk Broda played only three more games in the NHL after the Leafs won the Stanley Cup in 1951. He was elected to the Hockey Hall of Fame in 1967.

Turk Broda missed a week of action in November of 1949 because Maple Leafs management forced him to go on a diet. He got a shutout in his first game back and celebrated with a stack of pancakes!

Pavel Bure

Position: **Right Wing**   Height: **5'10" (178 cm)**   Weight: **189 lbs (86 kg)**   Born: **March 31, 1971 in Moscow, USSR.**

Regular Season									Playoffs						
Season	Team	GP	G	A	Pts	PIM	+/-		Season	Team	GP	G	A	Pts	PIM
1991-92	Vancouver	65	34	26	60	30	0		1991-92	Vancouver	13	6	4	10	14
1992-93	Vancouver	83	60	50	110	69	35		1992-93	Vancouver	12	5	7	12	8
1993-94	Vancouver	76	60	47	107	86	1		1993-94	Vancouver	24	16	15	31	40
1994-95	Vancouver	44	20	23	43	47	-8		1994-95	Vancouver	11	7	6	13	10
1995-96	Vancouver	15	6	7	13	8	-2		1995-96	Vancouver	—	—	—	—	—
1996-97	Vancouver	63	23	32	55	40	-14		1996-97	Vancouver	—	—	—	—	—
1997-98	Vancouver	82	51	39	90	48	5		1997-98	Vancouver	—	—	—	—	—
1998-99	Florida	11	13	3	16	4	3		1998-99	Florida	—	—	—	—	—
	NHL Totals:	439	267	227	474	332				Playoff Totals:	60	34	32	66	72

When the Vancouver Canucks announced that they finally had Pavel Bure's name on a contract in 1991, the fans on the Canadian west coast were excited, and they filled the arena the first time he skated with the team. There's nothing odd about that, except for the fact that his first appearance with the Canucks was only a practice! Fans just couldn't wait to get a glimpse of the young phenomenon the papers called "The Russian Rocket."

Bure is one of the most talented players to ever skate in the NHL. He's virtually unstoppable on a breakaway. No opening is too small for him to find, no defense too tight for him to stretch. When he's on the ice, the opposing team is so worried about stopping him that they drop their guard on the other players. That creates openings which, in turn, create goals. But it's Bure's speed that leaves everyone in awe. He can go from a standing start to top speed in the blink of an eye. Another key to his game is versatility. Bure can play every forward position with equal skill.

In 1991-92, Bure became the first Vancouver player to win a major NHL award when he took home the Calder Trophy as the league's top freshman. Since he moved from position to position so much, he was left off the All-Rookie Team, because the voters didn't know where to position him. The NHL then decided to drop the right wing, left wing, and center positions on the All-Rookie Team lineup card. That means the top three forwards in the league, regardless of their position, will make the All-Rookie Team.

A pair of 60-goal seasons in '92-93 and '93-94 followed his exciting rookie year. In 1994, Bure led a magical Stanley Cup run for Vancouver. He led all playoff scorers with 16 goals as the Vancouver Canucks came within a goalpost of winning the Stanley Cup. His next two seasons were plagued with injuries, but he returned to form in 1997-98, notching 51 goals and 90 points. In 1999, Vancouver traded Bure to Florida. In his first game in the Sunshine State, Bure scored a pair of goals and followed that up with a marvellous hat-trick that featured all his skills. The Bure era in Florida had just begun.

The explosive speed of "The Russian Rocket" makes it almost impossible for opposing players to catch him. Even if they do, his great balance makes it hard to knock him off the puck.

Chris Chelios

Position: **Defense**   Height: **6'1" (185 cm)**   Weight: **190 lbs (86 kg)**   Born: **January 25, 1962 in Chicago, IL.**

	Regular Season									Playoffs					
Season	Team	GP	G	A	Pts	PIM	+/-		Season	Team	GP	G	A	Pts	PIM
1983-84	Montreal	12	0	2	2	12	-5		1983-84	Montreal	15	1	9	10	17
1984-85	Montreal	74	9	55	64	87	11		1984-85	Montreal	9	2	8	10	17
1985-86	Montreal 🏆	41	8	26	34	67	4		1985-86	Montreal 🏆	20	2	9	11	49
1986-87	Montreal	71	11	33	44	124	-5		1986-87	Montreal	17	4	9	13	38
1987-88	Montreal	71	20	41	61	172	14		1987-88	Montreal	11	3	1	4	29
1988-89	Montreal	80	15	58	73	185	35		1988-89	Montreal	21	4	15	19	28
1989-90	Montreal	53	9	22	31	136	20		1989-90	Montreal	5	0	1	1	8
1990-91	Chicago	77	12	52	64	192	23		1990-91	Chicago	6	1	7	8	46
1991-92	Chicago	80	9	47	56	245	24		1991-92	Chicago	18	6	15	21	37
1992-93	Chicago	84	15	58	73	282	14		1992-93	Chicago	4	0	2	2	14
1993-94	Chicago	76	16	44	60	212	12		1993-94	Chicago	6	1	1	2	8
1994-95	Chicago	48	5	33	38	72	17		1994-95	Chicago	16	4	7	11	12
1995-96	Chicago	81	14	58	72	140	25		1995-96	Chicago	9	0	3	3	8
1996-97	Chicago	72	10	38	48	112	16		1996-97	Chicago	6	0	1	1	8
1997-98	Chicago	81	3	39	42	151	-7		1997-98	Chicago	—	—	—	—	—
1998-99	Chicago	65	8	26	34	89	-4		1998-99	Chicago	—	—	—	—	—
	Detroit	10	1	1	2	4	5			Detroit	10	0	4	4	14
	NHL Totals:	1076	165	633	798	2282				Playoff Totals:	173	28	92	120	333

When he just 16 years old, Chris Chelios was cut from three different teams in one season. For most players, that would be a sign that they were not good enough to play hockey. Chris Chelios decided to try again and was picked up by a junior team in Moose Jaw, Saskatchewan. Now Chelios is a six-time All-Star, a three-time winner of the Norris Trophy, and a certain Hockey Hall-of-Famer.

Chelios has never been a fancy skater or a tricky puck handler. He is, however, a gritty, hard-working defenseman who leaves every ounce of effort on the ice. He will skate through a player to get to a loose puck, he'll roll over an enemy forward to get him out the crease, and he'll flatten anyone who comes near his goalie. His fans love him. Their fans hate him. To Chelios, being booed in the other guy's rink is sweet music. It means he has done his job.

Chelios has plenty of offensive talent. He has scored 20 goals in his best season and has topped 70 points three times. Still, he's best known as a hard-pounding checker and a fearless shot blocker. Those skills have made him one of the best defensemen in hockey. His ability to play through pain has made him an inspirational leader to his teammates.

After a brief tour of duty with the U.S. Olympic Team, Chelios began his career with the Montreal Canadiens in 1983-84. Veteran defenseman Larry Robinson took the greenhorn under his wing and taught him the "Canadiens" way. Chelios was a good student. In just his third year with the Habs, Chelios won his first Stanley Cup title. In 1989 he won the Norris Trophy.

In a trade they will always regret, Montreal sent Chelios to Chicago in 1990. They have never really been able to replace him. Returning to his home town of Chicago was a perfect fit for Chelios.

He was the backbone of the Blackhawks for almost a decade, earning three First Team All-Star nods after coming home. He helped lead the Hawks to the Finals in 1992, and won Norris Trophy honors twice while wearing the Chicago

uniform. But with the Blackhawks struggling in 1998–99, Chelios was traded to the Red Wings. They won't be booing him in Detroit anymore.

Now a member of the Detroit Red Wings, Chris Chelios still has the talent to help out on offense, but it's his defensive skill in his own end that makes him so valuable.

King Clancy

Position: **Defense**   Height: **5'7" (170 cm)**   Weight: **155 lbs (70 kg)**   Born: **February 25, 1903 in Ottawa, ON.**

Regular Season								Playoffs						
Season	Team	GP	G	A	Pts	PIM	+/-	Season	Team	GP	G	A	Pts	PIM
1921-22	Ottawa	24	4	6	10	21		1921-22	Ottawa	2	0	0	0	2
1922-23	Ottawa 🏆	24	3	1	4	20		1922-23	Ottawa 🏆	8	1	0	1	2
1923-24	Ottawa	24	9	8	17	18		1923-24	Ottawa	2	0	0	0	4
1924-25	Ottawa	29	14	5	19	61		1924-25	Ottawa	—	—	—	—	—
1925-26	Ottawa	35	8	4	12	80		1925-26	Ottawa	2	1	0	1	8
1926-27	Ottawa 🏆	43	9	10	19	78		1926-27	Ottawa 🏆	6	1	1	2	14
1927-28	Ottawa	39	8	7	15	73		1927-28	Ottawa	2	0	0	0	6
1928-29	Ottawa	44	13	2	15	89		1928-29	Ottawa	—	—	—	—	—
1929-30	Ottawa	44	17	23	40	83		1929-30	Ottawa	2	0	1	1	2
1930-31	Toronto	44	7	14	21	63		1930-31	Toronto	2	1	0	1	0
1931-32	Toronto 🏆	48	10	9	19	61		1931-32	Toronto 🏆	7	2	1	3	14
1932-33	Toronto	48	13	12	25	79		1932-33	Toronto	9	0	3	3	14
1933-34	Toronto	46	11	17	28	62		1933-34	Toronto	3	0	0	0	8
1934-35	Toronto	47	5	16	21	53		1934-35	Toronto	7	1	0	1	8
1935-36	Toronto	47	5	10	15	61		1935-36	Toronto	9	2	2	4	10
1936-37	Toronto	6	1	0	1	4		1936-37	Toronto	—	—	—	—	—
	NHL Totals:	592	137	144	281	906			Playoff Totals:	61	9	8	17	92

King Clancy began his NHL career as an 18-year-old with the Ottawa Senators in 1921-22. He would remain actively involved in hockey for the next 66 years as a referee, a coach, and a team executive. But he began his career as a star player. At 5'7" (170 cm) and 155 pounds (70 kg), Clancy was small for a defenseman, but he never backed down from bigger opponents. He could take care of business in front of his goalie, and he could also score goals. Clancy was always among the top-scoring defensemen in the NHL.

King Clancy was born in Ottawa and began his hockey career there. His real name was Francis Michael Clancy. His father had been a star athlete who everyone called "King" and Clancy inherited the nickname from him. He started his career with the Ottawa Senators, and his feisty play helped his team win the Stanley Cup in 1923 and 1927. By 1929, though, the Senators were in trouble. The world economy was in a depression and Ottawa was having a hard time

supporting its hockey team. Soon the Senators were forced to sell their top stars to other teams. Shortly before the 1930-31 season, King Clancy was sold to the Toronto Maple Leafs. The price was $35,000 and two players. That might not sound like very much money today, but back then it was the most money ever paid for a hockey player!

Toronto Maple Leafs owner Conn Smythe hoped that King Clancy's spirited play would help his young team. It did exactly that. In just his second season in Toronto, Clancy helped the Leafs win the Stanley Cup. Following their victory in 1932, the Leafs reached the Finals three more times in the next four years. Clancy was a major reason behind their success. He had been a First-Team All-Star four years in a row (1930-31 to 1933-34), and continued to rank among the league's best defensemen until he retired in 1936-37.

After he left the Maple Leafs, King Clancy coached the Montreal Maroons in 1937-38, and then he became an NHL referee. In 1953, he returned to Toronto as the coach and later became the club's assistant general manager. During the 1960s, he helped run Toronto teams

that won the Stanley Cup in 1962, 1963, 1964, and 1967. Clancy was elected to the Hockey Hall of Fame in 1958 and remained with the Leafs as the club's "goodwill ambassador" until his death in 1986.

Like many players from hockey's early days, King Clancy later became a referee. Always a colorful character, Clancy could charm his way out of most problems with players and coaches.

Dit Clapper

Position: **Right Wing/Defense**　　Height: **6'2" (188 cm)**　　Weight: **195 lbs (88 kg)**　　Born: **February 9, 1907 in Newmarket, ON.**

	Regular Season								Playoffs				
Season	Team	GP	G	A	Pts	PIM	+/-	Season	Team	GP	G	A	Pts	PIM
1927-28	Boston	40	4	1	5	20		1927-28	Boston	2	0	0	0	2
1928-29	Boston	40	9	2	11	48		1928-29	Boston	5	1	0	1	0
1929-30	Boston	44	41	20	61	48		1929-30	Boston	6	4	0	4	4
1930-31	Boston	43	22	8	30	50		1930-31	Boston	5	2	4	6	4
1931-32	Boston	48	17	22	39	21		1931-32	Boston	—	—	—	—	—
1932-33	Boston	48	14	14	28	42		1932-33	Boston	5	1	1	2	2
1933-34	Boston	48	10	12	22	6		1933-34	Boston	—	—	—	—	—
1934-35	Boston	48	21	16	37	21		1934-35	Boston	3	1	0	1	0
1935-36	Boston	44	12	13	25	14		1935-36	Boston	2	0	1	1	0
1936-37	Boston	48	17	8	25	25		1936-37	Boston	3	2	0	2	5
1937-38	Boston	46	6	9	15	24		1937-38	Boston	3	0	0	0	12
1938-39	Boston	42	13	13	26	22		1938-39	Boston	12	0	1	1	6
1939-40	Boston	44	10	18	28	25		1939-40	Boston	5	0	2	2	2
1940-41	Boston	48	8	18	26	24		1940-41	Boston	11	0	5	5	4
1941-42	Boston	32	3	12	15	31		1941-42	Boston	—	—	—	—	—
1942-43	Boston	38	5	18	23	12		1942-43	Boston	9	2	3	5	9
1943-44	Boston	50	6	25	31	13		1943-44	Boston					
1944-45	Boston	46	8	14	22	16		1944-45	Boston	7	0	0	0	0
1945-46	Boston	30	2	3	5	0		1945-46	Boston	4	0	0	0	0
1946-47	Boston	6	0	0	0	0		1946-47	Boston	—	—	—	—	—
	NHL Totals:	833	228	246	474	462			Playoff Totals:	82	13	17	30	50

Dit Clapper was the first man to play 20 seasons in the NHL. He began his career with Boston as a 20-year-old in 1927-28 and didn't retire until he was 40. He had remained a Bruin for all of those years. At 6'2" (188 cm) and 195 pounds (89 kg), Clapper was one of the biggest players in hockey during his career and also one of the best. Dit played right wing during the first half of his career and then switched to defense. He was so good at both positions that he is the only man in NHL history to be named an All-Star both as a forward and a defenseman.

Boston had only been in the NHL for three years when Dit Clapper arrived in 1927. By 1928-29, the Bruins were Stanley Cup champions. Clapper starred on Boston's top line with Cooney Weiland and Dutch Gainor. Together, they were called the Dynamite Line because of their scoring power.

The NHL made an important rule change before the 1929-30 season. In the early days of hockey, players were not allowed to pass the puck forward. Passes behind them were allowed, but players could only advance the puck by skating with it. In 1929-30, forward passing was allowed, and no team used the new rule better than the Bruins.

Boston had a record of 38-5-1 during the 44-game season. All these years later, the Bruins' winning percentage of .875 is still the best in NHL history. If a team played that well during today's 82-game season they would have a record of 71-9-2 and 144 points! That year Clapper set a career high with 41 goals and 61 points. When the NHL first began to choose All-Stars in 1930-31, Clapper was named to the Second Team.

Prior to 1938-39, the Bruins added offensive stars like Bill Cowley and Milt Schmidt, allowing the Bruins to move Clapper to defense. He helped Boston win the Stanley Cup that season and again in 1940-41. He was also a First-Team All-Star at defense for three years in a row. In 1945-46, he

became the playing coach of the Bruins. When he finally retired as a player on February 12, 1947, Dit Clapper was immediately elected to the Hockey Hall of Fame.

Dit Clapper's number 5 is one of seven numbers retired by the Boston Bruins. The others belong to Eddie Shore (2), Lionel Hitchman (3), Bobby Orr (4), Phil Esposito (7), John Bucyk (9), and Milt Schmidt (15).

Bobby Clarke

Position: **Center**   Height: **5'10" (178 cm)**   Weight: **185 lbs (84 kg)**   Born: **August 13, 1949 in Flin Flon, MB.**

Season	Team	Regular Season GP	G	A	Pts	PIM	+/-	Season	Team	Playoffs GP	G	A	Pts	PIM
1969-70	Philadelphia	76	15	31	46	68	1	1969-70	Philadelphia	—	—	—	—	—
1970-71	Philadelphia	77	27	36	63	78	9	1970-71	Philadelphia	4	0	0	0	2
1971-72	Philadelphia	78	35	46	81	87	22	1971-72	Philadelphia	—	—	—	—	—
1972-73	Philadelphia	78	37	67	104	80	32	1972-73	Philadelphia	11	2	6	8	6
1973-74	Philadelphia	77	35	52	87	113	35	1973-74	Philadelphia	17	5	11	16	42
1974-75	Philadelphia	80	27	89	116	125	79	1974-75	Philadelphia	17	4	12	16	16
1975-76	Philadelphia	76	30	89	119	136	83	1975-76	Philadelphia	16	2	14	16	28
1976-77	Philadelphia	80	27	63	90	71	39	1976-77	Philadelphia	10	5	5	10	8
1977-78	Philadelphia	71	21	68	89	83	47	1977-78	Philadelphia	12	4	7	11	8
1978-79	Philadelphia	80	16	57	73	68	12	1978-79	Philadelphia	8	2	4	6	8
1979-80	Philadelphia	76	12	57	69	65	42	1979-80	Philadelphia	19	8	12	20	16
1980-81	Philadelphia	80	19	46	65	140	17	1980-81	Philadelphia	12	3	3	6	6
1981-82	Philadelphia	62	17	46	63	154	20	1981-82	Philadelphia	4	4	2	6	4
1982-83	Philadelphia	80	23	62	85	115	37	1982-83	Philadelphia	3	1	0	1	2
1983-84	Philadelphia	73	17	43	60	70	23	1983-84	Philadelphia	3	2	1	3	6
NHL Totals:		**1144**	**358**	**852**	**1210**	**1453**		**Playoff Totals:**		**136**	**42**	**77**	**119**	**152**

Bobby Clarke was the heart and soul of the Philadelphia Flyers during his 15-year career. Even though he suffered from diabetes, he never let his disease interfere with his dreams of playing in the NHL. His condition only made him work harder to achieve his goals.

Clarke played junior hockey in his hometown of Flin Flon, Manitoba. He led the Manitoba junior league in assists and points in his final two seasons. Although he was clearly one of the top young talents in the country, many scouts thought he was too fragile to play in the NHL. At the 1969 Amateur Draft, all 12 teams passed on selecting Clarke. Finally, the Philadelphia Flyers took a chance and chose him in the second round. That decision changed the hockey history of Philadelphia forever.

Almost from the first moment that Clarke put on a Flyers jersey, he became their on-ice leader. He was a brilliant playmaker who could skate, shoot, and score. But Clarke also had character and drive. He would plow into the corners to retrieve loose pucks, he could deliver punishing bodychecks, and he played every shift as though he might never play another. His determination won him a lot of fans and a lot of respect from opposing players and coaches.

In each of his first four seasons, Clarke consistently improved his goals, assists, and point totals of the year before. Named the Flyers captain in 1972, he became the first player from a post-1967 expansion team to record 100 points. In 1973-74, Clark won the Hart Trophy as league MVP. He went on to win the award again in 1975 and 1976, leading the Flyers to a pair of Stanley Cup titles along the way.

In 1979-80, Clarke became a playing assistant coach with the Flyers. He had to give up his captaincy, but it helped him to learn the front office ropes. It also meant a change in his style, and Clarke became one of the NHL's top two-way centers. In 1982-83, he won the Frank Selke Trophy as the league's top defensive forward.

The Flyers captain earned four All-Star Team berths, collected 50 or more assists nine times, and played in eight All-Star Games during his 15-year Hall of Fame career. Despite playing

a rough and rumble style, Clarke missed only 44 games in his entire career.

After his playing career was over, Clarke went on to become a well-respected general manager in Minnesota, Florida, and Philadelphia.

Bobby Clarke battles for the puck between Claire Alexander and George Ferguson (10) of the Toronto Maple Leafs. Determination and drive were the characteristics of this great Flyers captain.

Paul Coffey

Position: **Defense** Height: **6'0" (183 cm)** Weight: **190 lbs (86 kg)** Born: **June 1, 1961 in Weston, ON.**

	Regular Season								Playoffs					
Season	Team	GP	G	A	Pts	PIM	+/-	Season	Team	GP	G	A	Pts	PIM
1980-81	Edmonton	74	9	23	32	130	4	1980-81	Edmonton	9	4	3	7	22
1981-82	Edmonton	80	29	60	89	106	35	1981-82	Edmonton	5	1	1	2	6
1982-83	Edmonton	80	29	67	96	87	52	1982-83	Edmonton	16	7	7	14	14
1983-84	Edmonton 🏆	80	40	86	126	104	52	1983-84	Edmonton 🏆	19	8	14	22	21
1984-85	Edmonton 🏆	80	37	84	121	97	55	1984-85	Edmonton 🏆	18	12	25	37	44
1985-86	Edmonton	79	48	90	138	120	61	1985-86	Edmonton	10	1	9	10	30
1986-87	Edmonton 🏆	59	17	50	67	49	12	1986-87	Edmonton 🏆	17	3	8	11	30
1987-88	Pittsburgh	46	15	52	67	93	-1	1987-88	Pittsburgh	—	—	—	—	—
1988-89	Pittsburgh	75	30	83	113	195	-10	1988-89	Pittsburgh	11	2	13	15	31
1989-90	Pittsburgh	80	29	74	103	95	-25	1989-90	Pittsburgh	—	—	—	—	—
1990-91	Pittsburgh 🏆	76	24	69	93	128	-18	1990-91	Pittsburgh 🏆	12	2	9	11	6
1991-92	Pittsburgh	54	10	54	64	62	4	1991-92	Pittsburgh	—	—	—	—	—
	Los Angeles	10	1	4	5	25	-3		Los Angeles	6	4	3	7	2
1992-93	Los Angeles	50	8	49	57	50	9	1992-93	Los Angeles	—	—	—	—	—
	Detroit	30	4	26	30	27	7		Detroit	7	2	9	11	2
1993-94	Detroit	80	14	63	77	106	28	1993-94	Detroit	7	1	6	7	8
1994-95	Detroit	45	14	44	58	72	18	1994-95	Detroit	18	6	12	18	10
1995-96	Detroit	76	14	60	74	90	19	1995-96	Detroit	17	5	9	14	30
1996-97	Hartford	20	3	5	8	18	0	1996-97	Hartford	—	—	—	—	—
	Philadelphia	37	6	20	26	20	11		Philadelphia	17	1	8	9	6
1997-98	Philadelphia	57	2	27	29	30	3	1997-98	Philadelphia	—	—	—	—	—
1998-99	Chicago	10	0	4	4	0	-6	1998-99	Chicago	—	—	—	—	—
	Carolina	44	2	8	10	28	-7		Carolina	5	0	1	1	2
NHL Totals:		**1322**	**385**	**1102**	**1487**	**1732**		**Playoff Totals:**		**194**	**59**	**137**	**196**	**264**

Paul Coffey is the most dominant offensive defenseman of his era. He is the only rear guard to have two 40-goal seasons. Only Bobby Orr has more 100-point campaigns than Coffey. Coffey is the all-time leading scorer among defensemen and a major reason why the Edmonton Oilers rewrote the NHL record books in the mid-1980s.

The key to Coffey's success was his skating. He was the best skater to play in the NHL since Bobby Orr, and he shared a similar playing style. Coffey could lead an attack and still get back to protect his own zone. There are plenty of defensemen who can also speed back quickly, but Coffey always seemed to have a clear picture of where the attack was coming from.

The Edmonton Oilers selected Coffey sixth overall in the 1980 draft, inviting him to training camp that summer. Some teams would prefer to keep their young defensemen in junior or the minors. But the Oilers were a young team, and coach Glen Sather wanted to train the team to work together as a unit. Sather's plan worked, and the Oilers became a scoring machine, with Coffey at the steering wheel. He directed the attack with well-paced rushes and instinctive setups. Coffey scored at least 29 goals in five straight seasons with the Oilers, and set an NHL record for defensemen with 48 goals in 1985-86. In the 1985 playoffs, he set NHL records for goals (12), assists (25), and points (37) by a defenseman. He was voted as the NHL's top defenseman twice and helped the Oilers win three championships.

Early in the 1987-88 season, Coffey was traded to Pittsburgh where he was teamed with superstar Mario Lemieux. In 1990-91, Coffey helped the Pens take home the Cup for the first

time in franchise history. A brief reunion with Wayne Gretzky in Los Angeles was followed by a three-year stay with the Detroit Red Wings. One of Coffey's proudest moments came in 1994-95 when he won his third Norris Trophy award. It had been eight seasons since his last award. No player has ever gone so long between major awards.

Injuries slowed Coffey down during the last few years. Still, his name appears on the Stanley

Paul Coffey carries the puck up ice for the Carolina Hurricanes. Coffey's speed and his skill with the puck have allowed him to set all sorts of scoring records for NHL defensemen.

Cup four times, and he has appeared in the championship finals seven times with four different teams. Only one honor remains for Coffey — entry into the Hockey Hall of Fame.

Charlie Conacher

Position: **Right Wing**   Height: **6'1" (185 cm)**   Weight: **195 lbs (88 kg)**   Born: **December 20, 1910 in Toronto, ON.**

Regular Season								Playoffs					
Season	Team	GP	G	A	Pts	PIM	+/-	Season	Team	GP	G	A	Pts	PIM
1929-30	Toronto	38	20	9	29	48	—	1929-30	Toronto	—	—	—	—	—
1930-31	Toronto	37	31	12	43	78	—	1930-31	Toronto	2	0	1	1	0
1931-32	Toronto	44	34	14	48	66	—	1931-32	Toronto	7	6	2	8	6
1932-33	Toronto	40	14	19	33	64	—	1932-33	Toronto	9	1	1	2	10
1933-34	Toronto	42	32	20	52	38	—	1933-34	Toronto	5	3	2	5	0
1934-35	Toronto	47	36	21	57	24	—	1934-35	Toronto	7	1	4	5	6
1935-36	Toronto	44	23	15	38	74	—	1935-36	Toronto	9	3	2	5	12
1936-37	Toronto	15	3	5	8	13	—	1936-37	Toronto	2	0	0	0	5
1937-38	Toronto	19	7	9	16	6	—	1937-38	Toronto	—	—	—	—	—
1938-39	Detroit	40	8	15	23	39	—	1938-39	Detroit	5	2	5	7	2
1939-40	NY Americans	47	10	18	28	41	—	1939-40	NY Americans	3	1	1	2	8
1940-41	NY Americans	46	7	16	23	32	—	1940-41	NY Americans	—	—	—	—	—
	NHL Totals:	459	225	173	398	523			Playoff Totals:	49	17	18	35	49

Charlie Conacher was the best hockey player in one of Canada's greatest athletic families. Charlie is a member of the Hockey Hall of Fame, along with his younger brother Roy and his older brother Lionel. Not only that, Lionel is a member of the Canadian lacrosse, football, and sports halls of fame as well. In 1950, Lionel was chosen as Canada's greatest athlete of the first half of the 20th century. Lionel's son Brian also played in the NHL, as did Charlie's son Pete.

Charlie Conacher started his NHL career with the Toronto Maple Leafs in 1929-30. He was only 19 years old, but he was already a hockey hero in his hometown. Conacher had been a junior star with the Toronto Marlboros, and in 1928-29 he helped them win the Memorial Cup. He became an even bigger hero when he entered the NHL.

Conacher played right wing, and the Maple Leafs put him on a line with Busher Jackson and Joe Primeau. Because all three of them were so young, their line was called the Kid Line.

Conacher might have been a kid, but he was a big kid. He stood 6'1" (185 cm) and weighed 195 pounds (88 kg). People called him "The Big Bomber." His specialty was blasting in goals with his powerful wrist shot, but he was just as dangerous with a backhander. He also had shifty moves around the net and could beat goalies with a deke. Conacher scored 20 times in his rookie season. The next year he led the league with 31 goals. He played even better when the Leafs won the Stanley Cup in 1931-32. In fact, the entire Kid Line became stars that year: Conacher led the league with 34 goals; Joe Primeau led the league with 37 assists; and Busher Jackson was the NHL scoring leader with 53 points. Conacher would win two scoring titles of his own, and he would lead the league in goals three more times. In his best season, in 1934-35, he led the league with 36 goals and 57 points.

Charlie Conacher spent nine seasons with the Maple Leafs. During that time, he was the best right winger in the NHL. He was a First-Team All-Star three times and was named to the Second Team twice. He later played with the Detroit Red Wings and New York Americans before retiring in 1941.

Charlie Conacher greets former Toronto teammate Hap Day of the New York Americans when he returns to Maple Leaf Gardens. Conacher took over the Leafs' captaincy from Day in 1937-38.

Bill Cook

Position: **Right Wing**   Height: **5'10" (178 cm)**   Weight: **170 lbs (77 kg)**   Born: **October 9, 1896 in Brantford, ON.**

	Regular Season								Playoffs					
Season	Team	GP	G	A	Pts	PIM	+/-	Season	Team	GP	G	A	Pts	PIM
1926-27	NY Rangers	44	33	4	37	58	—	1926-27	NY Rangers	2	1	0	1	6
1927-28	NY Rangers 🏆	43	18	6	24	42	—	1927-28	NY Rangers 🏆	9	2	3	5	26
1928-29	NY Rangers	43	15	8	23	41	—	1928-29	NY Rangers	6	0	0	0	6
1929-30	NY Rangers	44	29	30	59	56	—	1929-30	NY Rangers	4	0	1	1	11
1930-31	NY Rangers	43	30	12	42	39	—	1930-31	NY Rangers	4	3	0	3	4
1931-32	NY Rangers	48	34	14	48	33	—	1931-32	NY Rangers	7	3	3	6	2
1932-33	NY Rangers 🏆	48	28	22	50	51	—	1932-33	NY Rangers 🏆	8	3	2	5	4
1933-34	NY Rangers	48	13	13	26	21	—	1933-34	NY Rangers	2	0	0	0	2
1934-35	NY Rangers	48	21	15	36	23	—	1934-35	NY Rangers	4	1	2	3	7
1935-36	NY Rangers	44	7	10	17	16	—	1935-36	NY Rangers	—	—	—	—	—
1936-37	NY Rangers	21	1	4	5	6	—	1936-37	NY Rangers	—	—	—	—	—
	NHL Totals:	474	229	138	367	386			Playoff Totals:	46	13	11	24	68

Bill Cook became a professional hockey star when he played with one of the game's legendary goal scorers. Newsy Lalonde became Cook's teammate with Saskatoon in the Western Canada Hockey League in 1922-23. (The Western league used to compete with the NHL for the Stanley Cup.) Bill scored only nine times in 30 games that year, but over the next three seasons he led the WCHL in scoring twice. Cook continued his high-scoring ways when he entered the NHL in 1926-27. Brothers Bill and Bun Cook both left Saskatoon for the New York Rangers that year. Bill was a right winger and Bun played left wing. Together with center Frank Boucher, they would become the best line in the league.

New York was a brand new team in the NHL in 1926-27 and Bill Cook was the captain. He was already 30 years old, but he quickly  proved that both he and the Rangers belonged in the league. In the team's very first game he scored the only goal in a 1–0 victory over the Stanley Cup champion Montreal Maroons. By the end of the season Cook was the NHL's leading scorer with 33 goals and 37 points in 44 games. In 1927-28, he helped the Rangers win the Stanley Cup.

Cook was always dangerous when he got the puck near the net. He had a hard wrist shot, but he could also score goals just as well with his backhand. In 1931-32, he reached a career-high with 34 goals in a 48-game season. That tied him with Charlie Conacher for the league lead. Cook's 28 goals and 50 points were both the league's best in 1932-33. Cook helped the Rangers win the Stanley Cup again when he scored the winning goal in overtime of the final game of the series.

The NHL started choosing an annual All-Star Team in 1930-31, and for the first three years Cook was picked as the First-Team right winger. He was a Second-Team All-Star in 1933-34. Cook continued to star with the Rangers until he was 40 years old, and was still the team captain during his final season in 1936-37. In 11 years, he had scored 229 goals with the Rangers and 88 goals in four seasons with Saskatoon. In total, Cook had 317 career goals. Only Nels Stewart scored more during this era. Bill Cook was elected to the Hockey Hall of Fame in 1958. His brother Bun was inducted in 1995.

Bill Cook scored the first goal in New York Rangers history on November 16, 1926. He retired in 1937 and remained the Rangers' all-time scoring leader for almost 20 years.

Yvan Cournoyer

Position: **Right Wing**   Height: **5'7" (170 cm)**   Weight: **178 lbs (81 kg)**   Born: **November 22, 1943 in Drummondville, QC.**

Regular Season								Playoffs						
Season	Team	GP	G	A	Pts	PIM	+/-	Season	Team	GP	G	A	Pts	PIM
1963-64	Montreal	5	4	0	4	0	—	1963-64	Montreal	—	—	—	—	—
1964-65	Montreal 🏆	55	7	10	17	10	—	1964-65	Montreal 🏆	12	3	1	4	0
1965-66	Montreal 🏆	65	18	11	29	8	—	1965-66	Montreal 🏆	10	2	3	5	2
1966-67	Montreal	69	25	15	40	14	—	1966-67	Montreal	10	2	3	5	6
1967-68	Montreal 🏆	64	28	32	60	23	19	1967-68	Montreal 🏆	13	6	8	14	4
1968-69	Montreal 🏆	76	43	44	87	31	19	1968-69	Montreal 🏆	14	4	7	11	5
1969-70	Montreal	72	27	36	63	23	1	1969-70	Montreal	—	—	—	—	—
1970-71	Montreal 🏆	65	37	36	73	21	20	1970-71	Montreal 🏆	20	10	12	22	6
1971-72	Montreal	73	47	36	83	15	23	1971-72	Montreal	6	2	1	3	2
1972-73	Montreal 🏆	67	40	39	79	18	50	1972-73	Montreal 🏆	17	15	10	25	2
1973-74	Montreal	67	40	33	73	18	16	1973-74	Montreal	6	5	2	7	2
1974-75	Montreal	76	29	45	74	32	16	1974-75	Montreal	11	5	6	11	4
1975-76	Montreal 🏆	71	32	36	68	20	37	1975-76	Montreal 🏆	13	3	6	9	4
1976-77	Montreal 🏆	60	25	28	53	8	27	1976-77	Montreal 🏆	—	—	—	—	—
1977-78	Montreal 🏆	68	24	29	53	12	39	1977-78	Montreal 🏆	15	7	4	11	10
1978-79	Montreal 🏆	15	2	5	7	2	5	1978-79	Montreal 🏆	—	—	—	—	—
	NHL Totals:	968	428	435	863	255			Playoff Totals:	147	64	63	127	47

Yvan Cournoyer was called "The Roadrunner" during his Hall-of-Fame career. He had speed to burn and the hockey sense to know where to be to make the big play. Cournoyer stood only 5'7" (170 cm) and weighed less than 180 pounds (81 kg). Today, he might not even get a chance to play in the NHL. Today, the average NHL player is over six feet tall (183 cm) and weighs 220 pounds (100 kg). If he played today, the Roadrunner would be grounded before he could even get started.

Yvan Cournoyer was a product of the rich Montreal Canadiens' farm system. He scored 63 goals in only 53 games for the Junior Canadiens in 1963-64. Although he was gifted offensively, the Canadiens brought Cournoyer along slowly. Cournoyer's gradual development paid off and he never had a negative plus/minus season during his entire 16 years of service for the Canadiens.

In 1966-67, the Drummondville, Quebec native became one of the NHL's first power-play specialists. Although he saw limited action in even-strength situations, Cournoyer scored a league-leading 20 power-play goals with the Habs. From 1968 to 1979, Cournoyer was a con-sistent all-round player who took pride in his ability to play at both ends of the rink.

Cournoyer's speed allowed him to survive in the body-crunching world of NHL hockey. The Roadrunner's quick skating allowed him to swoop into the corner and grab loose pucks. He was also a tricky stickhandler with exceptional balance.

One of the Roadrunner's finest moments came during the 1973 playoffs. Cournoyer led all post-season scorers in goals (15) and points (25) while helping the Canadiens win the Stanley Cup. That effort earned him the Conn Smythe Trophy as playoff MVP.

During his 16-year career, Cournoyer was a member of 10 Stanley Cup-winning teams. He scored at least 20 goals in 12 consecutive seasons and scored at least 10 power-play goals on nine occasions. His value and loyalty to the Montreal

Canadiens organization was recognized in 1975, when he was chosen to replace Henri Richard as team captain. Cournoyer wore the "C" with pride until a back injury forced him to retire in 1979.

The blazing speed of Yvan Cournoyer allowed him to compete with the big boys of the hard-hitting NHL. Here, Cournoyer zips into position in front of Rangers goalie Gilles Villemure.

Bill Cowley

Position: Center   **Height:** 5'10" (178 cm)   **Weight:** 165 lbs (75 kg)   **Born:** June 12, 1912 in Bristol, QC.

Regular Season								Playoffs						
Season	Team	GP	G	A	Pts	PIM	+/-	Season	Team	GP	G	A	Pts	PIM
1934-35	St. Louis	41	5	7	12	10	—	1934-35	St. Louis	—	—	—	—	—
1935-36	Boston	48	11	10	21	17	—	1935-36	Boston	2	2	1	3	2
1936-37	Boston	46	13	22	35	4	—	1936-37	Boston	3	0	3	3	0
1937-38	Boston	48	17	22	39	8	—	1937-38	Boston	3	2	0	2	0
1938-39	Boston	34	8	34	42	2	—	1938-39	Boston	12	3	11	14	2
1939-40	Boston	48	13	27	40	24	—	1939-40	Boston	6	0	1	1	7
1940-41	Boston	46	17	45	62	16	—	1940-41	Boston	2	0	0	0	0
1941-42	Boston	28	4	23	27	6	—	1941-42	Boston	5	0	3	3	5
1942-43	Boston	48	27	45	72	10	—	1942-43	Boston	9	1	7	8	4
1943-44	Boston	36	30	41	71	12	—	1943-44	Boston	—	—	—	—	—
1944-45	Boston	49	25	40	65	12	—	1944-45	Boston	7	3	3	6	0
1945-46	Boston	26	12	12	24	6	—	1945-46	Boston	10	1	3	4	2
1946-47	Boston	51	13	25	38	16	—	1946-47	Boston	5	0	2	2	0
	NHL Totals:	**549**	**195**	**353**	**548**	**143**			**Playoff Totals:**	**64**	**12**	**34**	**46**	**22**

Bill Cowley was the greatest playmaker in hockey during his 13 seasons in the NHL: he finished among the top 10 scorers seven times; he led the league in assists three times; he won one scoring title and earned the Hart Trophy as the NHL's most valuable player twice. Cowley's credentials would be even more impressive if he hadn't been injured so often. Even so, when he retired in 1947, Cowley was the leading scorer in NHL history.

Cowley began his NHL career in 1934-35 and joined the Boston Bruins the following year. The Bruins were using him as a left winger, but his skating speed and precise passes quickly convinced them to move him to center. By 1937-38, Cowley was a First-Team All-Star. In the 1938-39 season, Cowley led the NHL in assists for the first time. Boston won the Stanley Cup that year, and Cowley led all playoff performers with 14 points in 12 games. Three of his 11 playoff assists set up overtime goals by Mel Hill. To this day, "Sudden Death" Hill is still the only player to score three overtime goals in one playoff series. Cowley led the Bruins to another Stanley Cup title in 1940-41, the same year he won the scoring title and earned the Hart Trophy as NHL MVP.

A broken jaw sidelined Cowley for much of the 1941-42 season, but he returned better than ever the following year. He missed the scoring title by a single point in 1942-43, but still earned the Hart Trophy for the second time. Cowley would have had his greatest season ever in 1943-44, but injuries sidelined him again. He was only able to play 36 games that year, but he still established a career high 30 goals and 41 assists for a total of 71 points. At the time, the single-season scoring record was 73 points. If Cowley had been able to play all 50 games he might have reached 100 points!

Bill Cowley had another great season in 1944-45, but he missed more than half of the next year with a broken wrist. He was not up to his usual playing standard when he returned in 1946-47 and he retired after the season. At the time, his 353 assists and 548 points were the most in NHL history. He was elected to the Hockey Hall of Fame in 1968.

Bill Cowley's fancy footwork and precise passes resulted in plenty of points for the Boston Bruins. If injuries hadn't slowed him down, he might have been the first player to score 100 points in a season.

Cy Denneny

Position: **Left Wing**   Height: **5'7" (170 cm)**   Weight: **168 lbs (76 kg)**   Born: **December 23, 1891 in Farrow's Point, ON.**

Regular Season								Playoffs						
Season	Team	GP	G	A	Pts	PIM	+/-	Season	Team	GP	G	A	Pts	PIM
1917-18	Ottawa	20	36	10	46	80	—	1917-18	Ottawa	—	—	—	—	—
1918-19	Ottawa	18	18	6	24	55	—	1918-19	Ottawa	7	5	3	8	9
1919-20	Ottawa 🏆	24	16	6	22	31	—	1919-20	Ottawa 🏆	5	0	2	2	3
1920-21	Ottawa 🏆	24	34	5	39	10	—	1920-21	Ottawa 🏆	7	4	2	6	15
1921-22	Ottawa	22	27	12	39	20	—	1921-22	Ottawa	2	2	0	2	4
1922-23	Ottawa 🏆	24	21	10	31	20	—	1922-23	Ottawa 🏆	8	3	1	4	6
1923-24	Ottawa	21	22	1	23	10	—	1923-24	Ottawa	2	2	0	2	10
1924-25	Ottawa	28	27	15	42	16	—	1924-25	Ottawa	—	—	—	—	—
1925-26	Ottawa	36	24	12	36	18	—	1925-26	Ottawa	2	0	0	0	4
1926-27	Ottawa 🏆	42	17	6	23	16	—	1926-27	Ottawa 🏆	6	5	0	5	0
1927-28	Ottawa	44	3	0	3	12	—	1927-28	Ottawa	2	0	0	0	0
1928-29	Boston 🏆	23	1	2	3	2	—	1928-29	Boston 🏆	2	0	0	0	0
NHL Totals:		326	246	85	331	290		**Playoff Totals:**		43	21	8	29	51

Cy Denneny didn't look like a hockey star. He was short and pudgy and couldn't skate very well, but he was strong and had a hard, accurate shot. When Denneny retired after the 1928-29 season, he was the NHL's all-time leader with 246 goals and 331 points.

In the NHL's first season in 1917-18, Cy Denneny scored 36 goals in just 20 games. He finished second in the scoring race behind Joe Malone, who scored 44 goals. Over the next eight years, Denneny finished second in scoring four more times. He finally won the scoring title in 1923-24 when he scored 22 goals in 21 games. Only once in the NHL's first nine years did Denneny fall below the top 10 in scoring.

Cy Denneny's professional hockey career began three seasons before the NHL was formed. In 1914-15, he and his brother Corbett joined the Toronto Shamrocks of the National Hockey Association. The following year they became members of the Toronto Blueshirts. The two brothers played left and right wing on a line centered by Duke Keats, and together they became the top-scoring trio in the NHA. In 1916-17 the Denneny brothers joined the Ottawa Senators because Cy had an off-season job in Ottawa and preferred to play with the team there.

The Senators became one of the founding members of the NHL in 1917-18. During the 1920-21 season, the two Denneny brothers both scored six goals in a single game. (The NHL record of seven goals had been set by Joe Malone the season before.) Only five other players in NHL history have ever enjoyed a six-goal game. No other brother combination has ever accomplished the feat.

During Cy Denneny's time in Ottawa, the Senators were the best team in the NHL. Along with teammates Frank Nighbor, King Clancy, and Clint Benedict, Denneny helped the Senators win the Stanley Cup in 1920, 1921, 1923, and 1927. In 1927, Denneny led all playoff scorers with five goals in six games. The next year, he scored only three goals in 44 games, so Ottawa traded him to the Boston Bruins. Denneny was a player and an assistant coach in Boston, and he helped the Bruins win the Stanley Cup that year, but it was his final season as a player. Thirty years later, Cy Denneny was elected to the Hockey Hall of Fame.

Cy Denneny might not have looked like a hockey player, but he knew how to put the puck in the net. He also knew how to win, playing on five Stanley Cup champions in a 10-year span.

Marcel Dionne

Position: **Center**   Height: **5'9" (175 cm)**   Weight: **190 lbs (86 kg)**   Born: **August 3, 1951 in Drummondville, QC.**

Regular Season								Playoffs						
Season	Team	GP	G	A	Pts	PIM	+/-	Season	Team	GP	G	A	Pts	PIM
1971-72	Detroit	78	28	49	77	14	0	1971-72	Detroit	—	—	—	—	—
1972-73	Detroit	77	40	50	90	21	-4	1972-73	Detroit	—	—	—	—	—
1973-74	Detroit	74	24	54	78	10	-31	1973-74	Detroit	—	—	—	—	—
1974-75	Detroit	80	47	74	121	14	-15	1974-75	Detroit	—	—	—	—	—
1975-76	Los Angeles	80	40	54	94	38	2	1975-76	Los Angeles	9	6	1	7	0
1976-77	Los Angeles	80	53	69	122	12	10	1976-77	Los Angeles	9	5	9	14	2
1977-78	Los Angeles	70	36	43	79	37	-8	1977-78	Los Angeles	2	0	0	0	0
1978-79	Los Angeles	80	59	71	130	30	23	1978-79	Los Angeles	2	0	1	1	0
1979-80	Los Angeles	80	53	84	137	32	35	1979-80	Los Angeles	4	0	3	3	4
1980-81	Los Angeles	80	58	77	135	70	55	1980-81	Los Angeles	4	1	3	4	7
1981-82	Los Angeles	78	50	67	117	50	-10	1981-82	Los Angeles	10	7	4	11	0
1982-83	Los Angeles	80	56	51	107	22	10	1982-83	Los Angeles	—	—	—	—	—
1983-84	Los Angeles	66	39	53	92	28	8	1983-84	Los Angeles	—	—	—	—	—
1984-85	Los Angeles	80	46	80	126	46	11	1984-85	Los Angeles	3	1	2	3	2
1985-86	Los Angeles	80	36	58	94	42	-22	1985-86	Los Angeles	—	—	—	—	—
1986-87	Los Angeles	67	24	50	74	54	-8	1986-87	Los Angeles	—	—	—	—	—
	NY Rangers	14	4	6	10	6	-8		NY Rangers	6	1	1	2	2
1987-88	NY Rangers	67	31	34	65	54	-14	1987-88	NY Rangers	—	—	—	—	—
1988-89	NY Rangers	37	7	16	23	20	-6	1988-89	NY Rangers	—	—	—	—	—
NHL Totals:		1348	731	1040	1771	600		Playoff Totals:		49	21	24	45	17

It's been said that Marcel Dionne spent his entire career playing in the shadows. Despite all his success and his scoring records, there was always some other player that received the attention that Dionne deserved. But make no mistake, "The Little Beaver" was one of the best to ever play.

Dionne was short, but solid as a tree trunk. He was strong on his skates and could plough through the defense. After a great junior career with St. Catharines, Dionne was drafted by Detroit in the same year Guy Lafleur was drafted by Montreal. While "The Flower" gathered headlines, Dionne gathered goals and set an NHL rookie scoring record with 77 points. Yet, when it came time to hand out the top rookie award, Dionne was overshadowed by a lanky goalie for Montreal named Ken Dryden.

In each of his first four NHL campaigns, Dionne improved his overall play. He was named captain of the Wings in 1974-75 and set a Detroit single-season scoring record with 121 points that same season.

After his record-breaking season, Dionne decided to leave Detroit and sign with the Los

Angeles Kings. The league made sure the Red Wings received some good players in return for losing Dionne, but none of them were as good as the guy they lost. Dionne recorded eight 100-point seasons in Los Angeles, and he still holds the Kings' record for career goals, assists, points, and consecutive games played. In 1979-80, he won his only NHL scoring title, but once again his achievement was lost in the shadows. Even in his finest season, a kid named Gretzky stole most of the headlines.

Although the Kings had a solid team lineup, they never advanced very far in the playoffs. In March 1987, Dionne was traded to the New York Rangers. Dionne hoped the Broadway Blueshirts would give him a chance to win the elusive Stanley Cup, but he fell short of his goal. Like Gil Perreault, Harry Howell, and Bill

Gadsby, Dionne entered the Hall of Fame without a Stanley Cup ring on his finger, but like those players, he remains one of the game's all-time greatest.

Marcel Dionne may have been short, but he was sturdy enough to power his way past opposing players. Dionne's NHL totals of 731 goals and 1,771 points trail only Wayne Gretzky and Gordie Howe.

Ken Dryden

Position: **Goaltender**   Height: **6'4" (190 cm)**   Weight: **205 lbs (93 kg)**   Born: **August 8, 1947 in Hamilton, ON.**

| Regular Season | | | | | | | | | | Playoffs | | | | | | | |
Season	Team	GP	W	L	T	MINS	GA	SO	AVG.	Season	Team	GP	W	L	MINS	GA	SO	AVG.
1970-71	Montreal	6	6	0	0	327	9	0	1.65	1970-71	Montreal	20	12	8	1221	61	0	3.00
1971-72	Montreal	64	39	8	15	3800	142	8	2.24	1971-72	Montreal	6	2	4	360	17	0	2.83
1972-73	Montreal	54	33	7	13	3165	119	6	2.26	1972-73	Montreal	17	12	5	1039	50	1	2.89
1974-75	Montreal	56	30	9	16	3320	149	4	2.69	1974-75	Montreal	11	6	5	688	29	2	2.53
1975-76	Montreal	62	42	10	8	3580	121	8	2.03	1975-76	Montreal	13	12	1	780	25	1	1.92
1976-77	Montreal	56	41	6	8	3275	117	10	2.14	1976-77	Montreal	14	12	2	849	22	4	1.55
1977-78	Montreal	52	37	7	7	3071	105	5	2.05	1977-78	Montreal	15	12	3	919	29	2	1.89
1978-79	Montreal	47	30	10	7	2814	108	5	2.30	1978-79	Montreal	16	12	4	990	41	0	2.48
NHL Totals:		397	258	57	74	23352	870	48	2.24	Playoff Totals:		112	80	32	6846	274	10	2.40

At 6'4" (190 cm) and 205 pounds (93 kg), Ken Dryden was a big goalie. When he stretched out his arms and legs he could cover more of the net than anyone. His long reach made Phil Esposito refer to Dryden as an octopus.

Ken Dryden had all the makings of a great goalie, but he was also a good student. Although he was drafted by the Boston Bruins in 1964, Dryden chose to attend Cornell University instead. He was a three-time All-American at Cornell and later played for the Canadian national team. In 1970, he joined the Montreal Canadiens organization.

Dryden was called up to the NHL late in the 1970–71 season. He only played six games for Montreal that year, but the Canadiens decided they would go with the unproven youngster in the playoffs. Montreal's first opponent was Boston. The Bruins had set 37 new records that year, including Phil Esposito's 76 goals and 152 points. Boston was expected to beat the Canadiens easily, but Dryden led Montreal to a seven-game upset. When the Canadiens went on to win the Stanley Cup, Dryden won the Conn Smythe Trophy as the playoff MVP.

Despite his playoff heroics, Dryden was still considered a rookie when he played his first full season in 1971-72. That year he led the league with 39 wins and earned the Calder Trophy as rookie of the year. The next year, Dryden won the Vezina Trophy for the first of five times. He also led the Canadiens to another Stanley Cup championship.

While he was playing in the NHL Ken Dryden was also attending law school. In 1973-74 he sat out the NHL season in order to complete his studies. He returned to the Canadiens in 1974-75. From 1975-76 until he retired after the 1978-79 season Dryden helped Montreal win the Stanley Cup four years in a row. During that time, the Canadiens were perhaps the greatest team in NHL history. Dryden lost very few games in his career, and his lifetime record of 258 wins, 57 losses, and 74 ties adds up to a .758 winning percentage. That is by far the best in NHL history. Dryden was elected to the Hockey Hall of Fame in 1983.

Many people thought Ken Dryden would enter politics or law after his playing days, but he became an author instead. He later did some work for the Ontario government before returning to hockey as president of the Toronto Maple Leafs in 1997.

Ken Dryden was the biggest goalie in the NHL during the 1970s and could block the net better than anyone. Dryden only played eight seasons in the NHL, but he won the Stanley Cup six times.

Bill Durnan

Position: **Goaltender**   Height: **6'0" (183 cm)**   Weight: **190 lbs (86 kg)**   Born: **January 22, 1916 in Toronto, ON.**

	Regular Season									Playoffs						
Season	Team	GP	W	L	T	MINS	GA	SO	AVG.	Season	Team	GP	W	L	MINS	GA	SO	AVG.
1943-44	Montreal	50	38	5	7	3000	109	2	2.18	1943-44	Montreal	9	8	1	549	14	1	1.53
1944-45	Montreal	50	38	8	4	3000	121	1	2.42	1944-45	Montreal	6	2	4	373	15	0	2.41
1945-46	Montreal	40	24	11	5	2400	104	4	2.60	1945-46	Montreal	9	8	1	581	20	0	2.07
1946-47	Montreal	60	34	16	10	3600	138	4	2.30	1946-47	Montreal	11	6	5	720	23	1	1.92
1947-48	Montreal	59	20	28	10	3505	162	5	2.77	1947-48	Montreal	—	—	—	—	—	—	—
1948-49	Montreal	60	28	23	9	3600	126	10	2.10	1948-49	Montreal	7	3	4	468	17	0	2.18
1949-50	Montreal	64	26	21	17	3840	141	8	2.20	1949-50	Montreal	3	0	3	180	10	0	3.33
NHL Totals:		**383**	**208**	**112**	**62**	**22945**	**901**	**34**	**2.36**	**Playoff Totals:**		**45**	**27**	**18**	**2871**	**99**	**2**	**2.07**

Although he only spent seven seasons in the NHL, Bill Durnan won the Vezina Trophy as the league's best goalie six times. Only Jacques Plante has won it more often. Durnan was ambidextrous, which means he could use his stick or catch the puck equally well with both hands. He used specially designed goalie gloves because of this two-handed talent.

Bill Durnan had a long career as an amateur before he reached the NHL. He was born in Toronto and could have joined the Maple Leafs when he was only 20 years old, but they turned him down because of a knee injury. Durnan finally joined the league as a 28-year-old rookie with the Montreal Canadiens in 1943-44. At six feet (183 cm) tall and 190 pounds (86 kg), Durnan was a big man at a time when most goalies were small and quick. He had fast reflexes, but, more importantly, he trained himself to memorize the habits of the game's best players.

The Canadiens had been struggling for a long time before they finally convinced Durnan to turn pro. That year, he helped them win their first Stanley Cup in 13 years. Durnan tied an NHL record with 38 wins during the 1943-44 season and led the league with a 2.18 goals-against average. Durnan easily won the Vezina Trophy that year and was chosen as the goalie on the NHL's First All-Star Team. He received both honors again after each of the next three seasons. In 1945-46, he helped the Canadiens win another Stanley Cup title.

Turk Broda finally topped Durnan as the NHL's best goalie in 1947-48, but the Canadiens star bounced back better than ever. He led the league with 10 shutouts and a 2.10 goals-against average in 1948-49. Both marks were the best of his career. Durnan also set a modern NHL record that season when he had a shutout for four games in a row! He recaptured the Vezina Trophy that year and once again earned a spot as a First-Team All-Star. He received both honors for the sixth time with a 2.20 average and eight shutouts in 1949-50.

Great as he was, Bill Durnan did not like the pressure of being a goalie in the NHL. He decided to retire when the Rangers upset the Canadiens during the playoffs in 1950. In 1963, he was elected to the Hockey Hall of Fame.

Notice the webbing between the fingers and the thumb on the glove covering Bill Durnan's stick hand? Durnan had specially designed goalie gloves because he could catch the puck equally well with his left or right hand.

Babe Dye

Position: **Right Wing**   Height: **5'8" (173 cm)**   Weight: **150 lbs (68 kg)**   Born: **May 13, 1898 in Hamilton, ON.**

	Regular Season								Playoffs				
Season	Team	GP	G	A	Pts	PIM	+/-	Season	Team	GP	G	A	Pts	PIM
1919-20	Toronto St. Pats	23	11	3	14	10	—	1919-20	Toronto St. Pats	—	—	—	—	—
1920-21	Hamilton	1	2	0	2	0	—	1920-21	Hamilton	—	—	—	—	—
	Toronto St. Pats	23	33	5	38	32	—		Toronto St. Pats	2	0	0	0	7
1921-22	Toronto St. Pats	24	31	7	38	39	—	1921-22	Toronto St. Pats	7	11	1	12	5
1922-23	Toronto St. Pats	22	26	11	37	19	—	1922-23	Toronto St. Pats	—	—	—	—	—
1923-24	Toronto St. Pats	19	17	2	19	23	—	1923-24	Toronto St. Pats	—	—	—	—	—
1924-25	Toronto St. Pats	29	38	6	44	41	—	1924-25	Toronto St. Pats	2	0	0	0	0
1925-26	Toronto St. Pats	31	18	5	23	26	—	1925-26	Toronto St. Pats	—	—	—	—	—
1926-27	Chicago	41	25	5	30	14	—	1926-27	Chicago	2	0	0	0	2
1927-28	Chicago	10	0	0	0	0	—	1927-28	Chicago	—	—	—	—	—
1928-29	NY Americans	42	1	0	1	17	—	1928-29	NY Americans	2	0	0	0	0
1930-31	Toronto Maple Leafs	6	0	0	0	0	—	1930-31	Toronto Maple Leafs	—	—	—	—	—
	NHL Totals:	271	202	44	246	221			Playoff Totals:	15	11	1	12	14

Babe Dye was a great athlete. In addition to playing hockey, he had been a fine football player and a good enough baseball player to be offered a major league tryout. Dye turned down a $25,000 offer to play baseball in the majors. It would have been a huge salary in 1921, but he wanted to concentrate on hockey.

Babe Dye (his real name was Cecil) was born in Hamilton, Ontario, but grew up in Toronto. His NHL career began in 1919-20 with the Toronto St. Patricks. (This team would become the Toronto Maple Leafs in 1927.) Dye was not a strong skater, and he often found it difficult to get playing time as a rookie. Soon after his rookie year, Dye's superb stickhandling and his hard, accurate shot would make him a star.

Dye was loaned to the new NHL team in Hamilton to start the 1920-21 season. When he scored two goals in the first game, Toronto quickly asked for him back. The St. Pats sent Hamilton another player instead, which was a good move for Toronto because Dye went on to lead the

league with 35 goals in 24 games. He had 31 goals in 1921-22 and led the St. Pats to the Stanley Cup Final that year. Toronto played the Vancouver Millionaires of the Pacific Coast Hockey Association for the hockey championship, and Dye scored nine times in the five-game series. He had four goals in the final game as Toronto won the Stanley Cup with a 5-1 victory.

Over the next three seasons, Dye was the NHL's scoring leader two times. His best year was 1924-25 when he had a career-high 38 goals in 29 games. Twice, between 1921 and 1925, Dye scored five goals in a single game. He also had two streaks of 11 consecutive games with at least one goal during those seasons.

In 1926, Toronto sold Dye to the newest NHL team, the Chicago Blackhawks. Dye scored 25 goals for Chicago in 1926-27 but broke his leg during spring training with his baseball team in 1927. His hockey career was never the same. He played three more NHL seasons before he retired in 1930-31. In 1970, Babe Dye was elected to the Hockey Hall of Fame.

Babe Dye credited his success at two different sports to a surprising source: "My mother knew more about hockey than I ever did, and she could throw a baseball right out of the park."

Phil Esposito

Position: Center   **Height:** 6'1" (185 cm)   **Weight:** 205 lbs (93 kg)   **Born:** February 20, 1942 in Sault Ste. Marie, ON.

| Regular Season | | | | | | | | | Playoffs | | | | | |
Season	Team	GP	G	A	Pts	PIM	+/-		Season	Team	GP	G	A	Pts	PIM
1963-64	Chicago	27	3	2	5	2	—		1963-64	Chicago	4	0	0	0	0
1964-65	Chicago	70	23	32	55	44	—		1964-65	Chicago	13	3	3	6	15
1965-66	Chicago	69	27	26	53	49	—		1965-66	Chicago	6	1	1	2	2
1966-67	Chicago	69	21	40	61	40	—		1966-67	Chicago	6	0	0	0	7
1967-68	Boston	74	35	49	84	21	19		1967-68	Boston	4	0	3	3	0
1968-69	Boston	74	49	77	126	79	56		1968-69	Boston	10	8	10	18	8
1969-70	Boston	76	43	56	99	50	28		1969-70	Boston	14	13	14	27	16
1970-71	Boston	78	76	76	152	71	71		1970-71	Boston	7	3	7	10	6
1971-72	Boston	76	66	67	133	76	55		1971-72	Boston	15	9	15	24	24
1972-73	Boston	78	55	75	130	87	16		1972-73	Boston	2	0	1	1	2
1973-74	Boston	78	68	77	145	58	51		1973-74	Boston	16	9	5	14	25
1974-75	Boston	79	61	66	127	62	18		1974-75	Boston	3	4	1	5	0
1975-76	Boston	12	6	10	16	8	-1		1975-76	Boston	—	—	—	—	—
	NY Rangers	62	29	38	67	28	-39			NY Rangers	—	—	—	—	—
1976-77	NY Rangers	80	34	46	80	52	-28		1976-77	NY Rangers	—	—	—	—	—
1977-78	NY Rangers	79	38	43	81	53	-22		1977-78	NY Rangers	3	0	1	1	5
1978-79	NY Rangers	80	42	36	78	37	1		1978-79	NY Rangers	18	8	12	20	20
1979-80	NY Rangers	80	34	44	78	73	-13		1979-80	NY Rangers	9	3	3	6	8
1980-81	NY Rangers	41	7	13	20	20	-13		1980-81	NY Rangers	—	—	—	—	—
NHL Totals:		1282	717	873	1590	910			**Playoff Totals:**		130	61	76	137	138

Before there was Wayne Gretzky, there was Phil Esposito. Many of the records "The Great One" went on to break first belonged to a sharp-shooting sniper known around the NHL as "Espo."

The Chicago Blackhawks discovered Esposito in his hometown of Sault Ste. Marie, Ontario. They signed the 6'1" (185 cm), 205 pound (93 kg) center and watched him climb through the ranks. In 1964-65, Espo made the NHL to stay, but his team in Chicago was not a happy one. Although he finished among the NHL's top scorers in 1966-67, the Hawks thought Esposito was slow and lazy. In May 1967, they traded him to Boston, and it was the turning point of Esposito's career.

He was moving to a team that had Bobby Orr on defense, depth at all three forward positions, and great goaltending. In only his second season in Beantown, Espo set an NHL record for points (126). In the 1969 playoffs, Espo led all post-season scorers in goals, assists, and points, and the Bruins didn't even make the finals!

The secret of Esposito's success was his size and strength. Although he would be considered average by today's standards, he was the biggest man in the game in 1970. Espo could plant himself in the slot and stay there. With his long reach, he could scoop up rebounds and whip them into the net. It's not an exaggeration to suggest that 80% of his 717 career goals were scored within 10 feet of the net.

In 1970-71, Esposito rewrote the NHL record book, setting new marks for goals (76) and points (152). But perhaps his most impressive mark is the one that still stands. Espo set a new standard with 550 shots on goal. The closest players to Espo's record are Paul Kariya and Bobby and Brett Hull who, at best, managed to record 400 shots in a single season.

One of the defining moments of Esposito's Hall-of-Fame career came in September 1972. Prior to the 1972-73 season, he captained Team

Canada to an emotional victory over the Soviet Union in an eight-game exhibition series. After being booed during a loss in Vancouver, Esposito went on TV and pleaded for support from the Canadian fans. When the Team Canada players heard the speech, it gave them the motivational lift they needed to win the series.

During his 18-year, three-team NHL career, Esposito won five MVP awards and scored at

With his size and strength, it was almost impossible to move Phil Esposito once he had set himself up in the front of the net. Espo scored almost all of his goals from this area, known as the slot.

least 50 goals in five straight seasons. His final honor came in 1984 when he was inducted into the Hockey Hall of Fame.

Viacheslav Fetisov

Position: **Defense**   Height: **6'1" (185 cm)**   Weight: **220 lbs (100 kg)**   Born: **April 20, 1958 in Moscow, USSR.**

| | | | International Hockey and NHL Regular Season | | | | | | NHL Playoffs | | | | |
Year	Team	Event/League	GP	G	A	Pts	PIM	+/-	GP	G	A	Pts	PIM
1976-77	Soviet Union	World Championships	5	3	3	6	2	—	—	—	—	—	—
1977-78	Soviet Union	World Championships	10	4	6	10	11	—	—	—	—	—	—
1979-80	CSKA Moscow	Super Series	4	0	1	1	0	—	—	—	—	—	—
	Soviet Union	Olympics	7	5	4	9	10	—	—	—	—	—	—
1980-81	Soviet Union	World Championships	8	1	4	5	6	—	—	—	—	—	—
1981-82	Soviet Union	Canada Cup	7	1	7	8	10	—	—	—	—	—	—
	Soviet Union	World Championships	10	4	3	7	6	—	—	—	—	—	—
1982-83	CSKA Moscow	Super Series	6	1	4	5	10	—	—	—	—	—	—
	Soviet Union	World Championships	10	3	7	10	8	—	—	—	—	—	—
1983-84	Soviet Union	Olympics	7	3	8	11	8	—	—	—	—	—	—
1984-85	Soviet Union	World Championships	10	6	7	13	15	—	—	—	—	—	—
1985-86	Soviet Union	Super Series	6	3	3	6	6	—	—	—	—	—	—
	Soviet Union	World Championships	10	6	9	15	10	—	—	—	—	—	—
1986-87	Soviet Union	World Championships	10	2	8	10	2	—	—	—	—	—	—
1987-88	Soviet Union	Canada Cup	9	2	5	7	9	—	—	—	—	—	—
	Soviet Union	Olympics	8	4	9	13	6	—	—	—	—	—	—
1988-89	CSKA Moscow	Super Series	7	2	3	5	7	—	—	—	—	—	—
	Soviet Union	World Championships	10	2	4	6	17	—	—	—	—	—	—
1989-90	Soviet Union	World Championships	8	2	8	10	8	—	—	—	—	—	—
1975-1989	CSKA Moscow	Soviet Union League	479	153	220	373	374	—	—	—	—	—	—
1989-90	New Jersey	NHL	72	8	34	42	52	9	6	0	2	2	10
1990-91	New Jersey	NHL	67	3	16	19	62	5	7	0	0	0	17
	Soviet Union	World Championships	10	3	1	4	4	—	—	—	—	—	—
1991-92	New Jersey	NHL	70	3	23	26	108	11	6	0	3	3	8
1992-93	New Jersey	NHL	76	4	23	27	158	7	5	0	2	2	4
1993-94	New Jersey	NHL	52	1	14	15	30	14	14	1	0	1	8
1994-95	New Jersey	NHL	4	0	1	1	0	-2	—	—	—	—	—
	Detroit	NHL	14	3	11	14	2	3	18	0	8	8	14
1995-96	Detroit	NHL	69	7	35	42	96	37	19	1	4	5	34
1996-97	Detroit	NHL	64	5	23	28	76	26	20	0	4	4	42
1997-98	Detroit	NHL	58	2	12	14	72	4	21	0	3	3	10
Career Totals:			**1187**	**246**	**516**	**762**	**1185**	**Playoff Totals:**	**116**	**2**	**26**	**28**	**147**

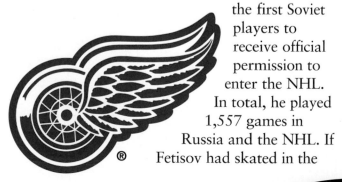

Viacheslav Fetisov was recognized as one of the best defensemen in hockey long before he made his NHL debut in 1989. The long-time captain of Moscow's Central Red Army team had been famous for years before he became one of the first Soviet players to receive official permission to enter the NHL. In total, he played 1,557 games in Russia and the NHL. If Fetisov had skated in the NHL for his entire career, only Gordie Howe would have played more games.

Slava Fetisov joined the Central Red Army as a 16-year-old junior in 1974-75. He played with the team until 1988-89. During that time, Fetisov won the Golden Stick Award as the best player in Europe three times. He also was named the Soviet player of the year three times. He was the Soviet League's best defenseman four times.

Good as he was in the Soviet League, it was Fetisov's success in international play that made him such a star. In 1978, he helped the Soviets win the World Junior Championships. He was named to the tournament All-Star team along

with future stars Wayne Gretzky and Anton Stastny. Fetisov also played for the Soviet National Team at the World Championships that year. It was the first of 11 times that Fetisov played at that tournament, and the first of seven times he won a gold medal. He was named the best defenseman at the World Championships five times and was a tournament All-Star eight times. Fetisov also represented the Soviet Union at the Olympics three times. He won two gold medals.

Although Soviet players were not officially allowed to play in the NHL in the early 1980s, many teams began drafting them. The New Jersey Devils selected Slava Fetisov in 1983. He refused to defect to the United States, but he did pressure Soviet officials for his legal release. The authori-

Though he was 40 years old in 1997, Viacheslav Fetisov was a key contributor to the Detroit Red Wings' Stanley Cup that year. He helped them repeat in 1998 before retiring that summer. Fetisov also won two Olympic gold medals during his career.

ties finally gave Fetisov permission in 1989. Though his best playing days were behind him, he played five full seasons for New Jersey. He then joined the Detroit Red Wings in 1994-95. Fetisov was one of five Russian players that helped the Red Wings win the Stanley Cup in 1997 and 1998. His success helped change the opinion that Russian players did not care enough about winning the Stanley Cup. Some day soon, Viacheslav Fetisov could become the first Russian head coach in the NHL.

Anatoli Firsov

Position: **Center/Left Wing**   **Height:** **5'9" (174 cm)**   **Weight:** **155 lbs (70 kg)**   **Born:** **February 1, 1941 in Moscow, USSR.**

Year	Team	Event/League	GP	G	A	Pts	PIM
1964	Soviet Union	Olympics	7	4	3	7	2
1965	Soviet Union	World Championships	6	5	4	9	8
1966	Soviet Union	World Championships	6	3	2	5	4
1967	Soviet Union	World Championships	7	11	11	22	2
1968	Soviet Union	Olympics	7	12	4	16	4
1969	Soviet Union	World Championships	10	10	4	14	6
1970	Soviet Union	World Championships	8	6	10	16	2
1971	Soviet Union	World Championships	10	11	8	19	4
1972	Soviet Union	Olympics	5	2	5	7	0
1958 - 1974	Spartak Moscow	Soviet Union League	474	344	—	—	—
	Career Totals:		540	408	—	—	—

For the Soviet Union, winning the World Championship in their first try, then winning a gold medal at the Olympics two years later, proved to be a hard act to follow. For the next few years, teams from Canada, the United States, and Sweden kept the Soviets from winning any more titles. But by 1963, the Soviets were ready to dominate international hockey again. The player that was most responsible for their return to the top was Anatoli Firsov.

Anatoli Firsov began his career with Spartak Moscow in 1958. In 1961, he joined the Central Red Army, which was the best team in the Soviet league. Firsov was a player who worked very hard in practice. Often he would remain on the ice to work on his skills long after all the other players had left. For Firsov, practice made perfect. He was already a brilliant skater, and with all his diligent work he also became the best stickhandler and hardest shooter in European hockey. In the days before

many goalies wore masks, a lot of them would worry more about protecting their heads than the net when Firsov wound up for a powerful blast! He once scored six goals in a single game during an exhibition series with the Canadian national team. In Soviet league play, Firsov scored 344 goals in 474 career games. He led his team to the Soviet championship nine times.

Firsov joined the Soviet national team in 1964. With him leading the way, they won the World Championship eight years in a row! Firsov was named the Best Forward at the tournament in 1967 and 1971. He was also named to the all-star team four times. During those years, the Olympics also counted as the World Championship, and Firsov led his team to Olympic gold medals in 1964 and 1968. His 12 goals in seven games led all Olympic performers in 1968. His 16 points were also tops that year. When the two tournaments became separate events in 1972, the Soviets won the Olympic title again, but fell to second place at the World Championships.

After his playing days, Firsov coached the Central Red Army junior team.

It takes two Swedish players to slow down Anatoli Firsov on this rush. Firsov was a speedy skater who trained himself to become the best stickhandler and hardest shooter in European hockey.

Peter Forsberg

Position: **Center**   Height: **6'0" (183 cm)**   Weight: **190 lbs (86 kg)**   Born: **July 20, 1973 in Ornskoldsvik, Sweden.**

Regular Season								Playoffs						
Season	Team	GP	G	A	Pts	PIM	+/-	Season	Team	GP	G	A	Pts	PIM
1994-95	Quebec	47	15	35	50	16	17	1994-95	Quebec	6	2	4	6	4
1995-96	Colorado	82	30	86	116	47	26	1995-96	Colorado	22	10	11	21	18
1996-97	Colorado	65	28	58	86	73	31	1996-97	Colorado	14	5	12	17	10
1997-98	Colorado	72	25	66	91	94	6	1997-98	Colorado	7	6	5	11	12
1998-99	Colorado	78	30	67	97	108	27	1998-99	Colorado	19	8	16	24	31
	NHL Totals:	344	128	312	440	338			Playoff Totals:	68	31	48	79	75

Few NHL teams have had more success with European-trained players than the Quebec Nordiques/Colorado Avalanche. From the Stastny brothers to Mats Sundin to Sandis Ozolinsh, the club has a knack for finding European talent. In 1992, the team went fishing for another goal-scoring gem. Using Eric Lindros as bait, the Nordiques were able to acquire the talented Peter Forsberg from Philadelphia. That trade was a major reason why the Avalanche became Stanley Cup champions in 1996, and why Forsberg has become one of the NHL's top talents.

The Nordiques knew Forsberg had breakout speed and great balance, but they felt he would eventually become a "four-tool" player. That meant Forsberg could be used in any of the four key situations in a game: penalty-killing, power play, four-on-four, and last minute holds or attacks.

By the time Forsberg finally came to the NHL in the 1994-95 season, the Nordiques were moving to Colorado. Team officials were pleasantly surprised as they watched Forsberg practice, because they realized he was already a "four-tool" player. Not only was he ready to play, he was ready to be a dominant player. Forsberg had spent five seasons in the Swedish Elite League, which made him a mature and confident player. He made an instant impact in the NHL. His 50 points in 47 games won him the Calder Trophy as the league's top freshman. The following season he was a playmaking maniac, setting up 86 goals and recording 116 points, the fifth highest total in the league. He added 21 points in the playoffs as the Avalanche swept the Florida Panthers to win the Stanley Cup. He has never had fewer than 58 assists in a season, except in his rookie campaign.

Forsberg loves physical play and doesn't really feel like he's in the game until he's delivered a big hit. Forsberg's a strong, durable player who can fend off a defenseman with one arm. Even with one arm tied up, he can still make great passes. He's even scored more than a few nice-looking one-handed goals!

Forsberg has been bothered by injuries in his career, yet he's still managed to put up great numbers. Despite missing 12 games in 1997-98, he still finished second in scoring with 91 points. In 1998-99, Forsberg's 97 points were the fourth highest total in the NHL. Forsberg preformed brilliantly in the playoffs, leading the league with 24 points despite losing to Dallas in the Conference Finals. With his talent, Forsberg is sure to keep the Avalanche on top of the NHL mountain.

People expected Peter Forsberg to be a great scorer, but his love of physical play was an added bonus. Forsberg can check like an NHL tough guy and still rank among the top 10 scorers.

Ron Francis

Position: **Center**   Height: **6'3" (191 cm)**   Weight: **200 lbs (91 kg)**   Born: **March 1, 1963 in Sault Ste Marie, ON.**

	Regular Season								Playoffs				
Season	Team	GP	G	A	Pts	PIM	+/-	Season	Team	GP	G	A	Pts	PIM
1981-82	Hartford	59	25	43	68	51	-13	1981-82	Hartford	—	—	—	—	—
1982-83	Hartford	79	31	59	90	60	-25	1982-83	Hartford	—	—	—	—	—
1983-84	Hartford	72	23	60	83	45	-10	1983-84	Hartford	—	—	—	—	—
1984-85	Hartford	80	24	57	81	66	-23	1984-85	Hartford	—	—	—	—	—
1985-86	Hartford	53	24	53	77	24	8	1985-86	Hartford	10	1	2	3	4
1986-87	Hartford	75	30	63	93	45	10	1986-87	Hartford	6	2	2	4	6
1987-88	Hartford	80	25	50	75	87	-8	1987-88	Hartford	6	2	5	7	2
1988-89	Hartford	69	29	48	77	36	4	1988-89	Hartford	4	0	2	2	0
1989-90	Hartford	80	32	69	101	73	13	1989-90	Hartford	7	3	3	6	8
1990-91	Hartford	67	21	55	76	51	-2	1990-91	Hartford	—	—	—	—	—
	Pittsburgh ⚱	14	2	9	11	21	0		Pittsburgh ⚱	24	7	10	17	24
1991-92	Pittsburgh ⚱	70	21	33	54	30	-7	1991-92	Pittsburgh ⚱	21	8	19	27	6
1992-93	Pittsburgh	84	24	76	100	68	6	1992-93	Pittsburgh	12	6	11	17	19
1993-94	Pittsburgh	82	27	66	93	62	-3	1993-94	Pittsburgh	6	0	2	2	6
1994-95	Pittsburgh	44	11	48	59	18	30	1994-95	Pittsburgh	12	6	13	19	4
1995-96	Pittsburgh	77	27	92	119	56	25	1995-96	Pittsburgh	11	3	6	9	4
1996-97	Pittsburgh	81	27	63	90	20	7	1996-97	Pittsburgh	5	1	2	3	2
1997-98	Pittsburgh	81	25	62	87	20	12	1997-98	Pittsburgh	6	1	5	6	2
1998-99	Carolina	82	21	31	52	34	-2	1998-99	Carolina	3	0	1	1	0
	NHL Totals:	1329	449	1037	1486	867			Playoff Totals:	133	40	83	123	87

Some players are content to play in the "shadows." These are the guys who prefer to stay outside the spotlight. They just get on the ice and do their jobs night in and night out. It's only fitting that Ron Francis falls into this category. It's been his ability to "shadow," or closely check, enemy forwards that has made him one of the NHL's top two-way players. Still, few fans outside of the city he plays in realize just how great his career has been.

Francis spent the first 10 years of his career toiling in relative obscurity with the Hartford Whalers. He never scored less than 20 goals and never set up fewer than 40 goals a year. Although he was traded to Pittsburgh in 1991, he remains the all-time leading scorer in the history of the Hartford franchise.

The secret to Francis' success has been his ability to excel in both ends of the rink. A ruthless checker and crafty playmaker, Francis' hard work makes every player on his team put in extra effort. Francis has always maintained that offense is created by defense. By pressuring the opposing defensemen as they carry the puck up ice, Francis forces them into making mistakes, then a turnover often ends up in the net. In 1994-95, the NHL recognized Francis's defensive ability when they awarded him the Selke Trophy.

As dominant as he has been in preventing goals, he's even better setting them up. Francis has collected at least 60 assists nine times and has twice led all NHL set-up artists in assists. He is one of only seven players to record over 1,000 career assists.

Francis' arrival in Pittsburgh at the trading deadline in 1990-91 was a turning point in the franchise's history. Francis gave the Penguins a top second-line center and a dominating defensive presence on the ice. He scored four game-winning goals in the 1991 playoffs as the Penguins won their first Stanley Cup title. In the 1991-92 playoffs, Francis notched a playoff-leading 19 assists in helping Pittsburgh repeat as champions. In 1994-95, he became the first

A Century of Hockey Heroes

player to win the Lady Byng Trophy and the Selke Trophy in the same season. The following year, he recorded a career-high 92 assists.

In the summer of 1998, Francis signed with the Carolina Hurricanes. Hockey is a new sport in Carolina, and its low profile is a fitting place

Because he's so good at the defensive part of the game, it is easy to overlook the offensive skills of Ron Francis. He's one of only seven players in NHL history with more than 1,000 assists.

for Francis to end what will almost certainly be a Hall-of-Fame career.

Bob Gainey

Position: **Left Wing**   Height: **6'2" (188 cm)**   Weight: **200 lbs (91 kg)**   Born: **December 13, 1953 in Peterborough, ON.**

| | Regular Season | | | | | | | | Playoffs | | | | |
Season	Team	GP	G	A	Pts	PIM	+/-	Season	Team	GP	G	A	Pts	PIM
1973-74	Montreal	66	3	7	10	34	-9	1973-74	Montreal	6	0	0	0	6
1974-75	Montreal	80	17	20	37	49	23	1974-75	Montreal	11	2	4	6	4
1975-76	Montreal	78	15	13	28	57	20	1975-76	Montreal	13	1	3	4	20
1976-77	Montreal	80	14	19	33	41	31	1976-77	Montreal	14	4	1	5	25
1977-78	Montreal	66	15	16	31	57	11	1977-78	Montreal	15	2	7	9	14
1978-79	Montreal	79	20	18	38	44	11	1978-79	Montreal	16	6	10	16	10
1979-80	Montreal	64	14	19	33	32	-2	1979-80	Montreal	10	1	1	2	4
1980-81	Montreal	78	23	24	47	36	13	1980-81	Montreal	3	0	0	0	2
1981-82	Montreal	79	21	24	45	24	37	1981-82	Montreal	5	0	1	1	8
1982-83	Montreal	80	12	18	30	43	7	1982-83	Montreal	3	0	0	0	4
1983-84	Montreal	77	17	22	39	41	10	1983-84	Montreal	15	1	5	6	9
1984-85	Montreal	79	19	13	32	40	13	1984-85	Montreal	12	1	3	4	13
1985-86	Montreal	80	20	23	43	20	10	1985-86	Montreal	20	5	5	10	12
1986-87	Montreal	47	8	8	16	19	0	1986-87	Montreal	17	1	3	4	6
1987-88	Montreal	78	11	11	22	14	8	1987-88	Montreal	6	0	1	1	6
1988-89	Montreal	49	10	7	17	34	13	1988-89	Montreal	16	1	4	5	8
	NHL Totals:	1160	239	262	501	585			Playoff Totals:	182	25	48	73	151

Before Bob Gainey came along, the term "two-way hockey" usually referred to those players who were constantly making the long trip from the farm to the big club. But Gainey changed all that. He was one of the first players to combine air-tight checking with opportunistic offense, and he used that style all the way to the Hockey Hall of Fame.

Early in his career, Gainey realized that his greatest strength was his natural instinct for the game. That's what made him such an effective defensive forward. The Peterborough, Ontario native was never a flashy skater or a top scorer, but he could sense how a play would unfold on the ice. By pressuring an attacker, Gainey could force a mistake, and that turnover usually resulted in a scoring chance for his team.

The Montreal Canadiens recognized these skills in Gainey and made him their first choice in the 1973 Amateur Draft. After only six games in the minors, Gainey was called up by the Habs and he never looked back. Gainey proved early on that he was a mature, confident student of the game. He could neutralize the other teams most dangerous forward. He could also turn the tempo of the game. Whether it was a bruising bodycheck, a key take-away, or blocked shot, Gainey did what it took to win and did it cleanly and effectively.

Gainey scored at least 10 goals in 14 of his 16 seasons, topping the 20-goal mark four times. In 1979, he won the Conn Smythe Trophy as playoff MVP. During the finals, he covered the Rangers' Phil Esposito like a blanket. Along the way, he collected a career-high 16 playoff points to help Montreal win their fourth straight Stanley Cup title. He continued his confident, consistent play throughout the 1980s, spending the majority of those years as captain of the Canadiens.

After he retired in 1989, a number of teams pursued Gainey to coach their club, but Gainey decided to spend a season in France. There he could learn the ropes of coaching outside the glare and pressure of the NHL. When he returned, he joined the Minnesota organization. He led the club to the Stanley Cup finals in

1992, as a coach, and when the team moved to Dallas, he built the club into a Stanley Cup champion as general manager.

Gainey was elected to the Hall of Fame in 1992.

Bob Gainey won the Frank Selke Trophy as the NHL's best defensive forward for the first four years it was presented. In his heyday, Russian hockey officials called Gainey the most complete hockey player in the world.

Mike Gartner

Position: **Right Wing**   Height: **6'0" (183 cm)**   Weight: **187 lbs (85 kg)**   Born: **October 29, 1959 in Ottawa, ON.**

| | Regular Season | | | | | | | | Playoffs | | | | |
Season	Team	GP	G	A	Pts	PIM	+/-	Season	Team	GP	G	A	Pts	PIM
1979-80	Washington	77	36	32	68	66	15	1979-80	Washington	—	—	—	—	—
1980-81	Washington	80	48	46	94	100	-5	1980-81	Washington	—	—	—	—	—
1981-82	Washington	80	35	45	80	121	-11	1981-82	Washington	—	—	—	—	—
1982-83	Washington	73	38	38	76	54	-2	1982-83	Washington	4	0	0	0	4
1983-84	Washington	80	40	45	85	90	22	1983-84	Washington	8	3	7	10	16
1984-85	Washington	80	50	52	102	71	17	1984-85	Washington	5	4	3	7	9
1985-86	Washington	74	35	40	75	63	-5	1985-86	Washington	9	2	10	12	4
1986-87	Washington	78	41	32	73	61	1	1986-87	Washington	7	4	3	7	14
1987-88	Washington	80	48	33	81	73	20	1987-88	Washington	14	3	4	7	14
1988-89	Washington	56	26	29	55	71	8	1988-89	Washington	—	—	—	—	—
	Minnesota	13	7	7	14	2	3		Minnesota	5	0	0	0	6
1989-90	Minnesota	67	34	36	70	32	-8	1989-90	Minnesota	—	—	—	—	—
	NY Rangers	12	11	5	16	6	4		NY Rangers	10	5	3	8	12
1990-91	NY Rangers	79	49	20	69	53	-9	1990-91	NY Rangers	6	1	1	2	0
1991-92	NY Rangers	76	40	41	81	55	11	1991-92	NY Rangers	13	8	8	16	4
1992-93	NY Rangers	84	45	23	68	59	-4	1992-93	NY Rangers	—	—	—	—	—
1993-94	NY Rangers	71	28	24	52	58	11	1993-94	NY Rangers	—	—	—	—	—
	Toronto	10	6	6	12	4	9		Toronto	18	5	6	11	14
1994-95	Toronto	38	12	8	20	6	0	1994-95	Toronto	5	2	2	4	2
1995-96	Toronto	82	35	19	54	52	5	1995-96	Toronto	6	4	1	5	4
1996-97	Phoenix	82	32	31	63	38	-11	1996-97	Phoenix	7	1	2	3	4
1997-98	Phoenix	60	12	15	27	24	-4	1997-98	Phoenix	5	1	0	1	18
	NHL Totals:	1432	708	627	1335	1159			Playoff Totals:	122	43	50	93	125

Mike Gartner was a scoring machine and the most consistent player to ever skate in the NHL. He scored at least 30 goals in each of his first 15 seasons in the league. His record may stand the test of time. Still, Mike Gartner played the majority of his career in total anonymity.

A product of the OHA's Niagara Falls Flyers, Gartner was one of the few teenagers who dared jump ship and sign with the World Hockey Association as an underage junior. After an excellent 27-goal season with the Cincinnati Stingers, Gartner was drafted by Washington. In his first NHL campaign, Gartner fired 36 goals, which was a rookie record at the time for the Capitals.

A smooth and graceful skater, Gartner had speed to burn. Few players could motor around the rink like Gartner. The speed record he set at the 1996 NHL Skills Competition still stands.

Gartner was blessed with a quick, deceptive shot that he was able to unleash from all angles. He could also score in any variety of ways. He was a demon in the slot and a sniper from the circle. He put 708 pucks behind enemy goaltenders. Only four other players in the history of the league found the back of the net more than Gartner.

Gartner played for five NHL teams in his career, and he scored at least 30 goals for each of them. He was also one of the most durable players of his era. Until a back injury forced him off the ice in his 19th and final NHL campaign, he had missed only 50 games. In fact, his consecutive 30-goal streak ended only because the NHL lockout prevented him from playing a full schedule in 1994-95.

Some critics feel that Gartner's failure to win a Stanley Cup ring meant he wasn't a clutch play-

er. Still, Gartner managed to collect 93 points in 122 post-season games. Ironically, his best chance at winning the Stanley Cup came in 1994, but the Rangers traded the Ottawa native to Toronto just weeks before they went on to win the Cup.

In every stop along the way during his 19-year career, Gartner was a respected and admired performer. His dedicated work during the troublesome lockout of 1994-95 paved the way for a

Sometimes defenders had to hold on because few players in hockey history were as fast as Mike Gartner. Not many have been better scorers either. Gartner topped 30 goals a record 17 times in his 19-year career.

settlement. He continues to work for the game and its players, adding a player's perspective to the boardroom. Thanks to players like Mike Gartner, hockey is a better game.

Bernie Geoffrion

Position: **Right Wing**   Height: **5'9" (175 cm)**   Weight: **166 lbs (75 kg)**   Born: **February 14, 1931 in Montreal, QC.**

	Regular Season								Playoffs				
Season	Team	GP	G	A	Pts	PIM	+/-	Season	Team	GP	G	A	Pts	PIM
1950-51	Montreal	18	8	6	14	9	—	1950-51	Montreal	11	1	1	2	6
1951-52	Montreal	67	30	24	54	66	—	1951-52	Montreal	11	3	1	4	6
1952-53	Montreal	65	22	17	39	37	—	1952-53	Montreal	12	6	4	10	12
1953-54	Montreal	54	29	25	54	87	—	1953-54	Montreal	11	6	5	11	18
1954-55	Montreal	70	38	37	75	57	—	1954-55	Montreal	12	8	5	13	8
1955-56	Montreal	59	29	33	62	66	—	1955-56	Montreal	10	5	9	14	6
1956-57	Montreal	41	19	21	40	18	—	1956-57	Montreal	10	11	7	18	2
1957-58	Montreal	42	27	23	50	51	—	1957-58	Montreal	10	6	5	11	2
1958-59	Montreal	59	22	44	66	30	—	1958-59	Montreal	11	5	8	13	10
1959-60	Montreal	59	30	41	71	36	—	1959-60	Montreal	8	2	10	12	4
1960-61	Montreal	64	50	45	95	29	—	1960-61	Montreal	4	2	1	3	0
1961-62	Montreal	62	23	36	59	36	—	1961-62	Montreal	5	0	1	1	6
1962-63	Montreal	51	23	18	41	73	—	1962-63	Montreal	5	0	1	1	4
1963-64	Montreal	55	21	18	39	41	—	1963-64	Montreal	7	1	1	2	4
1966-67	NY Rangers	58	17	25	42	42	—	1966-67	NY Rangers	4	2	0	2	0
1967-68	NY Rangers	59	5	16	21	11	1	1967-68	NY Rangers	1	0	1	1	0
NHL Totals:		**883**	**393**	**429**	**822**	**689**		**Playoff Totals:**		**132**	**58**	**60**	**118**	**88**

Bernie Geoffrion earned the nickname "Boom Boom" because of his booming slapshot. Blasts like his were very rare when Geoffrion joined the Montreal Canadiens in 1950-51. Almost everyone else relied on wrist shots and backhanders. Soon, the slapshot became a regular part of hockey.

Geoffrion's skill helped change the game, but unfortunately he almost never got the recognition he deserved. That's because he was a right winger at a time when Rocket Richard and Gordie Howe were starring in the league. Because Howe and Richard were such great players, Geoffrion was only chosen to the NHL All-Star Team three times. Still, his 393 career goals were the fifth highest in history when he retired in 1968. Geoffrion was also only the second NHL player to score 50 goals in a single season.

Geoffrion had been a great scorer right from the beginning of his career. In his first full season of 1951-52 he set a new rookie record with 30 goals and won the Calder Trophy as rookie-of-the-year. One year later, Boom Boom's six goals in

the playoffs helped the Canadiens win the Stanley Cup. In 1954-55, Geoffrion led the NHL with 38 goals and won the Art Ross Trophy as the league scoring leader with 75 points. Over the next five seasons, Geoffrion helped the Montreal Canadiens set an all-time record with five Stanley Cup championships in a row. The streak ended in 1960-61, but Geoffrion still managed to have the best season of his career that year.

Even though the NHL schedule had stretched from 50 games to 70, no one had yet duplicated the record of 50 goals set by Rocket Richard in 1944-45. Two players had a chance in 1960-61. Toronto's Frank Mahovlich made it to 48, while Geoffrion reached the magic 50. With 45 assists as well, his 95 points were just one short of that NHL record. That year, Geoffrion won the Art Ross Trophy for the second time and the Hart Trophy as the league's most valuable player.

After the 1963-64 season, Geoffrion retired to become coach of the Canadiens' farm team in Quebec City. He led the Aces to two straight titles. When Montreal didn't hire him as their new

A Century of Hockey Heroes

coach, he returned to the NHL as a player with the New York Rangers in 1966-67. Geoffrion played his final season in 1967-68 and also coached the Rangers that same year. In 1972, he was elected to the Hockey Hall of Fame. He finally got his chance to coach the Canadiens in 1979.

Booming blasts like this one earned Bernie Geoffrion his famous nickname. With his powerful slapshot, "Boom Boom" became just the second player in NHL history to score 50 goals in a single season.

Michel Goulet

Position: Left Wing   **Height:** 6'1" (185 cm)   **Weight:** 195 lbs (88 kg)   **Born:** April 21, 1960 in Peribonka, QC.

	Regular Season									Playoffs					
Season	Team	GP	G	A	Pts	PIM	+/-	Season	Team	GP	G	A	Pts	PIM
1979-80	Quebec	77	22	32	54	48	-10	1979-80	Quebec	—	—	—	—	—
1980-81	Quebec	76	32	39	71	45	0	1980-81	Quebec	4	3	4	7	7
1981-82	Quebec	80	42	42	84	48	35	1981-82	Quebec	16	8	5	13	6
1982-83	Quebec	80	57	48	105	51	31	1982-83	Quebec	4	0	0	0	6
1983-84	Quebec	75	56	65	121	76	62	1983-84	Quebec	9	2	4	6	17
1984-85	Quebec	69	55	40	95	55	10	1984-85	Quebec	17	11	10	21	17
1985-86	Quebec	75	53	51	104	64	6	1985-86	Quebec	3	1	2	3	10
1986-87	Quebec	75	49	47	96	61	-12	1986-87	Quebec	13	9	5	14	35
1987-88	Quebec	80	48	58	106	56	-31	1987-88	Quebec	—	—	—	—	—
1988-89	Quebec	69	26	38	64	67	-20	1988-89	Quebec	—	—	—	—	—
1989-90	Quebec	57	16	29	45	42	-33	1989-90	Quebec	—	—	—	—	—
	Chicago	8	4	1	5	9	1		Chicago	14	2	4	6	6
1990-91	Chicago	74	27	38	65	65	27	1990-91	Chicago	—	—	—	—	—
1991-92	Chicago	75	22	41	63	69	20	1991-92	Chicago	9	3	4	7	6
1992-93	Chicago	63	23	21	44	43	10	1992-93	Chicago	3	0	1	1	0
1993-94	Chicago	56	16	14	30	26	1	1993-94	Chicago	—	—	—	—	—
	NHL Totals:	1089	548	604	1152	825			Playoff Totals:	92	39	39	78	110

Although his name rarely comes up when discussing the greats of the game, Michel Goulet deserves a spot on that list. He ranks among the top-scoring left wingers of all time. Despite heavy competition, Goulet earned five All-Star berths in the 1980s, a testament to his talent and timely tallies.

During his 15-year career, Goulet was a consistent, all-round performer who scored at least 40 goals in six straight seasons. During the 1980s, only Gretzky, Bossy, and Jari Kurri scored more goals than Goulet. He was a smooth skater who could easily move past defenders with a mere shrug or quick deke. Once he was in the open with the puck on his stick, the red light behind the other team's goalie would often be glowing.

After serving a pair of seasons in the Quebec Remparts junior system, Goulet jumped ship and signed with the World Hockey Association's legendary Birmingham ® "Baby" Bulls.

Coached by John Brophy, the team featured teenage talents like Rick Vaive, Craig Hartsburg, and Rob Ramage. Goulet quickly learned to adapt to the rigors of the professional game. When he returned to Quebec in 1979-80, this time with the NHL's Nordiques, he was a mature, well-schooled player. The results of his hard work were proven on the score sheet.

The Peribonka, Quebec native hit the 40-goal plateau in his third season, and for the next six years, he was one of the NHL's top players. Although the Nordiques never managed to win a Stanley Cup title, Goulet played a key role in the post-season success they had. In 1982, he recorded eight goals as the Nordiques won their first Adams Division crown. Three years later, Goulet managed to collect 21 points despite a nagging groin injury, as the Nordiques reached the semifinals again.

In March, 1990, Goulet was traded to Chicago and he continued to be a productive, defensively sound winger in the Windy City. In 1991-92, he helped guide the Blackhawks into the Stanley Cup finals. Once they got there, however, a duo named Jagr and Lemieux were waiting. The Hawks fought bravely, but couldn't

match the offensive fireworks of the Penguins' powerful pair. On March 16, 1994, Goulet suffered a career-ending injury. He accepted his fate the same way he accepted his induction into the Hockey Hall of Fame — with humble honor and dignity.

Michel Goulet topped 100 points four times in his career and had more than 50 goals four years in a row. Only six players in NHL history have had more consecutive 50-goal seasons.

Wayne Gretzky

Position: **Center**   Height: **6'0" (183 cm)**   Weight: **185 lbs (84 kg)**   Born: **January 26, 1961 in Brantford, ON.**

	Regular Season									Playoffs					
Season	Team	GP	G	A	Pts	PIM	+/-		Season	Team	GP	G	A	Pts	PIM
1979-80	Edmonton	79	51	86	137	21	15		1979-80	Edmonton	3	2	1	3	0
1980-81	Edmonton	80	55	109	164	28	41		1980-81	Edmonton	9	7	14	21	4
1981-82	Edmonton	80	92	120	212	26	81		1981-82	Edmonton	5	5	7	12	8
1982-83	Edmonton	80	71	125	196	59	60		1982-83	Edmonton	16	12	26	38	4
1983-84	Edmonton 🏆	74	87	118	205	39	76		1983-84	Edmonton 🏆	19	13	22	35	12
1984-85	Edmonton 🏆	80	73	135	208	52	98		1984-85	Edmonton 🏆	18	17	30	47	4
1985-86	Edmonton	80	52	163	215	46	71		1985-86	Edmonton	10	8	11	19	2
1986-87	Edmonton 🏆	79	62	121	183	28	70		1986-87	Edmonton 🏆	21	5	29	34	6
1987-88	Edmonton 🏆	64	40	109	149	24	39		1987-88	Edmonton 🏆	19	12	31	43	16
1988-89	Los Angeles	78	54	114	168	26	15		1988-89	Los Angeles	11	5	17	22	0
1989-90	Los Angeles	73	40	102	142	42	8		1989-90	Los Angeles	7	3	7	10	0
1990-91	Los Angeles	78	41	122	163	16	30		1990-91	Los Angeles	12	4	11	15	2
1991-92	Los Angeles	74	31	90	121	34	-12		1991-92	Los Angeles	6	2	5	7	2
1992-93	Los Angeles	45	16	49	65	6	6		1992-93	Los Angeles	24	15	25	40	4
1993-94	Los Angeles	81	38	92	130	20	-25		1993-94	Los Angeles	—	—	—	—	—
1994-95	Los Angeles	48	11	37	48	6	-20		1994-95	Los Angeles	—	—	—	—	—
1995-96	Los Angeles	62	15	66	81	32	-7		1995-96	Los Angeles	—	—	—	—	—
	St. Louis	18	8	13	21	2	-6			St. Louis	13	2	14	16	0
1996-97	NY Rangers	82	25	72	97	28	12		1996-97	NY Rangers	15	10	10	20	2
1997-98	NY Rangers	82	23	67	90	28	-11		1997-98	NY Rangers	—	—	—	—	—
1998-99	NY Rangers	70	9	53	62	14	-23		1998-99	NY Rangers	—	—	—	—	—
	NHL Totals:	1487	894	1963	2875	577			Playoff Totals:	208	122	260	382	66

Wayne Gretzky was destined to be a superstar from the time he was a young boy practicing his skills on a backyard rink. Gretzky started playing organized hockey by the age of six. He was so small then that his father had to hitch up his sweater on the right side to keep it out of the way when he shot the puck. It worked, and by the time he was 11, Gretzky had scored 378 goals for his team in Brantford, Ontario.

By 17, Gretzky was ready to play professional hockey. The NHL does not allow players that young into the league, so Gretzky joined the rival World Hockey Association and played with men twice his age in the 1978-79 season. Still, Gretzky managed to finish third in the WHA scoring race. The next year, four WHA teams joined the NHL — including Gretzky's Edmonton Oilers.

Gretzky had been a star at every level of the game, but many experts doubted that a skinny 18 year old could succeed in the NHL. He wasn't very big or fast. His shot was only ordinary, and his style wasn't smooth.

Gretzky made a career of proving those experts wrong! He had incredible vision of the ice, uncanny anticipation of the play, and was always able to make the puck go wherever he wanted. He had 51 goals and 137 points in his rookie season of 1979-80 and won the Hart Trophy (for the first of nine times) as the NHL's most valuable player. Soon, he was rewriting the NHL record book.

In his second season, Gretzky won his first of 10 NHL scoring titles. He set new records with 109 assists and 164 points. In 1980-81, he smashed Phil Esposito's record of 76 goals when he scored an amazing 92 times! With 120 assists that year Gretzky had an incredible 212 points. Only Wayne himself has surpassed that mark, with 215 points (and a record 163 assists) in 1985-86.

A Century of Hockey Heroes

Gretzky led the Edmonton Oilers to four Stanley Cup titles during the 1980s, but on August 9, 1988 he was traded to Los Angeles. It was with the Kings that he broke Gordie Howe's career record of 1,850 points and 801 goals. Gretzky played three seasons with the New York Rangers before he retired in 1999. He ended his career with 894 goals. He also set up 1,963 goals for teammates, meaning that

Wayne Gretzky rewrote the NHL record book during his early days with the Edmonton Oilers, setting single season records for goals, assists, and points. He later broke all sorts of career records, including most career records, while playing with the Los Angeles Kings, St. Louis Blues and New York Rangers.

Wayne Gretzky had more assists than any other hockey player has ever had points!

George Hainsworth

Position: **Goaltender**   Height: **5'6" (168 cm)**   Weight: **150 lbs (68 kg)**   Born: **June 26, 1895 in Toronto, ON.**

	Regular Season											Playoffs								
Season	Team	GP	W	L	T	MINS	GA	SO	AVG.		Season	Team	GP	W	L	T	MINS	GA	SO	AVG.
1926-27	Mtl. Canadiens	44	28	14	2	2732	67	14	1.47		1926-27	Mtl. Canadiens	4	1	1	2	252	6	1	1.43
1927-28	Mtl. Canadiens	44	26	11	7	2730	48	13	1.05		1927-28	Mtl. Canadiens	2	0	1	1	128	3	0	1.41
1928-29	Mtl. Canadiens	44	22	7	15	2800	43	22	0.92		1928-29	Mtl. Canadiens	3	0	3	0	180	5	0	1.67
1929-30	Mtl. Canadiens	42	20	13	9	3008	108	4	2.15		1929-30	Mtl. Canadiens	6	5	0	1	481	6	3	0.75
1930-31	Mtl. Canadiens	44	26	10	8	2740	89	8	1.95		1930-31	Mtl. Canadiens	10	6	4	0	722	21	2	1.75
1931-32	Mtl. Canadiens	48	25	16	7	2998	110	6	2.20		1931-32	Mtl. Canadiens	4	1	3	0	300	13	0	2.60
1932-33	Mtl. Canadiens	48	18	25	5	2980	115	8	2.32		1932-33	Mtl. Canadiens	2	0	1	1	120	8	0	4.00
1933-34	Toronto	48	26	13	9	3010	119	3	2.37		1933-34	Toronto	5	2	3	0	302	11	0	2.19
1934-35	Toronto	48	30	14	4	2957	111	8	2.25		1934-35	Toronto	7	3	4	0	460	12	2	1.57
1935-36	Toronto	48	23	19	6	3000	106	8	2.12		1935-36	Toronto	9	4	5	0	541	27	0	2.99
1936-37	Toronto	3	0	2	1	190	9	0	2.84		1936-37	Toronto	—	—	—	—	—	—	—	—
	Mtl. Canadiens	4	2	1	1	270	12	0	2.67			Mtl. Canadiens	—	—	—	—	—	—	—	—
NHL Totals:		465	246	145	74	29415	937	94	1.91		Playoff Totals:		52	22	25	5	3486	112	8	1.93

As good as NHL goalies are today, none of them will ever match the shutout record George Hainsworth set in 1928-29. Hainsworth had 22 shutouts that year! Even more amazing, he did it during a 44-game season. Hainsworth played all 44 games for the Montreal Canadiens that year and only let in 43 goals. His goals-against that season was an amazing 0.92. His lifetime goals-against average was 1.91 over 11 NHL seasons.

George Hainsworth already had a long career before joining the NHL. He had been an amateur star who won championships at every level his teams played. In 1917-18, he led his team in Kitchener, Ontario to the Allan Cup. In those days the Allan Cup was as important a trophy as the Stanley Cup. It was awarded to the team that won Canada's senior amateur championship.

Hainsworth finally signed a professional contract in 1923-24 and spent the next three years playing with Saskatoon in the Western Canada Hockey League. Newsy Lalonde also played for

Saskatoon and had been a star with the Montreal Canadiens. When Montreal's legendary goalie Georges Vezina died in 1926, Lalonde recommended that the Canadiens sign Hainsworth as a replacement. It was a smart move.

Hainsworth joined the Canadiens for the 1926-27 season, and he quickly became the best goalie in the NHL. Hainsworth had 14 shutouts and a 1.47 goals-against average during his first season and won the Vezina Trophy (which was named after Georges Vezina). He won the Vezina Trophy again in 1927-28 after posting 13 shutouts and a 1.05 average. Hainsworth made it three trophies in a row with his record-setting season in 1928-29. The following year, the NHL decided it wanted more goals to be scored, so the rules were changed to allow more forward passing. After that, it was impossible for any goalie to match the statistics Hainsworth achieved in 1928-29.

Even with the new rules in place, Hainsworth remained a top goaltender. He helped the Canadiens win the Stanley Cup in 1929-30 and again in 1930-31. In 1933, the Canadiens traded Hainsworth to Toronto. He played three full seasons with the Maple Leafs and helped them reach the Stanley Cup Finals twice. He finally retired in 1936-37 at the age of 41. George Hainsworth had 94 shutouts during

his NHL career. It was a record that lasted almost 30 years. When Hainsworth's 10 shutouts in Saskatoon are added, he has 104 career shutouts, which is one more than Terry Sawchuk's current NHL record of 103.

Hainsworth was elected to the Hockey Hall of Fame in 1961.

George Hainsworth had 49 shutouts after just three seasons in the NHL. Through the 1998-99 season, only 15 goalies in NHL history have had more than 49 shutouts in their entire career!

Glenn Hall

Position: **Goaltender**   Height: **5'11" (180 cm)**   Weight: **180 lbs (82 kg)**   Born: **October 3, 1931 in Humboldt, SK.**

	Regular Season										Playoffs						
Season	Team	GP	W	L	T	MINS	GA	SO	AVG.	Season	Team	GP	W	L	MINS	GA	SO	AVG.
1952-53	Detroit	6	4	1	1	360	10	1	1.67	1952-53	Detroit	—	—	—	—	—	—	—
1954-55	Detroit	2	2	0	0	120	2	0	1.00	1954-55	Detroit	—	—	—	—	—	—	—
1955-56	Detroit	70	30	24	16	4200	148	12	2.11	1955-56	Detroit	10	5	5	604	28	0	2.78
1956-57	Detroit	70	38	20	12	4200	157	4	2.24	1956-57	Detroit	5	1	4	300	15	0	3.00
1957-58	Chicago	70	24	39	7	4200	202	7	2.89	1957-58	Chicago	—	—	—	—	—	—	—
1958-59	Chicago	70	28	29	13	4200	208	1	2.97	1958-59	Chicago	6	2	4	360	21	0	3.50
1959-60	Chicago	70	28	29	13	4200	180	6	2.57	1959-60	Chicago	4	0	4	249	14	0	3.37
1960-61	Chicago	70	29	24	17	4200	180	6	2.57	1960-61	Chicago	12	8	4	772	27	2	2.10
1961-62	Chicago	70	31	26	13	4200	186	9	2.66	1961-62	Chicago	12	6	6	720	31	2	2.58
1962-63	Chicago	66	30	20	15	3910	166	5	2.55	1962-63	Chicago	6	2	4	360	25	0	4.17
1963-64	Chicago	65	34	19	11	3860	148	7	2.30	1963-64	Chicago	7	3	4	408	22	0	3.24
1964-65	Chicago	41	18	17	5	2440	99	4	2.43	1964-65	Chicago	13	7	6	760	28	1	2.21
1965-66	Chicago	64	34	21	7	3747	164	4	2.63	1965-66	Chicago	6	2	4	347	22	0	3.80
1966-67	Chicago	32	19	5	5	1664	66	2	2.38	1966-67	Chicago	3	1	2	176	8	0	2.73
1967-68	St. Louis	49	19	21	9	2858	118	5	2.48	1967-68	St. Louis	18	8	10	1111	45	1	2.43
1968-69	St. Louis	41	19	12	8	2354	85	8	2.17	1968-69	St. Louis	3	0	2	131	5	0	2.29
1969-70	St. Louis	18	7	8	3	1010	49	1	2.91	1969-70	St. Louis	7	4	3	421	21	0	2.99
1970-71	St. Louis	32	13	11	8	1761	71	2	2.42	1970-71	St. Louis	3	0	3	180	9	0	3.00
	NHL Totals:	618	281	213	114	36204	1512	59	2.51		Playoff Totals:	94	41	52	5635	257	6	2.74

Glenn Hall was so good at his position that he became known as "Mr. Goalie." Good as he was though, Hall found the pressure of his position difficult to handle. He would get so nervous that he would vomit before almost every game! Yet he continued to play, and play, and play! In fact, Hall set one of the NHL's most amazing records by playing in 502 consecutive games. In the NHL these days, it's rare for a goalie to play more than 30 games in a row. Hall's streak lasted more than seven seasons before a back injury finally sidelined him on November 8, 1963.

Glenn Hall began his career with a few appearances in goal for Detroit in 1952-53 and 1954-55. At the time, Terry Sawchuk, the best goalie in the NHL played for the Red Wings. Sawchuk helped Detroit win the Stanley Cup in 1954-55, but Hall had been doing so well in the minor leagues that Detroit traded Sawchuk and gave his job to Glenn in 1955-56. He was an instant success that season with a 2.11 goals-against average and a league-leading 12 shutouts. Hall was rewarded with the Calder Trophy as the rookie of the year and a spot on the Second All-

Star Team. It was the first of 11 All-Star honors for him, including seven selections to the First All-Star Team. No other goalie in NHL history has ever been an All-Star so many times.

Despite his success, Detroit reacquired Terry Sawchuk prior to the 1957-58 season and traded Hall to Chicago. The Blackhawks had been the worst team in hockey for many years, but Hall helped to turn them around. In 1960-61, he helped Chicago win the Stanley Cup for the first time since 1938. In 1962-63 Hall won the Vezina Trophy as the NHL's top goalie. In 1966-67, he helped Chicago finish in first place in the regular-season standings. Hall split the Blackhawks' netminding duties with Dennis DeJordy that season, with whom he shared the Vezina Trophy.

When the NHL expanded from six teams to 12 in 1967-68, Glenn Hall joined the St. Louis

Blues. In 1968-69, he shared the St. Louis net with Jacques Plante, and together the veteran goalies earned the Vezina Trophy. Hall continued to star in St. Louis until retiring in 1971. He was elected to the Hockey Hall of Fame in 1975.

Glenn Hall played 15 seasons in the NHL without wearing a goalie mask. He finally put one on for the first time on November 13, 1968 – more than nine years after Jacques Plante first wore his.

Doug Harvey

Position: **Defense**   Height: **5'11" (180 cm)**   Weight: **187 lbs (85 kg)**   Born: **December 19, 1924 in Montreal, QC.**

Regular Season								Playoffs					
Season	Team	GP	G	A	Pts	PIM	+/-	Season	Team	GP	G	A	Pts	PIM
1947-48	Montreal	35	4	4	8	32	—	1947-48	Montreal	—	—	—	—	—
1948-49	Montreal	55	3	13	16	87	—	1948-49	Montreal	7	0	1	1	10
1949-50	Montreal	70	4	20	24	76	—	1949-50	Montreal	5	0	2	2	10
1950-51	Montreal	70	5	24	29	93	—	1950-51	Montreal	11	0	5	5	12
1951-52	Montreal	68	6	23	29	82	—	1951-52	Montreal	11	0	3	3	8
1952-53	Montreal 🏆	69	4	30	34	67	—	1952-53	Montreal 🏆	12	0	5	5	8
1953-54	Montreal	68	8	29	37	110	—	1953-54	Montreal	10	0	2	2	12
1954-55	Montreal	70	6	43	49	58	—	1954-55	Montreal	12	0	8	8	6
1955-56	Montreal 🏆	62	5	39	44	60	—	1955-56	Montreal 🏆	10	2	5	7	10
1956-57	Montreal 🏆	70	6	44	50	92	—	1956-57	Montreal 🏆	10	0	7	7	10
1957-58	Montreal 🏆	68	9	32	41	131	—	1957-58	Montreal 🏆	10	2	9	11	16
1958-59	Montreal 🏆	61	4	16	20	61	—	1958-59	Montreal 🏆	11	1	11	12	22
1959-60	Montreal 🏆	66	6	21	27	45	—	1959-60	Montreal 🏆	8	3	0	3	6
1960-61	Montreal	58	6	33	39	48	—	1960-61	Montreal	6	0	1	1	8
1961-62	NY Rangers	69	6	24	30	42	—	1961-62	NY Rangers	6	0	1	1	2
1962-63	NY Rangers	68	4	35	39	92	—	1962-63	NY Rangers	—	—	—	—	—
1963-64	NY Rangers	14	0	2	2	10	—	1963-64	NY Rangers	—	—	—	—	—
1966-67	Detroit	2	0	0	0	0	—	1966-67	Detroit	—	—	—	—	—
1967-68	St. Louis	—	—	—	—	—	—	1967-68	St. Louis	8	0	4	4	12
1968-69	St. Louis	70	2	20	22	30	11	1968-69	St. Louis	—	—	—	—	—
	NHL Totals:	1113	88	452	540	1216			Playoff Totals:	137	8	64	72	152

When people list the greatest defensemen in NHL history, three names usually come out on top. One is Bobby Orr. Another is Eddie Shore. But in terms of all around excellence, Doug Harvey may have been the best of them all. Harvey could take care of his own end better than anyone else in hockey during the 1950s. He could also lead his teammates on the attack by passing the puck better than any other defenseman. Harvey was so good with the puck that he could control the way everyone else had to play. When he slowed down, the pace of the entire game slowed down. When he sped up, everyone else on the ice moved faster, too.

Doug Harvey was also good enough at baseball to be offered a major league contract. He turned it down to concentrate on hockey and was soon the best defenseman on the best team in the NHL. Harvey joined the Montreal Canadiens in 1947-48 and was picked for the All-Star Team for the first time in 1951-52. He was an All-Star for 11 straight seasons after that! Ten of his selections were to the First All-Star Team. (Raymond

Bourque is the only defenseman with more All-Star honors than Harvey.) When the NHL began awarding the Norris Trophy to the league's best defenseman in 1954, Harvey won it six times in the first eight seasons. During that time he also helped Montreal win the Stanley Cup five years in a row between 1955-56 and 1959-60.

Harvey was named captain of the Canadiens in 1960-61. After the season, Montreal traded him to New York so that he could become the playing coach of the Rangers. He was good enough on the ice to win the Norris Trophy for the seventh time in 1961-62, and was good enough as a coach to lead the Rangers into the playoffs. After the season, Harvey decided he didn't like coaching. He spent two more years playing for the Rangers and then spent a few seasons in the minors. He was 43

years old when he returned to the NHL for the 1968 playoffs. Harvey helped the St. Louis Blues reach the Stanley Cup Finals that year. He retired after the 1968-69 season and was elected to the Hockey Hall of Fame in 1973.

Whether it was checking an opponent along the boards or leading his teammates on the attack, Doug Harvey was a defenseman who could do it all. Before Bobby Orr, Harvey's 540 points were the most ever by an NHL defenseman.

Dominik Hasek

Position: **Goaltender**   Height: **5'11" (180 cm)**   Weight: **168 lbs (76 kg)**   Born: **January 29, 1965 in Pardubice, Czechoslovakia.**

| Regular Season | | | | | | | | | | Playoffs | | | | | | | |
Season	Team	GP	W	L	T	MINS	GA	SO	AVG.	Season	Team	GP	W	L	MINS	GA	SO	AVG.
1990-91	Chicago	5	3	0	1	195	8	0	2.46	1990-91	Chicago	3	0	0	69	3	0	2.61
1991-92	Chicago	20	10	4	1	1014	44	1	2.60	1991-92	Chicago	3	0	2	58	8	0	3.04
1992-93	Buffalo	28	11	10	4	1429	75	0	3.15	1992-93	Buffalo	1	1	0	45	1	0	1.33
1993-94	Buffalo	58	30	20	6	3358	109	7	1.95	1993-94	Buffalo	7	3	4	484	13	2	1.61
1994-95	Buffalo	41	19	14	7	2416	85	5	2.11	1994-95	Buffalo	5	1	4	309	18	0	3.50
1995-96	Buffalo	59	22	30	6	3417	161	2	2.83	1995-96	Buffalo	—	—	—	—	—	—	—
1996-97	Buffalo	67	37	20	10	4037	153	5	2.27	1996-97	Buffalo	3	1	1	153	5	0	1.96
1997-98	Buffalo	72	33	23	13	4220	147	13	2.09	1997-98	Buffalo	15	10	5	948	32	1	2.03
1998-99	Buffalo	64	20	18	14	3817	119	9	1.87	1998-99	Buffalo	19	13	6	1217	36	2	1.77
NHL Totals:		414	185	139	62	23,903	901	42	2.26	Playoff Totals:		56	29	22	3383	116	5	2.06

It's safe to say the NHL has never seen anything like Dominik Hasek. When Hasek's in the crease, he will do anything to stop the puck. Hasek will roll, sprawl, dive, and stop goals with his mask if he has to! This in-crease acrobat stops more pucks on his back than he does standing up. Hasek's even been known to lay his goal stick across the goal line to keep slow rolling pucks from slipping by him. He has a spine like a Slinky and an arm span like a giant heron. It's no wonder he's the top goalie in the world.

Although he was drafted by Chicago in 1983, Hasek didn't come to North America until 1990-91. He stayed in Europe hoping to win an Olympic gold medal with Czechoslovakia. In 1988, he got his chance to play in the Olympics, but the Czechs finished sixth.

Hasek then decided he wanted to try and win the Stanley Cup and signed with Chicago. The Blackhawks made it to the finals in his second season, but lost to Pittsburgh. Since Ed Belfour started almost every game, Hasek never really felt like part of the team. After the 1992 finals, the Blackhawks traded Hasek to Buffalo. The Blackhawks have gone through four goalies since then, while the Buffalo Sabres have the first goalie in history to win the MVP award in back-to-back seasons.

After an average first season in Buffalo, Hasek quickly became the NHL's top goalie. In 1992-93, his goals-against average was 1.95, the lowest mark in nearly 20 years. He has led the league in shutouts three times, and in 1997-98, he had six shutouts in December alone. You have to go back 69 years to match that record!

Hasek's real value lies in how he has lifted the fortunes of the Sabres. Buffalo is an honest, hard-working team, but with Hasek in net, they've become a Stanley Cup contender.

In 1996-97, Hasek appeared in 67 games and won 37 of them. He was so outstanding, he became the first netminder since Jacques Plante to win the Hart Trophy as MVP. The following season, he suited up 72 times and once again was MVP.

But there was still another honor in store for Hasek. In the winter of 1998, the NHL stopped play so that the league's best could go to the Olympics. Hasek was given a second chance to play in goal for his home country. Hasek led the Czech Republic to their first gold medal and allowed only six goals in six games. With that goal reached, there's only one more left for Hasek. And if anybody can do it, Hasek can.

Dominik Hasek will do anything to stop the puck! He often drops his stick and sprawls along the ice to block shots, as he does here against Philadelphia. Hasek led Buffalo to the Stanley Cup Finals in 1999.

Bryan Hextall

Position: **Right Wing**   Height: **5'10" (178 cm)**   Weight: **180 lbs (82 kg)**   Born: **July 31, 1913 in Grenfell, SK.**

Regular Season								Playoffs						
Season	Team	GP	G	A	Pts	PIM	+/-	Season	Team	GP	G	A	Pts	PIM
1936-37	NY Rangers	3	0	1	1	0	—	1936-37	NY Rangers	—	—	—	—	—
1937-38	NY Rangers	48	17	4	21	6	—	1937-38	NY Rangers	3	2	0	2	0
1938-39	NY Rangers	48	20	15	35	18	—	1938-39	NY Rangers	7	0	1	1	4
1939-40	NY Rangers	48	24	15	39	52	—	1939-40	NY Rangers	12	4	3	7	11
1940-41	NY Rangers	48	26	18	44	16	—	1940-41	NY Rangers	3	0	1	1	0
1941-42	NY Rangers	48	24	32	56	30	—	1941-42	NY Rangers	6	1	1	2	4
1942-43	NY Rangers	50	27	32	59	28	—	1942-43	NY Rangers	—	—	—	—	—
1943-44	NY Rangers	50	21	33	54	41	—	1943-44	NY Rangers	—	—	—	—	—
1945-46	NY Rangers	3	0	1	1	0	—	1945-46	NY Rangers	—	—	—	—	—
1946-47	NY Rangers	60	20	10	30	18	—	1946-47	NY Rangers	—	—	—	—	—
1947-48	NY Rangers	43	8	14	22	18	—	1947-48	NY Rangers	6	1	3	4	0
NHL Totals:		449	187	175	362	227		Playoff Totals:		37	8	9	17	19

Bryan Hextall scored the winning goal in overtime when the New York Rangers won the Stanley Cup in 1940. As time went by, his goal became legendary because it took the Rangers 54 years to win another Stanley Cup! But Hextall was much more than a one-goal wonder. He topped 20 goals seven times in his eight NHL seasons. During his playing days a 20-goal scorer was as valuable as a 50-goal scorer is today. Hextall was also a solid bodychecker and was considered to be the hardest hitting forward in the NHL.

Hextall was a scoring star in the minor leagues before New York called him up for a three-game trial in 1936-37. He became a Rangers regular in the next season. Hextall scored 20 goals for the first time in 1938-39. In 1939-40, he led the NHL with 24 goals and was named to the First All-Star Team at right wing. He led the league with 26 goals the following year, then

topped the league with 56 points in 1941-42. Hextall was a First-Team All-Star both of those seasons, too. During those years, Hextall was starring on the Rangers' top line with Phil Watson and Lynn Patrick, who were All-Stars as well. In fact, when Hextall won the scoring title in 1941-42, Patrick led the NHL with 32 goals that season, while Watson was also tops with 37 assists. The Rangers finished in first place in the league standings. It would be another 50 years before a Rangers team topped the NHL standings again.

In 1942-43, Hextall scored a career-high 27 goals and was named to the Second All-Star Team. Unfortunately, the Rangers fell into last place in the NHL that year because many of their other top stars had become soldiers during World War II. Hextall played one more season before his career was also interrupted by military service. He returned to the Rangers late in the 1945-46 season. In 1946-47, he scored 20 goals, but he retired from the NHL after scoring only eight times in 43 games in 1947-48. He was elected to the Hockey Hall of Fame in 1969.

Bryan Hextall had been a well respected player during his career. He became a great ambassador for hockey after he retired. His sons Dennis and Bryan Jr. played in the NHL during the 1960s and '70s. Grandson Ron was a top goalie in the NHL through the 1980s and '90s.

Bryan Hextall shakes hands with Rangers coach and former star Frank Boucher after scoring the Stanley Cup-winning goal in 1940. Teammate Dutch Hiller flashes a big smile in the background.

Jiri Holecek

Position: **Goaltender**   Height: **6'0" (183 cm)**   Weight: **165 lbs (75 kg)**   Born: **March 18, 1944 in Prague, Czechoslovakia.**

Year	Team	Event	GP	Mins	GA	Avg
1966	Czechoslovakia	World Championships	2	116	5	2.58
1967	Czechoslovakia	World Championships	4	207	6	1.73
1971	Czechoslovakia	World Championships	8	440	12	1.64
1972	Czechoslovakia	Olympics	3	138	8	3.48
1972	Czechoslovakia	World Championships	6	360	10	1.67
1973	Czechoslovakia	World Championships	8	480	17	2.12
1974	Czechoslovakia	World Championships	6	340	10	1.76
1975	Czechoslovakia	World Championships	9	525	14	1.60
1976	Czechoslovakia	Olympics	5	263	9	2.05
1976	Czechoslovakia	World Championships	8	480	13	1.62
1977	Czechoslovakia	World Championships	4	200	14	4.20
1978	Czechoslovakia	World Championships	9	540	19	2.10
	Career Totals:		72	4086	137	2.21

Before being split up into the Czech Republic and Slovakia, these two countries had once formed one country known as Czechoslovakia. Czechoslovakia was one of the first European nations to develop star hockey players in the early years of the twentieth century. However, until the 1990s, the Communist government in Czechoslovakia did not allow its players to leave home for the NHL.

NHL stars like Jaromir Jagr and Dominik Hasek are two of the latest examples of great hockey players from the countries that once were Czechoslovakia. Hasek is now considered to be the greatest goalie in the world. Once, the same was true of Jiri Holecek. To this day many international hockey experts still consider Holecek to be one of the two greatest goalies ever to come from Europe. The other one is Vladislav Tretiak of Russia. If Holecek had been given as many opportunities as Tretiak to play tournaments against NHL stars, his name would be much more famous today.

Holecek played in the top league in Czechoslovakia from 1963 to 1978, and later spent three more years playing in Germany. He was the type of goalie that never seemed to let pressure bother him. No matter how exciting a game got, Holecek could keep calm. He was very good with his gloves, using his blocker to deflect pucks away or his catcher to grab them. His hands were so fast that Holecek was nick-named "The Magician."

Like all the great European stars of his era, what truly made Holecek stand out was his performance at international events. He was a member of the Czechoslovakian national team from 1966 to 1978. During that time, he helped his country win a silver medal at the 1976 Olympics and a bronze medal in 1972. Holecek also played at the World Championships 10 times. He was named Best Goalie at the tournament five times and earned five selections to the tournament's all-star team. Holecek helped Czechoslovakia win the world title in 1972, 1976, and 1977. His team finished the World Championships in second place five times, and in third place once. Holecek's only chance to face NHL opponents came at the 1976 Canada Cup hockey tournament, where Czechoslovakia reached the finals before losing to Team Canada.

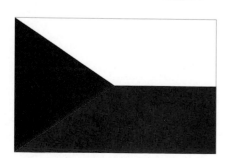

Jiri Holecek kicks this shot aside during the 1976 Canada Cup tournament. If Holecek had played more games against NHL opponents, his name would be as famous today as his chief European rival, Vladislav Tretiak.

Tim Horton

Position: **Defense**   Height: **5'10" (178 cm)**   Weight: **180 lbs (82 kg)**   Born: **January 12, 1930 in Cochrane, ON.**

Regular Season								Playoffs						
Season	Team	GP	G	A	Pts	PIM	+/-	Season	Team	GP	G	A	Pts	PIM
1949-50	Toronto	1	0	0	0	2	—	1949-50	Toronto	1	0	0	0	2
1951-52	Toronto	4	0	0	0	8	—	1951-52	Toronto	—	—	—	—	—
1952-53	Toronto	70	2	14	16	85	—	1952-53	Toronto	—	—	—	—	—
1953-54	Toronto	70	7	24	31	94	—	1953-54	Toronto	5	1	1	2	4
1954-55	Toronto	67	5	9	14	84	—	1954-55	Toronto	—	—	—	—	—
1955-56	Toronto	35	0	5	5	36	—	1955-56	Toronto	2	0	0	0	4
1956-57	Toronto	66	6	19	25	72	—	1956-57	Toronto	—	—	—	—	—
1957-58	Toronto	53	6	20	26	39	—	1957-58	Toronto	—	—	—	—	—
1958-59	Toronto	70	5	21	26	76	—	1958-59	Toronto	12	0	3	3	16
1959-60	Toronto	70	3	29	32	69	—	1959-60	Toronto	10	0	1	1	6
1960-61	Toronto	57	6	15	21	75	—	1960-61	Toronto	5	0	0	0	0
1961-62	Toronto 🏆	70	10	28	38	88	—	1961-62	Toronto 🏆	12	3	13	16	16
1962-63	Toronto 🏆	70	6	19	25	69	—	1962-63	Toronto 🏆	10	1	3	4	10
1963-64	Toronto 🏆	70	9	20	29	71	—	1963-64	Toronto 🏆	14	0	4	4	20
1964-65	Toronto	70	12	16	28	95	—	1964-65	Toronto	6	0	2	2	13
1965-66	Toronto	70	6	22	28	76	—	1965-66	Toronto	4	1	0	1	12
1966-67	Toronto 🏆	70	8	17	25	70	—	1966-67	Toronto 🏆	12	3	5	8	25
1967-68	Toronto	69	4	23	27	82	20	1967-68	Toronto	—	—	—	—	—
1968-69	Toronto	74	11	29	40	107	14	1968-69	Toronto	4	0	0	0	7
1969-70	Toronto	59	3	19	22	91	4	1969-70	Toronto	—	—	—	—	—
	NY Rangers	15	1	5	6	16	-7		NY Rangers	6	1	1	2	28
1970-71	NY Rangers	78	2	18	20	57	28	1970-71	NY Rangers	13	1	4	5	14
1971-72	Pittsburgh	44	2	9	11	40	5	1971-72	Pittsburgh	4	0	1	1	2
1972-73	Buffalo	69	1	16	17	56	12	1972-73	Buffalo	6	0	1	1	4
1973-74	Buffalo	55	0	6	6	53	5	1973-74	Buffalo	—	—	—	—	—
	NHL Totals:	1446	115	403	518	1611			Playoff Totals:	126	11	39	50	183

Tim Horton had one of the longest careers in hockey history. In fact, only Gordie Howe (who played for 26 seasons) spent more years in the NHL than Horton's total of 24. His 1,446 games was a record for the most games ever played by a defenseman. His record lasted from his final game in 1974 until the 1998-99 season, when Larry Murphy and Ray Bourque passed the mark.

Since he was not a flashy player, it was easy to overlook Horton's talent. But fans who knew the game well knew that Horton had everything it takes to be a great defenseman.

While he was a smooth skater, he could also hand out thumping bodychecks. When the pressure was on, Horton could stickhandle the puck out of his own end as well as anybody. He had a powerful slapshot and was good at passing the puck. During most of his long career, Horton was considered to be one of the strongest players in hockey, but he usually used his strength to stop fights rather than start them. When a player seemed ready to lose his temper, Horton would grab him in a powerful grip that became known as "The Horton Bear Hug."

Horton was a product of the Maple Leafs farm system, and he made two brief appearances for the Leafs before reaching the NHL to stay in 1952-53. He was named to the Second All-Star Team after just his second full season in the NHL, but injuries slowed him down for the next few years. By 1958-59, Horton was finally healthy again. Soon he was part of the best team in hockey, helping the Maple Leafs win the

Stanley Cup in 1962, 1963, and 1964. As for his own play, Horton was a Second-Team All-Star again in 1962-63 and was named to the First All-Star Team in 1963-64. When the Leafs won another Stanley Cup title in 1966-67, Horton was picked once again as a Second-Team All-Star.

Before the start of the 1967-68 season, the NHL added six new teams and grew to become a 12-team league. The Maple Leafs did not do well as a team after expansion, but Tim Horton continued to shine. He was named to the First All-

Tim Horton corrals the puck during a game against the Oakland Golden Seals in 1968. Though the Maple Leafs struggled after NHL expansion, Tim Horton was as good as ever.

Star Team in both 1967-68 and 1968-69. In 1969-70, Toronto traded him to the New York Rangers. Horton later played for the Pittsburgh Penguins and Buffalo Sabres before he was killed in a car accident in 1974. He was elected to the Hockey Hall of Fame in 1977.

Gordie Howe

Position: **Right Wing**   Height: **6'0" (183 cm)**   Weight: **205 lbs (93 kg)**   Born: **March 31, 1928 in Floral, SK.**

Regular Season								Playoffs					
Season	Team	GP	G	A	Pts	PIM	+/-	Season	Team	GP	G	A	Pts	PIM
1946-47	Detroit	58	7	15	22	52	—	1946-47	Detroit	5	0	0	0	18
1947-48	Detroit	60	16	28	44	63	—	1947-48	Detroit	10	1	1	2	11
1948-49	Detroit	40	12	25	37	57	—	1948-49	Detroit	11	8	3	11	19
1949-50	Detroit 🏆	70	35	33	68	69	—	1949-50	Detroit 🏆	1	0	0	0	7
1950-51	Detroit 🏆	70	43	43	86	74	—	1950-51	Detroit	6	4	3	7	4
1951-52	Detroit 🏆	70	47	39	86	78	—	1951-52	Detroit 🏆	8	2	5	7	2
1952-53	Detroit	70	49	46	95	57	—	1952-53	Detroit	6	2	5	7	2
1953-54	Detroit 🏆	70	33	48	81	109	—	1953-54	Detroit 🏆	12	4	5	9	31
1954-55	Detroit 🏆	64	29	33	62	68	—	1954-55	Detroit 🏆	11	9	11	20	24
1955-56	Detroit	70	38	41	79	100	—	1955-56	Detroit	10	3	9	12	8
1956-57	Detroit	70	44	45	89	72	—	1956-57	Detroit	5	2	5	7	6
1957-58	Detroit	64	33	44	77	40	—	1957-58	Detroit	4	1	1	2	0
1958-59	Detroit	70	32	46	78	57	—	1958-59	Detroit	—	—	—	—	—
1959-60	Detroit	70	28	45	73	46	—	1959-60	Detroit	6	1	5	6	4
1960-61	Detroit	64	23	49	72	30	—	1960-61	Detroit	11	4	11	15	10
1961-62	Detroit	70	33	44	77	54	—	1961-62	Detroit	—	—	—	—	—
1962-63	Detroit	70	38	48	86	100	—	1962-63	Detroit	11	7	9	16	22
1963-64	Detroit	69	26	47	73	70	—	1963-64	Detroit	14	9	10	19	16
1964-65	Detroit	70	29	47	76	104	—	1964-65	Detroit	7	4	2	6	20
1965-66	Detroit	70	29	46	75	83	—	1965-66	Detroit	12	4	6	10	12
1966-67	Detroit	69	25	40	65	53	—	1966-67	Detroit	—	—	—	—	—
1967-68	Detroit	74	39	43	82	53	12	1967-68	Detroit	—	—	—	—	—
1968-69	Detroit	76	44	59	103	58	45	1968-69	Detroit	—	—	—	—	—
1969-70	Detroit	76	31	40	71	58	23	1969-70	Detroit	4	2	0	2	2
1970-71	Detroit	63	23	29	52	38	-2	1970-71	Detroit	—	—	—	—	—
1979-80	Hartford	80	15	26	41	42	9	1979-80	Hartford	3	1	1	2	2
NHL Totals:		1767	801	1049	1850	1685		Playoff Totals:		157	68	92	160	220

Gordie Howe went to his first NHL training camp with the New York Rangers when he was only 15 years old. He signed his first contract with the Detroit Red Wings one year later. Howe's NHL records for goals, assists, and points have all been broken, but no one is likely to match his record-breaking 26 seasons in the league. When his six years in the World Hockey Association are included, Howe played a total of 32 years! No wonder he is known as "Mr. Hockey."

Gordie Howe was the strongest player in the game. He was tough and talented. After returning from a serious injury, Howe led the NHL with 43 goals and 86 points in 1950-51. It was the first of six times he would win the Art Ross Trophy as the league's scoring leader. Howe also won the Hart Trophy as the NHL's MVP six times in his career. Only Wayne Gretzky has won those awards more often.

In an era when defense dominated the NHL, Howe was the league's best all-around player. He and his teammates Sid Abel and Ted Lindsay were known as the Production Line because of their scoring skill. Howe's 49 goals in 1952-53 was the second-highest total in league history at the time. His 95 points set a new league record. The NHL did not have its first 100-point scorer until the 1967-68 season when Phil Esposito set a new league record with 126 points. Gordie Howe was already 41 years old that year, but he still managed to collect 103 points. He finished third in league scoring that year just behind Esposito and Bobby Hull.

Injuries finally slowed down Howe in 1970-71, and he retired after 25 years. He was immediately elected to the Hockey Hall of Fame. By 1973 he was back in the game. Howe was convinced to join the Houston Aeros of the World Hockey Association so that he could play on a line with his sons Mark and Marty. Gordie was still going strong six years later at the age of 51 when four WHA teams joined the NHL. Howe

Gordie Howe was the idol of millions of young hockey fans — including Wayne Gretzky. "The Great One" grew up to break most of Howe's records, but no one is likely to surpass "Mr. Hockey's" marks of 1,767 games and 26 NHL seasons.

scored 15 goals that year as a Hartford Whaler to give him 801 in his career. Howe's 1,049 assists give him a career total of 1,850 points in a record 1,767 games.

Bobby Hull

Position: **Left Wing**   Height: **5'10" (178 cm)**   Weight: **195 lbs (89 kg)**   Born: **January 3, 1939 in Point Anne, ON.**

| Regular Season | | | | | | | | Playoffs | | | | | | |
Season	Team	GP	G	A	Pts	PIM	+/-	Season	Team	GP	G	A	Pts	PIM
1957-58	Chicago	70	13	34	47	62	—	1957-58	Chicago	—	—	—	—	—
1958-59	Chicago	70	18	32	50	50	—	1958-59	Chicago	6	1	1	2	2
1959-60	Chicago	70	39	42	81	68	—	1959-60	Chicago	3	1	0	1	2
1960-61	Chicago 🏆	67	31	25	56	43	—	1960-61	Chicago 🏆	12	4	10	14	4
1961-62	Chicago	70	50	34	84	35	—	1961-62	Chicago	12	8	6	14	12
1962-63	Chicago	65	31	31	62	27	—	1962-63	Chicago	5	8	2	10	4
1963-64	Chicago	70	43	44	87	50	—	1963-64	Chicago	7	2	5	7	2
1964-65	Chicago	61	39	32	71	32	—	1964-65	Chicago	14	10	7	17	27
1965-66	Chicago	65	54	43	97	70	—	1965-66	Chicago	6	2	2	4	10
1966-67	Chicago	66	52	28	80	52	—	1966-67	Chicago	6	4	2	6	0
1967-68	Chicago	71	44	31	75	39	14	1967-68	Chicago	11	4	6	10	15
1968-69	Chicago	74	58	49	107	48	-7	1968-69	Chicago	—	—	—	—	—
1969-70	Chicago	61	38	29	67	8	20	1969-70	Chicago	8	3	8	11	2
1970-71	Chicago	78	44	52	96	32	34	1970-71	Chicago	18	11	14	25	16
1971-72	Chicago	78	50	43	93	24	54	1971-72	Chicago	8	4	4	8	6
1979-80	Winnipeg	18	4	6	10	0	-7	1979-80	Winnipeg	—	—	—	—	—
	Hartford	9	2	5	7	0	-3		Hartford	3	9	0	0	0
NHL Totals:		1063	610	560	1170	640		**Playoff Totals:**		119	62	67	129	102

By the time he was 10 years old, people were already predicting that Bobby Hull would play in the NHL. He made it to the NHL as an 18-year-old when he joined the Chicago Blackhawks in 1957-58. At the time, Chicago had missed the playoffs four years in a row. They had made the playoffs only once in 12 seasons. The Blackhawks were so bad that people were worried they would drop out of the NHL. When Bobby Hull joined the team he helped save the franchise. Soon, 18,000 fans were filling the Chicago Stadium. By 1961, the Blackhawks were Stanley Cup champions.

Bobby Hull had huge muscles that were developed by working on his family's farm. With his strong arms, he could shoot the puck faster than anybody in hockey history. His slapshot was timed at 120 miles per hour! Not only was it hard, it was tricky, too. Hull used a stick with a huge curve in the blade. The curve caused the puck to dip and dart as it moved through the air. (Curves as big as the one Hull used on his stick are no longer legal in the NHL.) In addition to his powerful shot, Hull was also the fastest skater in hockey. His great speed, combined with his blond good looks, made people call him "The Golden Jet."

In his 16 seasons in the NHL, Hull led the league in goals seven times. He also won the Art Ross Trophy for leading the league in points in 1959-60, 1961-62, and 1965-66. The 1961-62 season saw Hull become only the third player in history to score 50 goals in one season. In 1965-66, he set a new record with 54 goals. Bobby then broke that mark when he scored 58 times in 1968-69. He also became the second player in league history to top 100 points with 107 that season.

In 1972, Bobby Hull shocked hockey fans by joining a new league called the World Hockey Association, where he continued to star as a member of the Winnipeg Jets. In 1974-75, he set a new professional hockey record with 77 goals. When four WHA teams joined the NHL in 1979-80, Hull returned to the league for one last season. He retired after that year with 610 goals.

Bobby's son Brett now plays with the Dallas Stars. Bobby and Brett are the only father-and-son combination in hockey history to both reach the 500-goal milestone. Bobby Hull was elected to the Hockey Hall of Fame in 1983.

Note the huge hook in the blade of Bobby Hull's stick. Hull and his teammate Stan Mikita were the first to use the so-called "banana blade." Sticks with curves as big as this one are no longer allowed in the NHL.

Brett Hull

Position: Right Wing   **Height:** 5'10" (178 cm)   **Weight:** 201 lbs (91 kg)   **Born:** August 9, 1964 in Belleville, ON.

	Regular Season									Playoffs				
Season	Team	GP	G	A	Pts	PIM	+/-	Season	Team	GP	G	A	Pts	PIM
1985-86	Calgary	—	—	—	—	—	—	1985-86	Calgary	2	0	0	0	0
1986-87	Calgary	5	1	0	1	0	-1	1986-87	Calgary	4	2	1	3	0
1987-88	Calgary	52	26	24	50	12	10	1987-88	Calgary	—	—	—	—	—
	St. Louis	13	6	8	14	4	4		St. Louis	10	7	2	9	4
1988-89	St. Louis	78	41	43	84	33	-17	1988-89	St. Louis	10	5	5	10	6
1989-90	St. Louis	80	72	41	113	24	-1	1989-90	St. Louis	12	13	8	21	17
1990-91	St. Louis	78	86	45	131	22	23	1990-91	St. Louis	13	11	8	19	4
1991-92	St. Louis	73	70	39	109	48	-2	1991-92	St. Louis	6	4	4	8	4
1992-93	St. Louis	80	54	47	101	41	-27	1992-93	St. Louis	11	8	5	13	2
1993-94	St. Louis	81	57	40	97	38	-3	1993-94	St. Louis	4	2	1	3	0
1994-95	St. Louis	48	29	21	50	10	13	1994-95	St. Louis	7	6	2	8	0
1995-96	St. Louis	70	43	40	83	30	4	1995-96	St. Louis	13	6	5	11	10
1996-97	St. Louis	77	42	40	82	10	-9	1996-97	St. Louis	6	2	7	9	2
1997-98	St. Louis	66	27	45	72	26	-1	1997-98	St. Louis	10	3	3	6	2
1998-99	Dallas 🏆	60	32	26	58	30	19	1998-99	Dallas 🏆	22	8	7	15	4
	NHL Totals:	861	586	459	1045	328			**Playoff Totals:**	130	77	58	135	55

No one expected Brett Hull to become a star in the NHL. Although he was blessed with talent, he never took the game all that seriously. He even quit playing when he was a teenager. Hull himself will admit that early in his career, he didn't have the motivation to get better.

It wasn't that he couldn't score. Brett had three 50-goal seasons in junior, college, and minor pro before he even made it to the NHL. Still, some experts felt he was too slow and too lazy to ever make it to the NHL.

Like his famous father Bobby, Brett has a shot like a cannon. He also has a knack of finding open ice. When he spies a gap in the defense, he slides into it. And when his teammates put the puck on his stick, it's gone in a flash. And more often than not, it winds up behind the goalie. He has scored at least 30 goals in 10 of his 13 NHL seasons, including five straight 50-goal campaigns from 1989-90 to 1993-94.

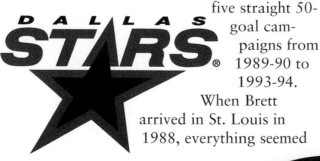

When Brett arrived in St. Louis in 1988, everything seemed to fall into place. Brett led the league in goals for three straight seasons in St. Louis, including an 86-goal performance in 1990-91. That year he was named league MVP. His dad was the NHL's MVP in 1965 and 1966. They are the only father-son duo to ever do that! He also shares another record with his dad. Brett and Bobby are the only players, other than Phil Esposito and Paul Kariya, to record more than 400 shots-on-goal in a single season.

In the last couple of seasons, "The Golden Brett" has shown a new sense of on-ice maturity. He has become an effective defensive forward who can anticipate how the flow of the game is going. That allows him to react a little quicker to break up passes or steal a loose puck. His offensive totals have suffered, but his all-round game is greatly improved.

After becoming a free agent in 1998, Brett signed with the Dallas Stars. Brett has always been a straight shooter — both on and off the ice — so he should have no trouble handling the Texas heat.

Mike Modano and Jere Lehtinen help Brett Hull celebrate the 1999 Stanley Cup-winning goal. Hull scored in triple overtime to end the second longest game in the history of the Stanley Cup Finals.

Jaromir Jagr

Position: **Right Wing**   Height: **6'2" (188 cm)**   Weight: **216 lbs (98 kg)**   Born: **February 15, 1972 in Kladno, Czechoslovakia.**

Regular Season								Playoffs						
Season	Team	GP	G	A	Pts	PIM	+/-	Season	Team	GP	G	A	Pts	PIM
1990-91	Pittsburgh	80	27	30	57	42	-4	1990-91	Pittsburgh	24	3	10	13	6
1991-92	Pittsburgh	70	32	37	69	34	12	1991-92	Pittsburgh	21	11	13	24	6
1992-93	Pittsburgh	81	34	60	94	61	30	1992-93	Pittsburgh	12	5	4	9	23
1993-94	Pittsburgh	80	32	67	99	61	15	1993-94	Pittsburgh	6	2	4	6	16
1994-95	Pittsburgh	48	32	38	70	37	23	1994-95	Pittsburgh	12	10	5	15	6
1995-96	Pittsburgh	82	62	87	149	96	31	1995-96	Pittsburgh	18	11	12	23	18
1996-97	Pittsburgh	63	47	48	95	40	22	1996-97	Pittsburgh	5	4	4	8	4
1997-98	Pittsburgh	77	35	67	102	64	17	1997-98	Pittsburgh	6	4	5	9	2
1998-99	Pittsburgh	81	44	83	127	66	17	1998-99	Pittsburgh	9	5	7	12	16
NHL Totals:		662	345	517	862	501		Playoff Totals:		113	55	64	119	97

When Jaromir Jagr joined the Pittsburgh Penguins in 1990-91, he asked if he could wear jersey #68. It was in 1968 that soldiers from the Soviet Union invaded his native country of Czechoslovakia. Although the invasion happened before he was born, his parents often told him about those dark and frightening days. Jagr told his folks that if he had a chance to play hockey in North America, he would wear #68 as a token of his respect for them and his country. That tells you what a special person Jagr is off the ice.

Few European-trained players have adapted to the NHL style of play better than Jagr. He won a Stanley Cup title in his rookie season and repeated the feat again as a sophomore. In 1994-95, Jagr won his first scoring title with 70 points in only 48 games and was the first winger to win the Art Ross Trophy since Guy Lafleur in 1977-78.

In 1997-98, Jagr was the only NHL player to crack the 100-point mark. In 1998-99, Jagr captured his third Art Ross Trophy with 127 points, along with his first Hart Trophy. Jagr has been selected to the All-Star Team five times.

There are only a handful of players who can command your attention every time they step on the ice, and Jagr is one of them. With his long hair, beaming smile, and post-goal bare-handed salute, it's clear he is having fun on the ice. The fans sense that, and even non-Penguin supporters have to admire his play.

Perhaps his most courageous performance came in the 1999 playoffs. Despite a serious groin injury and off-ice distractions due to the financial problems by the team, Jagr led the Penguins to a first-round upset over heavily favored New Jersey.

The legacy that Mario Lemieux helped create in Pittsburgh is safe in the hands of the Czech Republic's gentle giant, Jaromir Jagr.

Jaromir Jagr is the first player born and raised in Europe to win the NHL scoring title. Because he's got so much skill, it's easy to forgot how strong he is. Jagr is a big guy who can use his body to fend off checks.

Tumba Johansson

Position: **Center**   Height: **6'3" (191 cm)**   Weight: **205 lbs (93 kg)**   Born: **August 27, 1932 in Tumba, Sweden.**

Year	Team	Event/League	GP	G	A	Pts	PIM
1952	Sweden	Olympics	9	8	—	—	—
1953	Sweden	World Championships	4	6	—	—	—
1954	Sweden	World Championships	7	7	2	9	0
1955	Sweden	World Championships	8	9	—	—	—
1956	Sweden	Olympics	7	3	—	—	—
1957	Sweden	World Championships	7	6	—	—	—
1958	Sweden	World Championships	7	7	7	14	2
1960	Sweden	Olympics	6	6	1	7	5
1961	Sweden	World Championships	7	2	3	5	0
1962	Sweden	World Championships	7	7	6	13	2
1963	Sweden	World Championships	7	6	6	12	0
1964	Sweden	Olympics	7	8	3	11	0
1965	Sweden	World Championships	7	4	0	4	6
1966	Sweden	World Championships	5	2	3	5	0
1948 - 1966	Djurgardens IF Stockholm	Swedish League	—	—	—	—	—
Career Totals:			**95**	**81**	**31**	**80**	**15**

Sven Johansson is the greatest player in the history of Swedish hockey. He starred in Sweden's top hockey league from 1948 to 1966, and was a member of the Swedish national team from 1951 to 1966. His 14 appearances at the World Championships during that time are the most in hockey history. Johansson was from the town of Tumba, Sweden, and he was known as "Tumba" throughout his hockey career.

Big and strong, Tumba Johansson was a scoring star whose hockey style was similar to Gordie Howe. When he used his body like a battering ram, it was almost impossible to stop him!

Johansson helped his hockey team win the Swedish championship eight times in 18 years, including six titles in a row from 1958 to 1963. Internationally, he helped Sweden win the World Championship in 1953, 1957, and 1962. He was named the Best Forward at the tournament in 1957 and 1962. Johansson also helped Sweden finish in second place at the World Championships in 1963, and in third place in 1954, 1958, and 1965. During the Olympics, Johansson led Sweden to a bronze medal in 1952 and a silver medal in 1964.

In 1957, Johansson was given a chance to become the first European hockey star to play in the NHL. The Boston Bruins invited him to their

training camp and were impressed enough to offer him a contract with their minor league team in Quebec City. Johansson joined the Quebec Aces for a five-game trial and picked up four assists. If he wanted to remain with the team, Johansson would have had to sign a professional contract. In those days, professionals couldn't play international hockey so Johansson decided not to sign the contract. He left Quebec City and spent the rest of the 1957-58 season with a non-professional team in Chicago. He returned to Sweden in time to join the national team for the 1958 World Championship. It would be six more years before another Swedish hockey player would become the first European in the NHL. His name was Ulf Sterner, and he played four games for the New York Rangers during the 1964-65 season.

Tumba Johansson (right) poses with Sweden's third-place trophy at an international tournament in Canada during the 1963-64 season. Later that year, Johansson was the top scorer at the Olympics as Sweden won a silver medal.

Aurel Joliat

Position: **Left Wing**   Height: **5'7" (170 cm)**   Weight: **136 lbs (62 kg)**   Born: **August 29, 1901 in Ottawa, ON.**

Regular Season							
Season	Team	GP	G	A	Pts	PIM	+/-
1922-23	Mtl. Canadiens	24	13	9	22	31	—
1923-24	Mtl. Canadiens 🏆	24	15	5	20	19	—
1924-25	Mtl. Canadiens	24	29	11	40	85	—
1925-26	Mtl. Canadiens	35	17	9	26	52	—
1926-27	Mtl. Canadiens	43	14	4	18	79	—
1927-28	Mtl. Canadiens	44	28	11	39	105	—
1928-29	Mtl. Canadiens	44	12	5	17	59	—
1929-30	Mtl. Canadiens 🏆	42	19	12	31	40	—
1930-31	Mtl. Canadiens 🏆	43	13	22	35	73	—
1931-32	Mtl. Canadiens	48	15	24	39	46	—
1932-33	Mtl. Canadiens	48	18	21	39	53	—
1933-34	Mtl. Canadiens	48	22	15	37	27	—
1934-35	Mtl. Canadiens	48	17	12	29	18	—
1935-36	Mtl. Canadiens	48	15	8	23	16	—
1936-37	Mtl. Canadiens	47	17	15	32	30	—
1937-38	Mtl. Canadiens	44	6	7	13	24	—
NHL Totals:		**654**	**270**	**190**	**460**	**757**	

Playoffs						
Season	Team	GP	G	A	Pts	PIM
1922-23	Mtl. Canadiens	2	1	1	2	8
1923-24	Mtl. Canadiens 🏆	6	4	4	8	10
1924-25	Mtl. Canadiens	5	2	2	4	21
1925-26	Mtl. Canadiens	—	—	—	—	—
1926-27	Mtl. Canadiens	4	1	0	1	10
1927-28	Mtl. Canadiens	2	0	0	0	4
1928-29	Mtl. Canadiens	3	1	1	2	10
1929-30	Mtl. Canadiens 🏆	6	0	2	2	6
1930-31	Mtl. Canadiens 🏆	10	0	4	4	12
1931-32	Mtl. Canadiens	4	2	0	2	4
1932-33	Mtl. Canadiens	2	2	1	3	2
1933-34	Mtl. Canadiens	3	0	1	1	0
1934-35	Mtl. Canadiens	2	1	0	1	0
1935-36	Mtl. Canadiens	—	—	—	—	—
1936-37	Mtl. Canadiens	5	0	3	3	2
1937-38	Mtl. Canadiens	—	—	—	—	—
Playoff Totals:		**54**	**14**	**19**	**33**	**89**

Aurel Joliat is proof that sometimes good things come in small packages. He was barely 5'7" (170 cm) tall and weighed only 136 pounds (62 kg). Yet, through hard work and sheer determination, Joliat starred for 16 seasons in the NHL. Much of his career unfolded during a time when top players were still expected to play a full 60 minutes every game! Joliat became known as "The Mighty Atom" or "The Little Giant."

Aurel Joliat played football while growing up in his hometown of Ottawa. After suffering a broken leg in football, he soon began to focus on hockey instead. In 1922, Joliat was ready to begin his professional career. He was supposed to join the Saskatoon Sheiks of the Western Canada Hockey League. Instead, Saskatoon bought Newsy Lalonde from Montreal and sent Joliat to the Canadiens in his place. Aurel would spend his entire career with the Canadiens.

Joliat made an instant impression in the NHL. He finished among the top 10 scorers in the league during his rookie season of 1922-23.

The next year Montreal added Howie Morenz to the roster. With this new star at center, and Joliat on his left wing, the Canadiens won the Stanley Cup in 1924. Over the years, several right wingers would join their line, but it was Morenz and Joliat who made the Canadiens great. They led Montreal to back-to-back Stanley Cup championships in 1930 and 1931. The 1930-31 season saw the NHL begin to choose annual All-Stars. Both Morenz and Joliat were named to the First Team that year. Joliat would be a Second-Team All-Star three times.

He never won an NHL scoring title, but he did lead the Canadiens in goals four years in a row (1932-33 to 1935-36). He also won the Hart Trophy as the league's most valuable player in 1933-34.

Even though he was small, Aurel Joliat played a hard-hitting game. As a result, he suffered many injuries during his career, including six shoulder separations, three broken ribs, and five broken noses. By the 1936-37 season the Canadiens were forced to play him less often. He retired after the 1937-38 campaign. Joliat scored

270 goals during his career. At the time, he and his longtime teammate Howie Morenz were tied for second place on the NHL's all-time scoring list. Joliat was elected to the Hockey Hall of Fame in 1947.

Aurel Joliat stares at the empty locker of his friend and teammate Howie Morenz shortly after the death of the legendary "Stratford Streak." Before he died, Morenz told Joliat: "I'll be up there watching you guys in the playoffs."

Paul Kariya

Position: **Left Wing**　Height: **5'11" (180 cm)**　Weight: **175 lbs (80 kg)**　Born: **October 16, 1974 in Vancouver, BC.**

Regular Season									Playoffs					
Season	Team	GP	G	A	Pts	PIM	+/-		Season	Team	GP	G	A	Pts	PIM
1994-95	Anaheim	47	18	21	39	4	-17		1994-95	Anaheim	—	—	—	—	—
1995-96	Anaheim	82	50	58	108	20	9		1995-96	Anaheim	—	—	—	—	—
1996-97	Anaheim	69	44	55	99	6	36		1996-97	Anaheim	11	7	6	13	4
1997-98	Anaheim	22	17	14	31	23	12		1997-98	Anaheim	—	—	—	—	—
1998-99	Anaheim	82	39	62	101	40	17		1998-99	Anaheim	3	1	3	4	0
	NHL Totals:	302	168	210	378	93				Playoff Totals:	14	8	9	17	4

At 5'11" (180 cm) and 175 pounds (80 kg), Paul Kariya is considered a small player by today's NHL standards, but he's definitely one of the league's biggest talents. Kariya is a fast skater with a dangerously accurate shot. He is also an excellent puckhandler who can make accurate passes even when it seems he isn't looking. Kariya possesses a rare ability to see everything that's happening on the ice, and he's smart enough to make the right decision about what to do quickly. Kariya is the type of player who believes good things happen when you shoot the puck at the net, and he's usually among the league leaders in shots-on-goal.

Kariya was already a star player before he reached the NHL. He was named the Canadian Junior A player-of-the-year in 1991-92. Then he led the University of Maine hockey team to an American college championship in 1992-93. Kariya was the first freshman player to win the Hobey Baker award as the top player in U.S. college hockey. He also helped Canada win the World Junior Championship that same year. Kariya played for the Canadian national team in 1993-94. Kariya's trophy case also includes a silver medal from the Olympics and a gold medal from the World Championships.

The Mighty Ducks of Anaheim chose Paul Kariya with their first pick (the fourth choice overall) in the 1993 NHL Entry Draft. He entered the NHL in 1994-95 and was one of the league's top rookies. Before the next season began, Kariya started an exercise routine that

added 10 pounds of muscle to his body. The added strength made him one of the best players in the league. Kariya reached 50 goals and 100 points for the first time in 1995-96. That same year, Kariya was named to the NHL's First All-Star Team and won the Lady Byng Trophy as the league's most sportsmanlike player.

Injuries forced Kariya to miss 13 games in 1996-97, but he still reached 44 goals and 55 assists and finished third in the NHL with 99 points. Together with teammate Teemu Selanne, Kariya helped Anaheim make the playoffs for the first time in franchise history. Once again he was named to the First All-Star Team and won the Lady Byng. A serious concussion kept Kariya out for most of the 1997-98 season, and there were even worries that his career might be over. He returned better than ever in 1998-99 scoring 101 points, one of only three players to break the 100-point barrier.

Paul Kariya's ability to see everything that's happening on the ice makes him very dangerous. Kariya fired 429 shots on goal in 1998-99, the second-highest total in NHL history!

Red Kelly

Position: **Defense/Center**   Height: **5'11" (180 cm)**   Weight: **180 lbs (82 kg)**   Born: **July 9, 1927 in Simcoe, ON.**

Regular Season									Playoffs					
Season	Team	GP	G	A	Pts	PIM	+/-		Season	Team	GP	G	A	Pts	PIM
1947-48	Detroit	60	6	14	20	13	—		1947-48	Detroit	10	3	2	5	2
1948-49	Detroit	59	5	11	16	10	—		1948-49	Detroit	11	1	1	2	10
1949-50	Detroit 🏆	70	15	25	40	9	—		1949-50	Detroit 🏆	14	1	3	4	2
1950-51	Detroit 🏆	70	17	37	54	24	—		1950-51	Detroit	6	0	1	1	0
1951-52	Detroit 🏆	67	16	31	47	16	—		1951-52	Detroit 🏆	5	1	0	1	0
1952-53	Detroit	70	19	27	46	8	—		1952-53	Detroit	6	0	4	4	0
1953-54	Detroit 🏆	62	16	33	49	18	—		1953-54	Detroit 🏆	12	5	1	6	0
1954-55	Detroit 🏆	70	15	30	45	28	—		1954-55	Detroit 🏆	11	2	4	6	17
1955-56	Detroit	70	16	34	50	39	—		1955-56	Detroit	10	2	4	6	2
1956-57	Detroit	70	10	25	35	18	—		1956-57	Detroit	5	1	0	1	0
1957-58	Detroit	61	13	18	31	26	—		1957-58	Detroit	4	0	1	1	2
1958-59	Detroit	67	8	13	21	34	—		1958-59	Detroit	—	—	—	—	—
1959-60	Detroit	50	6	12	18	10	—		1959-60	Detroit	—	—	—	—	—
	Toronto	18	6	5	11	8	—			Toronto	10	3	8	11	2
1960-61	Toronto	64	20	50	70	12	—		1960-61	Toronto	2	1	0	1	0
1961-62	Toronto 🏆	58	22	27	49	6	—		1961-62	Toronto 🏆	12	4	6	10	0
1962-63	Toronto 🏆	66	20	40	60	8	—		1962-63	Toronto 🏆	10	2	6	8	6
1963-64	Toronto 🏆	70	11	34	45	16	—		1963-64	Toronto 🏆	14	4	9	13	4
1964-65	Toronto	70	18	28	46	8	—		1964-65	Toronto	6	3	2	5	2
1965-66	Toronto	63	8	24	32	12	—		1965-66	Toronto 🏆	4	0	2	2	0
1966-67	Toronto 🏆	61	14	24	38	4	—		1966-67	Toronto 🏆	12	0	5	5	2
	NHL Totals:	1316	281	542	823	327				Playoff Totals:	164	33	59	92	51

Red Kelly was a star defenseman who helped the Detroit Red Wings win the Stanley Cup four times. Later he was a member of the four-time Stanley Cup winning Toronto Maple Leafs while playing center. Very few players in NHL history have ever been as successful as Red Kelly at playing two different positions. With eight Stanley Cup titles, very few players have ever been as successful as Red Kelly, period!

Red Kelly (his real name is Leonard) began his career with Detroit in 1947-48. In 1948-49, he helped Detroit finish first in the regular-season standings. The Red Wings went on to lead the league for a record seven straight seasons. By Kelly's third season in 1949-50, Detroit won the Stanley Cup. Kelly was made a Second-Team All-Star that year and was an All-Star again for eight years in a row. In addition to being an All-Star, Kelly also won the Lady Byng

Trophy for sportsmanlike conduct three times. Very few defensemen have ever won that trophy.

When the Norris Trophy was presented to the NHL to honor the league's best defenseman in 1954, Red Kelly was the first player to win it. He was later made captain of the Red Wings in 1956-57 and 1957-58.

On February 7, 1960, Red Kelly was traded to Toronto. Kelly had always been an excellent checker and a great puck carrier in Detroit, but Maple Leafs coach Punch Imlach thought if he played center he could help check other team's top stars and still add power to the Leafs offense. He was right. As center on a line with Frank Mahovlich, Kelly helped "The Big M" set a Maple Leafs record with 48 goals in 1960-61. Kelly himself was second in the NHL with 50 assists and ranked sixth in the league scoring race. He won the Lady Byng Trophy for the fourth time that season. Kelly later helped the

A Century of Hockey Heroes

Leafs win the Stanley Cup in 1962, 1963, 1964, and 1967. From 1962 to 1965, Kelly also served as a Canadian politician in Ottawa while still playing hockey in Toronto.

Red Kelly's playing career finally ended after 20 years in 1967. He became coach of the Los Angeles Kings in the 1967-68 season and later coached the Pittsburgh Penguins. In 1973, he

An autograph from Red Kelly could be valuable indeed. He's the only player in NHL history to win eight Stanley Cup championships without ever playing for the Montreal Canadiens.

returned to Toronto and coached the Maple Leafs for four seasons. He was elected to the Hockey Hall of Fame in 1969.

Teeder Kennedy

Position: **Center**   Height: **5'11" (180 cm)**   Weight: **175 lbs (80 kg)**   Born: **December 12, 1925 in Humberstone, ON.**

Regular Season								Playoffs						
Season	Team	GP	G	A	Pts	PIM	+/-	Season	Team	GP	G	A	Pts	PIM
1942-43	Toronto	2	0	1	1	0	—	1942-43	Toronto	—	—	—	—	—
1943-44	Toronto	49	26	23	49	2	—	1943-44	Toronto	5	1	1	2	4
1944-45	Toronto	49	29	25	54	14	—	1944-45	Toronto	13	7	2	9	2
1945-46	Toronto	21	3	2	5	4	—	1945-46	Toronto	—	—	—	—	—
1946-47	Toronto	60	28	32	60	27	—	1946-47	Toronto	11	4	5	9	4
1947-48	Toronto	60	25	21	46	32	—	1947-48	Toronto	9	8	6	14	0
1948-49	Toronto	59	18	21	39	25	—	1948-49	Toronto	9	2	6	8	2
1949-50	Toronto	53	20	24	44	34	—	1949-50	Toronto	7	1	2	3	8
1950-51	Toronto	63	18	43	61	32	—	1950-51	Toronto	11	4	5	9	6
1951-52	Toronto	70	19	33	52	33	—	1951-52	Toronto	4	0	0	0	4
1952-53	Toronto	43	14	23	37	42	—	1952-53	Toronto					
1953-54	Toronto	67	15	23	38	78	—	1953-54	Toronto	5	1	1	2	2
1954-55	Toronto	70	10	42	52	74	—	1954-55	Toronto	4	1	3	4	0
1956-57	Toronto	30	6	16	22	35	—	1956-57	Toronto	—	—	—	—	—
	NHL Totals:	696	231	329	560	432			Playoff Totals:	78	29	31	60	32

Teeder Kennedy was one of the greatest stars in the history of the Toronto Maple Leafs. He won five Stanley Cup titles in seven seasons between 1944-45 and 1950-51. Kennedy became a hockey star through hard work and determination. He was not a smooth skater, but he had a hustling style and competitive spirit that fans loved. The shout "Come onnnnn, Teeder!" became a favorite battle cry in Toronto. To this day, Kennedy remains the last Maple Leaf to win the Hart Trophy as the NHL's most valuable player. He earned the honor in 1954-55.

Teeder Kennedy (whose real name is Ted) was originally part of the Montreal Canadiens. He attended their training camp in 1941 when he was only 16 years old. At 17 he was traded to Toronto. He played two games for the Leafs in 1942-43 and became a regular in the lineup the following season.

In 1944-45, Teeder led Toronto with 29 goals and 54 points. He helped the Leafs upset Montreal in the playoffs to win the Stanley Cup. Kennedy was the Leafs leading scorer again in 1946-47 with 28 goals and 60 points. Once again he helped Toronto defeat Montreal in the Stanley Cup Finals. That season Kennedy centered a line with Vic Lynn and Howie Meeker. They were called the new Kid Line because they were all so young. (Charlie Conacher, Busher Jackson, and Joe Primeau had been the original Kid Line in the 1930s.)

After another Stanley Cup victory in 1947-48, Teeder took over from Syl Apps as captain of the Maple Leafs. He was only 23 years old. By the 1949-50 season, hockey experts in other cities were beginning to recognize just how good Kennedy was. He was named to the Second All-Star Team that season, and earned the honor again when the Leafs won yet another Stanley Cup title in 1950-51. That season, Kennedy led the NHL with 43 assists and set a career-high with 61 points. Teeder was an All-Star for the final time in 1953-54.

Kennedy considered retirement in 1954, but was convinced to play one more season. His statistics did not rank him among the league leaders in 1954-55, but his inspirational effort made him a popular choice for the Hart Trophy. Kennedy did retire after that season but made a

brief comeback in 1956-57 because the Leafs had so many of their players injured that year. Teeder was elected to the Hockey Hall of Fame in 1966.

Teeder Kennedy tries to poke the puck past Boston goalie Sugar Jim Henry. Bill Quackenbush, Leo Boivin, and former Maple Leaf Gus Bodnar all try to push the Leafs captain out of the play.

Valeri Kharlamov

Position: **Left Wing**   Height: **5'8" (172 cm)**   Weight: **155 lbs (70 kg)**   Born: **January 14, 1948 in Moscow, USSR.**

Year	Team	Event/League	GP	G	A	Pts	PIM
1969	Soviet Union	World Championships	10	6	7	13	4
1970	Soviet Union	World Championships	9	7	3	10	4
1971	Soviet Union	World Championships	10	5	12	17	2
1972	Soviet Union	Olympics	5	9	7	16	2
1972	Soviet Union	World Championships	9	8	6	14	0
1972	Soviet Union	Summit Series	7	3	4	71	6
1973	Soviet Union	World Championships	10	9	14	23	31
1974	Soviet Union	World Championships	10	5	5	10	8
1975	Soviet Union	Summit Series	8	2	5	7	4
1975-76	Soviet Union	World Championships	9	10	6	16	4
1976	CSKA Moscow	Super Series	4	4	3	7	0
1976	Soviet Union	Olympics	6	3	6	9	6
1977	Soviet Union	World Championships	10	4	10	14	4
1978	Soviet Union	World Championships	10	9	7	16	4
1979	Soviet Union	World Championships	10	4	5	9	4
1979	Soviet Union	Challenge Cup	1	0	1	1	0
1979-80	Soviet Union	World Championships	8	7	7	14	4
1980	CSKA Moscow	Super Series	5	2	1	3	0
1980	Soviet Union	Olympics	7	3	8	11	2
1967 - 1981	CSKA Moscow	Soviet Union League	438	293	—	—	—
		Career Totals:	586	393	—	—	—

Valeri Kharlamov was a member of the Soviet national team from 1969 to 1980. During that time he never missed a single international event. He helped the Soviets win eight World Championships in 11 tries, and was named the Best Forward at the tournament in 1976. He was also named to the World Championship All-Star team three times. At the Olympics, Kharlamov played on gold medal-winning teams in 1972 and 1976. Sadly, Kharlamov was killed in a car accident in 1981.

Valeri Kharlamov was a brilliant stickhandler. He was not very big, but he was never afraid to go one-on-one against any of the game's toughest defensemen. During his career, Kharlamov played on one of the greatest lines in hockey history. The combination of Kharlamov, Boris Mikhailov, and Vladimir Petrov starred together with the Soviet national team and with the best team in the Soviet hockey league — the Central Red Army. Kharlamov's skill with the puck made him one of the top-scoring players in all of Soviet hockey. He had 293 goals in 438 games over a 14-year career with the Red Army. He also helped his team win the Soviet league title 11 times!

In 1972, Valeri Kharlamov was a member of the Soviet squad that faced Team Canada in a very special series. Until that time, no Soviet team had ever played against top NHL stars. Professional players were not yet allowed to appear in international events like the Olympics and the World Championships. Many people believed the only reason that the Soviets had replaced Canada as the top country in international hockey was because Canada had to use amateur players against them. The Soviets were fast skaters, slick stickhandlers, and pretty passers, but they had never had to face the hard hits of NHL hockey.

With top stars like Phil and Tony Esposito, Frank Mahovlich, and Yvan Cournoyer, many Canadian fans expected their team to beat the

Soviets in all eight games of the 1972 series. In the very first game, Canada had a 2–0 lead after only six minutes, but the lead didn't last. When Valeri Kharlamov scored twice in the second period, he gave the Soviets a 4–2 lead. The final score was 7–3. Team Canada eventually did win the series, but not until the final minute of the final game.

The skill of players like Valeri Kharlamov was one of the reasons why the Soviet Union surprised Canadian fans in 1972. Here, Pat Stapleton and Bill White of Team Canada cover Kharlamov during the Summit Series.

Jari Kurri

Position: **Right Wing** Height: **6'1" (185 cm)** Weight: **195 lbs (89 kg)** Born: **May 18, 1960 in Helsinki, Finland.**

	Regular Season								Playoffs					
Season	Team	GP	G	A	Pts	PIM	+/-	Season	Team	GP	G	A	Pts	PIM
1980-81	Edmonton	75	32	43	75	40	26	1980-81	Edmonton	9	5	7	12	4
1981-82	Edmonton	71	32	54	86	32	38	1981-82	Edmonton	5	2	5	7	10
1982-83	Edmonton	80	45	59	104	22	47	1982-83	Edmonton	16	8	15	23	8
1983-84	Edmonton 🏆	64	52	61	113	14	38	1983-84	Edmonton 🏆	19	14	14	28	13
1984-85	Edmonton 🏆	73	71	64	135	30	76	1984-85	Edmonton 🏆	18	19	12	31	6
1985-86	Edmonton	78	68	63	131	22	45	1985-86	Edmonton	10	2	10	12	4
1986-87	Edmonton 🏆	79	54	54	108	41	19	1986-87	Edmonton 🏆	21	15	10	25	20
1987-88	Edmonton 🏆	80	43	53	96	30	25	1987-88	Edmonton 🏆	19	14	17	31	12
1988-89	Edmonton	76	44	58	102	69	19	1988-89	Edmonton	7	3	5	8	6
1989-90	Edmonton 🏆	78	33	60	93	48	18	1989-90	Edmonton 🏆	22	10	15	25	18
1991-92	Los Angeles	73	23	37	60	24	-24	1991-92	Los Angeles	4	1	2	3	4
1992-93	Los Angeles	82	27	60	87	38	19	1992-93	Los Angeles	24	9	8	17	12
1993-94	Los Angeles	81	31	46	77	48	-24	1993-94	Los Angeles	—	—	—	—	—
1994-95	Los Angeles	38	10	19	29	24	-17	1994-95	Los Angeles	—	—	—	—	—
1995-96	Los Angeles	57	17	23	40	37	-12	1995-96	Los Angeles	—	—	—	—	—
	NY Rangers	14	1	4	5	2	-4		NY Rangers	11	3	5	8	2
1996-97	Anaheim	82	13	22	35	12	-13	1996-97	Anaheim	11	1	2	3	4
1997-98	Colorado	70	5	17	22	12	6	1997-98	Colorado	4	0	0	0	0
	NHL Totals:	1251	601	797	1398	545			**Playoff Totals:**	200	106	127	233	123

The NHL's first "Flying Finn" was an offensive dynamo named Jari Kurri. Not only was he a greyhound on skates, he had one of the most accurate shots of all time. Kurri never took many shots, but when he did decide to let one fly, no player could match his results. Between 1983-84 and 1986-87, Kurri scored on almost one out of every three shots he took. No other NHL player can match that. His scoring rate of 28.8 in 1985-86 is the highest mark ever recorded in the NHL.

Born in Helsinki, Finland, Kurri was a key member of the Finnish National Junior and Olympic Teams. He was named the best forward at the European Junior Tournament in 1978 and counted 11 points at the World Junior showdown in 1980. For many North American scouts, that tournament was the first time they had seen Kurri play. The Oilers were so impressed with his play that they made him their third choice in the 1980 draft.

Kurri collected 32 goals and 75 points as a rookie and improved on those totals in each of his first four seasons in Edmonton. In 1985-86, Kurri posted a league-best 68 goals while notching an impressive 131 points.

Despite all the regular-season success, Kurri saved his best for the playoffs. In each of the franchise's first four Cup wins, the top goal scorer on the club wasn't Messier, Anderson, or Gretzky — it was Jari Kurri. In the 1985 postseason, Kurri became only the second player to score 19 goals in a single playoff season. That was the same year that he single-handedly eliminated the Chicago Blackhawks from the postseason parade. In that six-game series, Kurri fired home an NHL record 12 goals. No one has come close to matching that mark.

In 1990-91, despite a 93-point season the year before, Kurri decided to play in Italy. One season later he returned to the NHL and was in Los Angeles reunited with Wayne Gretzky. The result was a trip to the finals in 1993. In May 1998, after brief stops in New York, Colorado,

and Anaheim, Kurri hung up the blades for good. With five All-Star nominations, 1,398 points, and 601 goals on his resume, it's a safe bet that Kurri will soon return to North America to accept his induction into the Hockey Hall of Fame.

Jari Kurri's success as a goal scorer made people forget that he was a great defensive forward. When Kurri played with Wayne Gretzky in Edmonton, it seemed like the two players could read each other's minds.

Elmer Lach

Position: **Center**   Height: **5'10" (178 cm)**   Weight: **165 lbs (75 kg)**   Born: **January 22, 1918 in Nokomis, SK.**

Regular Season										Playoffs					
Season	Team	GP	G	A	Pts	PIM	+/-		Season	Team	GP	G	A	Pts	PIM
1940-41	Montreal	43	7	14	21	16	—		1940-41	Montreal	3	1	0	1	0
1941-42	Montreal	1	0	1	1	0	—		1941-42	Montreal	—	—	—	—	—
1942-43	Montreal	45	18	40	58	14	—		1942-43	Montreal	5	2	4	6	6
1943-44	Montreal	48	24	48	72	23	—		1943-44	Montreal	9	2	11	13	4
1944-45	Montreal	50	26	54	80	37	—		1944-45	Montreal	6	4	4	8	2
1945-46	Montreal	50	13	34	47	34	—		1945-46	Montreal	9	5	12	17	4
1946-47	Montreal	31	14	16	30	22	—		1946-47	Montreal	—	—	—	—	—
1947-48	Montreal	60	30	31	61	72	—		1947-48	Montreal	—	—	—	—	—
1948-49	Montreal	36	11	18	29	59	—		1948-49	Montreal	1	0	0	0	4
1949-50	Montreal	64	15	33	48	33	—		1949-50	Montreal	5	1	2	3	4
1950-51	Montreal	65	21	24	45	48	—		1950-51	Montreal	11	2	2	4	2
1951-52	Montreal	70	15	50	65	36	—		1951-52	Montreal	11	1	2	3	4
1952-53	Montreal	53	16	25	41	56	—		1952-53	Montreal	12	1	6	7	6
1953-54	Montreal	48	5	20	25	28	—		1953-54	Montreal	4	0	2	2	0
NHL Totals:		664	215	408	623	478			Playoff Totals:		76	19	45	64	36

In the 1940s, when Rocket Richard was becoming the greatest goal scorer in hockey, the man passing him the puck was Elmer Lach. In fact, when Richard became the first player in NHL history to score 50 goals in 1944-45, Lach set a new league record with 54 assists. With 26 goals of his own that season, Lach was the NHL's scoring leader with 80 points in just 50 games. He was a quick and intelligent player who became the first man in NHL history to collect 400 career assists. He was also the first player to top 600 points. In his career, Lach had 215 goals and 408 assists for 623 points.

After playing amateur hockey in his home province of Saskatchewan, Elmer Lach joined the Montreal Canadiens in 1940-41. He made his first appearance among the league's top 10 scorers in 1943-44. That was the first year that Lach played center between Rocket Richard and Toe Blake. The powerful trio was dubbed the Punch Line, and they helped the Canadiens win the Stanley Cup that year.

In 1944-45, Lach, Richard, and Blake finished 1-2-3 in the NHL scoring race. All three were named to the First All-Star Team. Lach also won the Hart Trophy as the most valuable player in the NHL. He earned a selection to the Second All-Star Team in 1946 when Montreal won the Stanley Cup again. Lach led the league with 34 assists that season.

Two serious injuries kept Lach out of the Canadiens lineup for much of the 1946-47 season. When he returned in 1947-48, he won the Art Ross Trophy as the league's leading scorer. It was the first time that the NHL scoring leader was given a trophy. Lach had a career-high 30 goals that year and added 31 assists. Once again he was named to the First All-Star Team.

Injuries continued to slow Lach down over the next few seasons. Courageously, he kept coming back, and by 1951-52 he had regained his All-Star status. Lach led the league with 50 assists that season and finished third in scoring with 65 points. In 1952-53, he helped the Canadiens win the Stanley Cup again. Lach scored only one goal in 12 playoff games that year, but it was the Stanley Cup winner. The overtime goal in game five of the Finals gave

Montreal a 1–0 victory over the Boston Bruins. Lach retired after playing one more season. In 1966, Elmer Lach was elected to the Hockey Hall of Fame.

Elmer Lach was fast on his feet and a quick thinker. Rocket Richard and Toe Blake got the glory as goal scorers, but it was Lach's pretty passes that were the real power behind the Punch Line.

Guy Lafleur

Position: **Right Wing**   Height: **6'0" (183 cm)**   Weight: **185 lbs (84 kg)**   Born: **September 20, 1951 in Thurso, QC.**

	Regular Season								Playoffs					
Season	Team	GP	G	A	Pts	PIM	+/-	Season	Team	GP	G	A	Pts	PIM
1971-72	Montreal	73	29	35	64	48	27	1971-72	Montreal	6	1	4	5	2
1972-73	Montreal 🏆	69	28	27	55	51	16	1972-73	Montreal 🏆	17	3	5	8	9
1973-74	Montreal	73	21	35	56	29	10	1973-74	Montreal	6	0	1	1	4
1974-75	Montreal	70	53	66	119	37	52	1974-75	Montreal	11	12	7	19	15
1975-76	Montreal 🏆	80	56	69	125	36	68	1975-76	Montreal 🏆	13	7	10	17	2
1976-77	Montreal 🏆	80	56	80	136	20	89	1976-77	Montreal 🏆	14	9	17	26	6
1977-78	Montreal 🏆	78	60	72	132	26	73	1977-78	Montreal 🏆	15	10	11	21	16
1978-79	Montreal 🏆	80	52	77	129	28	56	1978-79	Montreal 🏆	16	10	13	23	0
1979-80	Montreal	74	50	75	125	12	40	1979-80	Montreal	3	3	1	4	0
1980-81	Montreal	51	27	43	70	29	24	1980-81	Montreal	3	0	1	1	2
1981-82	Montreal	66	27	57	84	24	33	1981-82	Montreal	5	2	1	3	4
1982-83	Montreal	68	27	49	76	12	6	1982-83	Montreal	3	0	2	2	2
1983-84	Montreal	80	30	40	70	19	-14	1983-84	Montreal	12	0	3	3	5
1984-85	Montreal	19	2	3	5	10	-3	1984-85	Montreal	—	—	—	—	—
1988-89	NY Rangers	67	18	27	45	12	1	1988-89	NY Rangers	4	1	0	1	0
1989-90	Quebec	39	12	22	34	4	-15	1989-90	Quebec	—	—	—	—	—
1990-91	Quebec	59	12	16	28	2	-10	1990-91	Quebec	—	—	—	—	—
	NHL Totals:	1126	560	793	1353	399			Playoff Totals:	128	58	76	134	67

Few players have ever started their NHL careers under more pressure than Guy Lafleur. Not only was he expected be a superstar in Montreal, he was also supposed to replace the legendary Jean Beliveau. Lafleur eventually became a dominant player, but it wasn't easy.

Guy Lafleur could do it all on the ice. He had speed and an explosive shot. He could dip and dash through traffic and feather a pass through a maze of sticks. Only one ingredient was missing when made his debut in 1971-72. Confidence.

In his first three NHL seasons, Lafleur showed only glimpses of the superstar he was to become. After his third campaign, Lafleur decided to play without a helmet. He felt that if he was forced to play a little scared, he might play with desperation. His idea worked. A view of Lafleur steaming down the right wing with his blond hair flying behind him was a sight that electrified the Montreal Forum.

From 1974-75 to 1979-80, Lafleur was the NHL's best player. He reached the 50-goal plateau and collected 100 points in six straight seasons. He led the league in scoring for three consecutive years, and he helped the Montreal Canadiens win five

Stanley Cup titles in seven years. In the playoffs, he was an awesome weapon. Lafleur had a knack for scoring timely goals when the situation looked hopeless.

The 1980s were a disappointment to the Thurso, Quebec legend. The Canadiens were struggling on the ice and Lafleur struggled with them. In November 1984, with only five points in 19 games, he hung up the skates. Although Lafleur still had the skill, he had lost the will.

Lafleur felt he had given up on the game too early. On the night he was inducted into the Hockey Hall of Fame in 1988, Lafleur announced he was coming back to the NHL. "The Flower" spent one season with the New York Rangers before joining Montreal's rival the

Quebec Nordiques. While he wasn't quite the old Lafleur, on certain nights all the magic came back. In his first return to Montreal, he scored a pair of goals. In his final visit to Toronto, he scored his 545th career goal to move past his idol, Maurice Richard, on the all-time goals-

The sight of Guy Lafleur streaking down the right wing, blond hair flying in the breeze, was enough to make fans at the Montreal Forum leap to their feet.

scored list. When he retired for good in 1991, he did so as a contented and respected legend.

Newsy Lalonde

Position: **Center**   Height: **5'9" (175 cm)**   Weight: **168 lbs (76 kg)**   Born: **October 31, 1888 in Cornwall, ON.**

	Regular Season									Playoffs				
Season	Team	GP	G	A	Pts	PIM	+/-	Season	Team	GP	G	A	Pts	PIM
1917-18	Mtl. Canadiens	14	23	7	30	51		1917-18	Mtl. Canadiens	2	4	2	6	17
1918-19	Mtl. Canadiens	17	23	10	33	42		1918-19	Mtl. Canadiens	10	17	1	18	18
1919-20	Mtl. Canadiens	23	37	9	46	34		1919-20	Mtl. Canadiens	—	—	—	—	0
1920-21	Mtl. Canadiens	24	32	11	43	2		1920-21	Mtl. Canadiens	—	—	—	—	—
1921-22	Mtl. Canadiens	20	9	5	14	20		1921-22	Mtl. Canadiens	—	—	—	—	—
1926-27	NY Americans	1	0	0	0	2		1926-27	NY Americans	—	—	—	—	—
	NHL Totals:	99	124	42	166	151			Playoff Totals:	12	21	3	24	35

In the early years of professional hockey there was no greater scorer than Newsy Lalonde. He was the NHL's scoring leader twice during the league's first four seasons. His best years, though, came before the NHL was formed. During the pre-NHL era, Lalonde was the scoring leader in three different professional leagues. When he left the NHL in 1922-23, he immediately topped his new league in goals. In a total of six different professional leagues, Newsy Lalonde scored 449 times. The next highest scorer in hockey during this time period was Joe Malone who only had 343 goals.

Newsy Lalonde earned his nickname while working in a newsprint factory as a boy in Cornwall, Ontario. (His real name was Edouard.) His hockey career also began in Cornwall, but soon took him all over Ontario. His first scoring title came in 1907-08 when he was playing in Toronto and led the Ontario Professional Hockey League with 29 goals in 11 games. Two years later he joined a brand-new team called the Montreal Canadiens in a league called the National Hockey Association. Halfway through the 1909-10 season Lalonde was traded

to the Renfrew Millionaires where he joined stars like Lester Patrick and Cyclone Taylor. Lalonde scored nine goals for

Renfrew in a single game on March 11, 1910. He finished the year with 38 goals in 11 games and won the NHA scoring title. Newsy's next scoring title came in 1911-12 with Vancouver of the rival Pacific Coast Hockey Association. The following season Lalonde returned to Montreal where he remained with the Canadiens for 10 years. His great speed and skill was one of the reasons people began calling the Canadiens the "Flying Frenchmen."

Lalonde was a great goal scorer, but he was not always a popular player. He could be very mean on the ice and would sometimes argue with teammates and fight with opposing players. Still, he was a star, and he helped the Canadiens win their first Stanley Cup title in 1915-16. After the NHL was formed in 1917, Lalonde continued to star with the Canadiens and often coached the team as well. In 1922, Newsy was traded to Saskatoon of the Western Canada Hockey League, in exchange for Aurel Joliat. Lalonde returned to the NHL as coach of the New York Americans in 1926-27. He later coached the Ottawa Senators and the Canadiens before retiring in 1935. He was elected to the Hockey Hall of Fame in 1950.

Though he played with many teams, Newsy Lalonde is best remembered as a member of the Montreal Canadiens. One of the original "Flying Frenchmen," Lalonde was a great talent with a temper to match.

John LeClair

Position: **Left Wing**   Height: **6'3" (191 cm)**   Weight: **226 lbs (103 kg)**   Born: **July 5, 1969 in St Albans, VT.**

Regular Season								Playoffs					
Season	Team	GP	G	A	Pts	PIM	+/-	Season	Team	GP	G	A	Pts	PIM
1990-91	Montreal	10	2	5	7	2	1	1990-91	Montreal	3	0	0	0	0
1991-92	Montreal	59	8	11	19	14	5	1991-92	Montreal	8	1	1	2	4
1992-93	Montreal	72	19	25	44	33	11	1992-93	Montreal	20	4	6	10	14
1993-94	Montreal	74	19	24	43	32	17	1993-94	Montreal	7	2	1	3	8
1994-95	Montreal	9	1	4	5	10	-1	1994-95	Montreal	—	—	—	—	—
	Philadelphia	37	25	24	49	20	21		Philadelphia	15	5	7	12	4
1995-96	Philadelphia	82	51	46	97	64	21	1995-96	Philadelphia	11	6	5	11	6
1996-97	Philadelphia	82	50	47	97	58	44	1996-97	Philadelphia	19	9	12	21	10
1997-98	Philadelphia	82	51	36	87	32	30	1997-98	Philadelphia	5	1	1	2	8
1998-99	Philadelphia	76	43	47	90	30	35	1998-99	Philadelphia	6	3	0	3	12
NHL Totals:		**583**	**269**	**269**	**539**	**295**		**Playoff Totals:**		**94**	**31**	**33**	**64**	**66**

John LeClair has a lot in common with Hall-of-Famer Phil Esposito. Like Espo, LeClair loves the action right in front of the net. And like Espo, LeClair reached his potential after being traded to a new team. Unlike Esposito, who was banished by the Blackhawks for poor play in the post-season, LeClair excelled in the playoffs. It was in the regular season, though, that LeClair seemed to have some problems.

A lot was expected of LeClair when he arrived in Montreal. He had the size and strength to become a star and was touted as the club's long-needed sniper. In the early going, LeClair lived up to his billing. In 1993, he became the first player in 43 years to score back-to-back overtime goals in the Stanley Cup finals.

Perhaps that performance put too much pressure on the bulky forward. Whatever it was, LeClair struggled.

LeClair's game was driving down the wing to the net. He is so strong on his skates, opposing defenders have to tackle him to bring him down. Sometimes LeClair just parks himself in front of the net where, with his great reflexes, he tips pucks and grabs rebounds. With his size, LeClair screens the goalie and lets his teammates blast long shots from the point.

But LeClair's game stalled in Montreal, and soon the Canadiens got rid of him. In February 1995, the Habs sent LeClair to Philadelphia. Once LeClair reported to the Flyers, his fortunes seemed to change overnight. Skating on a line with Eric Lindros and Mikael Renberg, LeClair scored 25 goals in 37 games, a new career high. The trio were quickly known as The Legion of Doom. With Lindros skating under, over, and through the defense, and Renberg delivering picture-perfect passes, LeClair parked himself in the slot and just kept blasting the puck.

The St. Albans, Vermont native has became a consistent 50-goal scorer and is now a dominant left winger in the game. He has gone from being a bench-warmer in Montreal to being a four-time All-Star in Philly. With his presence on the ice, Stanley Cup fever is still alive in Philadelphia.

Not everyone is willing to take the hits in front of the net, but John LeClair is more than tough enough. LeClair loves to camp out in front, screening goalies and picking up points off rebounds and deflections.

Mario Lemieux

Position: **Center**   Height: **6'4" (193 cm)**   Weight: **225 lbs (102 kg)**   Born: **October 5, 1965 in Montreal, QC.**

Regular Season								Playoffs					
Season	Team	GP	G	A	Pts	PIM	+/-	Season	Team	GP	G	A	Pts	PIM
1984-85	Pittsburgh	73	43	57	100	54	-35	1984-85	Pittsburgh	—	—	—	—	—
1985-86	Pittsburgh	79	48	93	141	43	-6	1985-86	Pittsburgh	—	—	—	—	—
1986-87	Pittsburgh	63	54	53	107	57	13	1986-87	Pittsburgh	—	—	—	—	—
1987-88	Pittsburgh	77	70	98	168	92	23	1987-88	Pittsburgh	—	—	—	—	—
1988-89	Pittsburgh	76	85	114	199	100	41	1988-89	Pittsburgh	11	12	7	19	16
1989-90	Pittsburgh	59	45	78	123	78	-18	1989-90	Pittsburgh	—	—	—	—	—
1990-91	Pittsburgh	26	19	26	45	30	8	1990-91	Pittsburgh	23	16	28	44	16
1991-92	Pittsburgh	64	44	87	131	94	27	1991-92	Pittsburgh	15	16	18	34	2
1992-93	Pittsburgh	60	69	91	160	38	55	1992-93	Pittsburgh	11	8	10	18	10
1993-94	Pittsburgh	22	17	20	37	32	-2	1993-94	Pittsburgh	6	4	3	7	2
1995-96	Pittsburgh	70	69	92	161	54	10	1995-96	Pittsburgh	18	11	16	27	33
1996-97	Pittsburgh	76	50	72	122	65	27	1996-97	Pittsburgh	5	3	3	6	4
NHL Totals:		**745**	**613**	**881**	**1494**	**737**		**Playoff Totals:**		**89**	**70**	**85**	**155**	**83**

Simply put, Mario Lemieux was one of the most creative players to ever play in the NHL. No player could score more goals, in more ways, with more flair than the Magnificent Mario.

The legacy of Mario Lemieux began before he even played his first shift in the league. In his final season as a junior, Lemieux scored an unbelievable 133 goals and 282 points in 70 games. That's an average of four points a game! Every NHL club wanted him, but only the last-place Pittsburgh Penguins were able to get him.

In Lemieux's first shift of his first NHL game in 1984-85, he stole the puck from Boston's Ray Bourque in the Penguins' zone and skated the length of the rink and scored a goal. In another game against New Jersey in 1988, Lemieux scored five goals in five different ways — on the power play, short-handed, on a penalty shot, at even strength, and into an empty net. No one in hockey history has ever done that. In the final game of the 1987 Canada Cup tournament, Lemieux scored the series-winning goal in the final minute to give Canada a thrilling 6-5 win. He also won a pair of Conn Smythe awards as playoff MVP. During his career, Lemieux averaged an NHL record 2.01 points a game.

Lemieux was born to be a hockey player. Tall and agile, with long arms and legs, he was almost impossible to defend. He could reach past players to grab rebounds or slip the puck into the corner of the net. He was also very strong. Lemieux could power his way to the net even if there were two defenders hanging onto him. Opposing defenders resorted to tackling, hooking, and slashing Lemieux in attempts to slow him down. Lemieux hoped the league would crack down on that type of player interference. The league eventually did, but not before they lost their marquee star. The physical punishment eventually took its toll on Lemieux and forced an early end to his career.

In 1994, Mario was diagnosed with Hodgkin's disease, a form of cancer. He spent the 1994-95 season treating and recovering from the disease. Lemieux overcame the disease and returned in 1995-96 leading the league with 161 points. After another NHL-best 122 points in 1996-97, Lemieux decided to retire. In November 1997, Lemieux went out on top and was inducted into the Hockey Hall of Fame without having to serve the traditional three-year waiting period.

Mario Lemieux was a magician with the puck. Though injuries cut short his career, Lemieux averaged about 62 goals per season, giving him the best scoring rate in NHL history.

Eric Lindros

Position: **Center**   Height: **6'4" (193 cm)**   Weight: **236 lbs (107 kg)**   Born: **February 28, 1973 in London, ON.**

Regular Season								Playoffs						
Season	Team	GP	G	A	Pts	PIM	+/-	Season	Team	GP	G	A	Pts	PIM
1992-93	Philadelphia	61	41	34	75	147	28	1992-93	Philadelphia	—	—	—	—	—
1993-94	Philadelphia	65	44	53	97	103	16	1993-94	Philadelphia	—	—	—	—	—
1994-95	Philadelphia	46	29	41	70	60	27	1994-95	Philadelphia	12	4	11	15	18
1995-96	Philadelphia	73	47	68	115	163	26	1995-96	Philadelphia	12	6	6	12	43
1996-97	Philadelphia	52	32	47	79	136	31	1996-97	Philadelphia	19	12	14	26	40
1997-98	Philadelphia	63	30	41	71	134	14	1997-98	Philadelphia	5	1	2	3	17
1998-99	Philadelphia	71	40	53	93	120	36	1998-99	Philadelphia	—	—	—	—	—
NHL Totals:		431	263	337	600	863		Playoff Totals:		48	23	33	56	118

Before he even played a single shift in the NHL, Eric Lindros was being called "The Next One." People thought Lindros was the player who would take the torch from Gretzky and Lemieux. He still may do that, but the road has been rocky for Lindros.

Lindros was discovered while playing local hockey in Toronto. He was over six feet (180 cm) tall and weighed nearly 200 pounds (91 kg), and on the ice, he was definitely in control. Off the ice, Lindros was the same way and was determined to choose the direction his career would take.

When he was selected first overall by the Quebec Nordiques in 1991, Lindros refused to play for the team and returned to junior. In September 1991, Lindros became the first non-NHL player to play for Team Canada in the Canada Cup tournament. Although he wasn't dominant, he proved he belonged in the NHL. In June, the Nordiques traded Lindros to Philadelphia for a lot of money and a half-dozen players, including Peter Forsberg.

Philly fans liked what they saw in Lindros.

He loved to be in the heat of the action. He steamrolled over everyone in his path. He brushed defenders off his back like flies. But that style of play was tough on Lindros. While there were few players who could match him, his problem was not being able to keep healthy.

In his rookie season, "The Big E" scored 41 goals in only 61 games. He notched 97 points in his second campaign, but he missed 19 games. In 1994-95, he was able to avoid injuries and tied for the scoring lead and won the Hart Trophy as NHL MVP. The following year, he had a career-high 68 assists and 115 points. Although the Flyers lost in the 1997 Stanley Cup finals, Lindros led all playoff scorers with 26 points.

In 1998-99, Lindros showed up in training camp in the best shape of his life, and the results were evident on the ice. He played like he wanted to lift the entire team and carry it on his shoulders. He took control of game like he took control of his future in 1991. Unfortunately, Lindros suffered a collapsed lung in a late season game against the Nashville Predators. The serious injury kept Eric out of the playoffs where the Flyers lost in the first round to Toronto. Eric's — and Philly's — dream of lifting Lord Stanley's Mug will have to wait.

No hockey player has ever combined size and skill like Eric Lindros. The Flyers' captain is tricky enough to out-maneuver his opponents, and strong enough to knock them down when he has to.

Ted Lindsay

Position: **Left Wing**   Height: **5'8" (173 cm)**   Weight: **163 lbs (74 kg)**   Born: **July 29, 1925 in Renfrew, ON.**

Regular Season								Playoffs						
Season	Team	GP	G	A	Pts	PIM	+/-	Season	Team	GP	G	A	Pts	PIM
1944-45	Detroit	45	17	6	23	43	—	1944-45	Detroit	14	2	0	2	6
1945-46	Detroit	47	7	10	17	14	—	1945-46	Detroit	5	0	1	1	0
1946-47	Detroit	59	27	15	42	57	—	1946-47	Detroit	5	2	2	4	10
1947-48	Detroit	60	33	19	52	95	—	1947-48	Detroit	10	3	1	4	6
1948-49	Detroit	50	26	28	54	97	—	1948-49	Detroit	11	2	6	8	31
1949-50	Detroit 🏆	69	23	55	78	141	—	1949-50	Detroit 🏆	13	4	4	8	16
1950-51	Detroit	67	24	35	59	110	—	1950-51	Detroit	6	0	1	1	8
1951-52	Detroit 🏆	70	30	39	69	123	—	1951-52	Detroit 🏆	8	5	2	7	8
1952-53	Detroit	70	32	39	71	111	—	1952-53	Detroit	6	4	4	8	6
1953-54	Detroit 🏆	70	26	36	62	110	—	1953-54	Detroit 🏆	12	4	4	8	14
1954-55	Detroit 🏆	49	19	19	38	85	—	1954-55	Detroit 🏆	11	7	12	19	12
1955-56	Detroit	67	27	23	50	161	—	1955-56	Detroit	10	6	3	9	22
1956-57	Detroit	70	30	55	85	103	—	1956-57	Detroit	5	2	4	6	8
1957-58	Chicago	68	15	24	39	110	—	1957-58	Chicago	—	—	—	—	—
1958-59	Chicago	70	22	36	58	184	—	1958-59	Chicago	6	2	4	6	13
1959-60	Chicago	68	7	19	26	91	—	1959-60	Chicago	4	1	1	2	0
1964-65	Detroit	69	14	14	28	173	—	1964-65	Detroit	7	3	0	3	34
NHL Totals:		1068	379	472	851	1808		Playoff Totals:		133	47	49	96	194

When fans called him "Terrible Ted," it was not because Ted Lindsay was a bad player — it was because he had a bad temper. Lindsay stood just 5'8" (173 cm) and weighed only 163 pounds (74 kg), but he was never afraid to battle anyone in the NHL. He almost always ranked among the league's top penalty leaders, but he also finished high on the list of leading scorers. Lindsay helped Detroit finish in first place in the regular-season standings for seven years in a row from 1948-49 to 1954-55. The Red Wings won the Stanley Cup four times during those years. "Terrible Ted" was so good that he was the NHL's All-Star left winger nine times. Eight of his selections were to the First All-Star Team. Bobby Hull is the only left winger in NHL history with more All-Star honors.

Ted Lindsay entered the NHL with the Detroit Red Wings in 1944-45. Two years later, he was teamed on a line with center Sid Abel and right winger Gordie Howe. Lindsay cracked the top 10 in scoring during their second season together in 1947-48. The next year the three players were dubbed the Production Line. The nickname came about because of their scoring skill, as well as the city of Detroit's fame in producing cars.

In 1949-50, Lindsay led the NHL in scoring with 78 points. Sid Abel finished second and Gordie Howe was third in the league that season. In the playoffs, the Production Line led Detroit to the Stanley Cup title. The Red Wings won again in 1951-52, while Howe and Lindsay finished 1-2 in the season scoring race that year. In 1952-53, Lindsay took over from Sid Abel as captain of the Red Wings and led Detroit to Stanley Cup victories again in 1954 and 1955.

In 1957, Detroit traded Lindsay to the Chicago Blackhawks, who were the worst team in the league at the time. He quickly helped them become one of the best teams in the NHL, but he decided to retire in 1960. Lindsay lived in Detroit after his retirement, and would sometimes work out with the Red Wings. His former teammate

A Century of Hockey Heroes

Sid Abel was the team's coach and general manager, and in 1964 he convinced Lindsay to make a comeback. Though he'd been out of the NHL for four years, he helped Detroit finish in first place in 1964-65. He retired for good after the season. One year later, Ted Lindsay was elected to the Hockey Hall of Fame.

Ted Lindsay tries to kick the puck up to his stick while two Toronto defenders attempt to push him away from Maple Leafs goalie Harry Lumley. Lindsay was the captain and inspirational leader of the great Detroit teams of the mid-1950s.

Al MacInnis

Position: **Defense**   Height: **6'2" (188 cm)**   Weight: **196 lbs (89 kg)**   Born: **July 11, 1963 in Inverness, NS.**

Regular Season								Playoffs					
Season	Team	GP	G	A	Pts	PIM	+/-	Season	Team	GP	G	A	Pts	PIM
1981-82	Calgary	2	0	0	0	0	0	1981-82	Calgary	—	—	—	—	—
1982-83	Calgary	14	1	3	4	9	0	1982-83	Calgary	—	—	—	—	—
1983-84	Calgary	51	11	34	45	42	0	1983-84	Calgary	11	2	12	14	13
1984-85	Calgary	67	14	52	66	75	7	1984-85	Calgary	4	1	2	3	8
1985-86	Calgary	77	11	57	68	76	38	1985-86	Calgary	21	4	15	19	30
1986-87	Calgary	79	20	56	76	97	20	1986-87	Calgary	4	1	0	1	0
1987-88	Calgary	80	25	58	83	114	13	1987-88	Calgary	7	3	6	9	18
1988-89	Calgary	79	16	58	74	126	38	1988-89	Calgary	22	7	24	31	46
1989-90	Calgary	79	28	62	90	82	20	1989-90	Calgary	6	2	3	5	8
1990-91	Calgary	78	28	75	103	90	42	1990-91	Calgary	7	2	3	5	8
1991-92	Calgary	72	20	57	77	83	13	1991-92	Calgary					
1992-93	Calgary	50	11	43	54	61	15	1992-93	Calgary	6	1	6	7	10
1993-94	Calgary	75	28	54	82	95	35	1993-94	Calgary	7	2	6	8	12
1994-95	St. Louis	32	8	20	28	43	19	1994-95	St. Louis	7	1	5	6	10
1995-96	St. Louis	82	17	44	61	88	5	1995-96	St. Louis	13	3	4	7	20
1996-97	St. Louis	72	13	30	43	65	2	1996-97	St. Louis	6	1	2	3	4
1997-98	St. Louis	71	19	30	49	80	6	1997-98	St. Louis	8	2	6	8	12
1998-99	St. Louis	82	20	42	62	70	33	1998-99	St. Louis	13	4	8	12	20
NHL Totals:		1142	290	775	1065	1296		Playoff Totals:		142	36	102	138	219

Al MacInnis can thank the Calgary Flames' patience for his tremendous career. Even though MacInnis had just helped his junior team win the Memorial Cup championship in 1981, the Flames resisted the temptation to put the hard-shooting defenseman in their lineup right away. When he finally did join the Flames for good in 1984-85, MacInnis was ready. He helped Calgary reach the Stanley Cup Finals in 1985–86. In 1986–87, he was named to the Second All-Star Team.

Al MacInnis has one of the hardest shots in hockey. When he leans into a slapshot, his stick almost bends in two. That's what gives the puck its extra snap. His powerful blueline blasts have so far resulted in seven seasons with 20 goals or more, including 1998–99. MacInnis knows to keep his shots low, and since he's so accurate, teammates are able to redirect the puck. This technique helped MacInnis top 50 assists for eight straight seasons.

Good as it is, there is more to Al MacInnis than just his shot. Over the years, he has matured into one of the NHL's most highly respected blue-liners. He has the ability and skill to keep forwards to the outside. This keeps the slot clear and helps his goalie see every shot. MacInnis can also carry the puck well, and he's an above average passer. He'll also sacrifice his body to help his goalie by dropping down to block shots. Still, it's his offensive skills that have made MacInnis a six-time All-Star.

The Cape Breton native scored 20 goals in only his third full season in the league. In 1988-89, he became the first defenseman to lead all post-season scorers when he collected 31 points in 22 games. MacInnis' performance was a key reason why the Flames won the Stanley Cup. Big Al was named the playoffs MVP. In 1990-91, he reached another milestone when he became only the fifth defenseman to reach the 100-point plateau.

In 1994, the Flames traded MacInnis to St. Louis. It marked an important change in his career. The Blues play a tight defensive system, and that

has forced MacInnis to become a better defender. In 1998-99, these abilities were recognized when he won his first Norris Trophy. MacInnis and young Chris Pronger now form St. Louis' twin towers. They have helped make the Blues' blueline one of the best and most feared in the game.

Al MacInnis has one of the hardest slapshots in hockey, but he can do much more than just blast the puck. His all-around skill as a defenseman has earned MacInnis six All-Star selections and the Norris Trophy in 1998-99.

Frank Mahovlich

Position: **Left Wing**   Height: **6'0" (183 cm)**   Weight: **205 lbs (93 kg)**   Born: **January 10, 1938 in Timmins, ON.**

Regular Season

Season	Team	GP	G	A	Pts	PIM	+/-
1956-57	Toronto	3	1	0	1	2	—
1957-58	Toronto	67	20	16	36	67	—
1958-59	Toronto	63	22	27	49	94	—
1959-60	Toronto	70	18	21	39	61	—
1960-61	Toronto	70	48	36	84	131	—
1961-62	Toronto 🏆	70	33	38	71	87	—
1962-63	Toronto 🏆	67	36	37	73	56	—
1963-64	Toronto 🏆	70	26	29	55	66	—
1964-65	Toronto	59	23	28	51	76	—
1965-66	Toronto	68	32	24	56	68	—
1966-67	Toronto 🏆	63	18	28	46	44	—
1967-68	Toronto	50	19	17	36	30	1
	Detroit	13	7	9	16	2	3
1968-69	Detroit	76	49	29	78	38	46
1969-70	Detroit	74	38	32	70	59	16
1970-71	Detroit	35	14	18	32	30	3
	Montreal 🏆	38	17	24	41	11	4
1971-72	Montreal	76	43	53	96	36	42
1972-73	Montreal 🏆	78	38	55	93	51	42
1973-74	Montreal	71	31	49	80	47	16
NHL Totals:		**1181**	**533**	**570**	**1103**	**1056**	

Playoffs

Season	Team	GP	G	A	Pts	PIM
1956-57	Toronto	—	—	—	—	—
1957-58	Toronto	—	—	—	—	—
1958-59	Toronto	12	6	5	11	18
1959-60	Toronto	10	3	1	4	27
1960-61	Toronto	5	1	1	2	6
1961-62	Toronto 🏆	12	6	6	12	29
1962-63	Toronto 🏆	9	0	2	2	8
1963-64	Toronto 🏆	14	4	11	15	20
1964-65	Toronto	6	0	3	3	9
1965-66	Toronto	4	1	0	1	10
1966-67	Toronto 🏆	12	3	7	10	8
1967-68	Toronto	—	—	—	—	—
	Detroit	—	—	—	—	—
1968-69	Detroit	—	—	—	—	—
1969-70	Detroit	4	0	0	0	2
1970-71	Detroit	—	—	—	—	—
	Montreal 🏆	20	14	13	27	18
1971-72	Montreal	6	3	2	5	2
1972-73	Montreal 🏆	17	9	14	23	6
1973-74	Montreal	6	1	2	3	0
Playoff Totals:		**137**	**51**	**67**	**118**	**163**

People predicted that Frank Mahovlich would be an NHL star from the time he was a teenager. "The Big M" beat out Bobby Hull for the Calder Trophy as rookie-of-the-year in 1957-58. He went on to score 533 goals in his career. He was the left winger on either the First or Second NHL All-Star Team nine different times. Still, people always felt that Mahovlich should have been better. His problem was that he was so good, he made the game look too easy!

Mahovlich helped the Toronto Maple Leafs win the Stanley Cup in 1962, 1963, 1964, and 1967. In those days he was the only true superstar in the Leafs lineup. He led the team in goals for six straight seasons from 1960-61 to 1965-66. No player since Rocket Richard in 1944-45 had scored 50 goals in the NHL, but both Mahovlich and Boom Boom Geoffrion took a run at the record in 1960-61. Geoffrion made it, but Mahovlich came up just short. Still, his 48 goals that season remained a Maple Leafs record for 21 years.

In 1968, Toronto traded Mahovlich to Detroit where he joined a roster that included his younger brother Pete. Frank was teamed on a line with Gordie Howe and Alex Delvecchio. In 1968-69 he set a career high with 49 goals. He also helped the 41-year-old Howe become just the third player in NHL history to top 100 points in a single season.

Despite his success in Detroit, the Red Wings traded the aging Mahovlich to Montreal for two younger players during the 1970-71 season. Once again Mahovlich joined his brother Pete, who had been traded to Montreal the year before. "The Big M" helped Montreal win the Stanley Cup. His 14 playoff goals in 1971 set a modern NHL record, while his 27 points tied Phil Esposito's all-time mark.

In Montreal, Mahovlich was transformed from a great goal scorer into a premier playmak-

Even flying through the air, Frank Mahovlich was dangerous around the net. Like Mahovlich, Red Wings defensemen Marcel Pronovost (3) and Bill Gadsby, as well as goalie Terry Sawchuk, are all members of the Hockey Hall of Fame.

er. During his three full seasons with the Canadiens, he led the club in assists every year. Even so, with such a strong farm system, Montreal allowed Mahovlich to return to Toronto in 1974. He wasn't a Maple Leaf, though. He was a member of the Toronto Toros in the rival league known as the World Hockey Association. Mahovlich played four years in the WHA and retired in 1978 at the age of 40. He was elected to the Hockey Hall of Fame in 1981.

Joe Malone

Position: **Center/Left Wing**   Height: **5'10" (178 cm)**   Weight: **150 lbs (68 kg)**   Born: **February 28, 1890 in Quebec City, QC.**

Regular Season								Playoffs						
Season	Team	GP	G	A	Pts	PIM	+/-	Season	Team	GP	G	A	Pts	PIM
1917-18	Mtl. Canadiens	20	44	4	48	30	—	1917-18	Mtl. Canadiens	2	0	0	0	0
1918-19	Mtl. Canadiens	8	7	2	9	3	—	1918-19	Mtl. Canadiens	5	5	1	6	3
1919-20	Quebec	24	39	10	49	12	—	1919-20	Quebec	—	—	—	—	—
1920-21	Hamilton	20	28	9	37	6	—	1920-21	Hamilton	—	—	—	—	—
1921-22	Hamilton	24	24	7	31	4	—	1921-22	Hamilton	—	—	—	—	—
1922-23	Mtl. Canadiens	20	1	0	1	2	—	1922-23	Mtl. Canadiens	2	0	0	0	0
1923-24	Mtl. Canadiens	9	0	0	0	0	—	1923-24	Mtl. Canadiens	—	—	—	—	—
	NHL Totals:	125	143	32	175	57			Playoff Totals:	9	5	1	6	3

Joe Malone was the first player to lead the NHL in scoring. He had an amazing 44 goals in 20 games in 1917-18. His total remained a record until Rocket Richard scored 50 goals in 50 games in 1944-45. No one has ever come close to matching Malone's scoring average of 2.2 goals per game that season. Of course, in those days, top stars were expected to play the entire 60 minutes of a game!

Joe Malone was a slick stickhandler and a smooth skater with shifty moves. He was so skilled at slipping past his opponents that he was called "The Phantom." Malone was a great scorer who believed in fair play. His sense of sportsmanship was rare in the rough-and-tumble days of early pro hockey.

Malone began his hockey career in his hometown of Quebec City. He was a member of the Quebec Bulldogs when that team joined the National Hockey Association in 1910-11. One year later, Quebec won the NHA championship and the Stanley Cup. Malone was the team's scoring leader with 21 goals in 18 games. In 1912-13, he led the entire NHA with 43 goals in 20 games. In the playoffs that year he scored nine goals in a game! The Bulldogs beat a team from

Sydney, Nova Scotia 14-3 that night. Quebec easily won the Stanley Cup that year, but the team struggled after that season. When the NHA was reorganized as the NHL in 1917-18, Quebec decided not to operate its team anymore, and Malone joined the Montreal Canadiens. In the NHL's first ever game on December 19, 1917, he scored five goals. The Canadiens beat the Ottawa Senators 7-4.

In the NHL's third season of 1919-20, the Bulldogs decided to run their team again. Malone returned to Quebec City and won his second scoring title that year with 39 goals and 49 points. He also set a league record that still stands with seven goals in a single game on January 31, 1920. Still, his team had a terrible season with four wins and 20 losses in 24 games. In 1920-21, the team moved to Hamilton, Ontario. Malone remained one of the league's best scorers for two more seasons, but the Hamilton Tigers were the NHL's worst team. Malone returned to Montreal in 1922-23, by which time he was no longer a star.

When Joe Malone retired in 1923-24, he was the NHL's career scoring leader with 143 goals. In his entire career, he had scored 343 times. "The Phantom" was elected to the Hockey Hall of Fame in 1950.

Malone and the Canadiens might have won the Stanley Cup in 1919, but the series against the Seattle Metropolitans was cancelled due to a worldwide influenza epidemic.

Alexander Maltsev

Position: **Center/Right Wing**   Height: **5'10" (178 cm)**   Weight: **173 lbs (79 kg)**   Born: **April 20, 1949 in Kirovo-Chepetsk, USSR.**

Year	Team	Event/League	GP	G	A	Pts	PIM
1970	Soviet Union	World Championships	10	5	6	11	0
1971	Soviet Union	World Championships	10	15	6	21	8
1972	Soviet Union	World Championships	10	10	6	16	2
1972	Soviet Union	Olympics	5	4	3	7	0
1972	Soviet Union	Summit Series	8	0	5	5	0
1973	Soviet Union	World Championships	10	10	12	22	0
1974	Soviet Union	World Championships	9	7	6	13	12
1974	Soviet Union	Summit Series	8	4	0	4	4
1975	Soviet Union	World Championships	10	6	4	10	2
1975-76	Soviet Union	World Championships	10	8	6	14	2
1976	CSKA	Super Series	4	1	1	2	0
1976	Soviet Union	Canada Cup	5	3	4	7	2
1976	Soviet Union	Olympics	6	7	7	14	0
1977	Soviet Union	World Championships	5	3	3	6	0
1978	Soviet Union	World Championships	8	1	9	10	2
1979-80	Soviet Union	World Championships	10	5	8	13	0
1980	Dynamo Moscow	Super Series	4	3	1	4	2
1981	Soviet Union	Olympics	7	6	4	10	0
1981	Soviet Union	Canada Cup	4	1	1	2	0
1982-83	Soviet Union	World Championships	8	6	7	13	2
1983	Soviet Union	Super Series	1	0	0	0	0
1983	Soviet Union	World Championships	8	1	3	4	0
1967 - 1984	Dynamo Moscow	Soviet Union League	530	329	—	—	—
	Career Totals:		**690**	**438**	**—**	**—**	**—**

NHL players from Russia, and international stars from the Soviet Union, have always been known for their abilities when handling the puck. The greatest stickhandler in the history of Soviet hockey was Alexander Maltsev.

Maltsev was a speedy forward who was equally at home at center, or on one of the wings. He was not a very physical player, and that gave him some difficulty when the Soviet national team took on Canadian teams with hard-hitting NHL stars. Still, he is considered to be one of greatest hockey players of all time. His 329 goals in 530 Soviet league games rank him among the all-time leaders. Unlike most Soviet superstars, who played with the Central Red Army, Maltsev was a member of the Moscow Dynamo from 1967 to 1984.

Maltsev was also a member of the Soviet national team from 1969 to 1983. During that

time, he helped his team win the Olympic gold medal in 1972 and 1976. In 1980, he was a member of the Soviet team that had to settle for a silver medal after being upset by the United States. Maltsev also played at the World Championships 12 times and helped his team win the title on nine occasions. He was named the Best Forward at the tournament in 1970, 1972, and 1981. He was selected to the all-star team five times.

Maltsev faced his first NHL opponents when the Soviet Union took on Team Canada in 1972. He tied for the team lead with five assists in eight games. Only NHL superstar Phil Esposito had more assists in the series. Espo set up six goals for Team Canada.

The Soviets nearly beat Team Canada in 1972, but their team was not as strong at the Canada Cup hockey tournament in 1976. This event featured Sweden, Finland, Czechoslovakia,

and the United States, as well as Canada and the Soviets. The Soviets finished third behind Canada and Czechoslovakia, but Maltsev's play was good enough to earn a selection to the tournament's all-star team. Maltsev was a veteran player on the Soviet team that took part in the Canada Cup tournament in 1981. That year, the

The slick stickhandling of Alexander Maltsev made this Soviet superstar one of the top hockey players in the world. He helped the Soviet national team win nine World Championships and was a five-time All-Star at the tournament.

Soviet Union won the event with a stunning 8–1 victory over Canada in the final game.

Frank McGee

Position: **Rover**   Height: **5'6" (168 cm)**   Weight: **(unknown)**   Born: **November 4, 1882 in Ottawa, ON.**

Season	Club	League	GP	G	A	Pts	PIM	GP	G	A	Pts	PIM
			Regular Season					**Playoffs**				
1902-03	Ottawa Silver Seven 🏆	CAHL	6	14	—	14	—	4	7	—	7	—
1903-04	Ottawa Silver Seven 🏆	CAHL	4	12	—	12	—	8	21	—	21	—
1904-05	Ottawa Silver Seven 🏆	CAHL	6	17	—	17	—	4	18	—	18	—
1905-06	Ottawa Silver Seven	CAHL	7	28	—	28	—	6	17	—	17	—
	Career Totals:		23	71	—	71	—	22	63	—	63	—

The name Frank McGee is legendary in hockey history. He could only see out of one eye, but he was still a spectacular goal scorer. He was the star of the first hockey dynasty of the 20th century — the Ottawa Silver Seven.

Ottawa won its first Stanley Cup title in 1903. In those days, the Stanley Cup did not belong to just one league. It was a challenge trophy. That meant that the champion of any top hockey league could arrange a series with the Stanley Cup winner. Usually, a team would only defend the Stanley Cup once or twice during one hockey season. The Silver Seven faced 10 Stanley Cup challengers before they were beaten in 1906.

Frank McGee was fast on his feet and a superb stickhandler. He joined the Silver Seven for the 1902-03 season and scored 14 goals in just six games. (The hockey season was only eight games long back then!) In the playoffs, he scored seven goals in four games as Ottawa beat two teams for the Stanley Cup. In 1904, McGee scored 21 goals in eight playoff games as the Silver Seven faced four different Stanley Cup challengers. Still, his greatest moment was yet to come!

The Ottawa Silver Seven faced a team from Dawson City, Yukon, in a Stanley Cup challenge match in 1905. The team had to travel across Canada by bicycle and dogsled, on foot and by train. In the first game on January 13, the Silver Seven beat Dawson City 9-2, but Frank McGee

scored only one goal. Some of the Dawson City players were heard to say that the great scoring star didn't seem so good. He proved them wrong in game two when, on January 16, 1905, "one-eyed" Frank McGee poured in 14 goals to lead Ottawa to a 23-2 win. It is a Stanley Cup scoring record that will never be matched!

The next season was McGee's best. He scored 28 goals in seven games in 1905-06. In the playoffs, he scored 15 times in four Stanley Cup games before the Silver Seven finally lost to the Montreal Wanderers. McGee retired after the season. In his four years with Ottawa, he had scored 71 goals in just 23 regular-season games. In the playoffs, he had 63 goals in 22 games. Hockey was a high-scoring game in this era, but few could match McGee's heroics. In 1945, he was one of the first 12 men elected to the Hockey Hall of Fame.

Frank McGee was a scoring sensation even though he could only see out of one eye. Despite his handicap, McGee became a soldier in World War One. Sadly, he was killed in battle in 1916.

Mark Messier

Position: **Center**   Height: **6'1" (185 cm)**   Weight: **205 lbs (93 kg)**   Born: **January 18, 1961 in Edmonton, AB.**

Regular Season								Playoffs						
Season	Team	GP	G	A	Pts	PIM	+/-	Season	Team	GP	G	A	Pts	PIM
1979-80	Edmonton	75	12	21	33	120	-10	1979-80	Edmonton	3	1	2	3	2
1980-81	Edmonton	72	23	40	63	102	-12	1980-81	Edmonton	9	2	5	7	13
1981-82	Edmonton	78	50	38	88	119	21	1981-82	Edmonton	5	1	2	3	8
1982-83	Edmonton	77	48	58	106	72	19	1982-83	Edmonton	15	15	6	21	14
1983-84	Edmonton 🏆	73	37	64	101	165	40	1983-84	Edmonton 🏆	19	8	18	26	19
1984-85	Edmonton 🏆	55	23	31	54	57	8	1984-85	Edmonton 🏆	18	12	13	25	12
1985-86	Edmonton	63	35	49	84	68	36	1985-86	Edmonton	10	4	6	10	18
1986-87	Edmonton 🏆	77	37	70	107	73	21	1986-87	Edmonton 🏆	21	12	16	28	16
1987-88	Edmonton 🏆	77	37	74	111	103	21	1987-88	Edmonton 🏆	19	11	23	34	29
1988-89	Edmonton	72	33	61	94	130	-5	1988-89	Edmonton	7	1	11	12	8
1989-90	Edmonton 🏆	79	45	84	129	79	19	1989-90	Edmonton 🏆	22	9	22	31	20
1990-91	Edmonton	53	12	52	64	34	15	1990-91	Edmonton	18	4	11	15	16
1991-92	NY Rangers	79	35	72	107	76	31	1991-92	NY Rangers	11	7	7	14	6
1992-93	NY Rangers	75	25	66	91	72	-6	1992-93	NY Rangers	—	—	—	—	—
1993-94	NY Rangers 🏆	76	26	58	84	76	25	1993-94	NY Rangers 🏆	23	12	18	30	33
1994-95	NY Rangers	46	14	39	53	40	8	1994-95	NY Rangers	10	3	10	13	8
1995-96	NY Rangers	74	47	52	99	122	29	1995-96	NY Rangers	11	4	7	11	16
1996-97	NY Rangers	71	36	48	84	88	12	1996-97	NY Rangers	15	3	9	12	6
1997-98	Vancouver	82	22	38	60	58	-10	1997-98	Vancouver	—	—	—	—	—
1998-99	Vancouver	59	13	35	48	33	-12	1998-99	Vancouver	—	—	—	—	—
	NHL Totals:	1413	610	1050	1660	1687			Playoff Totals:	236	109	186	295	244

Mark Messier's father Doug was his hockey coach and mentor when he was growing up. Doug Messier was a good player in his day, but he couldn't make the leap to the NHL. His advice to Mark was simple: play every shift as though it is your last. Messier has never taken his success for granted, and that is what made him one the greatest on-ice leaders ever.

It took Messier longer than most players to find his confidence. In his first season as a pro in the World Hockey Association, Messier scored only one goal in 52 games. But, by his third NHL campaign, Messier had turned into a 50-goal scorer. He reached the 100-point plateau five times with the Oilers. When the Oilers finally won their first championship in 1984, it wasn't Gretzky, Coffey, or Kurri who was named playoff MVP, it was Messier. His desire to win drove the Oiler ® machine. He took the reins again in 1989-90 when he guided the post-Gretzky Oilers to the Stanley Cup title.

In October 1991, the Oilers traded Messier to the New York Rangers. Messier proved he still had plenty of energy by winning the Hart Trophy in his first season in New York. During the 1994 playoffs, the Rangers were one game away from elimination, when Messier guaranteed the fans that the team would not lose. He then went out and scored three goals in a 4-2 Ranger win. New York went on to win the series and the Stanley Cup. It was their first championship in 54 years.

In July 1998, Messier signed with Vancouver as a free agent.

In 20 NHL seasons, Messier scored at least 20 goals sixteen times. He is the only player to earn an All-Star Team berth as both a winger and a center. And he's the only player to captain two different teams to a Stanley Cup championship.

Not many people have captained three different NHL teams. Mark Messier wore the "C" in Edmonton and New York before joining the Vancouver Canucks in 1997.

Stan Mikita

Position: **Center**   Height: **5'9" (175 cm)**   Weight: **169 lbs (77 kg)**   Born: **May 20, 1940 in Sokolce, Czechoslovakia.**

	Regular Season								Playoffs					
Season	Team	GP	G	A	Pts	PIM	+/-	Season	Team	GP	G	A	Pts	PIM
1958-59	Chicago	3	0	1	1	4	—	1958-59	Chicago	—	—	—	—	—
1959-60	Chicago	67	8	18	26	119	—	1959-60	Chicago	3	0	1	1	2
1960-61	Chicago	66	19	34	53	100	—	1960-61	Chicago	12	6	5	11	21
1961-62	Chicago	70	25	52	77	97	—	1961-62	Chicago	12	6	15	21	19
1962-63	Chicago	65	31	45	76	69	—	1962-63	Chicago	6	3	2	5	2
1963-64	Chicago	70	39	50	89	146	—	1963-64	Chicago	7	3	6	9	8
1964-65	Chicago	70	28	59	87	154	—	1964-65	Chicago	14	3	7	10	53
1965-66	Chicago	68	30	48	78	58	—	1965-66	Chicago	6	1	2	3	2
1966-67	Chicago	70	35	62	97	12	—	1966-67	Chicago	6	2	2	4	2
1967-68	Chicago	72	40	47	87	14	-3	1967-68	Chicago	11	5	7	12	6
1968-69	Chicago	74	30	67	97	52	17	1968-69	Chicago	—	—	—	—	—
1969-70	Chicago	76	39	47	86	50	29	1969-70	Chicago	8	4	6	10	2
1970-71	Chicago	74	24	48	72	85	21	1970-71	Chicago	18	5	13	18	16
1971-72	Chicago	74	26	39	65	46	16	1971-72	Chicago	8	3	1	4	4
1972-73	Chicago	57	27	56	83	32	31	1972-73	Chicago	15	7	13	20	8
1973-74	Chicago	76	30	50	80	46	24	1973-74	Chicago	11	5	6	11	8
1974-75	Chicago	79	36	50	86	48	14	1974-75	Chicago	8	3	4	7	12
1975-76	Chicago	48	16	41	57	37	-4	1975-76	Chicago	4	0	0	0	4
1976-77	Chicago	57	19	30	49	20	-9	1976-77	Chicago	2	0	1	1	0
1977-78	Chicago	76	18	41	59	35	18	1977-78	Chicago	4	3	0	3	0
1978-79	Chicago	65	19	36	55	34	3	1978-79	Chicago	—	—	—	—	—
1979-80	Chicago	17	2	5	7	12	2	1979-80	Chicago	—	—	—	—	—
	NHL Totals:	1394	541	926	1467	1270			Playoff Totals:	155	59	91	150	169

Stan Mikita came to Canada from Czechoslovakia without his parents as an eight-year-old boy. He lived in the city of St. Catharines, Ontario with his aunt and uncle. Later he became a junior hockey star in his new hometown and went on to become one of the greatest players in NHL history. Mikita never forgot the difficulty of having to learn to speak English. He said it was so hard for him to understand English that when people spoke he felt like he was deaf. As a result of his feelings, Mikita established a charity to help hearing-impaired children.

Stan Mikita's NHL career began when he played three games for Chicago in 1958-59. He became a regular in the lineup the following season. The Blackhawks were the NHL's worst team for many years, but with scoring stars like Mikita and Bobby Hull on their roster, they became Stanley Cup champions in 1961.

At 5'9" (175 cm) and 169 pounds (77 kg), Mikita was a small player. He was talented, but he was also tough. He wanted to prove that he could take care of himself, so in addition to piling up points, he was also picking up plenty of penalty minutes. In fact, in 1963-64 Mikita won the Art Ross Trophy as the league's leading scorer, but also finished among the league leaders in penalty minutes. The same thing happened when Mikita topped the scoring race again in 1964-65.

During the 1965-66 season, Mikita talked about hockey with his daughter Meg, and she asked him why he spent so much time by himself in the penalty box. Mikita realized that he was setting a bad example and decided to clean up his play. In 1966-67, he won the Art Ross Trophy once again when he tied the NHL single-season

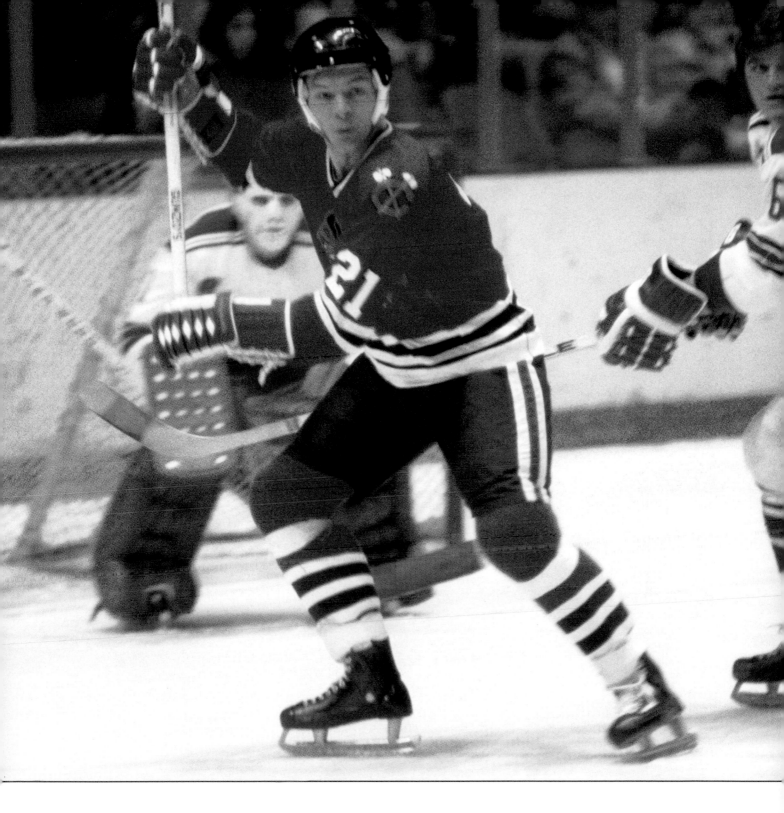

record with 97 points. That year he had only six penalties all season long! Once one of the league's bad boys, he now earned the Lady Byng Trophy for his outstanding sportsmanship. When he was also presented with the Hart Trophy as the league's MVP, Mikita became the first player to win three major NHL awards in one season. To prove it was no fluke, he won all three trophies again in 1967-68.

Stan Mikita maneuvers into position in front of the Rangers', goal. Mikita holds the Blackhawks' records for most seasons, most games, most assists, and most points. Only Bobby Hull had more goals for Chicago.

Stan Mikita continued to star for Chicago until 1979-80. When he retired, he ranked high among the NHL's all-time leaders with 541 goals, 926 assists, and 1,467 points. He was elected to the Hockey Hall of Fame in 1983.

Mike Modano

Position: **Center**   Height: **6'3" (191 cm)**   Weight: **200 lbs (91 kg)**   Born: **June 7, 1970 in Livonia, MI.**

| Regular Season | | | | | | | | | Playoffs | | | | | |
Season	Team	GP	G	A	Pts	PIM	+/-		Season	Team	GP	G	A	Pts	PIM
1988-89	Minnesota	—	—	—	—	—	—		1988-89	Minnesota	2	0	0	0	0
1989-90	Minnesota	80	29	46	75	63	-7		1989-90	Minnesota	7	1	1	2	12
1990-91	Minnesota	79	28	36	64	65	2		1990-91	Minnesota	23	8	12	20	16
1991-92	Minnesota	76	33	44	77	46	-9		1991-92	Minnesota	7	3	2	5	4
1992-93	Minnesota	82	33	60	93	83	-7		1992-93	Minnesota	—	—	—	—	—
1993-94	Dallas	76	50	43	93	54	-8		1993-94	Dallas	9	7	3	10	16
1994-95	Dallas	30	12	17	29	8	7		1994-95	Dallas	—	—	—	—	—
1995-96	Dallas	78	36	45	81	63	-12		1995-96	Dallas	—	—	—	—	—
1996-97	Dallas	80	35	48	83	42	43		1996-97	Dallas	7	4	1	5	0
1997-98	Dallas	52	21	38	59	32	25		1997-98	Dallas	17	4	10	14	12
1998-99	Dallas 🏆	77	34	47	81	44	29		1998-99	Dallas 🏆	23	5	18	23	16
NHL Totals:		710	311	424	735	500			**Playoff Totals:**		95	32	47	79	76

When the Minnesota North Stars drafted Mike Modano first overall in the 1988 Entry Draft, they knew he was an exciting, skilled player. On any given night, he could be the most exciting player on the ice. He had speed, agility, and the impressive ability to change speed and direction at will. Yet, for the first four years of his career, he often fell short of expectations.

Although he averaged 31 goals and 77 points a year, something was missing, and Modano's mind always seemed to be somewhere else. Modano often played lazy or would make mental mistakes. But most of all, he just didn't seem to be enjoying himself on the ice.

Midway through the 1995 season, Ken Hitchcock took over as coach of the Stars, and his first project was to turn Modano into a franchise player. Hitchcock's plan was to create offense through defense. By pressuring the puck with aggressive forechecking, the Stars forced the other team into making mistakes. Those mistakes turned into scoring chances, and those chances turned into goals for the Stars.

The plan was just the kick Modano needed because the system gave him lots of ice time. By constantly attacking the puck carrier, Modano had lots of scoring chances. It's strange how working hard at stopping goals actually helped Modano score them. Now the brightest light in the Stars' arena is the smile on Modano's face.

With the exception of the lockout season of 1994-95, Modano has never scored fewer than 20 goals or collected less than 38 assists in a season. Like many NHL stars, Modano became an elite superstar in 1998-99 after leading the Stars to the Stanley Cup. He preformed with a powerful combination of grit and finesse, scoring 23 points along the way.

A 50-goal scorer early in his career, Mike Modano became an even better player when he learned to improve his defensive game. Modano helped the Dallas Stars win their first Stanley Cup title in 1999.

Dickie Moore

Position: **Left Wing**   Height: **5'10" (178 cm)**   Weight: **168 lbs (76 kg)**   Born: **January 16, 1931 in Montreal, QC.**

Season	Team	Regular Season GP	G	A	Pts	PIM	+/-	Season	Team	Playoffs GP	G	A	Pts	PIM
1951-52	Montreal	33	18	15	33	44	—	1951-52	Montreal	11	1	1	2	12
1952-53	Montreal	18	2	6	8	19	—	1952-53	Montreal	12	3	2	5	13
1953-54	Montreal	13	1	4	5	12	—	1953-54	Montreal	11	5	8	13	8
1954-55	Montreal	67	16	20	36	32	—	1954-55	Montreal	12	1	5	6	22
1955-56	Montreal	70	11	39	50	55	—	1955-56	Montreal	10	3	6	9	12
1956-57	Montreal	70	29	29	58	56	—	1956-57	Montreal	10	3	7	10	4
1957-58	Montreal	70	36	48	84	65	—	1957-58	Montreal	10	4	7	11	4
1958-59	Montreal	70	41	55	96	61	—	1958-59	Montreal	11	5	12	17	8
1959-60	Montreal	62	22	42	64	54	—	1959-60	Montreal	8	6	4	10	4
1960-61	Montreal	57	35	34	69	62	—	1960-61	Montreal	6	3	1	4	4
1961-62	Montreal	57	19	22	41	54	—	1961-62	Montreal	6	4	2	6	8
1962-63	Montreal	67	24	26	50	61	—	1962-63	Montreal	5	0	1	1	2
1964-65	Toronto	38	2	4	6	68	—	1964-65	Toronto	5	1	1	2	6
1967-68	St. Louis	27	5	3	8	9	-8	1967-68	St. Louis	18	7	7	14	15
NHL Totals:		**719**	**261**	**347**	**608**	**652**		**Playoff Totals:**		**135**	**46**	**64**	**110**	**122**

Dickie Moore was a swift skater and stylish stickhandler. He also had a hard, accurate shot. With this collection of skills, it's not surprising that Moore was one of the top offensive talents during the NHL's six-team era. He was also one of the game's toughest players. Moore was called "Digging Dickie" because of the way he would dig in the corners to battle for the puck. His aggressive style resulted in lots of injuries, but Moore usually played even if he was in pain.

Moore was born in Montreal and was a star in his hometown even before he signed with the Canadiens. He helped two different Montreal teams win the Memorial Cup as Canada's junior hockey champion before he entered the NHL in 1951-52.

He helped the Canadiens win the Stanley Cup in 1952-53, but he did not earn a regular spot on the Montreal roster until 1954-55. Over the next five seasons, Moore was one of the key reasons why the Canadiens set an all-time record with five consecutive Stanley Cup championships. In 1956-57, Moore made his first appearance

among the NHL's scoring leaders. One year later, he was the best in the league. Moore led the NHL with 38 goals in 1957-58 and won the Art Ross Trophy with 84 points, despite playing the final three weeks of the season with a cast on his broken left wrist. In 1958-59 Moore led the league with 41 goals and added 55 assists to win his second straight scoring title. His 96 points that year set a new NHL record. (It would be another 10 years before the NHL had its first 100-point players.) Moore was the First-Team All-Star at left wing in both 1957-58 and 1958-59. He was a Second-Team All-Star in 1960-61.

Dickie Moore retired after the 1962-63 season, but he couldn't stay away from the game. When Toronto coach Punch Imlach invited him to make a comeback, Moore joined the Maple Leafs in 1964-65 but retired again after the season. In 1967-68, the NHL added six new expansion teams, and Moore returned to the league as a member of the St. Louis Blues. He helped St. Louis make it to the Stanley Cup Finals that year, then retired for good after the Blues lost to Montreal. Moore was elected to the Hockey Hall of Fame in 1974.

Dickie Moore's 96 points in 1958-59 would prove to be the second-highest total of the NHL's pre-expansion era. Both Bobby Hull and Stan Mikita would tally 97 points in the 1960s.

Howie Morenz

Position: **Center**   Height: **5'9" (175 cm)**   Weight: **165 lbs (75 kg)**   Born: **June 21, 1902 in Mitchell, ON.**

Regular Season								Playoffs						
Season	Team	GP	G	A	Pts	PIM	+/-	Season	Team	GP	G	A	Pts	PIM
1923-24	Mtl. Canadiens 🏆	24	13	3	16	20	—	1923-24	Mtl. Canadiens 🏆	6	7	2	9	10
1924-25	Mtl. Canadiens	30	27	7	34	31	—	1924-25	Mtl. Canadiens	6	7	1	8	10
1925-26	Mtl. Canadiens	31	23	3	26	39	—	1925-26	Mtl. Canadiens	—	—	—	—	—
1926-27	Mtl. Canadiens	44	25	7	32	49	—	1926-27	Mtl. Canadiens	4	1	0	1	4
1927-28	Mtl. Canadiens	43	33	18	51	66	—	1927-28	Mtl. Canadiens	2	0	0	0	12
1928-29	Mtl. Canadiens	42	17	10	27	47	—	1928-29	Mtl. Canadiens	3	0	0	0	6
1929-30	Mtl. Canadiens 🏆	44	40	10	50	72	—	1929-30	Mtl. Canadiens 🏆	6	3	0	3	10
1930-31	Mtl. Canadiens 🏆	39	28	23	51	49	—	1930-31	Mtl. Canadiens 🏆	10	1	4	5	10
1931-32	Mtl. Canadiens	48	24	25	49	46	—	1931-32	Mtl. Canadiens	4	1	0	1	4
1932-33	Mtl. Canadiens	46	14	21	35	32	—	1932-33	Mtl. Canadiens	2	0	3	3	2
1933-34	Mtl. Canadiens	39	8	13	21	21	—	1933-34	Mtl. Canadiens	2	1	1	2	0
1934-35	Chicago	48	8	26	34	21	—	1934-35	Chicago	2	0	0	0	0
1935-36	Chicago	23	4	11	15	20	—	1935-36	Chicago	—	—	—	—	—
	NY Rangers	19	2	4	6	6	—		NY Rangers	—	—	—	—	—
1936-37	Mtl. Canadiens	30	4	16	20	12	—	1936-37	Mtl. Canadiens	—	—	—	—	—
	NHL Totals:	550	270	197	467	531			Playoff Totals:	47	21	11	32	68

Back in 1950, Howie Morenz was voted Canada's best hockey player of the first half of the twentieth century. He was the biggest star in hockey during the 1920s and 1930s, which was an important time for the NHL. The league was expanding outside of Canada and into the United States for the first time, and the speedy exploits of Howie Morenz helped draw American fans to the game. He was called "The Babe Ruth of Hockey" because people bought tickets just to see him play. Morenz had many other nicknames, all of which were inspired by his blazing speed. His most famous nickname was "The Stratford Streak" because Morenz was the fastest player many had ever seen. He was also a great goal scorer, and his 270 career goals were the most anyone had ever scored in the NHL at that time. Morenz was also one of the first players elected to the Hockey Hall of Fame in 1945.

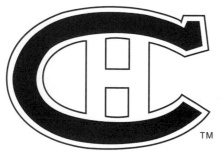

Morenz was born in Mitchell, Ontario, but first attracted the NHL's attention while playing hockey in nearby Stratford. He signed his first professional contract with the Canadiens for the 1923-24 season and immediately led Montreal to the Stanley Cup. In 1924-25, he collected 27 goals during a 30-game schedule. Morenz would lead the Canadiens in scoring every season for the next seven years. In both 1927-28 and 1930-31, he was also the NHL's top scorer. In 1930 and 1931, he led the Canadiens to back-to-back Stanley Cup titles. Morenz first won the Hart Trophy as the NHL player who was most valuable to his team in 1927-28, and then won it again in 1930-31 and 1931-32.

Morenz was an aggressive player throughout his career and old injuries finally began to catch up with him. Montreal traded him to Chicago before the 1934-35 season, and then the Blackhawks dealt him to the New York Rangers the following year. With Morenz gone, the Canadiens began to slump, so they brought him back to Montreal in 1936-37. He was no longer the star he had once been, but he helped the Canadiens, and the fans still flocked to see him. In fact, Montreal was leading the league until Morenz suffered a broken leg during a game on

January 28, 1937. The break was so bad that Morenz knew he would never be able to play hockey again. Morenz died while still in the hospital on March 8, 1937. Some people say he died of a broken heart.

Howie Morenz attacks the puck in front of New York Rangers goalie Andy Aikenhead. Morenz was the player most fans wanted to watch during the 1920s and '30s.

Vaclav Nedomansky

Position: Right Wing **Height:** 6'2" (188 cm) **Weight:** 205 lbs (93 kg) **Born:** March 14, 1944 in Hodonin, Czechoslovakia.

		International Hockey and NHL Regular Season							NHL Playoffs				
Year	Team	Event/League	GP	G	A	Pts	PIM	+/-	GP	G	A	Pts	PIM
1964-65	Czechoslovakia	World Championships	7	4	2	6	2	—	—	—	—	—	—
1965-66	Czechoslovakia	World Championships	7	5	2	7	8	—	—	—	—	—	—
1966-67	Czechoslovakia	World Championships	7	1	2	3	14	—	—	—	—	—	—
1967-68	Czechoslovakia	Olympics	7	5	2	7	4	—	—	—	—	—	—
1968-69	Czechoslovakia	World Championships	10	9	2	11	10	—	—	—	—	—	—
1969-70	Czechoslovakia	World Championships	10	10	7	17	11	—	—	—	—	—	—
1970-71	Czechoslovakia	World Championships	10	10	7	17	—	—	—	—	—	—	—
1971-72	Czechoslovakia	Olympics	6	8	3	11	0	—	—	—	—	—	—
	Czechoslovakia	World Championships	9	9	6	15	0	—	—	—	—	—	—
1972-73	Czechoslovakia	World Championships	10	9	3	12	2	—	—	—	—	—	—
1973-74	Czechoslovakia	World Championships	10	10	3	13	4	—	—	—	—	—	—
1977-78	Detroit	NHL	63	11	17	28	2	-17	7	3	5	8	0
1978-79	Detroit	NHL	80	38	35	73	19	-13	—	—	—	—	—
1979-80	Detroit	NHL	79	35	39	74	13	-5	—	—	—	—	—
1980-81	Detroit	NHL	74	12	20	32	30	-35	—	—	—	—	—
1981-82	Detroit	NHL	68	12	28	40	22	-15	—	—	—	—	—
1982-83	NY Rangers	NHL	1	1	0	1	0	—	—	—	—	—	—
	St. Louis	NHL	22	2	9	11	2	-8	—	—	—	—	—
	NY Rangers	NHL	34	11	8	19	0	1	—	—	—	—	—
	Career Totals:		514	202	195	397	143		**Playoff Totals:**	7	3	5	8	0

Hockey first became popular in Europe in the early years of the twentieth century. In those days, countries like England, Germany, Switzerland, and France were considered international hockey's best, so it was a big surprise when the country called Bohemia won the European Championship in 1911. They won it again in 1914. Its name has changed a few times since them, but that region is still producing great hockey players. Nowadays, the area is known as Slovakia and the Czech Republic.

Vaclav Nedomansky (whose first name is pronounced "Vatzlav") was the type of dominant hockey player that Jaromir Jagr is today. At 6'2" (188 cm) and 205 pounds (93 kg), Nedomansky was big and strong. He was also a slick stickhandler with a booming shot. Nedomansky was the best player ever produced during the 70 years when Slovakia and the Czech Republic were combined as the country of Czechoslovakia.

Nedomansky joined the Slovan Bratislava team in Czechoslovakia's top hockey league in 1962. In 12 seasons with the team, he played 419 games, had 369 goals, and won the league scoring title four times. In international play, Nedomansky starred with the Czechoslovakian national team from 1965 to 1974. He led his team to an Olympic silver medal in 1968 and a bronze medal in 1972. Nedomansky also played at ten World Championship tournaments and helped Czechoslovakia win a medal nine times. His team won the world title in 1972, and finished in second place on five occasions. Over the years, Nedomansky played 93 games at the World Championships and scored 78 goals. He was named to the tournament all-star team three times, and was selected as the Best Forward in 1974.

Nedomansky never returned to Czechoslovakia after the 1974 World

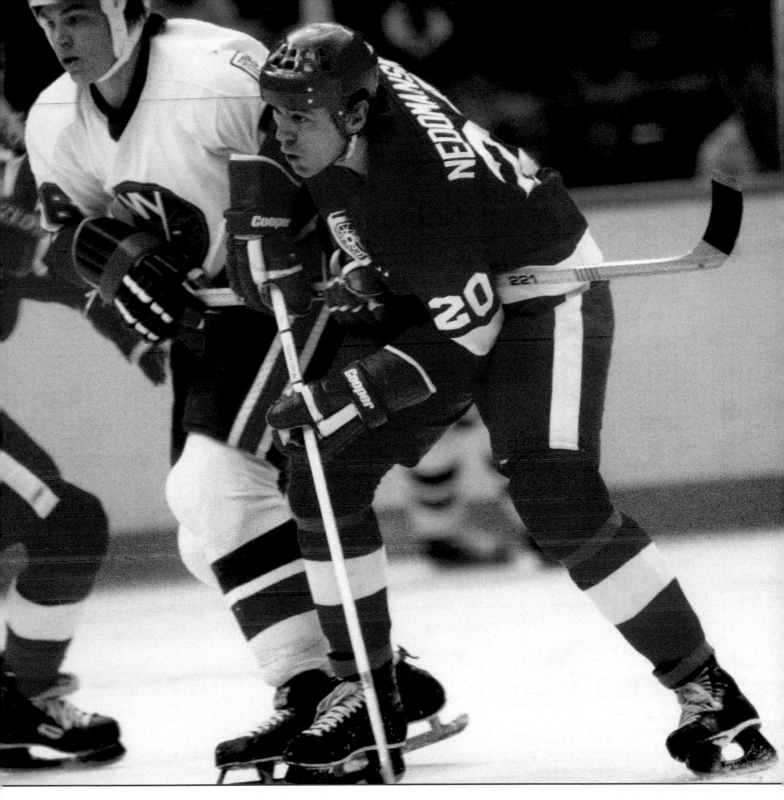

Championships. Instead, he snuck away from his teammates and came to Canada. Once in Canada, Nedomansky signed with the Toronto Toros of the World Hockey Association. "Big Ned," as he became known, led the Toros with 41 goals in 1974-75. He ranked third in the entire WHA with 56 goals in 1975-76.

During his fourth season in the WHA, Nedomansky asked his team to release him so

Vaclav Nedomansky was a great star in Czechoslovakia who later enjoyed success in the NHL at a time when players from his homeland were not supposed to leave their country.

that he could play in the NHL. Though he was now in his mid-30s, Nedomansky enjoyed two 30-goal seasons with the Detroit Red Wings. He later played for the Rangers and St. Louis before retiring in 1983.

Frank Nighbor

Position: **Center**　Height: **5'9" (175 cm)**　Weight: **160 lbs (73 kg)**　Born: **January 26, 1893 in Pembroke, ON.**

	Regular Season								Playoffs					
Season	Team	GP	G	A	Pts	PIM	+/-	Season	Team	GP	G	A	Pts	PIM
1917-18	Ottawa	10	11	8	19	6	—	1917-18	Ottawa	—	—	—	—	—
1918-19	Ottawa	18	18	9	27	30	—	1918-19	Ottawa	2	0	2	2	3
1919-20	Ottawa	23	26	15	41	18	—	1919-20	Ottawa	5	6	1	7	2
1920-21	Ottawa	24	19	10	29	10	—	1920-21	Ottawa	7	1	4	5	2
1921-22	Ottawa	20	8	10	18	4	—	1921-22	Ottawa	2	2	1	3	4
1922-23	Ottawa	22	11	7	18	16	—	1922-23	Ottawa	8	1	2	3	10
1923-24	Ottawa	20	10	3	13	14	—	1923-24	Ottawa	2	0	1	1	2
1924-25	Ottawa	26	5	2	7	18	—	1924-25	Ottawa	—	—	—	—	—
1925-26	Ottawa	35	12	13	25	40	—	1925-26	Ottawa	2	0	0	0	2
1926-27	Ottawa	38	6	6	12	26	—	1926-27	Ottawa	6	1	1	2	0
1927-28	Ottawa	42	8	5	13	46	—	1927-28	Ottawa	2	0	0	0	2
1928-29	Ottawa	30	1	4	5	22	—	1928-29	Ottawa	—	—	—	—	—
1929-30	Ottawa	19	0	0	0	0	—	1929-30	Ottawa	—	—	—	—	—
	Toronto	22	2	0	2	2	—		Toronto	—	—	—	—	—
NHL Totals:		349	137	92	229	252		Playoff Totals:		36	11	12	23	27

Frank Nighbor was one of the most popular players in the early days of the NHL. Others might have been better scorers than he was, but no one could match his two-way play. In fact, Nighbor's fans often wondered if it was better to use him to help score goals or to try and prevent them. He was one of the first players to use the hook check to knock the puck away from other players. When he had the puck, he was such a good stickhandler that it was hard for anyone to take the puck away from him.

Frank Nighbor was the first winner of two of the NHL's most important awards. He won the Hart Trophy as most valuable player when it was first donated to the league in 1923-24. The next season he won the brand new Lady Byng Trophy for his sportsmanlike play. He won the Lady Byng again in 1925-26. Nighbor was also a member of the Stanley Cup-winning Ottawa Senators in 1920, 1921, 1923, and 1927.

Nighbor's professional hockey career began five years before the NHL was formed. He started with the Toronto Blueshirts of the National Hockey Association in 1912-13. The next year he joined the Vancouver Millionaires of the Pacific Coast Hockey Association, where he was a PCHA All-Star in 1914-15 and helped the Millionaires win the Stanley Cup that year. Nighbor was so good against Ottawa in the Finals that the Senators offered him a contract. Ottawa was near his hometown, so he was happy to sign with them. Nighbor was from Pembroke, Ontario, and his nickname was "The Pembroke Peach." (Peach was an expression that meant something was very good.) Sometimes he was also called "The Flying Dutchman" after the mystical sailing ship of the same name that could not be stopped.

In 1916-17, Nighbor scored 41 goals for Ottawa and tied Joe Malone for the NHA scoring title that year. Next season the NHA became the NHL, but injuries slowed down Nighbor that year. Once he was healthy again he ranked as one of the league's top scorers for three seasons in a row. His final season in the NHL was 1929-30. He was elected to the Hockey Hall of Fame in 1947.

Frank Nighbor was just a young player in Pembroke when this picture was taken around 1910. Nighbor became one of the most popular players in hockey during the NHL's early days.

Bobby Orr

Position: **Defense**   Height: **6'0" (183 cm)**   Weight: **197 lbs (89 kg)**   Born: **March 20, 1948 in Parry Sound, ON.**

Regular Season								Playoffs						
Season	Team	GP	G	A	Pts	PIM	+/-	Season	Team	GP	G	A	Pts	PIM
1966-67	Boston	61	13	28	41	102	—	1966-67	Boston	—	—	—	—	—
1967-68	Boston	46	11	20	31	63	30	1967-68	Boston	4	0	2	2	2
1968-69	Boston	67	21	43	64	133	65	1968-69	Boston	10	1	7	8	10
1969-70	Boston	76	33	87	120	125	54	1969-70	Boston	14	9	11	20	14
1970-71	Boston	78	37	102	139	91	124	1970-71	Boston	7	5	7	12	25
1971-72	Boston	76	37	80	117	106	86	1971-72	Boston	15	5	19	24	19
1972-73	Boston	63	29	72	101	99	56	1972-73	Boston	5	1	1	2	7
1973-74	Boston	74	32	90	122	82	84	1973-74	Boston	16	4	14	18	28
1974-75	Boston	80	46	89	135	101	80	1974-75	Boston	3	1	5	6	2
1975-76	Boston	10	5	13	18	22	10	1975-76	Boston	—	—	—	—	—
1976-77	Chicago	20	4	19	23	25	6	1976-77	Chicago	—	—	—	—	—
1978-79	Chicago	6	2	2	4	4	2	1978-79	Chicago	—	—	—	—	—
NHL Totals:		657	270	645	915	953		Playoff Totals:		74	26	66	92	107

No one changed the way the game of hockey was played more than Robert Gordon Orr. Before the Parry Sound native joined the Boston Bruins in 1966-67, defensemen rarely journeyed into the offensive zone. Rear guards were taught to stay in their own end and defend their own zone. Orr proved that defensemen could play a prominent role at both ends of the ice. Orr could lead a rush and still be back in his own zone in time to stop an enemy attack. Orr also had alarming accuracy and could fire the puck from any angle and at any speed.

Wisely, the Bruins allowed Orr to play his own style. In his first season, Orr recorded 41 points and won the Calder Trophy as rookie-of-the-year. But he also suffered a knee injury that would bother him for the rest of his career.

Over the next eight seasons, Bobby Orr was hockey's most exciting performer. His end-to-end rushes captivated fans. In 1969-70, Orr became the first defenseman to record 100 points, leading the league in scoring. No other defenseman in NHL history has ever done that. Orr won the Norris Trophy as the league's top defense-man for eight straight seasons. He also won the Hart Trophy as MVP three times.

As dominant as he was in the regular season, Orr often saved his best hockey for the playoffs. In the 1970 finals, he scored the Stanley Cup-winning goal against St. Louis. The photo of Orr flying through the air seconds after slipping the puck past Blues goalie Glenn Hall to win the Stanley Cup is hockey's best-known image. He repeated his Stanley Cup heroics in 1972 by once again tapping home the Cup-winning goal. It's not surprising that he was named playoff MVP in both years.

Despite his talent, Orr knew he wasn't going to have a long career. Because he played at such a breakneck pace, he suffered numerous injuries. He was forced to have surgery on both knees as well as his shoulder and back. In the last three seasons of his career, he could only play 36 games.

In November 1978, at the age of 30, Bobby Orr was forced to retire. The Hockey Hall of Fame acknowledged Orr's place in history by automatically inducting him into the Hall without him having to serve the traditional waiting period.

In one of the most memorable moments in hockey history, Bobby Orr scores the Stanley Cup-winning goal against St. Louis in 1970 and celebrates while flying through the air. In the top photo, you can see the St. Louis player's stick under Orr's skate as Orr is tripped while scoring the goal.

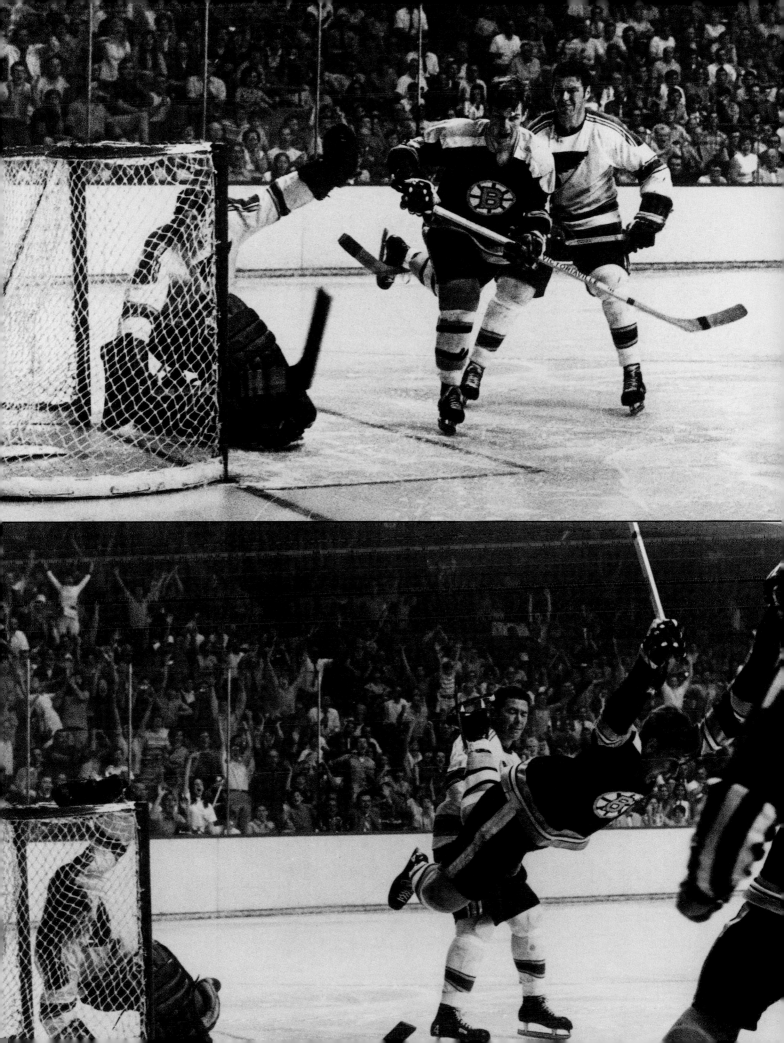

Brad Park

Position: **Defense**   Height: **6'0" (183 cm)**   Weight: **200 lbs (86 kg)**   Born: **July 6, 1948 in Toronto, ON.**

Regular Season								Playoffs					
Season	Team	GP	G	A	Pts	PIM	+/-	Season	Team	GP	G	A	Pts	PIM
1968-69	NY Rangers	54	3	23	26	70	12	1968-69	NY Rangers	4	0	2	2	7
1969-70	NY Rangers	60	11	26	37	98	23	1969-70	NY Rangers	5	1	2	3	11
1970-71	NY Rangers	68	7	37	44	114	25	1970-71	NY Rangers	13	0	4	4	42
1971-72	NY Rangers	75	24	49	73	130	62	1971-72	NY Rangers	16	4	7	11	21
1972-73	NY Rangers	52	10	43	53	51	31	1972-73	NY Rangers	10	2	5	7	8
1973-74	NY Rangers	78	25	57	82	148	18	1973-74	NY Rangers	13	4	8	12	38
1974-75	NY Rangers	65	13	44	57	104	6	1974-75	NY Rangers	3	1	4	5	2
1975-76	NY Rangers	13	2	4	6	23	-4	1975-76	NY Rangers	—	—	—	—	—
	Boston	43	16	37	53	95	23		Boston	11	3	8	11	14
1976-77	Boston	77	12	55	67	67	47	1976-77	Boston	14	2	10	12	4
1977-78	Boston	80	22	57	79	79	68	1977-78	Boston	15	9	11	20	14
1978-79	Boston	40	7	32	39	10	28	1978-79	Boston	11	1	4	5	8
1979-80	Boston	32	5	16	21	27	11	1979-80	Boston	10	3	6	9	4
1980-81	Boston	78	14	52	66	111	21	1980-81	Boston	3	1	3	4	11
1981-82	Boston	75	14	42	56	82	11	1981-82	Boston	11	1	4	5	4
1982-83	Boston	76	10	26	36	82	20	1982-83	Boston	16	3	9	12	18
1983-84	Detroit	80	5	53	58	85	-29	1983-84	Detroit	3	0	3	3	0
1984-85	Detroit	67	13	30	43	53	-15	1984-85	Detroit	3	0	0	0	11
NHL Totals:		1113	213	683	896	1429		Playoff Totals:		161	35	90	125	217

If Brad Park had played at any other time during the 87-year history of the NHL, he may have been called the game's best defenseman. But since he had to share the spotlight with Bobby Orr, he really didn't receive the attention he deserved.

While Orr was touted as a future superstar when he was still a teenager, Park was relatively unknown. A Toronto native, Park's original rights should have belonged to the Maple Leafs. However, a front office foul-up by the Leafs allowed Park to slip through their fingers. The New York Rangers believed Park would become a steady rear guard after some practice in the minors. But after only 17 games in the minors, Park was promoted, and he never looked back.

Part of Park's early appeal was his work ethic. He loved laying out thunderous body checks and he was a demon in the corners. He also could fire low, accurate shots at the net that were easy to tip but hard to defend. But what impressed his coaches most was his confidence.

By his second season, he was already the team's on-ice general who controlled the ice and the tempo of the game. The Rangers' offensive system depended on Park's ability to lug the puck from end-to-end. Sure, he made mistakes. But he never made excuses.

Over the next 17 years, Park earned nine trips to the All-Star Game. He scored 10 or more goals 12 times, including three 20-goal campaigns. An aggressive playmaker who could take a hit to make a clean pass, Park earned at least 40 assists in nine different seasons.

In November 1975, Park was dealt to Boston, ironically, to replace Bobby Orr, whose knees were giving out on him. Park continued to play intelligent, effective hockey under the guidance of coach Don Cherry. In 1977-78, he tied a career-high with 57 assists and was one of a record 11 Boston players to record at least 20 goals. In the 1978 playoffs, he led the Bruins in scoring with nine goals and 20 points, but the Bruins were still unable to win the Stanley

Cup title that Park wanted so badly. Despite three trips to the finals during his career, Park was never able to sip Stanley Cup champagne.

Overshadowed by Bobby Orr during his years with the New York Rangers, Brad Park actually replaced the great Boston blueliner when he joined the Bruins in 1975.

Lester Patrick

Position: **Defense**　Height: **6'1" (185 cm)**　Weight: **180 lbs (82 kg)**　Born: **December 31, 1883 in Drummondville, QC.**

			Regular Season					Playoffs				
Season	Club	League	GP	G	A	Pts	PIM	GP	G	A	Pts	PIM
1903-04	Brandon	NWHL	2	0	0	0	—	—	—	—	—	—
1904-05	Westmount	CAHL	8	4	0	4	—	—	—	—	—	—
1905-06	Mtl. Wanderers	ECAHA	9	17	0	17	—	2	3	0	3	—
1906-07	Mtl. Wanderers	ECAHA	9	11	0	11	—	6	10	0	10	—
1907-08	Nelson	Sr.	2	1	0	1	—	—	—	—	—	—
1908-09	Edmonton	Sr.	—	—	—	—	—	2	1	—	1	—
1908-09	Nelson	Sr.	—	—	—	—	—	—	—	—	—	—
1909-10	Renfrew Millionaires	NHA	12	23	—	23	25	—	—	—	—	—
1910-11	Nelson	SR.	—	—	—	—	—	—	—	—	—	—
1911-12	Victoria Aristocrats	PCHA	16	10	0	10	—	—	—	—	—	—
1912-13	Victoria Aristocrats	PCHA	15	14	5	19	9	—	—	—	—	—
1913-14	Victoria Aristocrats	PCHA	9	5	5	10	12	3	4	0	4	—
1914-15	Victoria Aristocrats	PCHA	17	12	5	17	0	3	2	0	2	—
1915-16	Victoria Aristocrats	PCHA	18	13	11	24	15	—	—	—	—	—
1916-17	Spokane	PCHA	23	10	11	21	27	—	—	—	—	—
1917-18	Seattle	PCHA	17	2	8	10	15	—	—	—	—	—
1918-19	Victoria Aristocrats	PCHA	9	2	5	7	15	2	0	1	1	0
1919-20	Victoria Aristocrats	PCHA	11	2	2	4	3	—	—	—	—	—
1920-21	Victoria Aristocrats	PCHA	5	2	3	5	13	—	—	—	—	—
1921-22	Victoria Aristocrats	PCHA	2	0	0	0	0	—	—	—	—	—
1925-26	Victoria Aristocrats	WHL	23	5	8	13	20	1	0	0	0	2
1926-27	NY Rangers	NHL	1	0	0	0	2	—	—	—	—	—
1927-28	NY Rangers	NHL	—	—	—	—	—	1	0	0	0	0
	Career Totals:		208	133	63	196	156	20	20	1	21	2

Lester Patrick was a player, coach, owner, and league executive during a hockey career that lasted from 1904 to 1954. Patrick first gained fame as a hockey player in Brandon, Manitoba when his team lost the Stanley Cup to the Ottawa Silver Seven in 1904. He was a defenseman at a time when defensemen were expected to remain in front of their goaltender all game long. Patrick would help take care of his own end, but he could also stickhandle the puck up the ice to help his forwards on the attack.

After Brandon, Lester returned to his family home in Montreal. He became a star with the Montreal Wanderers and helped them win the Stanley Cup in ® 1906 and 1907.

After a season in Edmonton, Lester joined brother Frank in 1909-10 to play for the Renfrew Millionaires. Lester was the captain of the star-studded team that also featured Newsy Lalonde and Cyclone Taylor. After the season, he and Frank returned to British Columbia, and in 1911, they organized the Pacific Coast Hockey Association.

The PCHA introduced many rules that helped modernize hockey. It was the first league to allow players to pass the puck forward and the first to keep track of assists. Lester was a player, coach, general manager, and owner of the Victoria Aristocrats. He continued to play in the PCHA until the 1921-22 season. That year, he even made an appearance as a goaltender. In 1926-27, Lester Patrick entered the NHL as the coach and general manager of the New York Rangers. One season later, his goaltending experience came in handy.

The Rangers had reached the Stanley Cup Final in just their second season of 1927-28. Unfortunately, their goalie was injured in the second game. Teams didn't carry a backup goaltender back then, so 44-year-old Lester decided that he would go in net. It is one of the most famous moments in hockey history. The Rangers won the game 2-1 in overtime and went on to win the Stanley Cup.

A member of one of hockey's most promi-

A star as both a forward and a defenseman during his playing career, 44-year-old Lester Patrick was coach of the New York Rangers when he made an emergency appearance in goal during the 1928 Stanley Cup Finals.

nent families, Lester was elected to the Hockey Hall of Fame in 1947. Brother Frank was inducted in 1958. Son Lynn was elected in 1980. Today, Pittsburg Penguins General Manager Craig Patrick is Lester's grandson.

Jacques Plante

Position: **Goaltender**   Height: **6'0" (183 cm)**   Weight: **175 lbs (79 kg)**   Born: **January 17, 1929 in Shawinigan Falls, QC.**

Regular Season											Playoffs									
Season	Team	GP	W	L	T	MINS	GA	SO	AVG.		Season	Team	GP	W	L	T	MINS	GA	SO	AVG.
1952-53	Montreal 🏆	3	2	0	1	180	4	0	1.33		1952-53	Montreal 🏆	4	3	1		240	7	1	1.75
1953-54	Montreal	17	7	5	5	1020	27	5	1.59		1953-54	Montreal	8	5	3		480	15	2	1.88
1954-55	Montreal	52	31	13	7	3080	110	5	2.14		1954-55	Montreal	12	6	4		640	30	0	2.81
1955-56	Montreal 🏆	64	42	12	10	3840	119	7	1.86		1955-56	Montreal 🏆	10	8	2		600	18	2	1.80
1956-57	Montreal 🏆	61	31	18	12	3660	123	9	2.02		1956-57	Montreal 🏆	10	8	2		616	18	1	1.75
1957-58	Montreal 🏆	57	34	14	8	3386	119	9	2.11		1957-58	Montreal 🏆	10	8	2		618	20	1	1.94
1958-59	Montreal 🏆	67	38	16	13	4000	144	9	2.16		1958-59	Montreal 🏆	11	8	3		670	28	0	2.51
1959-60	Montreal 🏆	69	40	17	12	4140	175	3	2.54		1959-60	Montreal 🏆	8	8	0		489	11	3	1.35
1960-61	Montreal	40	22	11	7	2400	112	2	2.80		1960-61	Montreal	6	2	4		412	16	0	2.33
1961-62	Montreal	70	42	14	14	4200	166	4	2.37		1961-62	Montreal	6	2	4		360	19	0	3.17
1962-63	Montreal	56	22	14	19	3320	138	5	2.49		1962-63	Montreal	5	1	4		300	14	0	2.80
1963-64	NY Rangers	65	22	36	7	3900	220	3	3.38		1963-64	NY Rangers	—	—	—		—	—	—	—
1964-65	NY Rangers	33	10	17	5	1938	109	2	3.37		1964-65	NY Rangers	—	—	—		—	—	—	—
1968-69	St. Louis	37	18	12	6	2139	70	5	1.96		1968-69	St. Louis	10	8	2		589	14	3	1.43
1969-70	St. Louis	32	18	9	5	1839	67	5	2.19		1969-70	St. Louis	6	4	1		324	8	1	1.48
1970-71	Toronto	40	24	11	4	2329	73	4	1.88		1970-71	Toronto	3	0	2		134	7	0	3.13
1971-72	Toronto	34	16	13	5	1965	86	2	2.63		1971-72	Toronto	1	0	1		60	5	0	5.00
1972-73	Toronto	32	8	14	6	1717	87	1	3.04		1972-73	Toronto	—	—	—		—	—	—	—
	Boston	8	7	1	0	480	16	2	2.00			Boston	2	0	2		120	10	0	5.00
NHL Totals:		837	434	247	146	49533	1965	82	2.38		Playoff Totals:		112	71	37		6652	240	14	2.16

Very few players in hockey history have changed the game as much as Jacques Plante. He was one of the first goalies who moved outside of the crease, stopped pucks behind the net, or made passes to his defensemen. He was also the first man to make the mask a regular piece of his equipment.

Jacques Plante suffered from asthma, a disease that makes it hard to breathe. To protect his nose, he began wearing a mask in practice during the 1957-58 season. Management of the Montreal Canadiens didn't want him using it during games because they thought a mask would block his vision. Plante was finally allowed to wear his mask in a game on November 1, 1959, after he suffered a bad cut on his face. Teams didn't have backup goalies in those days, and the Canadiens needed Plante to play. Montreal went 10 games in a row without losing after Plante started wearing his mask, so the Canadiens gave him permission to wear it all the time. Within a few years, goalies everywhere were wearing masks.

Jacques Plante's NHL career began with Montreal in 1952-53. He played only a few games, but helped the Canadiens win the Stanley Cup. After another brief appearance in 1953-54, he took over Montreal's goaltending job in 1954-55. Soon, he was the top goalie in the NHL. From 1955-56 to 1959-60, Plante helped Montreal win the Stanley Cup five years in a row. During that stretch he also won the Vezina Trophy as the league's leading goaltender five years in a row. Plante won the Vezina Trophy for the sixth time in 1961-62. His play was so good that season that he also won the Hart Trophy as the NHL's most valuable player. No goalie would win the Hart Trophy again until Dominik Hasek did in 1996-97.

In 1963, Montreal traded Plante to the New York Rangers where he retired two years later. In 1968-69, the St. Louis Blues convinced him to make a comeback. Plante shared goaltending duties with Glenn Hall and won the Vezina Trophy for a record seventh time. He later played for the

A Century of Hockey Heroes

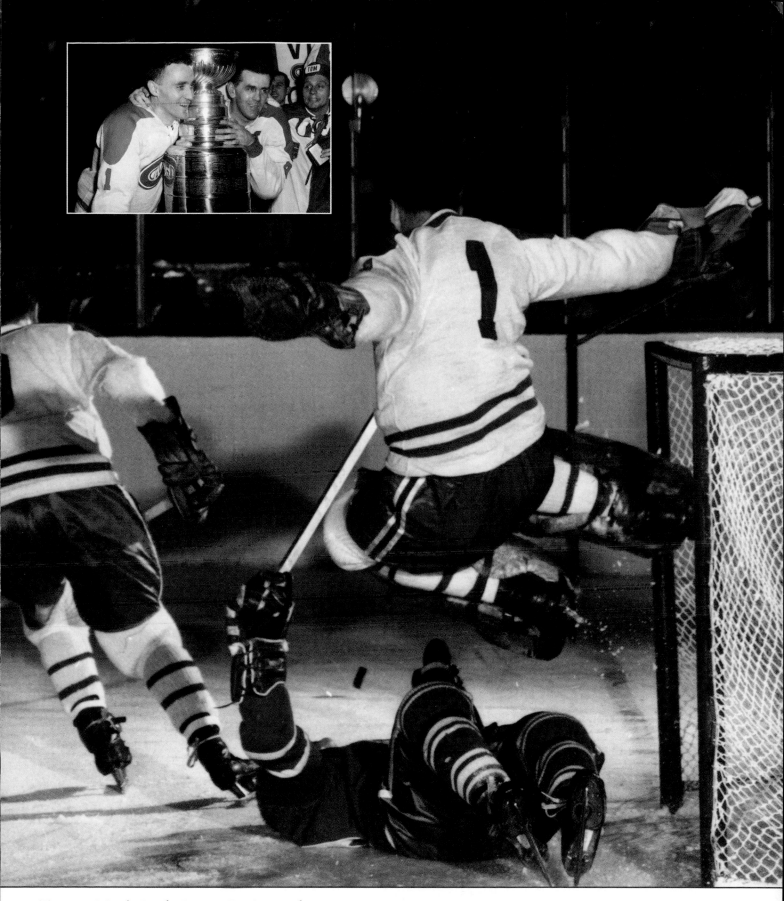

Toronto Maple Leafs, Boston Bruins, and
Edmonton Oilers (when they were in the World
Hockey Association) before retiring for good in
1975. Jacques Plante was elected to the Hockey
Hall of Fame in 1978.

*Jacques Plante was an acrobatic goalie who loved to
move around on the ice. His unorthodox style helped the
Montreal Canadiens win the Stanley Cup five years in a
row. Inset: Plante poses with Rocket Richard and the
Stanley Cup.*

Denis Potvin

Position: **Defense**   Height: **6'0" (183 cm)**   Weight: **205 lbs (93 kg)**   Born: **October 29, 1953 in Ottawa, ON.**

Regular Season								Playoffs						
Season	Team	GP	G	A	Pts	PIM	+/-	Season	Team	GP	G	A	Pts	PIM
1973-74	NY Islanders	77	17	37	54	175	-16	1973-74	NY Islanders	—	—	—	—	—
1974-75	NY Islanders	79	21	55	76	105	28	1974-75	NY Islanders	17	5	9	14	30
1975-76	NY Islanders	78	31	67	98	100	12	1975-76	NY Islanders	13	5	14	19	32
1976-77	NY Islanders	80	25	55	80	103	42	1976-77	NY Islanders	12	6	4	10	20
1977-78	NY Islanders	80	30	64	94	81	57	1977-78	NY Islanders	7	2	2	4	6
1978-79	NY Islanders	73	31	70	101	58	71	1978-79	NY Islanders	10	4	7	11	8
1979-80	NY Islanders	31	8	33	41	44	13	1979-80	NY Islanders	21	6	13	19	24
1980-81	NY Islanders	74	20	56	76	104	38	1980-81	NY Islanders	18	8	17	25	16
1981-82	NY Islanders	60	24	37	61	83	38	1981-82	NY Islanders	19	5	16	21	30
1982-83	NY Islanders	69	12	54	66	60	32	1982-83	NY Islanders	20	8	12	20	22
1983-84	NY Islanders	78	22	63	85	87	55	1983-84	NY Islanders	20	1	5	6	28
1984-85	NY Islanders	77	17	51	68	96	36	1984-85	NY Islanders	10	3	2	5	10
1985-86	NY Islanders	74	21	38	59	78	34	1985-86	NY Islanders	3	0	1	1	0
1986-87	NY Islanders	58	12	30	42	70	-6	1986-87	NY Islanders	10	2	2	4	21
1987-88	NY Islanders	72	19	32	51	112	26	1987-88	NY Islanders	5	1	4	5	6
NHL Totals:		1060	310	742	1052	1356		Playoff Totals:		185	56	108	164	253

One of the only players to ever come close to having Bobby Orr's talent was Denis Potvin. Like Orr, Potvin started playing junior hockey at the age of 14. In his final season with the Ottawa 67's in 1972-73, Potvin broke one of Orr's most prized marks by recording an OHA record-breaking 123 points.

When Potvin joined the New York Islanders the following season, it was clear that he had the skill to dominate at both ends of the rink. Blessed with a sturdy physique and quick reflexes, Potvin also found himself on a young, growing team. The coaches gave him all the ice time he wanted and needed to develop. He won the Calder Trophy as the NHL's top rookie in 1973-74 and reached the 20-goal mark in his second season. It was the first of nine seasons with 20 or more goals, including three 30-goal seasons, for Potvin.

During the 1970s, the Islanders suffered some humbling playoff losses, but that only gave them a greater drive to win. When Potvin was named captain in 1979, he made it his goal to lead the team to the Stanley Cup winner's circle. By the 1982-83 season, the Isles had turned their fortunes around and won four consecutive Stanley Cup titles. They became the only team other than the Montreal Canadiens to reach the finals in five straight years. Potvin was selected to the First All-Star Team five times and was chosen as the league's top defenseman three times. He was the first defenseman to score 300 goals and the first to reach the 1,000-point mark. Though his offensive totals dipped late in his career, Potvin remained a dependable defenseman until he retired in 1988. Potvin was the highest-scoring defenseman of all time when he was elected to the Hockey Hall of Fame in 1991.

Denis Potvin was a junior sensation who took his high-scoring ways to the NHL with the New York Islanders. Potvin was as tough as he was talented and could deliver bone-crunching body checks.

Henri Richard

Position: **Center**   Height: **5'7" (170 cm)**   Weight: **160 lbs (73 kg)**   Born: **February 29, 1936 in Montreal, QC.**

| Regular Season | | | | | | | | Playoffs | | | | | |
Season	Team	GP	G	A	Pts	PIM	+/-	Season	Team	GP	G	A	Pts	PIM
1955-56	Montreal	64	19	21	40	46	—	1955-56	Montreal	10	4	4	8	21
1956-57	Montreal	63	18	36	54	71	—	1956-57	Montreal	10	2	6	8	10
1957-58	Montreal	67	28	52	80	56	—	1957-58	Montreal	10	1	7	8	11
1958-59	Montreal	63	21	30	51	33	—	1958-59	Montreal	11	3	8	11	13
1959-60	Montreal	70	30	43	73	66	—	1959-60	Montreal	8	3	9	12	9
1960-61	Montreal	70	24	44	68	91	—	1960-61	Montreal	6	2	4	6	22
1961-62	Montreal	54	21	29	50	48	—	1961-62	Montreal	—	—	—	—	—
1962-63	Montreal	67	23	50	73	57	—	1962-63	Montreal	5	1	1	2	2
1963-64	Montreal	66	14	39	53	73	—	1963-64	Montreal	7	1	1	2	9
1964-65	Montreal	53	23	29	52	43	—	1964-65	Montreal	13	7	4	11	24
1965-66	Montreal	62	22	39	61	47	—	1965-66	Montreal	8	1	4	5	2
1966-67	Montreal	65	21	34	55	28	—	1966-67	Montreal	10	4	6	10	2
1967-68	Montreal	54	9	19	28	16	4	1967-68	Montreal	13	4	4	8	4
1968-69	Montreal	64	15	37	52	45	25	1968-69	Montreal	14	2	4	6	8
1969-70	Montreal	62	16	36	52	61	24	1969-70	Montreal	—	—	—	—	—
1970-71	Montreal	75	12	37	49	46	13	1970-71	Montreal	20	5	7	12	20
1971-72	Montreal	75	12	32	44	48	10	1971-72	Montreal	6	0	3	3	4
1972-73	Montreal	71	8	35	43	21	34	1972-73	Montreal	17	6	4	10	14
1973-74	Montreal	75	19	36	55	28	7	1973-74	Montreal	6	2	2	4	2
1974-75	Montreal	16	3	10	13	4	9	1974-75	Montreal	6	1	2	3	4
	NHL Totals:	1256	358	688	1046	928			Playoff Totals:	180	49	80	129	181

Even at a time when hockey players were smaller than they are today, Henri Richard was smaller than most. He stood only 5'7" (170 cm) and weighed just 160 pounds (73 kg). Richard was tiny but he was talented too. He was not afraid to battle for the puck with players that were much bigger than he was. Richard's smooth skating and stickhandling skill allowed him to play for 20 seasons in the NHL. He spent all of that time with the Montreal Canadiens and helped them win the Stanley Cup 11 times! No player in NHL history has played for as many Stanley Cup champions as Henri Richard.

Henri joined the Montreal Canadiens in 1955-56. At that time, his older brother Maurice was the team's biggest star and one of the NHL's greatest players. Together, the Richard brothers helped the Canadiens win the Stanley Cup five years in a row between 1956 and 1960. Henri did not have the same goal-scoring talent as Maurice but he proved to be a much better playmaker. "The Pocket Rocket," as he was called (his brother was "The Rocket"), led the NHL in

assists during his third season of 1957-58, and he consistently ranked among the league's point leaders in the years that followed. In addition to his offensive talent, Henri was also an excellent checker. He was often used by the Canadiens to help kill penalties. He was named to either the NHL's First or Second All-Star Teams four times between 1958 and 1963.

Richard continued to star with Montreal throughout the 1960s and helped them win the Stanley Cup again in 1965, 1966, 1968, and 1969. He played on his tenth championship team in 1971 when the Canadiens battled the Chicago Blackhawks in a Stanley Cup series that went all seven games. It was Henri Richard who scored the game-winning goal in the deciding seventh game.

Jean Beliveau retired from the Canadiens before the 1971-72 season and Richard took his place as team captain. The following year, he helped Montreal win the Stanley Cup once again. In his career, Henri Richard played 1,256 games. That is more than any other player in Montreal Canadiens history. He scored 358 goals and had 688 assists for 1,046 points to rank among

St. Louis Blues goalie Glenn Hall watches anxiously as Henri Richard chases a loose puck into the corner. Richard played for a record 11 Stanley Cup champions during his career.

Montreal's all-time leaders in those categories as well. He retired after the 1974-75 season and was elected to the Hockey Hall of Fame in 1979.

Maurice Richard

Position: **Right Wing**   Height: **5'10" (178 cm)**   Weight: **170 lbs (77 kg)**   Born: **August 4, 1921 in Montreal, QC.**

Regular Season							
Season	Team	GP	G	A	Pts	PIM	+/-
1942-43	Montreal	16	5	6	11	4	
1943-44	Montreal 🏆	46	32	22	54	45	
1944-45	Montreal	50	50	23	73	46	
1945-46	Montreal 🏆	50	27	21	48	50	
1946-47	Montreal	60	45	26	71	69	
1947-48	Montreal	53	28	25	53	89	
1948-49	Montreal	59	20	18	38	110	
1949-50	Montreal	70	43	22	65	114	
1950-51	Montreal	65	42	24	66	97	
1951-52	Montreal	48	27	17	44	44	
1952-53	Montreal 🏆	70	28	33	61	112	
1953-54	Montreal	70	37	30	67	112	
1954-55	Montreal	67	38	36	74	125	
1955-56	Montreal 🏆	70	38	33	71	89	
1956-57	Montreal 🏆	63	33	29	62	74	
1957-58	Montreal 🏆	28	15	19	34	28	
1958-59	Montreal 🏆	42	17	21	38	27	
1959-60	Montreal 🏆	51	19	16	35	50	
NHL Totals:		978	544	421	965	1.285	

Playoffs						
Season	Team	GP	G	A	Pts	PIM
1942-43	Montreal	—	—	—	—	
1943-44	Montreal 🏆	9	12	5	17	10
1944-45	Montreal	6	2	8	10	
1945-46	Montreal 🏆	9	7	4	11	15
1946-47	Montreal	10	6	5	11	44
1947-48	Montreal	—	—	—	—	
1948-49	Montreal	7	2	1	3	14
1949-50	Montreal	5	1	1	2	6
1950-51	Montreal	11	9	4	13	13
1951-52	Montreal	11	4	2	6	6
1952-53	Montreal 🏆	12	7	1	8	2
1953-54	Montreal	11	3	0	3	22
1954-55	Montreal	—	—	—	—	
1955-56	Montreal 🏆	10	5	9	14	24
1956-57	Montreal 🏆	10	8	3	11	8
1957-58	Montreal 🏆	10	11	4	15	10
1958-59	Montreal 🏆	4	0	0	0	2
1959-60	Montreal 🏆	8	1	3	4	2
Playoff Totals:		133	82	44	126	188

Maurice Richard was the heart and soul of the Montreal Canadiens. No player in hockey could match the fierce determination or the scoring skill of the man called "The Rocket." Richard had the speed to race past other team's defensemen and the strength to push past them if they got in his way. No one was ever as dangerous as Richard was when he got close to the net. He was the first player in hockey history to score 50 goals in a single season, and the first to score 500 in his career.

It was in the 1944-45 season that Rocket Richard became a true hockey legend. The NHL record of 44 goals had been set by Joe Malone in the league's first season of 1917-18, and it finally fell to Richard in 1944-45 when he totaled 50 goals during the 50-game schedule. It was the first of five times the Rocket would

lead the NHL in goals. During his playing days, 20 goals was considered to be a very good season, and Richard topped 30 on nine occasions! One year, during the semifinals against the Toronto Maple Leafs, Richard scored five goals in one playoff game. For his performance that night Richard was named the first, second, and third star during the three-star selection.

The Rocket was always at his best when a game meant the most. His 82 playoff goals were a long-time NHL record while his six playoff overtime goals remain an NHL record to this day. Richard helped the Canadiens win the Stanley Cup eight times in his career. He retired after the Canadiens won their record fifth straight NHL championship in 1960 and was elected to the Hockey Hall of Fame one year later.

Maurice Richard played hockey with an intensity that could be seen in the fiery glare of his eyes. No one was ever as dangerous as "The Rocket" when he got the puck close to the net.

Larry Robinson

Position: **Defense**   Height: **6'4" (193 cm)**   Weight: **225 lbs (102 kg)**   Born: **June 2, 1951 in Winchester, ON.**

| Regular Season | | | | | | | | Playoffs | | | | | | |
Season	Team	GP	G	A	Pts	PIM	+/-	Season	Team	GP	G	A	Pts	PIM
1972-73	Montreal	36	2	4	6	20	3	1972-73	Montreal	11	1	4	5	9
1973-74	Montreal	78	6	20	26	66	32	1973-74	Montreal	6	0	1	1	26
1974-75	Montreal	80	14	47	61	76	61	1974-75	Montreal	11	0	4	4	27
1975-76	Montreal	80	10	30	40	59	50	1975-76	Montreal	3	3	3	6	10
1976-77	Montreal	77	19	66	85	45	120	1976-77	Montreal	14	2	10	12	12
1977-78	Montreal	80	13	52	65	39	71	1977-78	Montreal	15	4	17	21	6
1978-79	Montreal	67	16	45	61	33	50	1978-79	Montreal	16	6	9	15	8
1979-80	Montreal	72	14	61	75	39	38	1979-80	Montreal	10	0	4	4	2
1980-81	Montreal	65	12	38	50	37	46	1980-81	Montreal	3	0	1	1	2
1981-82	Montreal	71	12	47	59	41	57	1981-82	Montreal	5	0	1	1	8
1982-83	Montreal	71	14	49	63	33	33	1982-83	Montreal	3	0	0	0	2
1983-84	Montreal	74	9	34	43	39	4	1983-84	Montreal	15	0	5	5	22
1984-85	Montreal	76	14	33	47	44	33	1984-85	Montreal	12	3	8	11	8
1985-86	Montreal	78	19	63	82	39	29	1985-86	Montreal	20	0	13	13	22
1986-87	Montreal	70	13	37	50	44	24	1986-87	Montreal	17	3	17	20	6
1987-88	Montreal	53	6	34	40	30	26	1987-88	Montreal	11	1	4	5	4
1988-89	Montreal	74	4	26	30	22	23	1988-89	Montreal	21	2	8	10	12
1989-90	Los Angeles	64	7	32	39	34	7	1989-90	Los Angeles	10	2	3	5	10
1990-91	Los Angeles	62	1	22	23	16	22	1990-91	Los Angeles	12	1	4	5	15
1991-92	Los Angeles	56	3	10	13	37	1	1991-92	Los Angeles	2	0	0	0	0
NHL Totals:		1384	208	750	958	793		**Playoff Totals:**		227	28	116	144	211

Few defensemen in the post-expansion era can match the accomplishments of Larry "Big Bird" Robinson. "Big Bird" was the first rear guard since Tim Horton to play for 20 seasons. He played on six Stanley Cup-winning teams, earned five All-Star nominations, and was voted as the NHL's top rear guard twice. But few people know that he never played defense until he was a pro.

When Robinson was a junior, he played both center and left wing. His production wasn't all that impressive, so it was no surprise that every team passed on him in the 1971 Amateur Draft. Montreal finally took Robinson with their fourth pick because they liked his size.

At 6'4" (193 cm) and 225 pounds (102 kg), Robinson was an imposing sight on the ice. While he had a powerful skating stride and a booming shot, coach Scotty Bowman wanted Robinson to play defense so the Habs sent Robinson to the minors, where he spent almost two full seasons learning to play the blueline. When he finally got the call to join the big club, he was ready.

Even though he was a key element in the Habs' five Stanley Cup titles in the 1970s, Robinson's finest moments may have come in 1985-86 when he collected 63 assists and recorded 82 points — his highest numbers in nine years. But the best was still to come for Robinson. In the 1986 playoffs, Robinson anchored the defense as the Canadiens began the journey to their only Stanley Cup title of the decade. Robinson performed in the playoffs with the heart of a champion. He guided his young team past Boston, Hartford, the New York Rangers, and Calgary, setting up 13 goals along the way. When the final whistle blew, the Habs had won their 23rd title. At the time, that was more championships than any other professional sports franchise in history.

Robinson ended his playing career with the Los Angeles Kings. After he retired, New Jersey

hired Larry as an assistant coach, where he helped the team win their first championship. Robinson then returned to the west coast to become head coach of the Kings.

Coach Scotty Bowman of the Montreal Canadiens thought Larry Robinson's booming shot would be more valuable from the blueline. He was right, and Robinson became one of the best defensemen in NHL history.

Art Ross

Position: **Defense**   Height: **5'11" (180 cm)**   Weight: **190 lbs (86 kg)**   Born: **January 13, 1886 in Naughton, ON.**

			Regular Season					Playoffs				
Season	Club	League	GP	G	A	Pts	PIM	GP	G	A	Pts	PIM
1904-05	Montreal	Sr.	8	10	0	10	—	—	—	—	—	—
	Westmount	CAHL	—	—	—	—	—	—	—	—	—	—
1905-06	Brandon	MSHL	7	6	0	6	—	—	—	—	—	—
1906-07	Kenora Thistles 🏆	SMHL	2	0	0	0	—	—	—	—	—	—
	Brandon	MPHL	9	5	0	5	—	—	—	—	—	—
1907-08	Mtl. Wanderers 🏆	ECAHA	10	8	0	8	5	4	0	4	4	—
	Pembroke	Sr.	1	5	0	5	—	—	—	—	—	—
1908-09	Mtl. Wanderers	ECHA	9	2	0	2	30	—	—	—	—	—
	Mtl. Wanderers	NY	2	2	0	2	3	—	—	—	—	—
	Cobalt	TPHL	2	0	—	0	—	—	—	—	—	—
1909-10	Haileybury	NHA	12	6	0	6	31	—	—	—	—	—
	All- Montreal	CHA	4	4	0	4	3	—	—	—	—	—
1910-11	Mtl. Wanderers	NHA	11	4	0	4	24	—	—	—	—	—
1911-12	Mtl. Wanderers	NHA	18	16	0	16	35	—	—	—	—	—
1912-13	Mtl. Wanderers	NHA	19	11	0	11	58	—	—	—	—	—
1913-14	Mtl. Wanderers	NHA	18	4	5	9	74	—	—	—	—	—
1914-15	Ottawa Senators	NHA	16	3	1	4	55	2	—	2	2	—
1915-16	Ottawa Senators	NHA	21	8	8	16	69	—	—	—	—	—
1916-17	Mtl. Wanderers	NHA	16	6	3	9	63	—	—	—	—	—
1917-18	Mtl. Wanderers	NHL	3	1	0	1	12	—	—	—	—	—
	Career Totals:		186	103	17	118	462	6	0	6	6	—

The man who donated the trophy for the NHL scoring leader was a defenseman who only had one goal in his NHL career! Of course, he only played three games in the league because he played most of his career before the NHL was even formed. He was one of the top stars of hockey during the early days of the twentieth century.

Art Ross grew up in Montreal and began his hockey career there in 1904-05. Like childhood friend Lester Patrick, Ross was a defenseman who liked to help out on offense. This was very unusual at the time because defensemen were expected to remain in their end of the ice at all times.

After one season in Montreal, Ross moved west to Brandon, Manitoba. In 1907, he was loaned to a team called the Kenora Thistles when they challenged the Montreal Wanderers for the Stanley Cup. Ross helped the Thistles sweep the series and become the team from the tiniest town ever to win the prized trophy. (Kenora's population was only 4,000!) Ross then returned to

Montreal in 1908 and helped the Wanderers regain the Stanley Cup.

During this time hockey experienced major changes. Organized hockey had begun in the 1880s as an amateur sport, which meant that players weren't paid any salary for playing. After the Stanley Cup was donated in 1893, cities began to realize that they could take pride in having a championship hockey team. By the early 1900s, teams began offering money for good players to join their team. Top stars like Art Ross were always in demand. In his first two seasons with the Wanderers, Ross would sometimes accept money from teams in other leagues to play games against their biggest rivals. In those days, hockey players were only paid a few hundred dollars per season, but Ross could make as much as $1,000 for these extra games! Still, he spent most of his career in Montreal and was still with the

Wanderers when they joined the NHL in 1917-18. Unfortunately, the team dropped out of hockey during the league's first year when its home arena burned down.

After his playing days, Ross became a hockey coach and was hired by the Boston Bruins when they joined the NHL in 1924. Ross built

Though Art Ross was often on the move during his playing days, he spent most of his career with the Montreal Wanderers. He later became a great coach and general manager with the Boston Bruins.

Boston into a championship team in the 1930s and '40s. In 1945, he was one of the first 12 men elected to the Hockey Hall of Fame.

Patrick Roy

Position: **Goaltender**   Height: **6'0" (183 cm)**   Weight: **192 lbs (87 kg)**   Born: **October 5, 1965 in Quebec City, QC.**

| | Regular Season | | | | | | | | |
Season	Team	GP	W	L	T	MINS	GA	SO	AVG.
1984-85	Montreal	1	1	0	0	20	0	0	0.00
1985-86	Montreal 🏆	47	23	18	3	2651	148	1	3.35
1986-87	Montreal	46	22	16	6	2686	131	1	2.93
1987-88	Montreal	45	23	12	9	2586	125	3	2.90
1988-89	Montreal	48	33	5	6	2744	113	4	2.47
1989-90	Montreal	54	31	16	5	3173	134	3	2.53
1990-91	Montreal	48	25	15	6	2835	128	1	2.71
1991-92	Montreal	67	36	22	8	3935	155	5	2.36
1992-93	Montreal 🏆	62	31	25	5	3595	192	2	3.20
1993-94	Montreal	68	35	17	11	3867	161	7	2.50
1994-95	Montreal	43	17	20	6	2566	127	1	2.97
1995-96	Montreal	22	12	9	1	1260	62	1	2.95
	Colorado 🏆	39	22	15	1	2305	103	1	2.68
1996-97	Colorado	62	38	15	7	3698	143	7	2.32
1997-98	Colorado	65	31	19	13	3835	153	4	2.39
1998-99	Colorado	61	32	19	8	3648	139	5	2.29
NHL Totals:		778	412	243	95	45,404	2014	46	2.66

| | Playoffs | | | | | | | | |
Season	Team	GP	W	L	T	MINS	GA	SO	AVG.
1984-85	Montreal	—	—	—		—	—	—	—
1985-86	Montreal 🏆	20	15	5		1218	39	1	1.92
1986-87	Montreal	6	4	2		330	22	0	4.00
1987-88	Montreal	8	3	4		430	24	0	3.35
1988-89	Montreal	19	13	6		1206	42	2	2.09
1989-90	Montreal	11	5	6		641	26	1	2.43
1990-91	Montreal	13	7	5		785	40	0	3.06
1991-92	Montreal	11	4	7		686	30	1	2.62
1992-93	Montreal 🏆	20	16	4		293	46	0	2.13
1993-94	Montreal	6	3	3		375	16	0	2.56
1994-95	Montreal	—	—	—		—	—	—	—
1995-96	Montreal	—	—	—		—	—	—	—
	Colorado 🏆	22	16	6		1454	51	3	2.10
1996-97	Colorado	17	10	7		1034	38	3	2.21
1997-98	Colorado	7	3	4		430	18	0	2.51
1998-99	Colorado	19	11	8		1173	52	1	2.66
Playoff Totals:		179	110	67		11,055	444	12	2.41

Playing goal in Montreal takes more than talent. The pressure is intense. So, Patrick Roy relieved that pressure with some odd on-ice antics. He would stretch his neck like a bird. Stare at his net. Talk to his goalposts. The fans and the press focused on this funny new goalie's mannerisms. By the time they got around to talking about his play, he was already a Forum folk-hero.

When "Saint Patrick" came along, goaltending equipment was undergoing amazing changes. Light-weight leg pads. Form-fitting body armor. Rounded helmet-mask combinations. Goalies were now perfectly protected.

Roy was always an observant player, and one day he realized that a majority of goals were scored from close to the net. With modern equipment, he reasoned, a goalie could stay low to the ice and not get hurt. So Roy perfected his own style of "butterfly" goaltending that would allow him to cover the bottom of the net. By spreading his legs in an inverted V-shape, he realized he could cover both corners. That freed him up to stop slapshots from the point and flip shots from the slot. Even when being screened, Roy still had a lot of the net covered.

Roy's new style really worked and in his rookie season, he guided the Canadiens to the Stanley Cup championship. He was the first goalie since Ken Dryden to do that. Roy won 15 games in the playoffs that year and captured the Conn Smythe Trophy. During the 1993 playoffs, the Montreal Canadiens won 10 straight overtime games because Roy would tell them: "Just to go out and play. I won't be letting in another goal." They did and he didn't.

Over the course of his remarkable career, Roy has earned five All-Star berths, won three Vezina Trophy awards, and has been the playoff MVP twice. In 1998-99, he became only the fifth goalie to win 400 games.

In 1995-96, Roy was traded to Colorado. Where he played a big role in helping Colorado win their first Stanley Cup.

By spreading his legs in an inverted V, Patrick Roy can drop to the ice to cover both corners of the bottom of the net. This "butterfly" style has made him one of the greatest goalies of all time.

Joe Sakic

Position: **Center**   Height: **5'11" (180 cm)**   Weight: **185 lbs (84 kg)**   Born: **July 7, 1969 in Burnaby, BC.**

Regular Season								Playoffs						
Season	Team	GP	G	A	Pts	PIM	+/-	Season	Team	GP	G	A	Pts	PIM
1988-89	Quebec	70	23	39	62	24	-36	1988-89	Quebec	—	—	—	—	—
1989-90	Quebec	80	39	63	102	27	-40	1989-90	Quebec	—	—	—	—	—
1990-91	Quebec	80	48	61	109	24	-26	1990-91	Quebec	—	—	—	—	—
1991-92	Quebec	69	29	65	94	20	5	1991-92	Quebec	—	—	—	—	—
1992-93	Quebec	78	48	57	105	40	-3	1992-93	Quebec	6	3	3	6	2
1993-94	Quebec	84	28	64	92	18	-8	1993-94	Quebec	—	—	—	—	—
1994-95	Quebec	47	19	43	62	30	7	1994-95	Quebec	6	4	1	5	0
1995-96	Colorado	82	51	69	120	44	14	1995-96	Colorado	22	18	16	34	14
1996-97	Colorado	65	22	52	74	34	-10	1996-97	Colorado	17	8	17	25	14
1997-98	Colorado	64	27	36	63	50	0	1997-98	Colorado	6	2	3	5	6
1998-99	Colorado	73	41	55	96	29	23	1998-99	Colorado	19	6	13	19	8
	NHL Totals:	792	375	604	979	340			Playoff Totals:	76	41	53	94	44

The term "quiet superstar" wasn't invented to describe Joe Sakic, but it could have been. It refers to a player who, despite great personal numbers, goes unnoticed. That is true of Joe Sakic. In Quebec, Sakic was a consistent 100-point scorer. Yet, few fans knew of him. He was also quiet off the ice. A teammate once said, "Joe never uses three words if two will do the trick."

When the club moved to Denver and won the Stanley Cup, the spotlight changed. But Sakic didn't. He still lets his play on the ice speak for him.

Sakic was playing junior hockey in Swift Current, Saskatchewan when, on December 30, 1986, his team bus slipped off a bridge ramp and crashed to the ground. Four of his teammates were killed. From that moment on, Sakic dedicated his career to the memory of his friends. Sakic decided that if he could make an impact in the NHL, their names — Kresse, Kruger, Mantyka, and Ruff — would never be forgotten. When he was selected 15th overall by Quebec in 1987, he knew he could go all the way.

Interestingly, Sakic's reserved personality is reflected in how he plays. Since he's not a big guy, he has to play smart. He has no time for flashy moves or take-a-chance passes. That's not his style. He excels in the face-off circle. He can bob and weave through any defensive scheme. His greatest asset is his deceptive acceleration. He seems to reach top speed with a single thrust. That really helps him find holes in the defense. He can get through them before the defenders have time to react.

In his first six seasons in Quebec, Sakic averaged 36 goals and 95 points a season. However, in 1995-96, he had a breakout year. He set a career-high for goals (51), assists (69), and points (120) and was even better in the playoffs where he led the Avalanche to a surprising Stanley Cup Championship. That year he led all post-season snipers with 18 goals and 34 points. Those totals earned the Colorado captain the Conn Smythe Trophy as playoff MVP. The following season, he led all playoff playmakers with 17 assists, even though the Avalanche never made it to the finals.

Joe Sakic shares a laugh with his Colorado teammates. Usually a quiet guy, Sakic's reserved personality is reflected in the intelligent way he plays the game.

Denis Savard

Position: **Center**   Height: **5'10" (178 cm)**   Weight: **175 lbs (80 kg)**   Born: **February 4, 1961 in Pointe Gatineau, QC.**

Regular Season								Playoffs						
Season	Team	GP	G	A	Pts	PIM	+/-	Season	Team	GP	G	A	Pts	PIM
1980-81	Chicago	76	28	47	75	47	27	1980-81	Chicago	3	0	0	0	0
1981-82	Chicago	80	32	87	119	82	0	1981-82	Chicago	15	11	7	18	52
1982-83	Chicago	78	35	86	121	99	26	1982-83	Chicago	13	8	9	17	22
1983-84	Chicago	75	37	57	94	71	-13	1983-84	Chicago	5	1	3	4	9
1984-85	Chicago	79	38	67	105	56	16	1984-85	Chicago	15	9	20	29	20
1985-86	Chicago	80	47	69	116	111	7	1985-86	Chicago	3	4	1	5	6
1986-87	Chicago	70	40	50	90	108	15	1986-87	Chicago	4	1	0	1	12
1987-88	Chicago	80	44	87	131	95	4	1987-88	Chicago	5	4	3	7	17
1988-89	Chicago	58	23	59	82	110	-5	1988-89	Chicago	16	8	11	19	10
1989-90	Chicago	60	27	53	80	56	8	1989-90	Chicago	20	7	15	22	41
1990-91	Montreal	70	28	31	59	52	-1	1990-91	Montreal	13	2	11	13	35
1991-92	Montreal	77	28	42	70	73	6	1991-92	Montreal	11	3	9	12	8
1992-93	Montreal 🏆	63	16	34	50	90	1	1992-93	Montreal 🏆	14	0	5	5	4
1993-94	Tampa Bay	74	18	28	46	106	-1	1993-94	Tampa Bay	—	—	—	—	—
1994-95	Tampa Bay	31	6	11	17	10	-6	1994-95	Tampa Bay	—	—	—	—	—
	Chicago	12	4	4	8	8	3		Chicago	16	7	11	18	10
1995-96	Chicago	69	13	35	48	102	20	1995-96	Chicago	10	1	2	3	8
1996-97	Chicago	64	9	18	27	60	-10	1996-97	Chicago	6	0	2	2	2
	NHL Totals:	1196	473	865	1338	1336			Playoff Totals:	169	66	109	175	256

Even before he made it to the NHL, Denis Savard was a hockey legend. A member of the powerhouse Montreal Jr. Canadiens, Savard played on one of the greatest forward units in the history of junior hockey. They were known as "les Trois Denis." Not only was each member of the line named Denis, they were all born on the same day and grew up in the same neighborhood!

The Montreal Canadiens had the first selection in the 1980 draft, and every Habs fan expected them to chose Savard. They were wrong. The Habs decided to select a player from western Canada instead of their local hero. Savard ended up in Chicago, where he would go on to delight Blackhawk fans for full decade.

Some scouts had felt that Savard was too small for the NHL. But bigger doesn't always mean better. Savard played hockey with pride and determination.

He knew that he was small, and that in order to play his game — driving to the net, snaking in and out of heavy traffic in the slot — he would have to pay a physical price. Still he went all out, all the time.

Savard was a joy to watch on the ice. He could dip, doodle, deke, and draw — seemingly all at the same time! Nobody could match the moves he made. Savard could skate up ice, slam on the brakes, and idle, waiting for the opposing defender to make a move. Then, in a flash, he would spin past the confused defenseman, step into the slot, and fire a shot on goal or set up a teammate.

During his first decade with the Hawks, Savard never scored fewer than 23 goals in a season. He reached the 100-point plateau four times and played in five All-Star Games.

In June 1990, the Hawks traded Savard to Montreal. Although he was in the late stages of his career, the Habs' fans were delighted to finally have their long-lost hero wearing the bleu, blanc, et rouge.

The move paid dividends for Savard, too. In 1992-93, he fulfilled his dream of winning the

Stanley Cup. The only downside was that he suffered a broken ankle in the finals and couldn't play in the Cup-clinching game. He later suited up for Tampa Bay before returning for an encore tour with Chicago. He retired in 1997.

Most people thought Montreal would draft Denis Savard in 1980, but he wound up with the Blackhawks instead. Denis' dazzling moves delighted fans in Chicago and around the NHL.

Terry Sawchuk

Position: **Goaltender**   Height: **5'11" (180 cm)**   Weight: **195 lbs (89 kg)**   Born: **December 28, 1929 in Winnipeg, MB.**

Regular Season										Playoffs									
Season	Team	GP	W	L	T	MINS	GA	SO	AVG.	Season	Team	GP	W	L	T	MINS	GA	SO	AVG.
1949-50	Detroit	7	4	3	0	420	16	1	2.29	1949-50	Detroit	—	—	—	—	—	—	—	—
1950-51	Detroit	70	44	13	13	4200	139	11	1.99	1950-51	Detroit	6	2	4		463	13	1	1.68
1951-52	Detroit	70	44	14	12	4200	133	12	1.90	1951-52	Detroit	8	8	0		480	5	4	0.63
1952-53	Detroit	63	32	15	16	3780	120	9	1.90	1952-53	Detroit	6	2	4		372	21	1	3.39
1953-54	Detroit	67	35	19	13	4004	129	12	1.93	1953-54	Detroit	12	8	4		751	20	2	1.60
1954-55	Detroit	68	40	17	11	4080	132	12	1.94	1954-55	Detroit	11	8	3		660	26	1	2.36
1955-56	Boston	68	22	33	13	4080	181	9	2.66	1955-56	Boston	—	—	—	—	—	—	—	—
1956-57	Boston	34	18	10	6	2040	81	2	2.38	1956-57	Boston	—	—	—	—	—	—	—	—
1957-58	Detroit	70	29	29	12	4200	207	3	2.96	1957-58	Detroit	4	0	4		252	19	0	4.52
1958-59	Detroit	67	23	36	8	4020	209	5	3.12	1958-59	Detroit	—	—	—	—	—	—	—	—
1959-60	Detroit	58	24	20	14	3480	156	5	2.69	1959-60	Detroit	6	2	4		405	20	0	2.96
1960-61	Detroit	37	12	16	8	2150	113	2	3.17	1960-61	Detroit	8	5	3		465	18	1	2.32
1961-62	Detroit	43	14	21	8	2580	143	5	3.33	1961-62	Detroit	—	—	—	—	—	—	—	—
1962-63	Detroit	48	22	16	7	2775	119	3	2.57	1962-63	Detroit	11	5	6		660	36	0	3.27
1963-64	Detroit	53	25	20	7	3140	138	5	2.64	1963-64	Detroit	13	6	5		677	31	1	2.75
1964-65	Toronto	36	17	13	6	2160	92	1	2.56	1964-65	Toronto	1	0	1		60	3	0	3.00
1965-66	Toronto	27	10	11	3	1521	80	1	3.16	1965-66	Toronto	2	0	2		120	6	0	3.00
1966-67	Toronto	28	15	5	4	1409	66	2	2.81	1966-67	Toronto	10	6	4		565	25	0	2.65
1967-68	Los Angeles	36	11	14	6	1936	99	2	3.07	1967-68	Los Angeles	5	2	3		280	18	1	3.86
1968-69	Detroit	13	3	4	3	641	28	0	2.62	1968-69	Detroit	—	—	—	—	—	—	—	—
1969-70	NY Rangers	8	3	1	2	412	20	1	2.91	1969-70	NY Rangers	3	0	1		80	6	0	4.50
NHL Totals:		971	447	330	172	57228	2401	103	2.52	Playoff Totals:		106	54	48		6290	267	12	2.55

Terry Sawchuk played more games in goal than any man in NHL history. He was the first goalie to win 400 games (300 is a major milestone!), and he is the NHL's all-time shutout leader. With 103 in his career, Sawchuk's shutout record is not likely to be broken.

Terry Sawchuk was the rookie-of-the-year in two different minor leagues before he reached the NHL as a 20-year-old in 1949-50. Harry Lumley was Detroit's regular goalie that year, and he led the Red Wings to the Stanley Cup, but the team was so confident in Sawchuk that they traded Lumley to make Terry their goalie in 1950-51. It proved to be a smart move when Sawchuk won the Calder Trophy that year as NHL rookie-of-the-year. The following year, Sawchuk led Detroit all the way to the Stanley Cup Championship and was awarded the Vezina Trophy as the top goalie. Sawchuk had four shutouts in eight games during the playoffs.

Over the next three years, Detroit won two more Stanley Cup titles, and Sawchuk won the Vezina Trophy two more times. During his first five seasons in the NHL, his yearly goals-against average was never higher than 1.99! Sawchuk was a goaltender with lightning-fast reflexes. He stood bent over in a deep crouch in front of his net, and liked to drop down to his knees to block shots. Today, this low position is called "the butterfly," and lots of goalies use it, but Sawchuk was the first. No other goalie liked to play so low to the ice because back then goalies didn't wear masks!

As great as he was, the Red Wings traded Sawchuk in 1955-56. He played two years for the Boston Bruins before Detroit brought him back in 1957-58. Sawchuk spent seven more seasons in Detroit, then became a member of the Toronto Maple Leafs in 1964-65. That season, he and Johnny Bower starred in goal for Toronto and

shared the Vezina Trophy. In 1967, both goalies helped the Maple Leafs win the Stanley Cup.

When the NHL added six new expansion teams for the 1967-68 season, Terry Sawchuk joined the Los Angeles Kings. He later played for Detroit again and then with the New York Rangers. Sawchuk was killed in an accident after

Terry Sawchuk relaxes in the dressing room after he and his partner Johnny Bower led Toronto to the 1967 Stanley Cup title. Sawchuk had won the Stanley Cup three times with Detroit in the 1950s.

the 1969-70 season, and he was elected to the Hockey Hall of Fame the very next year.

Milt Schmidt

Position: **Center/Defense** Height: **6'0" (183 cm)** Weight: **185 lbs (84 kg)** Born: **March 5, 1918 in Kitchener, ON.**

Regular Season									Playoffs						
Season	Team	GP	G	A	Pts	PIM	+/-		Season	Team	GP	G	A	Pts	PIM
1936-37	Boston	26	2	8	10	15	—		1936-37	Boston	3	0	0	0	0
1937-38	Boston	44	13	14	27	15	—		1937-38	Boston	3	0	0	0	0
1938-39	Boston	41	15	17	32	13	—		1938-39	Boston	12	3	3	6	2
1939-40	Boston	48	22	30	52	37	—		1939-40	Boston	6	0	0	0	0
1940-41	Boston	45	13	25	38	23	—		1940-41	Boston	11	5	6	11	9
1941-42	Boston	36	14	21	35	34	—		1941-42	Boston	—	—	—	—	—
1945-46	Boston	48	13	18	31	21	—		1945-46	Boston	10	3	5	8	2
1946-47	Boston	59	27	35	62	40	—		1946-47	Boston	5	3	1	4	4
1947-48	Boston	33	9	17	26	28	—		1947-48	Boston	5	2	5	7	2
1948-49	Boston	44	10	22	32	25	—		1948-49	Boston	4	0	2	2	8
1949-50	Boston	68	19	22	41	41	—		1949-50	Boston	—	—	—	—	—
1950-51	Boston	62	22	39	61	33	—		1950-51	Boston	6	0	1	1	7
1951-52	Boston	69	21	29	50	57	—		1951-52	Boston	7	2	1	3	0
1952-53	Boston	68	11	23	34	30	—		1952-53	Boston	10	5	1	6	6
1953-54	Boston	62	14	18	32	28	—		1953-54	Boston	4	1	0	1	20
1954-55	Boston	23	4	8	12	26	—		1954-55	Boston	—	—	—	—	—
NHL Totals:		**776**	**229**	**346**	**575**	**466**			**Playoff Totals:**		**86**	**24**	**25**	**49**	**60**

Milt Schmidt was only 18 years old when he began his NHL career with the Boston Bruins in 1936-37. The next year, he became a regular player in the Bruins lineup along with his friends Bobby Bauer and Woody Dumart. All three had grown up together in Kitchener, Ontario, and soon they were the best forward line in the NHL. Because they were all from German families, the combination of Schmidt, Dumart, and Bauer was called the Kraut Line.

Milt Schmidt was a strong skater and a clever stickhandler. He was always dangerous around the net because he was just as good at passing to his wingers as he was at blasting a shot on goal. As tough as he was talented, it proved almost impossible to knock him off the puck.

Schmidt helped the Bruins win the Stanley Cup for the first time in 10 years in 1938-39. The next year, he was the best player in the NHL when he led the league in scoring with 52 points (22 goals, 30 assists) in 48 games. His linemates finished second and third in the scoring race, and all three were selected as All-Stars that year. In 1940-41, Boston won the Stanley Cup again, and Schmidt was one of five Bruins to finish among the NHL's top 10 in scoring.

Schmidt, Dumart, and Bauer continued to star with the Bruins until the 1941-42 season. That year they all left Boston to join the Royal Canadian Air Force. The three players helped the Ottawa RCAF hockey team win the Allan Cup that year as Canada's amateur hockey champions. Then they began their military service in World War II. When the war ended, all three players returned to Boston.

By 1946-47, Schmidt was back on top, finishing fourth in the league with 62 points and was named to the First All-Star Team. In 1950-51 he was named captain of the Bruins and enjoyed another great season. Not only was he a First-Team All-Star that year, he also won the Hart Trophy as the most valuable player in the NHL. Schmidt continued to star for the Bruins until he announced his retirement on Christmas Day in 1954. After his retirement, Schmidt was

hired to be the Bruins head coach. In 1961, Milt Schmidt was elected to the Hockey Hall of Fame.

Milt Schmidt captained the Boston Bruins from 1950 until his retirement on Christmas day in 1954. Note the odd placement of the "C" in the middle of Schmidt's sweater.

Teemu Selanne

Position: **Right Wing**   Height: **6'0" (183 cm)**   Weight: **200 lbs (91 kg)**   Born: **July 3, 1970 in Helsinki, Finland.**

Regular Season									Playoffs						
Season	Team	GP	G	A	Pts	PIM	+/-		Season	Team	GP	G	A	Pts	PIM
1992-93	Winnipeg	84	76	56	132	45	8		1992-93	Winnipeg	6	4	2	6	2
1993-94	Winnipeg	51	25	29	54	22	-23		1993-94	Winnipeg	—	—	—	—	—
1994-95	Winnipeg	45	22	26	48	2	1		1994-95	Winnipeg	—	—	—	—	—
1995-96	Winnipeg	51	24	48	72	18	3		1995-96	Winnipeg	—	—	—	—	—
	Anaheim	28	16	20	36	4	2			Anaheim	—	—	—	—	—
1996-97	Anaheim	78	51	58	109	34	28		1996-97	Anaheim	11	7	3	10	4
1997-98	Anaheim	73	52	34	86	30	12		1997-98	Anaheim	—	—	—	—	—
1998-99	Anaheim	75	47	60	107	30	18		1998-99	Anaheim	4	2	2	4	2
	NHL Totals:	485	313	331	644	195			Playoff Totals:	21	13	7	20	8

In the 1988 Entry Draft, the Winnipeg Jets selected a little-known Finnish kid named Teemu Selanne with their first pick. Still, Selanne was not tempted to leave Finland to play in the NHL until he thought he was ready. He spent five full seasons playing in the Jokerit Helsinki system, and as he moved from junior to the elite level, he refined his game. In 1992-93, Selanne finally felt ready for the NHL.

No player ever had a rookie season like the one Teemu Selanne had in 1992-93. "The Finnish Flash" broke a ton of freshman records, including most goals (76), points (132), and power-play goals (24). All of Selanne's extra work and patience had paid off. Selanne was a unanimous winner of the Calder Trophy as the league's top newcomer. He also earned a spot on the NHL's First All-Star Team.

Selanne's greatest asset is speed. When the Flash shifts into top gear, no one can catch him. He plays a complete game. He has an assortment of dekes and dips that keep defenders guessing. And he's an expert at the art of the "touch" pass. Selanne's delicate feeds always seem to hit their mark, and he has a variety of other weapons, from a booming slapshot to a deadly wrister.

In his sophomore campaign, Selanne suffered a torn Achilles tendon, which is one of the worst hockey injuries you can get because it takes so long to heal. Selanne tried to come back too soon, and he never seemed able to regain his form. As he struggled to find his scoring touch, he lost his confidence and soon was traded to Anaheim.

When Selanne arrived in California, he was paired with Paul Kariya, the Ducks' slick playmaker. They proved to be a perfect fit. The Finnish Flash scored 50 goals in each of his first two full seasons in Anaheim. All of Selanne's clever moves and creative plays have returned and his 47 goals in 1998-99 were the most in the NHL. With Selanne on board, the Ducks should be mighty for years to come.

It's almost impossible to catch "The Finnish Flash" when he's skating at top speed. Teemu Selanne is also great with the puck, stickhandling around opponents to get into position for a shot or a pass.

Eddie Shore

Position: **Defense**   Height: **5'11" (180 cm)**   Weight: **190 lbs (86 kg)**   Born: **November 25, 1902 in Fort Qu'Appelle, SK.**

Regular Season								Playoffs					
Season	Team	GP	G	A	Pts	PIM	+/-	Season	Team	GP	G	A	Pts	PIM
1926-27	Boston	40	12	6	18	130		1926-27	Boston	8	1	1	2	40
1927-28	Boston	43	11	6	17	165		1927-28	Boston	2	0	0	0	8
1928-29	Boston	39	12	7	19	96		1928-29	Boston	5	1	1	2	28
1929-30	Boston	42	12	19	31	105		1929-30	Boston	6	1	0	1	26
1930-31	Boston	44	15	16	31	105		1930-31	Boston	5	2	1	3	24
1931-32	Boston	45	9	13	22	80		1931-32	Boston	—	—	—	—	—
1932-33	Boston	48	8	27	35	102		1932-33	Boston	5	0	1	1	14
1933-34	Boston	30	2	10	12	57		1933-34	Boston	—	—	—	—	—
1934-35	Boston	48	7	26	33	32		1934-35	Boston	4	0	1	1	2
1935-36	Boston	45	3	16	19	61		1935-36	Boston	2	1	1	2	12
1936-37	Boston	20	3	1	4	12		1936-37	Boston	—	—	—	—	—
1937-38	Boston	48	3	14	17	42		1937-38	Boston	3	0	1	1	6
1938-39	Boston	44	4	14	18	47		1938-39	Boston	12	0	4	4	19
1939-40	Boston	4	2	1	3	4		1939-40	Boston	—	—	—	—	—
	NY Americans	10	2	3	5	9			NY Americans	3	0	2	2	2
NHL Totals:		**550**	**105**	**179**	**284**	**1047**		**Playoff Totals:**		**55**	**6**	**13**	**19**	**181**

Eddie Shore was born in Fort Qu'Appelle, Saskatchewan. He played his early hockey in Western Canada before coming to Boston in 1926-27. The Bruins were only in their third NHL season and were not a very good team. Other players helped, but it was Shore more than anybody that turned Boston into a top team. He led the Bruins to their first Stanley Cup championship in 1928-29. Ten years later, he was still a star when Boston won the Stanley Cup again. In the years in between, Shore had led Boston to first place in the NHL's American Division eight times.

When the NHL began naming an annual All-Star Team in 1930-31, Shore was picked for the team eight times in the first nine years. Seven of those selections were to the First Team. The only time Shore wasn't picked during those years was in 1936-37 when he missed most of that season with a broken bone in his back. Shore recovered before the next season and returned to hockey as good as ever. To prove it, he won the Hart Trophy as the NHL's most valuable player. It was the fourth time in his career that he had earned that honor. No other defenseman in NHL history has won the Hart Trophy more than three times.

Shore skated with long strides that moved him with blazing speed. Even though he was a defenseman, he was one of the best puck carriers in the NHL. This was still a very rare combination in the NHL during the 1920s and '30s. Shore's playing style resulted in lots of points — and even more penalty minutes. Before he retired in 1940, he had outscored every defenseman in the NHL. But during his career, only Red Horner of the Toronto Maple Leafs got more penalties.

As good as he was, Eddie Shore is often remembered for an awful play. On December 12, 1933 he knocked down Ace Bailey when the Toronto player wasn't looking. Bailey fell on his head and broke his skull, which ended his career. Many people were mad at Shore, but Ace Bailey forgave him and even shook his hand. In 1947, Shore was elected to the Hockey Hall of Fame.

The Bruins were a struggling new franchise when Eddie Shore arrived in Boston in 1926. Three years later, they were Stanley Cup champions. Shore's tough play was what got them there.

Darryl Sittler

Position: **Center**   Height: **6'0" (183 cm)**   Weight: **190 lbs (86 kg)**   Born: **September 18, 1950 in Kitchener, ON.**

Regular Season								Playoffs						
Season	Team	GP	G	A	Pts	PIM	+/-	Season	Team	GP	G	A	Pts	PIM
1970-71	Toronto	49	10	8	18	37	3	1970-71	Toronto	6	2	1	3	31
1971-72	Toronto	74	15	17	32	44	-4	1971-72	Toronto	3	0	0	0	2
1972-73	Toronto	78	29	48	77	69	-11	1972-73	Toronto	—	—	—	—	—
1973-74	Toronto	78	38	46	84	55	12	1973-74	Toronto	4	2	1	3	6
1974-75	Toronto	72	36	44	80	47	-10	1974-75	Toronto	7	2	1	3	15
1975-76	Toronto	79	41	59	100	90	12	1975-76	Toronto	10	5	7	12	19
1976-77	Toronto	73	38	52	90	89	8	1976-77	Toronto	9	5	16	21	4
1977-78	Toronto	80	45	72	117	100	34	1977-78	Toronto	13	3	8	11	12
1978-79	Toronto	70	36	51	87	69	9	1978-79	Toronto	6	5	4	9	17
1979-80	Toronto	73	40	57	97	62	3	1979-80	Toronto	3	1	2	3	10
1980-81	Toronto	80	43	53	96	77	-8	1980-81	Toronto	3	0	0	0	4
1981-82	Toronto	38	18	20	38	24	-14	1981-82	Toronto	—	—	—	—	—
	Philadelphia	35	14	18	32	50	-1		Philadelphia	4	3	1	4	6
1982-83	Philadelphia	80	43	40	83	60	17	1982-83	Philadelphia	3	1	0	1	4
1983-84	Philadelphia	76	27	36	63	38	13	1983-84	Philadelphia	3	0	2	2	7
1984-85	Detroit	61	11	16	27	37	-10	1984-85	Detroit	2	0	2	2	0
	NHL Totals:	1096	484	637	1121	948			Playoff Totals:	76	29	45	74	137

For over a decade, Darryl Sittler was the emotional and offensive leader of the Toronto Maple Leafs. To this day, he remains the franchise's all-time leader in goals (389) and points (916).

Even when he was still learning the NHL ropes, Sittler had the poise of a veteran. By his third season he was one of the game's top young talents. In 1975-76, he became the first Maple Leaf player to hit the 100-point mark.

The year of 1976 was a very special one for Darryl Sittler. From February 7 to September 15, he had three unforgettable nights.

On February 7, the Leafs were facing the Boston Bruins, who were using a rookie goalie named Dave Reece. As it turns out, Reece had the best seat in the house for the most remarkable single-game performance in NHL history. The Leafs' captain scored six goals and assisted on four others as the Leafs pounded the Bruins 11-4. Sittler scored a hat-trick in both the second and third period, a feat that has never been duplicated. Even the magnificent Mario and the great Gretzky couldn't equal Sittler's 10-point masterpiece.

On April 22, 1976, Sittler added another milestone to his growing record book. Facing elimination at the hands of the Philadelphia Flyers, Sittler single-handedly kept the Leafs' hopes alive by blasting five pucks behind Bernie Parent in an 8-5 win. Only three other players have ever done that!

Those performances helped earn him a berth on Team Canada in the first Canada Cup Tournament, which was held prior to the 1976-77 season. In the series' final game on September 15, 1976, Sittler won the game with an overtime goal that still ranks as one of the highlight moments in hockey history.

Sittler went on to record 10 seasons of 30 or more goals, all but two of them wearing a Leafs uniform. In August 1991, after almost a decade away from the team, Sittler returned to the Leafs to work as a special consultant. He was elected to the Hockey Hall of Fame in 1989.

TORONTO MAPLE LEAFS

Darryl Sittler's best years in Toronto were spent with Lanny McDonald on his right wing. Here, they battle for the puck with Phil Esposito (77) of the New York Rangers. Sittler's total of 10 points in one game is an NHL record that could last for a long time.

Peter Stastny

Position: **Center**   Height: **6'1" (185 cm)**   Weight: **200 lbs (91 kg)**   Born: **September 18, 1956 in Bratislava, Czechoslovakia.**

| | Regular Season | | | | | | | | | Playoffs | | | | |
Season	Team	GP	G	A	Pts	PIM	+/-	Season	Team	GP	G	A	Pts	PIM
1980-81	Quebec	77	39	70	109	37	11	1980-81	Quebec	5	2	8	10	7
1981-82	Quebec	80	46	93	139	91	-10	1981-82	Quebec	12	7	11	18	10
1982-83	Quebec	75	47	77	124	78	28	1982-83	Quebec	4	3	2	5	10
1983-84	Quebec	80	46	73	119	73	22	1983-84	Quebec	9	2	7	9	31
1984-85	Quebec	75	32	68	100	95	23	1984-85	Quebec	18	4	19	23	24
1985-86	Quebec	76	41	81	122	60	2	1985-86	Quebec	3	0	1	1	2
1986-87	Quebec	64	24	53	77	43	-21	1986-87	Quebec	13	6	9	15	12
1987-88	Quebec	76	46	65	111	69	2	1987-88	Quebec	—	—	—	—	—
1988-89	Quebec	72	35	50	85	117	-23	1988-89	Quebec	—	—	—	—	—
1989-90	Quebec	62	24	38	62	24	-45	1989-90	Quebec	—	—	—	—	—
	New Jersey	12	5	6	11	16	-1		New Jersey	6	3	2	5	2
1990-91	New Jersey	77	18	42	60	53	0	1990-91	New Jersey	7	3	4	7	2
1991-92	New Jersey	66	24	38	62	42	6	1991-92	New Jersey	7	3	7	10	19
1992-93	New Jersey	62	17	23	40	22	-5	1992-93	New Jersey	5	0	2	2	2
1993-94	St. Louis	17	5	11	16	4	-2	1993-94	St. Louis	4	0	0	0	2
1994-95	St. Louis	6	1	1	2	0	1	1994-95	St. Louis	—	—	—	—	—
	NHL Totals:	977	450	789	1239	824			Playoff Totals:	93	33	72	105	123

The very fact that Peter Stastny was able to play in the NHL is the stuff of legend. The details of his flight from communist Czechoslovakia read like the plot of a spy novel. In 1980, defection often meant death. If Stastny had been caught while leaving Czechoslovakia, he would have been shot. No questions asked.

Luckily for the Quebec Nordiques and hockey fans everywhere, Stastny, his family, and his brother Anton arrived safely in Canada. When the Quebec Nordiques began planning to get Stastny out of Europe, they knew they were getting a top talent. What they got was a superstar. Stastny's skill and ability would change the face of the NHL forever.

Peter Stastny took the NHL by storm in 1980-81 and set a rookie record with 109 points. Stastny had at least 100 points in seven of his first eight seasons.

When Stastny joined the Nords, he had already played six years with Slovan Bratislava, an elite Czech club. So when Stastny showed up in training camp in 1980 he was already a seasoned pro. It was Stastny's ability to adapt his style to the NHL game that opened the door for the hundreds of European players who have followed him.

Like many European-trained players, Stastny was an excellent skater and precise passer. In his first nine years in the NHL, he averaged 70 assists a season. Only Wayne Gretzky had more points than Stastny during the 1980s.

An era in Quebec came to a close in March 1990 when Stastny was traded to New Jersey. He put in three steady, though not spectacular, seasons with the Devils before returning to Europe.

After a brilliant performance in the 1994 Winter Olympics for Slovakia, the St. Louis Blues signed him for the rest of the 1993-94 season. He managed 16 points in 17 games, but he found his legs and his desire to win were gone. When he retired, he was the all-time leading scorer among European players. He was inducted into the Hall of Fame with his Nordique teammate Michel Goulet in 1998.

Only Wayne Gretzky had more points than Peter Stastny during the 1980s. Peter and his brother Anton were joined by a third Stastny, Marian, during their second season with the Quebec Nordiques.

Nels Stewart

Position: **Center**　　Height: **6'1" (185 cm)**　　Weight: **195 lbs (89 kg)**　　Born: **December 29, 1902 in Montreal, QC.**

Regular Season								Playoffs						
Season	Team	GP	G	A	Pts	PIM	+/-	Season	Team	GP	G	A	Pts	PIM
1925-26	Mtl. Maroons 🏆	36	34	8	42	119	—	1925-26	Mtl. Maroons 🏆	8	6	3	9	24
1926-27	Mtl. Maroons	43	17	4	21	133	—	1926-27	Mtl. Maroons	2	0	0	0	4
1927-28	Mtl. Maroons	41	27	7	34	104	—	1927-28	Mtl. Maroons	9	2	2	4	13
1928-29	Mtl. Maroons	44	21	8	29	74	—	1928-29	Mtl. Maroons	—	—	—	—	—
1929-30	Mtl. Maroons	44	39	16	55	81	—	1929-30	Mtl. Maroons	4	1	1	2	2
1930-31	Mtl. Maroons	42	25	14	39	75	—	1930-31	Mtl. Maroons	2	1	0	1	6
1931-32	Mtl. Maroons	38	22	11	33	61	—	1931-32	Mtl. Maroons	4	0	1	1	2
1932-33	Boston	47	18	18	36	62	—	1932-33	Boston	5	2	0	2	4
1933-34	Boston	48	22	17	39	68	—	1933-34	Boston	—	—	—	—	—
1934-35	Boston	47	21	18	39	45	—	1934-35	Boston	4	0	1	1	0
1935-36	NY Americans	48	14	15	29	16	—	1935-36	NY Americans	5	1	2	3	4
1936-37	Boston	11	3	2	5	6	—	1936-37	Boston	—	—	—	—	—
	NY Americans	32	20	10	30	31	—		NY Americans	—	—	—	—	—
1937-38	NY Americans	48	19	17	36	29	—	1937-38	NY Americans	6	2	3	5	2
1938-39	NY Americans	46	16	19	35	43	—	1938-39	NY Americans	2	0	0	0	0
1939-40	NY Americans	35	6	7	13	6	—	1939-40	NY Americans	3	0	0	0	0
NHL Totals:		650	324	191	515	953		**Playoff Totals:**		54	15	13	28	61

Nels Stewart was a big man at a time when most hockey players were much smaller than they are today. He stood 6'1" (185 cm) and weighed 195 pounds (89 kg), and was not a very graceful skater. However, Stewart was very dangerous when he got the puck on his stick. People called him "Old Poison" because his shot was so deadly accurate. For many years he ranked as the NHL's all-time scoring leader.

Nels Stewart was born in Montreal, but he grew up in Toronto where he played junior hockey. In 1920, he joined the Cleveland Indians hockey team in the United States Amateur Hockey Association. Stewart played five seasons in the USAHA and led the league in scoring four times. During his years with Cleveland, he scored 100 goals in 102 games.

Stewart began his NHL career as a member of the Montreal Maroons in 1925-26. The Maroons had joined the NHL as an expansion team in 1924-25. They had been terrible that year, going 9-19-2 during the 30-game season. After Stewart was added, the team improved dramatically. The Maroons finished second in the NHL with a record of 20-11-5. They went on to win the Stanley Cup. Nels Stewart was the main reason for the Maroons' success. He led the NHL with 34 goals in 36 games winning the point scoring title. Stewart also won the Hart Trophy as the NHL's most valuable player. In the play-offs, he scored both goals in the Maroons' 2-0 victory that clinched the Stanley Cup. In 1929-30, the Maroons teamed Nels Stewart with Babe Siebert and Hooley Smith. The combination became known as the S-Line. Stewart responded with a career-high 39 goals in 44 games and won the Hart Trophy for the second time.

The S-Line remained one of the best in hockey until Stewart was sold to the Boston Bruins in 1932-33. Stewart was later traded to the New York Americans where, in 1936-37, he once again led the NHL in scoring. That year he also broke Howie Morenz' career record of 270 goals. By the time he retired in 1939-40, Stewart had scored 324 goals. His total would

remain the most in NHL history until Rocket Richard scored his 325th goal in 1952. In 1962, Nels Stewart was elected to the Hockey Hall of Fame.

It wasn't his skating skill that made Nels Stewart a star. It was his ability to shoot the puck. Stewart was known as "Old Poison" because of the effect his accurate shot had on opposing goaltenders.

Mats Sundin

Position: Center/Right Wing   **Height:** 6'4" (193 cm)   **Weight:** 215 lbs (98 kg)   **Born:** February 13, 1971 in Bromma, Sweden.

Regular Season								Playoffs						
Season	Team	GP	G	A	Pts	PIM	+/-	Season	Team	GP	G	A	Pts	PIM
1990-91	Quebec	80	23	36	59	58	-24	1990-91	Quebec	—	—	—	—	—
1991-92	Quebec	80	33	43	76	103	-19	1991-92	Quebec	—	—	—	—	—
1992-93	Quebec	80	47	67	114	96	21	1992-93	Quebec	6	3	1	4	6
1993-94	Quebec	84	32	53	85	60	1	1993-94	Quebec	—	—	—	—	—
1994-95	Toronto	47	23	24	47	14	-5	1994-95	Toronto	7	5	4	9	4
1995-96	Toronto	76	33	50	83	46	8	1995-96	Toronto	6	3	1	4	4
1996-97	Toronto	82	41	53	94	59	6	1996-97	Toronto	—	—	—	—	—
1997-98	Toronto	82	33	41	74	49	-3	1997-98	Toronto	—	—	—	—	—
1998-99	Toronto	82	31	52	83	58	22	1998-99	Toronto	17	8	8	16	16
NHL Totals:		693	296	419	715	543		**Playoff Totals:**		36	19	14	33	30

In 1989, Mats Sundin was the first European to be selected first overall in the NHL Entry Draft. Sundin played one more year in his native Sweden before joining the Quebec Nordiques for the 1990–91 NHL season. His 23 goals that year ranked him among the league's rookie scoring leaders. He upped his total to 33 goals in his second season and added 43 assists. Sundin topped the 100-point plateau in 1992–93, scoring 47 goals and collecting 67 assists. But after the 1993-94 season, the Nordiques decided they had too many finesse players. They needed some grit, so they swapped Sundin to the Maple Leafs for Wendel Clark.

Sundin knew he was coming into a pressure-packed situation in Toronto. He was expected to replace a player who was a Maple Leafs legend. The big Swede proved to be a joy to watch on the ice, and he won over both teammates and fans with his brilliant playmaking. He's an elegant skater who can easily weave through traffic. Sundin's daring cuts to the net with his long legs extended to ward off checkers always bring the fans to their feet. But it's his backhand shot that sets Mats Sundin apart from other players.

Backhanders are the hardest shot for a goalie to stop, but scoring with a backhand shot has become a lost art in the NHL. Players today all use curved sticks. That makes it tough to get the puck up on the backhand. Sundin uses a straight blade and has exceptionally strong wrists. He can snap the puck upstairs on the backhand with ease. It's a weapon he has used to score some of his prettiest goals.

Sundin has led the Leafs in scoring every season since he arrived in Toronto. He has great vision, which means he can see the whole ice surface. That helps him decide where to go with the puck and where to pass it. He rarely makes a bad pass or a poor decision. He's also an excellent face-off man and a key penalty killer.

In 1997, Sundin became the first European to be named captain of the Maple Leafs, a great honor. Even former Leafs great and fellow Swede Borje Salming did not get that honor. Now that he's got his "C," Sundin hopes he can bring Leaf fans the other big "C": the Stanley Cup. Toronto's surprising success in 1998–99 is certainly a step in the right direction.

Mats Sundin uses his size and strength to advantage, warding off checkers with his long legs and snapping his strong wrists to lift backhand shots into the top of the net.

Cyclone Taylor

Position: **Rover**   Height: **5'8" (173 cm)**   Weight: **165 lbs (75 kg)**   Born: **June 24, 1883 in Tara, ON.**

Season	Club	League	GP	G	A	Pts	PIM	GP	G	A	Pts	PIM
1905-06	Portage Lakes	MHL Sr.	4	4	0	4	—	—	—	—	—	—
	Portage Lakes	IHL	6	11	0	11	4	—	—	—	—	—
1906-07	Portage Lakes	IHL	23	18	7	25	31	—	—	—	—	—
1907-08	Ottawa Senators	ECAHA	10	9	0	9	—	—	—	—	—	—
1908-09	Pittsburgh	WPHL	3	0	0	0	0	—	—	—	—	—
	Ottawa Senators 🏆	ECHA	11	9	0	9	28	—	—	—	—	—
1909-10	Renfrew Millionaires	CHA	1	1	0	1	5	—	—	—	—	—
	Renfrew Millionaires	NHA	12	9	0	9	14	—	—	—	—	—
1910-11	Renfrew Millionaires	NHA	16	12	0	12	21	—	—	—	—	—
1912-13	Vancouver Millionaires	PCHA	14	10	8	18	5	—	—	—	—	—
1913-14	Vancouver Millionaires	PCHA	16	24	15	39	18	—	—	—	—	—
1914-15	Vancouver Millionaires 🏆	PCHA	16	23	22	45	9	7	3	10	3	—
1915-16	Vancouver Millionaires	PCHA	18	22	13	35	9	—	—	—	—	—
1916-17	Vancouver Millionaires	PCHA	11	14	15	29	12	—	—	—	—	—
1917-18	Vancouver Millionaires	PCHA	18	32	11	43	0	9	2	11	15	—
1918-19	Vancouver Millionaires	PCHA	20	23	13	36	12	1	0	1	0	—
1919-20	Vancouver Millionaires	PCHA	10	6	6	12	0	0	0	0	0	—
1920-21	Vancouver Millionaires	PCHA	6	5	1	6	0	0	1	1	0	—
1922-23	Vancouver Millionaires	PCHA	1	0	0	0	0	—	—	—	—	—
	Career Totals:		216	232	111	343	168	17	6	23	18	—

Cyclone Taylor earned his nickname because of his blazing speed and furious rushes. He learned to play hockey as a boy in Listowel, Ontario, and became hockey's first superstar after he joined the Ottawa Senators in 1908-09. Taylor had usually played forward, but the Senators moved him to a position called cover point. (Defensemen used to be called point and cover point in the early days of hockey.) Cyclone was so fast that he could lead Ottawa's forwards up the ice and still speed back in time to help out in his own end. He led the Senators to the Stanley Cup in 1909. Then a new league called the National Hockey Association was formed for the 1909-10 season.

Even though he was a superstar in Ottawa,  Cyclone Taylor left the Senators to sign with the NHA team in nearby Renfrew. His decision made the NHA the top league in hockey. Renfrew paid Taylor $5,250 for the season, which was the highest salary in hockey history. Soon fans began calling his new team the Renfrew Millionaires. Taylor played two seasons in Renfrew, before he joined an even newer hockey league.

The Pacific Coast Hockey Association had been formed in 1911. It was organized by Frank and Lester Patrick. The two brothers had been teammates of Taylor's during his first year in Renfrew. In 1912, he joined Frank Patrick's hockey team, the Vancouver Millionaires. In 1914, PCHA teams began to play NHA teams for the hockey championship, and one year later, Cyclone Taylor led Vancouver to the Stanley Cup.

In 1917-18 the NHA became the NHL. Taylor was happy where he was and he decided to stay. He played in Vancouver until he was 40 years old and finally retired in 1922-23. Taylor returned to the position of forward again while playing for Vancouver. In 10 years in the PCHA, he led the league in scoring five times. Cyclone Taylor was elected to the Hockey Hall of Fame in 1947.

Cyclone Taylor was almost as fast skating backward as he was skating forward. Old-timers claimed to have seen Taylor score a goal by deking around the whole other team while skating backwards!

Vladislav Tretiak

Position: **Goaltender**   Height: **6'1" (185 cm)**   Weight: **177 lbs (80 kg)**   Born: **April 25, 1952 in Dmitrovo, USSR.**

Year	Team	Event	GP	Mins	GA	Avg
1970	Soviet Union	World Championships	6	215	4	1.12
1971	Soviet Union	World Championships	5	241	6	1.49
1972	Soviet Union	Olympics	4	240	10	2.50
1972	Soviet Union	World Championships	8	430	15	2.09
1972	Soviet Union	Summit Series	8	480	31	3.88
1973	Soviet Union	World Championships	7	420	14	2.00
1974	Soviet Union	World Championships	8	440	12	1.64
1975	Soviet Union	World Championships	8	449	18	2.40
1976	Soviet Union	Canada Cup	5	300	14	2.80
1976	Soviet Union	Olympics	4	240	10	2.50
1976	Soviet Union	World Championships	10	577	19	1.97
1977	Soviet Union	World Championships	9	482	17	2.11
1978	Soviet Union	World Championships	8	480	21	3.01
1979	Soviet Union	World Championships	7	407	12	1.77
1980	Soviet Union	Olympics	5	220	9	2.45
1981	Soviet Union	Canada Cup	6	360	8	1.33
1981	Soviet Union	World Championships	7	420	13	1.86
1982	Soviet Union	World Championships	8	464	19	2.45
1983	Soviet Union	World Championships	7	420	4	0.57
1984	Soviet Union	Olympics	6	360	4	0.67
1969 - 1984	CSKA Moscow	Soviet Union League	482	28920	1158	2.40
	Career Totals:		618	36565	1418	2.33

Vladislav Tretiak is the greatest goaltender in the history of Russian hockey. He played at a time when Russia was part of the Soviet Union, so he was never allowed to join an NHL team. Still, Tretiak is considered one of the best goalies in hockey history.

Though he never did play in the NHL, Tretiak did play against NHL stars in several tournaments. The first one was in 1972 when the Soviet national team played a team made up Canadian All-Stars. Many people thought Canada would win all eight games, but Tretiak and his teammates were too good. It took until the last minute of the last game for Canada to finally clinch the series. Tretiak was a big man with fast reflexes who could cover all of the net, but what made him so good was his mental toughness. He could always think his way out of trouble and was able to play his best when the game mattered the most. He always gave his teammates the feeling that he could stop every shot.

Tretiak started to play hockey when he was 11 years old. By the time he was 15, he was already good enough to practice with Moscow's Central Red Army hockey team — the best team in all of Russia. He became a team member in 1968-69 at only 17. Tretiak was the Red Army's starting goaltender by the very next year. In 16 seasons, he helped the Red Army win 13 Soviet League championships! For 14 straight seasons, from 1970-71 to 1983-84, he was selected as the goaltender on the First All-Star Team. Tretiak won the Golden Stick Award as the best player in Europe for three years in a row from 1981 to 1983.

Tretiak became a member of the Soviet national team in 1970 and played in every major event with the team until 1984. He played at the Olympics four times and helped the Soviets win the gold medal in 1972, 1976, and 1984. He earned a silver medal in 1980 when the United States beat the Soviet Union in one of the great-

est upsets in hockey history. Tretiak also played at the World Championships 13 times and helped the Soviets take the world title on 10 occasions. In 1989, Tretiak became the first Russian player to be elected to the Hockey Hall of Fame.

Team Canada had been told that the Soviets were weak in goal before the famous Summit Series in 1972. Vladislav Tretiak proved the scouts wrong and kept on proving it for years to come.

Bryan Trottier

Position: **Center**   Height: **5'11" (180 cm)**   Weight: **195 lbs (89 kg)**   Born: **July 17, 1956 in Val Marie, SK.**

Regular Season								Playoffs						
Season	Team	GP	G	A	Pts	PIM	+/-	Season	Team	GP	G	A	Pts	PIM
1975-76	NY Islanders	80	32	63	95	21	28	1975-76	NY Islanders	13	1	7	8	8
1976-77	NY Islanders	76	30	42	72	34	28	1976-77	NY Islanders	12	2	8	10	2
1977-78	NY Islanders	77	46	77	123	46	52	1977-78	NY Islanders	7	0	3	3	4
1978-79	NY Islanders	76	47	87	134	50	76	1978-79	NY Islanders	10	2	4	6	13
1979-80	NY Islanders	78	42	62	104	68	31	1979-80	NY Islanders	21	12	17	29	16
1980-81	NY Islanders	73	31	72	103	74	49	1980-81	NY Islanders	18	11	18	29	34
1981-82	NY Islanders	80	50	79	129	88	70	1981-82	NY Islanders	19	6	23	29	40
1982-83	NY Islanders	80	34	55	89	68	37	1982-83	NY Islanders	17	8	12	20	18
1983-84	NY Islanders	68	40	71	111	59	70	1983-84	NY Islanders	21	8	6	14	49
1984-85	NY Islanders	68	28	31	59	47	5	1984-85	NY Islanders	10	4	2	6	8
1985-86	NY Islanders	78	37	59	96	72	29	1985-86	NY Islanders	3	1	1	2	2
1986-87	NY Islanders	80	23	64	87	50	3	1986-87	NY Islanders	14	8	5	13	12
1987-88	NY Islanders	77	30	52	82	48	10	1987-88	NY Islanders	6	0	0	0	10
1988-89	NY Islanders	73	17	28	45	44	-7	1988-89	NY Islanders	—				
1989-90	NY Islanders	59	13	11	24	29	-11	1989-90	NY Islanders	4	1	0	1	4
1990-91	Pittsburgh	52	9	19	28	24	5	1990-91	Pittsburgh	23	3	4	7	49
1991-92	Pittsburgh	63	11	18	29	54	-11	1991-92	Pittsburgh	21	4	3	7	8
1993-94	Pittsburgh	41	4	11	15	36	-12	1993-94	Pittsburgh	2	0	0	0	0
NHL Totals:		**1279**	**524**	**901**	**1425**	**912**		**Playoff Totals:**		**221**	**71**	**113**	**184**	**277**

While there's no doubt that Bryan Trottier was a skilled athlete, it seems that he was driven to succeed by a power that could not be measured. It was his dedication to hard work that allowed Trottier to excel in the NHL. One newspaper reporter put it best when he wrote, "Bryan Trottier looks like an angel and plays like the Devil."

Although he wasn't big or particularly quick, Trottier was smart. He loved to battle in the corners and never gave up a loose puck without a fight. "Trotts" was the emotional leader and playmaking quarterback of the four-time Stanley Cup champion New York Islanders.

Every NHL team had passed on Trottier in the 1974 draft, but the Islanders saw his great potential. He rewarded them by winning the NHL's top rookie award in 1975-76. His 95 points (32 goals, 63 assists) set a new record for a first-year player at the time. Trottier reached the 50-assist mark 11 times in his first 13 seasons. In his third year, he led the NHL with 77 assists and topped 100 points (123) for the first of six times. In 1978-79, Trottier had 87 assists and led the league with 134 points. He not only won the scoring title that year, he also captured the Hart Trophy as league MVP. In 1979-80, Trottier led all playoff performers with 12 goals and 29 points and earned the Conn Smythe Trophy when the Islanders won the Stanley Cup for the first time. Despite playing center in the same era as Gretzky, Lemieux, and Dionne, Trottier still managed to earn four All-Star Team berths. When the Islanders decided not to re-sign him in 1990, he joined the Pittsburgh Penguins.

When he retired after the 1993-94 season, Trottier stood sixth on the all-time NHL points ladder with 524 goals and 901 assists. He was elected to the Hockey Hall of Fame in 1997.

Bryan Trottier had two careers in one. With the Islanders, he was one of the highest-scoring players in the NHL. In Pittsburgh he was a defensive specialist.

Valeri Vasiliev

Position: **Defense**   Height: **6'0" (183 cm)**   Weight: **190 lbs (86 kg)**   Born: **August 3, 1949 in Bor, USSR.**

Year	Team	Event/League	GP	G	A	Pts	PIM
1970	Soviet Union	World Championships	6	0	0	0	2
1972	Soviet Union	Summit Series	6	1	2	3	6
1972	Soviet Union	Olympics	2	0	0	0	2
1972	Soviet Union	World Championships	9	2	2	4	2
1973	Soviet Union	World Championships	10	0	7	7	6
1974	Soviet Union	World Championships	10	0	6	6	16
1974	Soviet Union	Summit Series	8	3	1	4	4
1975	Soviet Union	World Championships	10	2	4	6	0
1976	Soviet Union	Canada Cup	5	0	3	3	6
1976	Soviet Union	Olympics	6	1	2	3	4
1976	Soviet Union	World Championships	10	5	2	7	8
1977	Soviet Union	World Championships	10	1	2	3	8
1978	Soviet Union	World Championships	10	3	3	6	6
1979	Soviet Union	World Championships	8	1	3	4	0
1980	Soviet Union	Olympics	7	2	1	3	2
1981	Soviet Union	Canada Cup	6	0	1	1	4
1981	Soviet Union	World Championships	8	0	0	0	2
1982	Soviet Union	World Championships	10	1	2	3	0
1967 - 1984	Dynamo Moscow	Soviet Union League	619	71	—	—	—
	Career Totals:		760	93	—	—	—

Valeri Vasiliev was a Russian player who was similar in style to NHL legend Tim Horton. Like Horton, Vasiliev was a defenseman who had the ability to handle the puck and score goals, but he was much happier when he was stopping other players from scoring. Vasiliev loved the physical part of the game. He was probably the toughest player in the history of Soviet hockey.

Valeri Vasiliev was a member of the Soviet national team from 1970 to 1982 and was a captain of the team for part of that time. He won Olympic gold medals in 1972 and 1976, and a silver in 1980. Vasiliev played at the World Championships on 11 occasions and helped the Soviets win the title nine times. He was named the Best Defenseman at the tournament in 1973, 1977, and 1979. Five times he was chosen to the World Championship All-Star team. Most stars of the Soviet national team played with the Central Red Army in the Soviet

league, but Vasiliev played with Dynamo Moscow. His team never won a league title, but he led them to six second-place finishes and seven third-place seasons between 1967 and 1984.

Vasiliev was a member of the Soviet squad for the historic 1972 series against Team Canada and also at the first Canada Cup tournament in 1976. Because he was such a physical player, Valeri Vasiliev loved to play against NHL competition. During the 1978-79 hockey season, Vasiliev took part in a mid-season tournament that replaced the NHL All-Star Game. The 1979 Challenge Cup pitted the Soviet Union against the NHL All-Star Team. Facing such talented players as Guy Lafleur, Mike Bossy, and Darryl Sittler, the Soviets won the best-of-three series two games to one.

In 1981, Vasiliev was a member of the Soviet Team that won the second Canada Cup tournament. His solid defensive play helped

shut down stars like Wayne Gretzky and Marcel Dionne when the Soviets beat Team Canada 8–1 in the final game.

Teams from the old Soviet Union were built around speed and skill, but Valeri Vasiliev loved to check people. He was probably the toughest player in the history of Soviet hockey.

Georges Vezina

Position: **Goaltender**   Height: **5'6" (168 cm)**   Weight: **185 lbs (84 kg)**   Born: **January 21, 1887 in Chicoutimi, QC.**

Regular Season										Playoffs									
Season	Team	GP	W	L	T	MINS	GA	SO	AVG.	Season	Team	GP	W	L	T	MINS	GA	SO	AVG.
1917-18	Mtl. Canadiens	21	12	9	0	1282	84	1	3.93	1917-18	Mtl. Canadiens	2	1	1	0	120	10	0	5.00
1918-19	Mtl. Canadiens	18	10	8	0	1117	78	1	4.19	1918-19	Mtl. Canadiens	10	6	3	1	636	37	1	3.49
1919-20	Mtl. Canadiens	24	13	11	0	1456	113	0	4.66	1919-20	Mtl. Canadiens	—	—	—	—	—	—	—	—
1920-21	Mtl. Canadiens	24	13	11	0	1436	99	1	4.14	1920-21	Mtl. Canadiens	—	—	—	—	—	—	—	—
1921-22	Mtl. Canadiens	24	12	11	1	1468	94	0	3.84	1921-22	Mtl. Canadiens	—	—	—	—	—	—	—	—
1922-23	Mtl. Canadiens	24	13	9	2	1488	61	2	2.46	1922-23	Mtl. Canadiens	2	1	1	0	120	3	0	1.50
1923-24	Mtl. Canadiens	24	13	11	0	1459	48	3	1.97	1923-24	Mtl. Canadiens	6	6	0	0	360	6	2	1.00
1924-25	Mtl. Canadiens	30	17	11	2	1860	56	5	1.81	1924-25	Mtl. Canadiens	6	3	3	0	360	18	1	3.00
1925-26	Mtl. Canadiens	1	0	0	0	20	0	0	0.00	1925-26	Mtl. Canadiens	—	—	—	—	—	—	—	—
	NHL Totals	190	103	81	5	11,586	633	13	3.28		NHL Playoffs	26	17	8	1	1596	74	4	2.78

Georges Vezina is the most famous goalie from the early days of professional hockey. That's because every season since 1926-27, the best goalie in the NHL has been presented with the Vezina Trophy. The trophy was donated to the league after Georges Vezina died on March 26, 1926. Vezina had never missed a game — regular season or playoffs — in his entire career with the Montreal Canadiens until a serious illness forced him to retire. It was a streak that lasted 367 games. These days, very few goalies play more than 30 straight games without getting a rest.

During much of Vezina's career, goaltenders had to remain standing at all times and were not allowed to drop down to the ice to make a save. Also, their equipment was much poorer than it is today. Except for their leg pads, goaltenders' equipment was not much different than any other player's. For those reasons Vezina's goals-against average usually seems high to today's fans. But in his day, Vezina was considered one

of the very best. In 1945 he was one of the first 12 men elected to the Hockey Hall of Fame. Georges Vezina began

playing hockey in his hometown of Chicoutimi, Quebec. He joined the Canadiens for the 1910-11 season of the National Hockey Association. Montreal was a struggling young franchise then, but Vezina helped them to improve quickly. Because he was so calm under pressure, people called him "The Chicoutimi Cucumber." By 1915-16, the Canadiens were Stanley Cup champions for the first time. One year later, Vezina and the Canadiens were back in the Finals. This time, though, they were beaten by the Seattle Metropolitans of the rival Pacific Coast Hockey Association.

The NHA became the NHL in 1917-18 and the Canadiens' success continued. Vezina led the new league with a 3.93 goals-against average the first year, then he helped the Canadiens reach the Stanley Cup Final again in 1919. Vezina posted a 1.97 average in 1923-24 and led the Canadiens to another Stanley Cup title that year. Vezina was even better the next year with a 1.81 average and five shutouts. Unfortunately for Vezina, Montreal lost to the PCHA's Victoria Cougars in the Stanley Cup Final.

Goalie equipment wasn't much different from any other hockey player's in Georges Vezina's day. Skimpy protection and old-fashioned rules meant higher goals-against averages in the NHL's early days.

Steve Yzerman

Position: **Center**   Height: **5'11" (180 cm)**   Weight: **185 lbs (84 kg)**   Born: **May 9, 1965 in Cranbrook, BC.**

		Regular Season								Playoffs				
Season	Team	GP	G	A	Pts	PIM	+/-	Season	Team	GP	G	A	Pts	PIM
1983-84	Detroit	80	39	48	87	33	-17	1983-84	Detroit	4	3	3	6	0
1984-85	Detroit	80	30	59	89	58	-17	1984-85	Detroit	3	2	1	3	2
1985-86	Detroit	51	14	28	42	16	-24	1985-86	Detroit	—	—	—	—	—
1986-87	Detroit	80	31	59	90	43	-1	1986-87	Detroit	16	5	13	18	8
1987-88	Detroit	64	50	52	102	44	30	1987-88	Detroit	3	1	3	4	6
1988-89	Detroit	80	65	90	155	61	17	1988-89	Detroit	6	5	5	10	2
1989-90	Detroit	79	62	65	127	79	-6	1989-90	Detroit	—	—	—	—	—
1990-91	Detroit	80	51	57	108	34	-2	1990-91	Detroit	7	3	3	6	4
1991-92	Detroit	79	45	58	103	64	26	1991-92	Detroit	11	3	5	8	12
1992-93	Detroit	84	58	79	137	44	33	1992-93	Detroit	7	4	3	7	4
1993-94	Detroit	58	24	58	82	36	11	1993-94	Detroit	3	1	3	4	0
1994-95	Detroit	47	12	26	38	40	6	1994-95	Detroit	15	4	8	12	0
1995-96	Detroit	80	36	59	95	64	29	1995-96	Detroit	18	8	12	20	4
1996-97	Detroit 🏆	81	22	63	85	78	22	1996-97	Detroit 🏆	20	7	6	13	4
1997-98	Detroit 🏆	75	24	45	69	46	3	1997-98	Detroit 🏆	22	6	18	24	22
1998-99	Detroit	80	29	45	74	42	8	1998-99	Detroit	10	9	4	13	0
	NHL Totals:	1178	592	891	1483	782			Playoff Totals:	145	61	87	148	68

When you think of Steve Yzerman, the first word that comes into mind is class. When he finally lifted the Stanley Cup over his head on June 7, 1997, hockey fans everywhere applauded. That's because Yzerman has always played the game with passion and respect. So when the Wings finally erased their 42-year-old curse in 1996-97, much of the acclaim was rightly laid at the skates of "Little Stevie Y."

When Yzerman joined the Red Wings in 1983-84, the team had missed the playoffs in 15 of the previous 17 seasons. (They have only missed the playoffs twice since.) The Detroit front office knew they were getting something special when they drafted Yzerman fourth overall in 1983. When he arrived in Detroit, he was a mature, clever player and set a team rookie

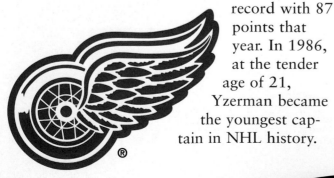

record with 87 points that year. In 1986, at the tender age of 21, Yzerman became the youngest captain in NHL history.

Now, he's also the longest-serving captain in the history of the game.

In 1987-88, Yzerman began a remarkable roll that would make him one of the NHL's elite players. He scored at least 45 goals and collected at least 102 points in each of the next six seasons. In 1988-89, he set team records for goals (65), assists (90), and points (155) in a single season. His fellow NHLers realized just how amazing that season was and awarded him the Lester Pearson Trophy as the players' MVP.

After countless playoff disappointments, the Red Wings finally got it right in 1996-97. With Yzerman playing terrific two-way hockey, Detroit swept the Philadelphia Flyers to win their first Stanley Cup title since 1955. They liked it so much, they did it all over again the following season. This time, Yzerman found himself playing a larger offensive role and led the club in playoff scoring with 24 points. Stevie Y captured the Conn Smythe Trophy as playoff MVP that year.

The Detroit Red Wings had not won the Stanley Cup in 42 years when Steve Yzerman led the team to victory in 1997. Stevie Y's guys made it two in a row in 1998.

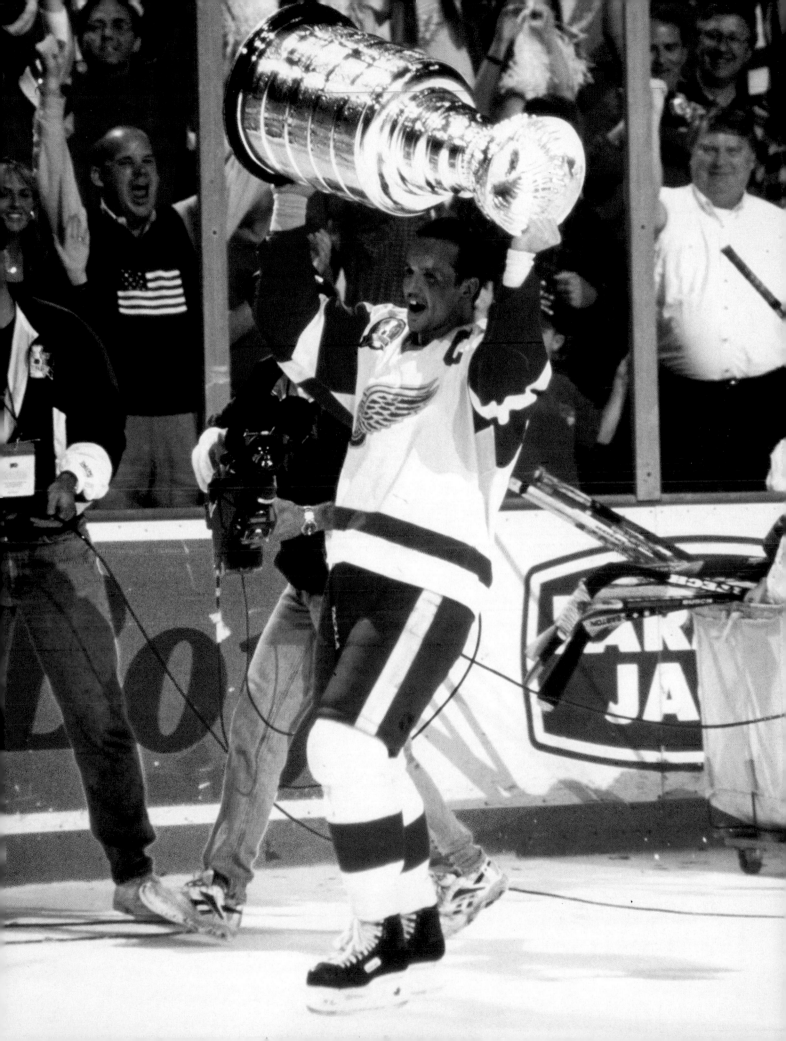

Notes on Statistical Information

Seasons: If a player was traded mid-season, that year's stats are shown on two lines, one for each team. If a player missed one or more seasons and then came back to play in the NHL, his missing seasons are not shown.

A note on +/-: the "Plus/Minus" statistic was first used in the 1967-68 season to measure a player's contribution to his team. A player's Plus/Minus rating reflects the total number of goals *scored* by a player's team while he is on the ice (at even strength or short-handed) less the total number of goals *allowed* by a player's team while he is on the ice (at even strength or on the power play).

In the playoffs, +/- statistics are not shown. The +/- rating is not a meaningful statistic in playoff hockey because the varying number of games played makes it impossible to compare players accurately. For example, in the 1998-99 playoffs, Brett Hull and John LeClair were both +3. Did they have equally successful playoffs? John LeClair played 6 games and scored 3 points.

Brett Hull played 22 games, and scored 15 points, including the Stanley Cup winning goal!

Goalie Playoff Ties: playoff games could end in a tie until the end of the 1935 playoffs. Prior to that, playoff rounds were often played under a two-game format in which the team that scored the most goals over both games combined won the series. Under this format two teams might play to a 2-2 tie in the first game, followed by a 1-0 win in game two, resulting in a combined score of 3-2.

International Players: these statistics include professional league totals, as well as International competition totals, by tournament or event. In many cases with International Players, full statistical data is either not available, or not reliable.

Pre-NHL Players: players from the early part of the century often have incomplete or unreliable statistics. The statistics included for these players are the most complete available.

Position Player Abbreviations

GP: Games Played
G: Goals
A: Assists
Pts: Points
PIM: Penalties in Minutes
+/- : Plus/Minus Rating

Goalie Abbreviations

GP: Games Played
W: Wins
L: Losses
T: Ties
AVG.: Goals Against Average
MINS: Minutes Played
GA: Goals Against
SO: Shut Outs

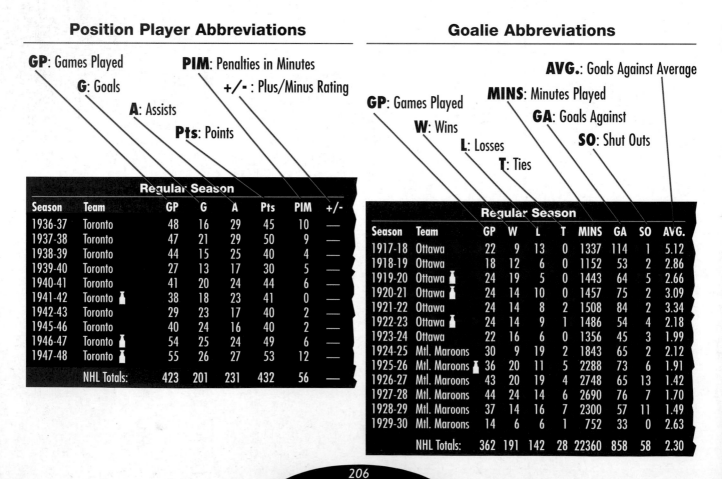

Regular Season							
Season	Team	GP	G	A	Pts	PIM	+/-
1936-37	Toronto	48	16	29	45	10	—
1937-38	Toronto	47	21	29	50	9	—
1938-39	Toronto	44	15	25	40	4	—
1939-40	Toronto	27	13	17	30	5	—
1940-41	Toronto	41	20	24	44	6	—
1941-42	Toronto	38	18	23	41	0	—
1942-43	Toronto	29	23	17	40	2	—
1945-46	Toronto	40	24	16	40	2	—
1946-47	Toronto	54	25	24	49	6	—
1947-48	Toronto	55	26	27	53	12	—
	NHL Totals:	423	201	231	432	56	—

Regular Season								
Season	Team	GP	W	L	T	MINS	GA	SO	AVG.
1917-18	Ottawa	22	9	13	0	1337	114	1	5.12
1918-19	Ottawa	18	12	6	0	1152	53	2	2.86
1919-20	Ottawa	24	19	5	0	1443	64	5	2.66
1920-21	Ottawa	24	14	10	0	1457	75	2	3.09
1921-22	Ottawa	24	14	8	2	1508	84	2	3.34
1922-23	Ottawa	24	14	9	1	1486	54	4	2.18
1923-24	Ottawa	22	16	6	0	1356	45	3	1.99
1924-25	Mtl. Maroons	30	9	19	2	1843	65	2	2.12
1925-26	Mtl. Maroons	36	20	11	5	2288	73	6	1.91
1926-27	Mtl. Maroons	43	20	19	4	2748	65	13	1.42
1927-28	Mtl. Maroons	44	24	14	6	2690	76	7	1.70
1928-29	Mtl. Maroons	37	14	16	7	2300	57	11	1.49
1929-30	Mtl. Maroons	14	6	6	1	752	33	0	2.63
	NHL Totals:	362	191	142	28	22360	858	58	2.30